Praise for *The Near Enemy*

"The Near Enemy is NOT fiction. John Ligato has painted a portrait of an America on a slippery slope caused by political correctness."
— Joe Pistone, FBI Special Agent, Retired
AKA, the real Donnie Brasco.

"The Near Enemy deals with lone wolf terrorists. They represent a direct threat to our homeland, family and freedom."
— Chris Hansen, former NBC Dateline
Correspondent and Host of *To Catch a Predator*.

"This is an action-packed read that is current, topical and on the mark concerning the 'new normal' of asymmetric warfare. John Ligato is a voice that America needs to hear."
— Lt. General Gary McKissock,
United States Marine Corps – Retired

"I served with John Ligato in Vietnam and his book should be a wake up call to our leaders."
— Major General Ray "E-Tool" Smith,
United States Marine Corps – Retired

Also by John Ligato
Dirty Boys

THE NEAR ENEMY

JOHN LIGATO

A POST HILL PRESS BOOK
ISBN: 978-1-68261-278-1
ISBN (eBook): 978-1-68261-279-8

Post Hill
PRESS

Post Hill Press
posthillpress.com

Published in the United States of America

ACKNOWLEDGEMENTS

Family, Friends, and Food make life worthwhile. I'd like to thank my wife Lorri, who has been beside me for 47 years and counting. She has already achieved sainthood on earth. My daughters, Gia and Dani, who have evolved into my good friends and enjoy hanging out with Dad. My sister Florence, who prays for me and loves me unconditionally. (I need the prayers.) Joe Pistone, aka Donnie Brasco, my mentor, who set the standard for covert operations. Thanks to my publisher and friend, Anthony Ziccardi, and to the many individuals who have influenced, encouraged, criticized, and loved me: Tony Daniels, James Kallstrom, AJ Perry, Gordon Batcheller, Ray Smith, Eddie Neas, Herbert Watkins, Gunny Canley, Paul Brown, Buck Stubbs, the late Nick Carangio, Jimmy Sullivan, Fred Snellings, and Al Gonzalez. Thanks also to my Jacksonville family of Mike Williams, Bruce Gombar, Gary McKissock, Rose and Mike Eagan, Bob and Lois Dupuis, Jerry Yanello, Dick Vercauteran, Efren Saenz, Bill Garrettt, Bobby Hayes, and Janelle and Horace Mann. There are some special individuals who sacrifice their time, money and sweat for an ideal. Mat Raymond and Joe Houle (USMC retired), are true Patriots who love their country and the Marine Corps. All of whom took many hours providing me good counsel on my writing and life. A 'shout out" to my miscellaneous geographically placed friends, Tom Koslowski, Dennis Hord, Harvey Senter, and to the best mayor in America, Gary Starr.

DEDICATION

This book is dedicated to our hero protectors in the military and law enforcement. Lately this word, HERO, is a misused and overused word in our society. A hero is *not* a baseball player, *not* an actor and definitely *not* some thug who robs a convenience store. A hero doesn't wear a cape, - they wear dog tags. If your job *requires* you to wear a bulletproof vest and your blood type around your neck, then you are on a path to heroism. Our veterans in law enforcement and the military represent Americans who raised their right hand and took an oath to defend our nation. From the Revolutionary War to the current War on Terror, Americans from all walks of life share the bond of their *oath*…an oath which ends with…."So help me God." The children of Mississippi farmers, Philadelphia cops, and Pittsburgh steel workers…answered our nations call and found themselves in locations like Belleau Woods, Tarawa, Iwo Jimo, the Chosen Reservoir, Inchon, Hue City, Khe Shan, Faluzzia, and Ramadi. And, as long as we still have Americans who will *raise* their right hand…the United States can *never* be defeated. Americans fight for their brothers on the battlefield, and if you've ever been at the destination end of an AK 47, then you understand this concept of brotherhood. The commitment to safeguard one another's lives in combat is non-negotiable. The willingness to die for another person is a form of love that even religions fail to inspire, and that experience changes a person forever.

WARNING

The Near Enemy is considered fiction, but much of it is based on facts. I have changed or consolidated names, locations, combined characters, and interwoven fact with fiction. The subject matter is lone wolf terrorists. The world is in a state of chaos as we await the next attack. America is no longer the shining beacon of hope and stability. Lone Wolf terrorists are creating a bunker mentality within the United States. They kill women, children, and babies indiscriminately, and our political leaders have tied the hands of law enforcement and military. Political correctness has replaced sanity and common sense.

Homegrown terrorists are defeating us from within our own borders. Imagine empty malls, airplanes, hotels, sports stadiums, and Fourth of July celebrations. Imagine schools protected by barbed wire, checkpoints on our highways, and sunset curfews. This will be the "new" America if lone wolf terrorists continue to multiply and create havoc.

Many of the situations, characters and dialogue in this book are authentic. They are a result of spending a lifetime with Marines, cops, and government decision makers. Many policy makers do not understand our enemy. The truth is that we *can* eliminate lone wolves but their solution is providing terrorists jobs and education. Terrorists' *only* goal is the destruction of the American way of life.

Lone wolves' present the greatest long-term threat to our country. So, as Wednesday Addams said in an *Addams Family* flick, "Be afraid… be very, very afraid."

"America will never be destroyed from the outside. If we falter and lose our freedoms, it will be because we destroyed ourselves."

–Abraham Lincoln

FOREWORD

Our country is in real trouble. We face a crisis in leadership. Radical Islamic forces have vowed to destroy America but we continue down the path of political correctness. Our enemies fight dirty but our leaders have tied the hands of the military and law enforcement. John Ligato has written a book which contains the blueprint for dealing with lone wolf terrorists. We should read and heed before it is too late.

Anthony Daniels
Assistant Director of the FBI – Retired

PROLOGUE

*"Terrorism is not an enemy, it is a belief.
So, can terrorism ever be defeated?"*

Raqqa Syria - The Present

The heat and human stench is overwhelming as 117 girls huddle together in the ISIS capital. The burqa covers Jennifer's entire face and body, leaving a small mesh screen through which she views her new world. Raqqa, Syria, the de facto capital of the Islamic State, is a city governed by strict Sharia law. It has been a long journey for Jennifer Wilson from Peoria, Illinois. She met Rashid on Facebook and her world changed. The handsome Iraqi complimented her silly posts and encouraged Jennifer to *'seek a destiny different from the rest.'*

Jen was slightly overweight and painfully shy when it came to boys. Rashid sent Jen photos of young men and women enjoying life in exotic places. The invisible radicalization didn't take long for the girl who felt an overwhelming need to belong. Jennifer studied the Koran and Sharia law. Her world *finally* had purpose. One year after meeting Rashid, the high school senior left a note on her pillow. Her parents didn't understand much of the rambling discourse of being *empowered,* but they *did* realize that their little girl had run away.

The auction is about to begin as several hundred Islamic jihadists arrive on slave market day. The girls in the large room range in age from 8 to 28. They're about to be bought as sexual slaves by ISIS fighters. The men enter the room and pay an official with guns, money, or a goat. They laugh and boast of their sexual prowess. After loud negotiations with the marketers, the men drag one or two of the girls away.

Jennifer Wilson is led to a small wooden rise in the center of the room. It's her turn. A large menacing man shoves two competitors aside and roughly grabs Jennifer's face. He lifts the burqa and forces her mouth open. He turns to the man collecting the money and smiles. A blonde hair, blue-eyed teenage girl with good teeth is the jackpot. Later that evening the girl from Illinois is savagely raped and passed like property among drunken men. Jennifer smiles and thinks, "I am doing Allah's will."

CHAPTER 1

"Radical Islamists use three major strategies to achieve their goal of world domination. The first is to fight The Near Enemy..."

Cleveland, Ohio – FBI Office – The Present

"Hey Booker. Who's the near enemy?"

I am FBI Special Agent John Anthony Booker. Eight months ago I was arrested for possessing 5 ki's of coke. A month later I saved 2 million New Yorkers from being incinerated by a nuclear bomb. Shit happens. I should also mention that I am *often* a sarcastic pain in the ass.

"Yo, Booker." Tommy Shoulders a bit louder. "You're the expert on sand monkeys. Who the hell is the *near* enemy?"

"Use to be anyone inside Islamic lands, but *now*, we'd be the near enemy."

"So we got upped by the jihadist?" Tommy wonders.

"It's not a good thing." I explain. "ISIS discovered social media and began recruiting Americans to do their dirty work. They use *YouTube* and produce slick videos glorifying beheadings. They even use Hip Hop music."

"Fuckin' idiots."

"That's the consensus, but ISIS is actually pretty sophisticated. They're shooting out over 90,000 messages into the ether-sphere every day to millions of people across the globe."

Sgt. Tommy Shoulders, Cleveland Police Department and member of the Joint Terrorism Task Force (JTTF) is waiving the latest FBI Intel bulletin. This is highly unusual for Tommy whose reading habits rarely include anything with footnotes. Seven months ago, Tommy whacked three terrorists who were about to purchase a nuclear suitcase bomb and kill 2 million New Yorkers. But I digress.

"Taliban, Al Qaida, ISIS, Boca Raton." Tommy argues. "What's the difference?"

"That's Boko Haram." I chuckle. "Boca Raton is a city in Florida, but there *is* a difference. Just like McDonalds, ISIS franchises its operation. Al-Qaida and the Taliban function in isolated cells with little or no communication, but ISIS communicates and makes their brand seem like an adventure. Some Americans view ISIS black flags as the new version of the golden arches."

Tommy counters with, "Just a bunch of pimple face losers who fall in love with towel heads on the internet and head to sand land thinking it's gonna be like some reality TV show."

That's what the public believes but the sad reality is that people attracted to ISIS run the gamut from rich to poor, educated to dropout, male to female, and teenaged to middle-aged. Once converted, they travel on a pilgrimage to caliphate shithole camps in Syria and believe that they're on some noble crusade.

"Unfortunately." I tell Tommy that, "The girls are raped and the men are forced to sever the heads of non-believers. Only then, it's too late to call mommy and fly first class back to Omaha." I sip my coffee and add, "A year or two later, when screaming infants being torched becomes background noise, they can't recognize the savage animals they've become."

"Great visual Booker. But those losers get what they deserve. I say, the *less* Q-tip heads in America, the better."

"You *do* realize that not *all* Muslims are terrorists?"

"Maybe, *but* most terrorists *seem* to be Muslims."

Although my friend is not *strictly* correct, his argument has teeth. Islam *is* different. No other religion inspires militancy than the *religion of peace*. Any war against non-believers is *justified* under Muslim law and the Koran. The number of terrorist attacks committed by Muslims since 9/11 is close to 17 a day. These incidents of deadly violence are committed purely out of *religious* duty.

Tommy asks again. "You *never* answered my question. If the near enemy used to be inside Islamic lands, how did we get to be the near enemy?"

"Because ISIS sends these programmed monsters back home to kill Americans. They are our cashiers, teachers, plumbers, and college students. We are no longer separated from our enemy by oceans and land masses. *We* are now the near enemy, and they are very, *very* near."

CHAPTER 2

"They're here!"...

Poltergeist, 1982

Agent 36 enters the JTTF office. Her given name is Gwen McNulty but she came factory equipped with a pair of perfect 36 Cs, thus her nickname. Dirty little FBI secret. When the Burea finally accepted female agents in 1972, lady G-men resembled East German weight lifters on steroids, only with more facial hair. But Agent 36 is the latest generation of improved models who are gorgeous, smart, and can shoot a flea off a dog at a hundred paces.

I should add that Agent 36 also has a pair of metaphorical testicles the size of beach balls. She strangled to death a 300-pound imam in Cairo just seven months ago with her bare hands. After the cleric took his last breath, Gwen announced that she was *hungry*. It seems that a lot went down seven months ago, but that's another story, and we really shouldn't discuss the details until the statute of limitation expires. *Unfortunately*, there is no statute of limitation on murder.

We are members of the JTTF (Joint Terrorism Task Force) in Cleveland, Ohio. These units are our nation's front line on terrorism: small cells of highly trained, locally based investigators, analysts, linguists, and other specialists from dozens of U.S. law enforcement and intelligence agencies.

When it comes to investigating terrorism, we do it all: chase down leads, gather evidence, make arrests, undercover ops, and respond to threats at a moment's notice. We also occasionally fuck up, but hey, nobody's perfect.

Our office space is the standard government low bid with tiny, sterile cubicles the bland color of Caucasian Barbie dolls. The walls, floor, ceiling, bathrooms, and even the computers are similar to drab elevator music. In the *old* days, desks were squeezed together in open squad bays. There was a frat house type of frenzy, which somehow worked. Older agents mentored younger agents and passed on the unwritten rules that made the Bureau great. But those days are gone.

Currently the task force is tracking several Iranian students gabbing on Facebook about bomb making. Although Tommy Shoulders wants to snatch them up and *'give them a beating,'* they haven't crossed the criminal line. Their electronic conversations comprise only one half of a criminal conspiracy, which is, *'two or more people who get together and plan illegal activities.'* The other half requires an *overt* act in furtherance of the spoken words. So basically, we have to wait until the terrorists purchase the materials to make a bomb, *then* we can snatch them up and give them a beating.

Our constitution is being assaulted by political correctness. The truth has become an insult within the country I love. In my opinion, the Iranian students, are foreign pond scum, thus have no fucking rights. But I am a FBI Special Agent and must play by the current rule-book, which seems to change at the whim of our leaders in DC.

"How was your weekend Gwen?"

"Some friends came in from Philly and we hit the Flats. I mixed vodka, brandy and tequila. Not good."

Tommy observes, "You *are* looking a little *green* today."

Agent 36 warns Shoulders, "Yea, I'm wearing a lovely shade of, *I slept like shit,* so don't piss me off." She smiles, playfully messes Tommy's hair and asks, "Whatta you boys discussing?"

"Booker was enlightening me on the number of American traitors who join ISIS and come back and plant pressure cooker bombs."

Gwen nods and offers. "The State Department estimates that 12,000 westerners have joined ISIS within the last 3 years, which includes about 3,700 Americans."

Agent 36 is a tall, lean version of Cameron Diaz with a law degree from Yale. She's dressed down today in jeans and a tight white sweater accessorized with a black 40 Cal. shoulder holster. The straps of the tight contraption circle her boobs and the effect is dual smiley faces.

The phone chirps and it's the wire room. Agent Pat Cloutier tells me that, "Your Iranian students just purchased a few hundred pounds of fertilizer and some blasting caps. Thought you'd want to know."

I hang up and announce, "Let's rock and roll."

On the way out the door, I inform Bruce Gombar that we are going to snatch up our Iranian friends. Bruce is the supervisor of the JTTF, a Harvard law grad, and good guy. He does have an annoying habit of inserting the word 'Harvard' into most conversations.

I should point out that FBI supervisors never leave the office, *except* for lunch. They're frustrated and live vicariously through the brick agents by scribbling their names on our reports. Eventually, they believe that paperwork is not only important but also terribly challenging. Their priorities get skewed and many confuse policy with mission.

Supervisors love meetings since it's the *only* time they get to assert their authority. Brick agents pacify these boy wonders by nodding thoughtfully but once we leave adult supervision, we *ignore* the entire conversation. I personally would rather discuss mortality rates with an insurance adjuster than attend meetings.

Bruce desires another brief as I'm jogging out the door to prevent an explosion in downtown Cleveland.

"I already briefed you."

"That was yesterday."

"Same shit different day," I say but am instantly annoyed. This is not the time for *dialogue* but lately our government has been *all* talk and no action.

Bruce whines. "I just need to keep you administratively pure."

Bureaucratic translation; *'I have to cover my ass in case you fuck up.'*

I tell Bruce, "Make it quick. I just hope the Iranian bombers wait until we finish our philosophy class."

Bruce ignores my sarcasm and consults a notepad on his desk. He asks:

"Do you have arrest warrants?"

"No."

"Are you taking the SWAT team?"

"No."

"The bomb techs?"

"No."

"Do you have an ops arrest plan?"

"No."

"Have you alerted the US Attorney's office?

"No."

"How about the Marshall's office."

"No."

"Need any additional manpower?"

"No."

I'd answered these identical questions yesterday so I interrupt Bruce and ask, "Do you know the most significant contribution *ever* made by a Harvard Law school grad?"

Bruce seems intrigued by the question and says, "I actually don't."

"Employees must wash their hands before returning to work."

Bruce shakes his head and says, "That's it?"

"That's it."

"I don't get it."

"I know. Goodbye."

CHAPTER 3

"Dear Karma...I have a list of people you missed"
Eddie Neas

On the way out the door I call Agent Sean Gregory. His father, FBI Special Agent *Fred* Gregory, was part of our little task force in Cairo last year when we arranged a meeting between 5 terrorists and 72 virgins. It's fair to say that they indeed, *'got fucked.'* The official FBI post op report stated that, *'they shot first, blah, blah blah."* *Unofficially,* that's not what really happened.

Dirty little FBI secret: Supervisors love *paper.* Their value is measured by bulk and not content. Reports are the bows on fictional gifts which brick agents present their supervisors. It makes them feel all warm and fuzzy so we feed them a steady stream of bullshit on federal documents. Our reports should *actually* begin with, *'Once upon a time…'*

Fred survived the great Cairo shootout, but was killed a few months later by a bank robber in DC. Life isn't fair. His son was recently sworn in as a special agent of the Federal Bureau of Investigation and I pulled some strings to get Sean assigned to the Cleveland Division. I owe Thumper, so I promise myself to look out for his boy.

I tell Sean to, "Grab the Mod squad, go to the armory and check out a bunch of lethal weapon stuff, then meet us at the staging area."

Gwen and I jump into my BU car and head east on Superior Avenue. Agent 36 is a member in good standing of the Mensa Society but often masks her genius IQ with an endearing quality some may call *ditzy*. A week ago Gwen and I received the brief from the Quantico lab nerds on fertilizer bombs. I was lost after the two scientists began with, "To understand Amide you must be familiar with a derivative of ammonia in which one or more hydrogens are replaced by alkyl."

As we turn onto Mayfield Ave I ask Agent 36 to re-brief me. "I flunked Shop at Bishop Neumann so give me the basic shit."

Gwen chuckles. "You made a funny. Shit, *fertilizer*, get it?" I smile and she begins the tutorial with. "Ammonium nitrate is the fertilizer compound used in explosives, but it *must* be in a pure form for a bomb."

"Is the pure stuff hard to find and are there any restrictions?"

"The Feds try to keep an eye on bulk sales but you can make ammonium nitrate from common household chemicals. Just mix some nitric acid with ammonia and bam!"

"Is it that easy?"

"Actually.' Gwen says. "There's an easier way. The feds don't track the sale of stump remover in any quantity."

"Gwen, I'm from South Philly. We had no trees, so we had no stumps."

Agent 36 informs me that, "You dissolve tree stumps with a toxic concoction which just happens to contain 100% potassium nitrate and, unfortunately, it works just as well as ammoniam nitrate for making bombs."

"Where can a terrorist, *or*, a stump removal guy buy this concoction?"

"Any Home Depot, Lowe's, Wal-Mart, but, if you're a lazy jihadist, you can even go online and Amazon will deliver it."

"This is *not* good." I say. "What's the other stuff they need for the explosion?"

Gwen sits in the passenger seat as we head to a staging area. Tommy Shoulders and the Mod Squad are close behind in two additional vehicles. Agent 36 explains that, "Fertilizer bombs need two components beside the fertilizer: a detonator and diesel fuel. The detonator must be able to generate sufficient energy."

"How is the bomb detonated?"

"Well, Timothy McVeigh used blasting caps and time delayed fuses. Our Iranian students intend to be suicide martyrs so they'll probably detonate it with a fuse igniter or even a match."

My mind was trying to process the technical information until Gwen mentioned Timothy McVeigh. Then it shifted to a time and place I'd rather forget. Until September 11, 2001, the 1995 Oklahoma City bombing was the worst terrorist attack to take place on U.S. soil.

I ask Gwen, "Where were you when the Murrah building exploded?"

"Sixth grade, but remember it well. I wrote a report on it."

"I was a rookie agent in Memphis. They sent our entire office to Oklahoma City a few hours after the explosion. The bottom line was 168 mangled bodies, 650 injured, and 300 buildings damaged or destroyed."

"It's amazing how two everyday items like fertilizer and gasoline can produce an explosion that powerful." Gwen asks, "What'd you do there?"

"My assignment was to pull bodies from the rubble. Pretty basic stuff."

Gwen softens her voice and says. "That must've been rough, Booker."

"It was, but I can control my emotions in crisis mode. Get the mission accomplished and all that macho stuff. I spent the first day picking through the rubble and found about 10 bodies. I wasn't really counting. That was rough enough until day 2."

"What happened on that day?"

"I've seen some bad shit in Iraq...," I pause, not wanting to go where this was going, but it was too late. "On day 2, my supervisor assigned me a particular section of the building."

"What section?" Gwen asks.

"For two days, I carried bodies out and gently placed them in plastic bags. And when the last body had gone to the morgue, I bawled my eyes out, then drank a shitload of Jim Beam."

"What section?" Gwen repeats.

I turn toward Agent 36 and ask, "Did your school report include the nursery with 56 babies?"

Silence fills the car and after I regain my composure I promise aloud. "That *ain't* gonna happen in Cleveland on our watch."

We stage behind the Holy Rosary church on Murray Hill in Little Italy. It's a safe bet that radical Muslims won't be attending Catholic Mass today. I review the known and unknown in my brain. Two months ago, a reliable source provided information that three University students were spouting ISIS propaganda. Unfortunately, this is not that unusual in today's climate of anti- Americanism. But, when one of the Iranians asked the source, "Where can we purchase some fertilizer?" our interest peaked.

As Tommy Shoulders shrewdly observed at the time, "*Something* ain't right. Isn't fertilizer human *shit* spread over asparagus on farms?"

I thought that a pretty accurate description and became suspicious since our college students *weren't* agriculture majors. We identify the students as: Mr. Jamal Ahmad, Mr. Al Badawi, and Miss Shirin Hamadei, which translates to *kind* and *sweet*. Tommy chimed in again with, "I once dated a Serbian girl whose name *should* have translated to *psychotic, crazy bitch*."

Now here's where it gets interesting. Jamal and Badawi are Iranian-born and studying in the U.S. on student VISAs, but Ms. Hamadei was born Brenda Carlsen, of Finnish descent, in Yankton, South Dakota. She joined some Muslim study group on campus and met the junior bin Ladens. The three amigos took the next semester off and traveled to Turkey. The blonde-haired Miss Carlsen departed the U.S. as Brenda and returned as Shirin Hamadei. Word was that the trio attended terrorist boot camp and earned their merit badge in bombs. Recent surveillance photos of them indicate Ms. 'kind and sweet' wearing a khimar, which is a type of headscarf. The two males, who I nickname Vinny and Bruno, resemble the typical pissed off, chest-pounding assholes parading around sand land on the nightly news.

"Why Vinny and Bruno?" Gwen wonders.

"In second grade, two fourth graders stole my chocolate milk every day. Their names were Vinny and Bruno. Bruno was as dumb as a head of lettuce but psychotic and Vinny was smart. Jamal resembles Vinny with a similar sleazy sneer, and Badawi has those vacant crazy eyes that Bruno had."

Agent 36 laughs and says, "You are not right John Booker."

"Maybe not, but Bruno is the wild card, and he ain't getting my milk today."

An aside: All three students are on full scholarships and receive food stamps, free health care, supplemental security income, and workers' compensation. The bogus worker's comp claim resulted after Jamal and Badawi worked one week as landscapers and allegedly fell off a gazebo. All benefits compliments of U.S. taxpayers. Dirty little FBI secret: Most FBI agents support a wall on our southern border, fracking, welfare reform, free market, less government, and nude volleyball. That last category is a personal favorite of mine.

My daughter Nikki attends Ohio State and I fork over $47,000 a year. I often suggest that she change her name to Salami O'Bami, declare herself transgender, and put marbles in her shoes. "Save me a lot of moola, honey."

Tommy arrives with three brand new agents. They recently graduated the FBI academy and still have that new agent smell. I facetiously christen them *The Mod Squad*, after a popular TV show in the 70s featuring three cops with tie-dye jeans, Afro haircuts, and bad attitudes. Actually, the three baby FBI agents are the exact *opposite*, hence the sarcasm. Dennis Hord, Sean Gregory, and Gianna Olson exit the car and head my way. Gia, born in Seoul, South Korea, was adopted as an infant by the Olson family from Zelienople, Pennsylvania. She is small in stature with silky, jet black hair and smiling, almondshaped eyes. A delicate porcelain doll comes to mind.

The three rookies are eager to mix it up with bad guys even though they look a lot like models in L. L. Bean catalogues. Tommy has taken them on as a project. He often complains, "They need to knock a few doors down on Kinsman Avenue. Get their fingernails dirty."

The new feds could do a lot worse than apprentice under Sgt. Shoulders. He's street smart and never met a regulation that he wouldn't massage. Tommy experiences mild seizures whenever The Mod Squad quote sections from MIOG, which stands for the FBI's Manual of Investigative Operations and Guidelines.

The group is standing in a semi-circle awaiting my brief. I tell them that, "Surveillance puts Brenda holed up in their apartment on Euclid. The boys are heading this way with a Ryder Truck filled with fertilizer. I look Gwen's way and add, "Or, stump remover. But under *no* circumstances do we allow fertilizer, gasoline, and detonator to end up at the same location." The group takes turn asking questions.

"Do we know the location of the gasoline and detonator?"

"Negative. Some vague phone conversations about a storage shed – location unknown."

"What radio frequency we working on?"

"Bravo four," I say. "I'll be monitoring surveillance on Bravo six."

"Do we take the truck down before it gets in the area?"

"Negative on that. We don't know if they can self-detonate and become one massive mobile suicide bomb."

"Should we hit the apartment and take down Ms. Hamedi?"

"That's an affirmative. Gwen's doing a ruse to gain entrance. Sean and I go in, Dennis and Gia cover the rear, and Tommy covers our six o'clock."

"Are they armed?"

"Affirmative. The males with AR 15s modified to auto and Ms. Kind and Sweet has a 45 cal pistol."

"What about the truck?"

"Surveillance squad figures we have 45 minutes to neutralize Hamedi. Then we deal with the truck."

"Why are we cutting it that close?"

"Cell phones are both a curse and a blessing. If we take Brenda down too soon, and the boys try to call her, we'll have a truck filled with explosives careening around a city filled with civilians. We lose control, so it's important that the truck reach the apartment on Euclid. Once the boys leave the truck, we take them down inside the vestibule of the apartment building."

Gia asks a very interesting question, "What happens if only one or neither of the males leave the truck?"

I smack my head and utter, "A blinding flash of the obvious Miss Gia. *And,* a good question." Options scroll through my brain and the solution is two feet away. I say, "Tommy Shoulders will deal with whoever sticks with the truck." I look at Tommy, and he gives me a subtle nod. No need to provide any further details. I conclude with, "Any *other* questions?"

I lock eyes with my team and recognize the look. It's the same thousand-yard stare that Marines get right before combat. The Mod Squad rookies seems ready to kick some terrorist ass. God Bless America. Fred's son asks the final question, "If they somehow get the fertilizer bomb together, do we know their target?"

I nod and tell Sean that, "The Convention Center is hosting a massive conference on pre-school development. There's gonna be close to 1500 people. Psychologists, educators, administrators, vendors, parents, and," I pause and finish with, "five hundred children between the ages of 1 and 5."

CHAPTER 4

"Fasten your seatbelts. It's going to be a bumpy night."
Bette Davis, All About Eve (1950)

Cleveland, Ohio has four seasons: *pre*-winter, winter, *still* winter, and construction. The October temperature is hovering in the mid 30s with the sun MIA for the past two weeks. The group saddles up and checks their gear: radios, rounds, Kevlar vests, and weapons. Sean lingers behind and says, "Can I ask something else?"

Sean looks nothing like his father. Thumper was a raging bull but Sean is a gazelle. He's taller and lankier than Fred and much more introspective. Thumper was a former combat Marine and Georgia State Trooper who earned the moniker of *Thumper* by *thumping* assholes. He was built like a vending machine and enjoyed swapping the most vile racist jokes. My sense is that Sean may be thin-skinned to *any* affront concerning his African American heritage.

I nod and Sean wonders, "Was it like this in Cairo?"

During the great Cairo shootout it was Fred who saved my ass, and I will be forever indebted to the man called Thumper. After the funeral Sean approached me and announced, "I'm applying to the Bureau."

"Have you discussed this with your mom?"

29

"She's against it. Told me that, '*the Bureau took away my husband but they won't take my son.*' "

"Listen to your mother, Sean." I say. "The Bureau's changed. It ain't no fun anymore."

"You're just saying that."

I realized that Sean couldn't be dissuaded, so I switched gears and wished him luck but hoping he'd have none. The Bureau has changed and not for the good. Things we routinely did 5 years ago are now firing offenses, and anything before that will get you indicted. Most bosses are terrified of making a mistake *so* they *won't* make a decision. It forces us brick agents to act minus authority because it's easier to gain forgiveness than permission. My FBI has morphed into this beautiful but treacherous woman who breaks your heart, and then does it again, and again. I started divorce proceedings when FBI Director Comey proclaimed Hillary Clinton brainless *but* innocent.

Sean breezed through the application process and finished top rookie in his new agent class. He asked if I would present his credentials on graduation day, and I was honored to do so. It struck me that Sean walked across the same stage his dad did so many years ago. He shook my hand and I presented him his FBI credentials. A Kodak moment just two short months ago captured forever inside the safe confines of the FBI Academy. Now he's on the mean streets of Cleveland hunting radical jihadists, just like his dad in Cairo.

I take a step toward Sean and rest my hand on his shoulder. "Do you know what went down in Cairo?"

"Every FBI agent knows how you and dad saved millions of people from certain death."

"But do you know what *really* happened there?"

"At the FBI Academy, instructors used your case as an example of a textbook terrorist investigation. Spent a week discussing the Intel bulletins, CIA murders, how you and dad turned the imam, *and* the shootout with the terrorists. Your task force came home heroes."

"But what they didn't tell you was that we worked *off* the books, that we violated every page of that MIOG manual you memorized, that we did shit that FBI agents should *never* do. Did they tell you that?"

"No but I'm not some naïve kid. I know that we sometimes have to do things that aren't *exactly* by the book."

I shake my head. "Have you watched the news lately, Sean? It's open season on law enforcement officers. You either get shot by some thug, or indicted by your own prosecutor for shooting the thug first. Only the asshole you shoot, with 17 prior arrests, is somehow transformed into a model citizen who sings in the church choir. Then the media plasters his third grade school photo on the 6 o'clock news but can't seem to find his latest arrest photo with the neck tattoos."

"So what are you saying? That I can't handle the pressure or maybe I'm not tough enough."

"You're plenty tough. You can probably outshoot me, outrun me, and kick my ass, but that's not enough nowadays. To stay alive, you have to fight dirty."

Sean body stiffens and he challenges me with, "What's that mean, to fight *dirty*? Plant evidence, lie under oath, or beat a confession out of someone?" He pauses and taunts me with, "I know, let's *really* play dirty and kill someone in cold blood."

My immediate thought is, '*My God, the kid knows everything we did in Cairo,*' but I doubt that Fred would *ever* share those details and place Sean in an ethical jackpot.

He takes a deep breath and finishes with, "I respect you Mr. Booker, but you *don't* have to fight dirty or break rules. You just need to do your *job*."

I am about to respond with, '*there was a time when that was true,*' but I hold my tongue. This is not the time *nor* place to be having this particular conversation. So, I smile and say, "You're right, Sean. I'm probably just a burnt-out geezer who glamorizes the good old days. Maybe I've been on the job too long." I pat his arm and end the conversation with, "I loved your dad, now go and be a chip off the old block." Stupid cliché, but it's the best I can do. It seems to give Fred's son some comfort.

Sean smiles back and tells me, "And my dad loved you. I'm sorry if I spoke out of line."

"That's what brick agents do son, we speak our minds. No one ever accused your dad of being shy."

Sean nods and heads toward his first dance with the devil.

As Gwen and I leave the parking lot I gaze up at the large crucifix sitting atop the Holy Rosary steeple. I silently make a request to God, "No more dead kids, and keep Sean safe, OK?" It may not have been your standard memorized prayer but God is understanding and a standup guy.

CHAPTER 5

"Do not speak to me of rules. This is war!"
The Bridge on the River Kwai (1957)

The apartment building on Euclid Avenue is a square, four-story crumbling structure. The occupants are a collection of college students, Section 8 welfare recipients, and a few old hookers. The Muslim owner of the corner convenience store is also the slum landlord of the apartment building. Muslims seem to be transplanting the Chinese, Italians, and Irish who preceded them in America's inner city. But, unlike their predecessors, who embraced their new culture, Muslims have no intention of assimilating. They remain insulated and hostile to the country that provides them a safe haven, rap music, and the Kardashians.

Gwen and I are about 2 blocks from Ms. Kind's and Sweet's place going over a list of *what ifs*. We're also monitoring the truck's journey on the Bravo 6 surveillance channel. Any cop or agent learns how to multitask with the radio in the background. A few can actually nap as radio chatter continues nonstop but will somehow hear their own call sign. Teenagers have developed a similar optic ability, like an iguana, with one eye up and one down that enables them to text and drive.

A surveillance agent with the call sign of *Catfish* reports: 'Target vehicle exiting I-77 and turning southbound on Fleet."

The surveillance team leader responds, "10-4"

A moment later the *'eye'* calls out. "Target vehicle entering some type of business."

"What business?"

"Standby, I have to make a 180."

Catfish fills the uneasy silence with, "The truck pulled into a gated parking lot. I'm doubling back to get an ID."

The team leader understands the significance of losing physical contact with the truck. His voice has sudden urgency, "What type of business?"

"Standby." A tense 2 minutes elapse before Catfish announces, "Some type of storage facility."

It is Gwen who sums up our new situation with "Holy fuck." She didn't have to say that the fertilizer, gasoline, and detonators have married and will soon honeymoon inside the back of that truck.

Our original plan assumed we'd be able to take the trio down *prior* to the storage stop. But plans often turn to shit in law enforcement, and you must adapt and improvise. This was always the wild card in the back of my mind anyway. "OK," I say to Gwen. "Our options have narrowed."

Agent 36 sums up our predicament with, "If the truck moves directly toward the target, we have to take it down before they reach the populated downtown area. But my money is they'll head here."

"The clock is ticking." I check my watch and say. "We have about ten minutes, max, to make a decision or that truck is back on public streets."

There is not enough time to poll the group over the radio so it's left to Gwen and I to think fast, *and* good.

I offer, "It's too dangerous to assume the truck comes here. I'm leaning toward having the surveillance units block their exit from the storage lot and take them down."

Gwen reasons, "If they detonate there, we still lose hundreds of civilians not to mention 6 FBI agents who are not only our colleagues but our friends."

I tell Gwen, "We now have five minutes and if that truck reaches I-77, with a straight shot to the Convention Center, we'll have another Oklahoma City on our hands."

Agent 36 chuckles which seems totally inappropriate given the circumstances, even for such a smart ass. She leans over, rubs my neck, and says, "Hey Booker, you're a little tense. I got this figured out. You trust me, don't you?"

"Last time you asked me that question a Muslim cleric and his son met mysterious deaths. I trust you to cover my back but your decision-making has been leaking oil lately."

Gwen becomes serious and runs it down minus any bullshit. "If they're heading here, they make a left on Fleet and turn on 65th street, but if they're headed toward the target they turn right on Fleet toward the interstate."

I nod and tell Gwen, "Wrap it up."

"Our source is convinced that Brenda is itching to be a bride martyr for Allah, which is why we always assumed she'd be in that truck." Gwen pauses and turns toward me. She adds, "So the truck will be here shortly. Trust me."

"That made sense *before*, but Brenda could've just gone with the boys. Why risk multiple stops?"

Gwen explains that, "Muslim men are rude, arrogant alpha males who huff and puff, but it's the *Bitch* who actually controls the litter. Remember, Brenda is *not* your typical submissive pajama mama."

I check my watch and say, "I know you're taking me somewhere with this, but move it along please."

Gwen tilts her head the way puppies do when they hear a unique sound and says, "Brenda may have switched teams but basically she'll always be a suburban brat from South Dakota."

My patience is running low. "Get to the point Gwen!"

"The truck is heading to the apartment to pick up Miss Kind and Sweet.'

"And how can you be so sure?"

"Because," Agent 36 explains, "Brenda wants to blow something up and her two greasy boyfriends ain't gonna ruin her party. She's probably up in that apartment taking a bubble bath, putting on makeup, and listening to music."

"You're not making sense." I scold. As I reach for the mic to order the takedown at the storage facility the radio squelches and Catfish announces that, "Target vehicle left on Fleet and heading toward the apartment."

Gwen smirks and says, "All men should consider castration after the age of 40."

I smile back and respond, "Fuck you."

CHAPTER 6

"I have come here to chew bubblegum and kick ass...and,
I'm all out of bubblegum."

They Live (1988)

I cue my mic and ask Tommy, "You copying this traffic?"

"Yep. The two diaper heads coming our way."

Time for another dirty little FBI secret. The law enforcement community is a fairly racist group. We routinely use phrases like *towel heads, sand maggots, camel jockey,* and an occasional *beaner.* We look forward to the FBI's required sensitivity and diversity training since it's an opportunity for new material. A month ago our *cultural sensitivity trainer* compared Reverend Al Sharpton to Reverend Martin Luther King, which prompted me to observe, *"Calling Al Sharpton a Reverend is like calling Jeffrey Dahmer a chef."* This did not go over well with management.

Tommy Shoulders has been to this rodeo before and sounds like he is ordering the combo at the takeout window at KFC. His nonchalant, flippant attitude lowers everyone's blood pressure and sends the message to the rookies that a massive bomb is routine shit.

Gia and Dennis are monitoring the conversation in a separate unit so I reach out and attempt to involve them by asking, "You guys having fun yet."

Gia responds with a tense, "10-4."

I ask Agent 36 her take on Special Agent Gianna Olson. Gwen tells me that, "Gia is a Phi Beta Kappa from John Carroll University. She was a financial analyst for some investment firm but her dad is a retired FBI agent, and her DNA kicked in." Agent 36 pauses and gives the addendum of, "A smart kid who probably chose the wrong career path."

"Why's that?"

"At the FBI Academy, she excelled at the academics, but had to take remedial training for both Firearms and Defensive Tactics."

I shake my head and say, "Well, now we'll find out if that remedial shit works."

"It's your fearless leader, boys and girls." I transmit on our secure frequency. "OK, one more time. The target apartment is on the ground floor. Dennis and Gia cover the back. Gwen knocks on the door and tells Brenda that the building is being evacuated due to a gas leak. Once the door opens I go first, then Sean and Gwen. Tommy, you cover the street in case Vinny and Bruno arrive before we secure the apartment. Channel 4 on the handi-talkies. Questions?"

Dennis politely inquires, "What happens if Brenda doesn't open the door?"

Tommy immediately responds with, "We kick it down." Then adds, "And they'll be none of those fucking blue raid jackets with FBI on the back. This ain't no recruiting visit to the ghetto."

Agent 36 chuckles and says, "I love Tommy Shoulders."

I switch radio channels from four to six and contact the Special Operations Group (SOG -surveillance) team leader. "Task Force one – SOG 6."

"Go TF one."

"Give me a 20 on the truck."

Skip Meindhart is the SOG team leader and good guy. We're both diehard Pittsburgh Steelers fans and occasionally get together on game day for pizza and Iron City beer. He says, "A block east of

65ᵗʰ and Carnegie. Good news is that they're barely doing 25 miles an hour, the bad news is traffic is light."

"Traffic is *never* light in Cleveland."

"Just your luck." Skip chuckles. "The ETA has changed from 45 to 35 minutes, so do your thing but, do it quickly."

"Thanks Skip. Keep me posted on their 20."

"Will do. Go Steelers - out."

Gwen gives me a shrug and says, "This thing's getting like Cairo. One surprise after another."

I smile and say, "But we better not kill *all* the bad guys this time. The Bureau is getting downright touchy about people's constitutional rights."

Brenda's apartment is unit 113 and located on the ground floor. It's the typical inner city apartment building with a dark hallway and ratty stained carpets. The only access to an individual apartment is via the hallway door but there is an outside window in the kitchen. I assign Dennis and Gia to cover Brenda's window, which faces a parking lot. "Just in case Ms. Kind and Sweet makes a break for it."

Dennis wonders, "What's our orders if she attempts to escape?"

I just know that Tommy is about to say, shoot her, so I cue the radio mic before Shoulders, and say, "Detain her." I pause and add. "But if she resists, then…shoot her." Followed by, "Just kidding." Sometimes I can't help myself.

I'm using Gwen for the ruse since females are less threatening to other females. We decide on the gas leak since it would be hard to ignore. It's show time and the team is in place. As I am about to run down the plan in my brain one last time, I decide, fuck it, let's not overthink this thing.

Gia alerts us that, "Team two in place."

"10-4. We're rolling."

Gwen exits the car and enters the outer apartment door. Agent 36 will wait in the vestibule until Sean and I approach. Once she eyeballs us she'll head to the target. We'll give her a 20-foot lead and catch up once she reaches unit 113. Detective Shoulders will remain in his car, monitor the surveillance frequency, and keep an eye out for Vinny and Bruno. As Sean and I walk pass Tommy's car he opens the window and asks, "What's the difference between Osama bin Laden and Mike Tyson?"

He waits a beat and deadpans with, "Mike Tyson can take a shot to the head."

Sean and I stare at him in disbelief. Sean's expression conveys, *The man's outta his mind,* but, I'm glad he's on the home team. I smile and say, "Not your best Tommy."

Shoulders gives me the finger and closes his window. This finger response seems to be a trend. Life is good, but not for long.

CHAPTER 7

"When you're gonna shoot, then shoot. Don't talk."
The Good, The Bad, and the Ugly (1966)

Agent 36 is wearing a Dominion Gas Company jacket and holding a flashlight, which is actually a Taser. Her *girl next door* beauty and perfect teeth belie a steel cadaver. She reaches Brenda's apartment, straightens her jacket, and raps on the door. "Gas Company," she says.

Sean and I are hugging the inside wall since the glass eye allows Brenda limited hallway vision. A female voice asks, "Who?"

"Gas Company, ma'am, there's a leak in the building."

A voice somewhere near the door counters with, "I don't smell any gas."

"That's because *natural* gas is odorless." Agent 36 later confesses that she has no idea if natural gas is odorless but assumed so, since it's *natural*.

"Can I just open a window?"

"This is an emergency. We must evacuate the building now!"

Brenda counters with, "OK, but I need about ten minutes."

Gwen uses her *outside* voice and barks, "You have exactly *one* minute before I call the police and they break the door down!"

My gut is screaming that a person can do a lot of bad things in one minute. After 15 seconds elapse I nudge Gwen aside, aim my foot at a spot a few inches besides the door handle and kick with all I've got. I bounce back and realize that the cheap wooden door must have multiple locks. I motion Sean beside me, point at the door and say, "Together, on three."

"One, two, three!"

Our combined weight rips the door from its hinges as wood and screws fly in every direction. I enter the room, move quickly to the right, followed by Sean who moves left. We scan the room and it appears empty but we know that Ms. Kind and Sweet is nearby. My eyes search out the deadly traps where Brenda can pop up like a whack a mole. Behind the couch, the bedroom door and kitchen are possible hot spots so our next move is to clear each room. Sean looks at me and I mouth, "bedroom." He nods just as my handi-talkie comes to life on my hip. It's Gia who excitedly broadcasts, "Subject exiting kitchen window into parking lot."

Sean and I race to the kitchen just as Ms. Kind and Sweet lands on the ground. She moves surprisingly well for a short, chubby terrorist from South Dakota. Gia and Dennis are out of their car and heading toward Brenda while screaming "FBI!" I leap the four feet from kitchen window to ground followed by Sean and Gwen. It's only 5:27 PM but dusk on a cloudy day turns the parking lot into a series of dark shadows. The lot is packed with cars, which Brenda uses for cover and concealment. She's about 40 yards from us but only 25 feet from Gia and Dan. The rookie agents are screaming compliance commands just as they were taught at Hogan's Alley. Of course, the bad guys at the FBI Academy are role players who *eventually* surrender.

My take is that Brenda is definitely not in surrender mode given her body language. It reeks of defiance. Then I see why. Brenda holds a pistol in one hand, while the other hand is cradling a cell phone. She is attempting to punch numbers into the cell phone with her gun hand while running. It's almost an impossible task. This strange configuration is somewhat unique in law enforcement and seems to confuse the rookies. During escapes, the bad guys usually point the gun at us and rarely have time for phone conversations. It takes me a second to figure out her intentions. I yell, "She's calling the truck!"

Since I don't have a clear shot I holler in the direction of Gia and Dennis and say, "Shoot her!"

Sean immediately countermands my order with, "No! She's not a threat!"

I can see Dennis and Gia attempting to process the conflicting commands, so I make my point with an emphatic, "*Shoot* that fucking bitch!"

Sean begins a sprint toward Brenda. He's holstered his weapon and seems to be in pre-tackle mode but five rows of parked cars make it difficult to travel in a straight line. Time is running out because if Brenda connects with the boys in the truck, they'll head directly toward the Convention Center and those 500 children. Ms. Kind and Sweet is having difficulty multi-tasking as she simultaneously attempts her escape while holding a gun and struggling to dial a cell phone. She stops to steady her hand and begins to tap Vinny's or Bruno's number.

Gwen and I are frozen in time taking on the unexpected role of observers. Sean closes the gap to about ten yards when Brenda suddenly turns and aims her 45-caliber pistol center mass at Fred Gregory's son. This just happens to be the person I had vowed to keep safe. The muzzle flash and explosion from such a large caliber weapon makes an impression. I focus my attention on Sean expecting him to fall in a heap *but* it is Brenda who drops like a sack of potatoes.

And, it is Special Agent Gianna Olson holding the smoking gun. Who'd a thought?

CHAPTER 8

"Hang on a minute, lads, I've got a great idea."
The Italian Job (1969)

I turn to Agent 36 and comment, "That remedial firearms training really *does* work."

Gwen and I race in between the cars toward Brenda and find Sean attempting CPR. Gia's 40 caliber round entered Ms. Kind and Sweet's back and made a nasty exit somewhere near the heart. I notice bright red blood gushing in spasms from her chest, which indicates major artery damage. In laymen's terms, Brenda is either dead or will be in the very near future. I kneel down, shove Terrence aside, and check Brenda's neck, wrist, and foot for a pulse. The blood quits gushing and I place my ear on her lips to hear or feel some sign of life. There is none so I pronounce her, "Dead."

I find Brenda's phone under a car some five feet away and determine that she never connected with the truck. Dennis and Gia are standing nearby with a glazed look. I approach Gia, look her in the eye and say, "Great job, you just saved the lives of 1500 people."

She looks confused so I clarify that, "Brenda was just about to contact the truck. If you didn't shoot her they who would've gone directly to the Convention Center."

It slowly sinks in and Gia nods her understanding. I finish with, "OK, we gotta act quick. Dennis, you and Sean lug Brenda back to her kitchen window and toss her inside. Gia, stay in the parking lot in case we get some gawkers. Badge them and insist they leave the area." I chuckle and add. "But just don't shoot anyone else today, unless you *really* have to."

Gia actually gives me a big smile and I'm beginning to think that we may have another Agent 36 on our hands.

Dennis grabs Brenda's lifeless torso but Sean remains still. He glares at me and asks, "Did we have to kill her?"

"The short answer is yes." I say. "But we don't have time for an ethics discussion, so get moving."

Just as Sean is about to spout off some bullshit, I warn, "Get your fucking ass in gear, son. Now!"

Sean gives me one last defiant stare and joins Dennis. Do I feel sympathy for the girl from South Dakota who lay dead on a ghetto parking lot on this cold dreary evening? Not really, but I feel deep sorrow for her parents. Life is about choices and Brenda Carlsen chose this outcome. The 500 toddlers at that Convention Center wouldn't have a choice if Brenda had her way. She is not a victim of jihadist brainwashing, nor any less culpable by virtue of some trendy psychological diagnosis that excuses irrational homicidal behavior. She's *not* even a misguided youth; she *is* evil. Her choice.

Gwen and I grab Brenda's weapon and cell phone and I comment, "So far so good."

Agent 36 shakes her golden mane and ruins my *feel-good* moment with, "You do realize that you're going to have to get real creative with the paperwork on this one."

I look at her and wonder, "Why's that?"

"Because the newspaper headlines will read, 'Ms. Brenda Carlsen, a 19-year-old college student from Yankton, South Dakota, was shot in the *back* by FBI agents.' And anything *after* that headline is irrelevant."

Gwen is a constitutional attorney so her cautionary warning has some bite. But, we have a bomb capable of leveling a city block due here in 15 minutes, so first things first. Some citizen may have dialed 911 with a "shots fired" call, although gunfire in this particular neighborhood is not that unusual. It's almost pitch black now since dusk has morphed into night. The moonless night and few working street lights provide us additional cover. Tommy Shoulders' number appears on my personal cell phone.

The veteran street cop can definitely recognize the sound of a gunshot and nonchalantly inquires, "Heard some caps, anyone dead?"

"Nobody on our side."

"Don't tell me that Ms. Kind and Sweet has joined the 72 Virgins in the great 7-11."

"That's a big 10-4."

"I'm beginning to think that there is only *one* 72-year-old toothless virgin with herpes and a mustache awaiting these assholes."

Tommy is street smart and used his cell phone in lieu of any government device due to prying bureaucratic ears. He understands that we may have to get our story straight so we can massage the facts if needed. I smile and say, "Tommy, call the district commander and put a kibosh on dispatching any units to this location."

"Got it."

"What's the truck's ETA?"

"Surveillance estimates 15 to 18 minutes."

"Stay put and we'll clean up here. Should take less than 5 minutes but I'm heading your way now."

I find Tommy sitting in his car. He asks what happened and I provide the abridged version. He simply nods and says, "Sounds like our little Gia may be corruptible."

"Remedially so." I chuckle then get serious with, "Let's go over the plan for the takedown."

Law Enforcement officers understand that taking down bad guys in a moving vehicle is a recipe for disaster. They're called felony car stops at the training academy and they usually turn to shit since most felons will attempt to escape at high speeds endangering innocent civilians and, if cornered, will turn their vehicle into battering rams. When you factor in several tons of explosives, it becomes imperative to separate the terrorists from their ride.

I tell Tommy, "It would make sense that the boys call Brenda when they get close but before they leave the truck."

Shoulders nods and says, "That's what I would do."

"So." I surmise. "If they can't reach her by phone my money is that they park and one or both go gather her."

"No way would I leave a truck alone in this neighborhood. Why risk some gangbanger thinking they hit the jackpot with some TVs, I-Pads, and leather recliners?"

"Agreed. So, they make the call to Brenda who is currently dead and thus, unavailable, which will force one of them to leave the truck and determine why Ms. Kind and Sweet is not answering her phone."

"I love this fuckin' job." Tommy comments. "Gia whacks some terrorist from South Dakota and now jihad Vinny and Bruno are coming right to us."

"It ain't over yet, Tommy." I cue the mic. "TF one to SOG."

"Go TF one."

"What's their ETA, Skip?"

"Two miles from your location. Ten minutes give or take with traffic."

"Give us a shout when they're a mile out."

"10-4 TF one. Be careful, that fertilizer smell is nasty and I'm a block away."

I look at Tommy and say, "You know what you gotta do. Want one of the baby agents with you?"

The street cop raises his eyebrows in a 'you dumb fuck' stare but says very businesslike, "Not really, I work better alone." Then adds, "But, in a pinch, I'd consider ol' trigger happy Gia."

I actually did generate a detailed ops plan several days ago but had never copied my supervisor. I can't explain my chronic insubordination but it probably has something to do with my lack of breastfeeding as an infant. Gwen and I surveyed the apartment building last week and agreed that the best place to take down armed terrorists is the vestibule. This building is typical of once-proud neighborhoods that have gone to seed. It has an outer door leading into a vestibule with a bunch of mailboxes and buzzers, but any electronic connection between lobby and apartment had long ago gone south. If we time it just right, then we trap the boys in the 8' by 8' vestibule. They either surrender or be shot like ducks in a barrel. I'm hoping they surrender but I doubt they will.

That's my ops plan and it looked good on my unofficial memo but as they say in football, the game still has to be played.

CHAPTER 9

"Whatever they're sellin', I don't want it."
Butch Cassidy and the Sundance Kid (1969)

It's 5:32 PM and we finalize our options just as surveillance gives us the heads up. "Target vehicle one mile from your location," which places the truck here at about 5:38. I cue the mic and it is Gia who responds. The three rookies are in Brenda's kitchen awaiting word on the grand finale. My instructions are as clear and direct as I can make them. I begin with, "Everyone hear me? A few muttered, "Yes'." And I continue, "OK; surveillance puts the truck here in about 5 minutes. If one subject remains in the vehicle, Tommy's responsible for that location. You three will leave Brenda's apartment once the truck arrives and position yourself according to our plan."

I rehash the plan just to be sure. "And that position is in the hallway next to the vestibule door. Sean and Dennis will be ready to engage the subject and Gia will keep any civilian tenants from becoming targets. Gwen and I will loosely follow the subject into the apartment building but stop before entering. This scenario should position the bad guy inside the vestibule, and thus, trapped with nowhere to go."

"Questions?"

There are none so I conclude with, "If the truck attempts to leave the area you three will stand down and have no role. Gwen, Tommy, and I will handle that situation. We clear on that?"

A few nervous 10-4s and I say, "Good, be careful and avoid any crossfire with Gwen and I. You guys are good to go."

Skip announces that, "Target vehicle eastbound on Euclid. Should be at your location in two minutes."

Gwen and I sit inside Tommy's vehicle, which is parked across the street and 30 yards from the apartment entrance. The final piece of this puzzle is predicting where Vinny and Bruno stop? Perhaps the parking lot where Brenda bit the big one but we immediately ruled that out. A 30-foot Ryder truck can't fit or maneuver in such a confined space. Euclid Avenue is a one-way, single lane street with parked cars on both sides, so Gwen feels, "They either find a rare parking space large enough to accommodate the truck or block traffic."

"The third option," I say, "is they stop in front of the apartment, one idiot goes to fetch Brenda and the truck circles the block."

Tommy Shoulders comments, "You fuckin' feds will '*what if*' this shit to death. Let's just improvise like we did in Cairo."

'That's what I'm afraid of."

Skip Meinhardt interrupts our discussion, "TF one, Target vehicle one block from your location."

"10 –4. Skipper. Good job. We'll take over. You guys bracket the area and standby." I switch the radio to channel four and ask, "You copy Team two?"

This time Dennis replies with, "Affirmative, we are exiting the apartment and will stand by in the lobby."

I turn my head and can see a yellow Ryder truck coming our way. The tension inside the car is palpable since a massive bomb is about to pass some three feet away. The silence is broken by Tommy Shoulders who, in his most somber voice, wonders, "Can I ask a question?"

This is somewhat unusual given the timing. I say, "Of course."

He turns his head to face both Gwen and I and asks, "Whatta you call a Muslim who owns 6 goats."

Gwen is already chuckling, "I don't know." She says. "What *do* you call a Muslim who owns six goats?"

"A pimp."

The truck stops directly in front of the apartment building and it's Vinny who jumps from the passenger seat. Bruno drives off just as Gwen and I exit Tommy's car. Shoulders alerts the surveillance units to keep a loose eye on the truck but, "expect it to circle the block." The timing of the plan is critical. The three rookies should prevent Vinny from entering the inner door, and we should prevent him from exiting the *outer* door. Simple enough.

Vinny half sprints up the three steps but suddenly stops on the top step and turns his head. He scans the area as Gwen and I close the gap while walking arm in arm. My hope is that we pass for an older couple out for a post dinner stroll. We're now about fifteen feet from Bruno when he finally enters the building. We're now in a full out sprint with weapons drawn. We reach the outer door and clearly hear Sean and Dennis screaming, "FBI, hands up!"

Vinny must not be the *hands up* kind of terrorist since I recognize the distinctive retort of an AR 15 on full auto followed by the sound of an MP5 and a high caliber handgun. There's only one option left for Vinny so I yell to Gwen, "He's coming our way."

On cue, Vinny burst through the front door clutching his AR 15 at port arms. He hesitates a split second as he attempts to process the image of a tall blonde and a suave, debonair gentleman pointing guns his way. Agent 36 frequently makes the observation that we are like two peas in a pod. After Cairo, I can no longer argue the point.

The fact that Vinny had already ignored the previous *hands up* request is a good indication that he will continue to be non-compliant, so we simultaneously shoot him. It actually sounds like a single gunshot. No verbal commands, no '*drop the gun*,' no, '*FBI*,' and not even a lousy stinkin', "*Halt!*"

Vinny staggers off the step onto a scraggly bush and temporarily out of sight. I rush over to make sure he won't pop up firing but find the terrorist prone and holding his stomach. When our eyes meet, I expect defiance, but see fear. He's still clutching the AR 15 in his right hand so I ask him, "This has to be a tough choice; 72 virgins or 72 guys raping you in the prison shower." Vinny doesn't seem to be in the mood to take one for Allah. As Mike Tyson once said, "Everybody's a tough guy until they get punched in the nose." Or, in Vinny's case, *shot in the stomach*.

Although it seems an eternity since the truck departed, only 20 seconds had elapsed. We have a good minute left before Bruno makes his orbit so I call out to Shoulders and say, "We're taking Vinny inside for some first aid, I'll be right back."

Tommy responds with, "I got this covered. Get that asshole inside before the *other* asshole shows."

I have no intention of deserting Tommy who'll be confronting a terrorist armed with an assault weapon and a bomb. I cue my handi-talkie and tell the Mod Squad that the, "Coast is clear, we need some bodies out here *now!*"

Dennis, Sean, and I hoist Vinny off the ground and lug him to Brenda's apartment, which is getting crowded with bleeding terrorists. I inspect the stomach wound and see two entry wounds a centimeter apart. I tell Gwen that, "You were off target a little."

Agent 36 chuckles and corrects me as she taps Vinny's belly. "*This* hole was caused by a 10MM Sig. The *other* wound was from some wussy Saturday night special usually carried by weak, older agents." Vinny moans as Gwen continues poking his open wound. She tells the terrorist, "Shut up. You're not going to die. What kinda wimp jihadist are you?"

The bullets entered the upper right portion of the stomach and don't seem life-threatening. Vinny has no difficulty breathing, is not coughing up blood, and is alert. My two tours in Iraq observing bullet wounds indicate that Vinny will survive. I turn to Dennis and Sean,

"Keep pressure on the wound *and* leave the cuffs on. Gia monitor our activities on Bravo 4 in case we need backup."

As we exit the front door the first thing that catches my eye is a traffic jam. It takes a few seconds to sort things out and realize that Tommy has positioned his car in the middle of the street. The hood is raised indicating engine trouble, and the Ryder truck is frozen four vehicles back. Cars are slowly forming a line behind the truck, making it impossible to back up. Tommy seems to be tugging and pulling at something on the engine when the first horn begins the serenade. The cop waits until other drivers join the chorus, then steps out from under the hood screaming and frantically waving his arms. A tough guy can whip another tough guy but they'll *always* avoid crazy. Tommy appears deranged and heads down the row of cars pounding on hoods until he reaches the truck. Then in one fluid motion he leaps up on the running board pulls out his 9MM and blast a cap into Bruno's cranium. I now understand why he wanted to act alone and why my official report may win an Oscar for best fictional screenplay in a foreign film.

I race to the truck and notice that Bruno's skull has been reorganized. He probably won't be requiring first aid. As I open the driver's door Bruno begins a slow-motion slump toward me. I prop him back into a sitting position and notice the AR 15 lying on the passenger seat. I snatch a dollar bill from my pocket and use it to grab the muzzle of the rifle. Ever so carefully, I slide the AR 15 onto Bruno's lap and close the door.

Tommy's psychotic one act play provided him the time needed to shoot first. Law enforcement officers are *required* to identify themselves and provide the opportunity for surrender. But, had Shoulders approached the truck holding a badge while screaming, *'police'*, Bruno could have set off the bomb or grabbed his automatic weapon. Many prosecutors would indict Tommy on premeditated murder, but they probably didn't have a kid sitting at the Convention Center.

A further inspection of the cab reveals a wire with an attached fuse igniter leading somewhere. My guess is that it will lead directly to the fertilizer and diesel fuel. I step away from the truck and contact the FBI dispatcher, "TF one to Base."

"Go TF one."

"Requesting three ambulances, our Evidence Response Team, ATF bomb techs, and notify JTTF supervisor to come on scene at 12738 Euclid Avenue."

"Roger that TF one."

Tommy has a shit-eating grin on his mug. He says, "You're really gonna like this one."

I nod and he asks me, "When's the only time you should wink at a Muslim?"

"Don't know. When *is* the only time you should wink at a Muslim?"

"When aiming."

CHAPTER 10

*"I was a fraud, a hypocrite, and a liar. I was practically
a member of Congress."*

Dave Barry

I never claimed that Tommy's jokes were funny but at this particular time and place, this one leaves me laughing hysterically. *"When aiming,"* I repeat, and begin laughing again. Some locals begin to gather on the perimeter of the scene. They sense that events have come to a safe conclusion. The adult move would be to evacuate the neighborhood so I ask Tommy to call the local precinct.

He says, "This is Sgt. Shoulders, patch me through to the shift commander." A few seconds elapse and Tommy continues, "Yeah Ron, we need some marked units for crowd and traffic control. ASAP."

My FBI training dictates that we protect the crime scene, but maybe some contamination could actually help matters. There's the back parking lot, Brenda's apartment, the vestibule, front entrance, the Ryder truck, and every inch between.

The FBI Evidence Response Team (ERT) is good, so it's important that evidence gathered at the crime scene match our reports. I cue my handi-talkie and say. "TF one to TF team?"

Sean responds, "Go."

"We need to maintain the crime scene. Have Gia remain in the apartment, Sean to the back parking lot, Dennis will seal off the lobby and front step."

Agent 36 joins us at the Ryder truck. She hops onto the running board, observes Bruno, and informs Tommy, "Good foot work for a tubby guy who doesn't work out."

I say, "In a few minutes this place will be swarming with official types, so, we need to get our stories *somewhat* coherent."

I look at Tommy and he begins with, "I whacked the truck turd 'cause when I jumped on the running board, asshole here," Tommy pauses and points at Bruno slumped in the truck. "could've grabbed his gun, or set off the bomb."

I think, close enough for government work, but look Tommy in the eye. I say, "His weapon was on his lap so you may want to change, *'could've* grabbed' to *'attempted* to grab.' "

Tommy immediately understands and says, "That's what I *meant* to say."

Dirty little FBI secret; agents occasionally fib on reports but only to convict the guilty.

Agent 36 places her index fingers in her ears and asks, "Are you boys done getting your story straight?"

Technically speaking, Tommy *should* have identified himself as law enforcement before giving Bruno a part in his hair. But I say, "We're good on the truck, so let's deal with the shootout on the front step."

Gwen, being an attorney, opines that, "Shooting Vinny on the front step met every standard of our deadly force policy. We identified ourselves as federal agents, and Vinny shot first. As he exited the apartment building with his AR 15, he presented an imminent threat to us and others. So, we write it up exactly how it went down."

"So far, so good." I observe.

"But," Gwen qualifies, "our real problem is Brenda. Gia and Dennis will say the right thing, namely that Brenda, aka the terrorist, was attempting to escape and when cornered she pointed her weapon at Agent Gregory, where upon Agent Olson discharged her weapon."

"That sounds like a winner." Tommy says.

"Except if Sean decides to stray too far from that narrative."

Tommy gets a little exercised and says, "But that's the fuckin' truth! It was a righteous shoot, even by fed standards."

Gwen tells Tommy, "I'm on your side so shut up and listen! We don't have much time. I agree with you but these are the questions they'll ask, so we better get our shit together on the answers now."

Agent 36 begins a cross examination. "Question 1: Did we verbally or physically identify ourselves as law enforcement before we broke Brenda's door down? Answer: No." Gwen pauses and clarifies, "We never stated that we were FBI nor did we wear identifying clothing." Question 2: Is it unusual for a single girl in this neighborhood to possess a gun for protection? Answer: No. Question 3: Does the gas company normally knock down your door? Answer: No. Question 4: Why couldn't six trained law enforcement officers subdue a female teenager without shooting her in the back? Question 5:," Gwen pauses and finishes with, "aw shit, I can go on for a while longer but you get the picture."

We can hear police and ambulance sirens in the background. I tell my two friends. "I'll take the hit on this. I'm the senior agent and it's my case."

"Cut the martyr act Saint Booker." Gwen serious. "We're in this together but Sean Gregory is our wild card. If we all get on the same page, it'll read that the JTTF saved the lives of 500 kids. We smile for the camera, get our ass kissed by bureaucrats, and celebrate with cheap tequila. If Sean decides that we murdered Brenda, it's several years of investigations, grand jury indictments, and possible jail. The media will eat us alive and we'll be pariahs even within the FBI."

Tommy is getting frustrated and whines, "But we *did* the right thing."

I tell Tommy, "The cops in Ferguson and Baltimore did the right thing, but in today's world, that ain't good enough anymore."

Gwen finishes our little legal conference with, "And now it's up to Sean to say the right thing."

"I'll go talk to him." Tommy says and takes a step before Gwen grabs his arm and tells him that, "Bad move. You'll face additional charges of obstruction, and threatening a federal officer."

Ten minutes later the scene on Euclid Avenue is chaos. Flashing strobe lights illuminate the dark night. There's police, ambulance, ATF, FBI, news vehicles, helicopters, and a few fire trucks scattered everywhere.

Bruce Gombar has us sequestered in a tight little circle about a half a block from the craziness. He begins with, "Great job. ATF bomb techs estimate there's enough fertilizer in that truck to take down three apartment buildings and damage twenty more." He pauses and asks me, "Talk to me, John, so I can brief the boss and the media."

I take the lead and provide the sanitized version. It rolls off my tongue and has my supervisor nodding like a bobblehead doll. Bruce smiles and looks at Gwen who repeats the company line only with bigger words. Then Tommy, Gia, and Dennis corroborate with minor variations. It's Sean's turn, and we hold our collective breath.

If the media spins the tale that Jihad Brenda was escaping the jaws of law enforcement and attempting to blow up 500 kids, it's a wrap. But if they paint her as some frightened teenager running from crazies in fear for her life, then *we* become the terrorists. And since our media is anti-law enforcement *and* deceitful, I'm not feeling too warm and fuzzy if Sean decides to make a hard left.

Fred Gregory's son locks eyes with me, hesitates a few seconds, and finally says, "It went down just as everybody stated Mr. Gombar. I have nothing to add."

I give him a subtle nod and think that Sean Gregory has more of his dad's DNA than I originally believed.

Tommy smiles and asks Gwen, "Is it time for the cheap tequila?"

CHAPTER 11

"Fat, drunk, and stupid is no way to go through life."
Dean Wormer – Animal House

Three hours later we leave the crime scene and head toward the *Arrow Café* on St. Clair Avenue. When last seen, Vinny was headed to Metro Hospital for a few hours of surgery accompanied by a gaggle of police officers. We'll interview him later. Brenda and Bruno were in route to the morgue for autopsies and seemed uncommunicative. Gwen, Tommy, and I share a vehicle followed by the Mod Squad. Gwen makes the observation, "We must be slipping."

"Why's that?" I ask.

"Because we only killed two out of three terrorists."

"And your point?"

We scored 100% in Cairo." She adds, "And that was an *away* game."

The Arrow Café received its name in honor of the great Wal-Mart shootout during the East Coast blackout. A fat plumber, holed up in sporting goods, attempted to impale Captain Ray Kopka of the Cleveland Police Department with an arrow. Captain Kopka's exact words at the time were, "We're the Cleveland Police department and not the fuckin' Texas Rangers, so my obituary ain't gonna include the word *arrow*."

Ray has since retired and is the proud owner of this choke and puke eating establishment. He's an old crusty street cop from a bygone era when the world was black and white. Kopka's also a charter member of the Cairo gun club, but more on that later.

"We'll if it ain't the boys and girls from my past life. Out slumming?"

I give Ray a hug and say, "Be nice or I'll call the health department."

The big cop smiles and tells me, "I can see in your faces that you've been out having some fun."

I make introductions to the Mod Squad who have yet to utter a single syllable. They seem tentative from having to transition from a major shootout to a saloon. In the old Bureau, anytime an agent fired their weapon, the evening concluded at some bar where we over imbibed and talked trash. The shooter caught nonstop smack about their firearms proficiency as they were plied with booze. This generation of agent seems to graduate the FBI Academy armed with a flawed honor code that discourages the brotherhood of occasionally getting shit faced on duty.

New FBI guidelines mandate a visit with a Bureau shrink following the discharge of your weapon. They usually diagnose us with PTSD and recommend Prozac and some Buddhist chant. Just for the record, getting tipsy with the boys and girls is a lot less costly *and* more therapeutic.

In today's politically correct world, any cop or agent involved in a *questionable* shoot is immediately placed on administrative leave, lawyers up, and becomes isolated from their support system. They often get indicted, sued civilly, and resign. This makes law enforcement officers very tentative *and* it also leaves them vulnerable.

Kopka directs us to a table where we bunch together and rehash the evening's events. The old police captain listens, nods, and when we finish, he says, "Sometimes, I miss that shit."

It's 9:51 PM and the restaurant is absent customers. I tell him, "From what I've heard, this joint is empty at noon. You can always come back to the JTTF."

Kopka shakes his large head and scans the vacant room. He chuckles and sarcastically offers, "And give up all of this." The good captain stands, moseys into the kitchen, and returns holding a 700-ml bottle of Maraska Kruskovac liquor.

He informs us that it's, "Croatia's finest booze. It may not be a Coma, but it'll knock your ass out." Kopka pours out a few fingers of booze in water glasses. The Mod Squad seems reluctant to imbibe, until Gia Olson grabs her glass of Maraska, stands and offers. "A toast." She waits until our glasses are raised and says. "The good guys won."

Agent 36 adds, "*And*, to our remedially challenged friend here, Gia Olson, who whacked Jihad Brenda with a perfect bulls-eye to the back."

We all mumble and repeat, "To the good guys and Gia Olson who whacked Jihad Brenda. Saluda!"

The group chugs the tart liquor and slam our glasses on the table. Gia squints her eyes, shakes her head, and concludes her toast with, "Fuck Brenda!"

CHAPTER 12

"I'm too old for this shit."
Dannny Glover - Lethal Weapon

I awake with a throbbing headache and rethink the Bureau's guideline prohibiting getting shit-faced after a shootout. It now seems like a sound guiding principle. My initial craving includes caffeine, so I make my way to the kitchen and find my darling wife.

Lorri pours me a cup of coffee and asks rhetorically, "Have fun last night."

"Just a little bonding with the new agents."

She smirks and tells me to, "Cut the crap. It's been all over the morning news. You could've at least called so I knew you were alive."

"Well, I knew that someone would've called you if I *wasn't*." My logic, though somewhat skewed, is probably true.

My beautiful wife of twenty years has heard all my bullshit, so she gives me a hug and tells me, "You really make it difficult, but I *do* love you John Booker."

It hasn't all been hugs and I love you. We'd reached a point in the marriage where we were marking time. I'd just returned from a long-term undercover assignment and was still in asshole mode. I compounded that condition by chasing some Muslim college professor with big boobs who was eventually murdered by terrorists.

I could go on, but it gets muddled with a nuclear suitcase bomb, avian bird flu, and the murder of the chief justice of the Supreme Court. It culminated with a major shootout in Cairo and though the good guys prevailed, the marriage endured some stress fractures.

Lorri heads off to her job as a counselor who works with abused and neglected children. She's charged with the distasteful task of having to deal with parents who abuse their children. It's not the career I'd choose since beating the snot out of some parent who battered their kid would be frowned upon by management.

On the way to the FBI office, I stop at the local Starbucks and am greeted by Donnie Osmond. His name is actually Harvey Greenberg but he bears a striking resemblance to the singer. Donnie refers to himself as the "Gay Barista," which is both a reference to his sexual preference and an Italian term translating to coffee mixologist. When I was facing ten years in jail, it was the Gay Barista who comped me free Venti double mochas and cheered me up with droll banter.

"The usual John?"

"Naw, in a hurry, just a Grande, black."

Donnie smiles mischievously and says, "I'd like a big black one too."

"I'm hung over. Quit the gay innuendos and get my fucking coffee before I beat you straight."

Donnie pouts and feigns an injured look. "That's so mean, John." He says then, smiles and asks. "Did you have anything to do with that shootout last night?"

"Nope."

"You're lying, John. I can smell the gunpowder from here."

"That's my Glock aftershave. I get it at the Dollar Store."

Donnie hands me my coffee and I tell him, "Later."

It's going to be a busy day. Interview Vinny, visit the US Attorney's office, process the evidence, a noon debrief with the FBI shooting team, and write a ream of FD 302 reports. These undertakings will, in all likelihood, be interrupted by well meaning squad mates who'll want to discuss every detail of last evening's shootout.

My cell phone chirps and caller ID indicates that the Deputy Director of the FBI is reaching out to yours truly. Tony Daniels s says, "Hey roomie, congratulations."

"News travels quickly in the B."

"I was updated every 15 minutes. Was gonna call you last night but a birdie told me that you were celebrating at some dive chugging ethnic antifreeze."

"Let me guess. Your snitch has bodacious tatas and a law degree from Yale."

"When you put it that way, it sounds both sleazy *and* cerebral."

Deputy Director Anthony "Tony" Daniels is the second highest ranking official in the Federal Bureau of Investigation. Tony was my roommate at new agent training, where he shamelessly cheated off me in a Forensics exam. He's also a *good shit*, which is actually a high compliment among law enforcement types.

"You always seem to be in the right place at the right time."

"Cairo was not exactly a chance happening."

Tony chuckles and agrees, "I stand corrected, and one of these days, you're gonna have to tell me what happened there."

"I'm shocked." I say seriously. "Are you implying that my official reports did not accurately and truthfully portray the events in Egypt?"

"I highly doubt it." Tony laughs and asks. "What's left on the fertilizer case?"

"I'm not following you."

Tony's voice loses its playfulness. "I have an assignment for you John. It's sensitive and crucial to our national security."

I knew not to push Tony on the details of a case on a cell phone, so I answer his question. "Well, two of the subjects are dead and I'll interview the remaining idiot today or tomorrow. Don't anticipate he'll cooperate and even if he does, it'll probably be a dead end."

"Why's that?"

"Our intelligence indicates that these three idiots were lone wolfs and acted in a vacuum. We may get some bullshit leads with the usual sandbox surnames but ISIS is too smart to share anything useful with low level mopes."

"Agreed. So, you have three days to tie up the loose ends and get your butt to DC. I already cleared it with your S.A.C. (Special Agent in Charge). I'm assigning you TDY (Temporary Duty) to Headquarters."

"I'll think about it."

"Well then, think about being reassigned to work the Migratory Bird Act for the remainder of your career."

"I like birdies."

"Give my best to Lorri, wiseass."

"Likewise to Nancy," I say. "See you in the Seat of Power."

The SOP, or Seat of Power, was J. Edgar Hoover's designation for FBI Headquarters. I've since re-named it The Obstruction Palace, since it reminds me of Halloween straw mazes where kids get lost and begin sobbing.

CHAPTER 13

"Insanity runs in my family. It sometimes gallops."
Arsenic and Old Lace (1944)

When I arrive at the JTTF office Bruce Gombar seems impatient. "Been calling you, where've you been?"

"Was feeling sluggish so met my gay mojo supplier."

Bruce raises his eyebrow and says, "Whatever. The Bureau Psychologist has been waiting to interview you."

"Why?"

"You were involved in a shootout."

"I've been involved in lots of shootouts."

Bruce puts on his official puss and whines, "It's new FBI policy that anyone involved in a deadly force incident must be cleared for duty."

"Why?"

"Because you may have suffered trauma associated with the incident."

"I've got no problem shooting some maggot but I *am* experiencing trauma with this conversation."

"Just go." Bruce getting impatient. "May do you some good."

'If I have to spend several hours with some civilian tree hugger who wants to know why I wet the bed and once had sex with a unicorn in Bangkok, then I *will* go postal."

Bruce cocks his head and asks, "You are kidding, right?"

I smile and say, "Only about the bed wetting." I pause and ask Bruce to, "Tell them I'm trauma free and too busy."

"Look John," Bruce counsels, "you get away with a lot of shit because you produce and your friend is the Deputy Director, but *only* the shrink can clear you for field duty, and I know how much you love the office."

I realize that Bruce is on firm regulatory ground. I'm a brick agent and get cold sweats after two hours in an enclosed setting. Two years ago, FBI attorneys deemed that any agent involved in deadly force must be pronounced sane in case they go on a post-traumatic rampage. It is classic legal ass covering, so I'm off to see the wizard, whether I like it or not.

I inform Bruce, "I'll go."

Bruce smiles and as he leaves utters, "Have fun."

I fire off a childish, "Harvard sucks." But Bruce is gone.

As I head to the conference room for my head shrinking session, I think, *'All I gotta do is convince the Bureau psychologist that I'm sane. Shouldn't be too hard.'*

I knock on the door and hear, "Come in."

As I enter the SAC's conference room, a tall, slender, stunning lady stands and offers her hand, "I'm Doctor Linda Alvarez." Jet black hair, olive complexion, dark eyes, she looks a lot like the actress, Penelope Cruz or an older Selena. I notice tan muscular legs, which are my personal favorites, but tiny tits. I'll have to ask Agent 36 if she'll donate a cup size to our new Bureau shrink.

It's a firm, warm handshake and as we part I scan her left ring finger for a wedding band. Men are curious pigs and consider checking out a pretty girl's marital status a natural impulse. No ring, but in today's world, that means little. Linda sports a delicate ensemble of bracelets, hoop earrings, and a pearl necklace. I also detect a faint fragrance that reminds me of vanilla.

She points to a chair opposite some notepads, pens, and I notice my personnel file. It somehow annoys me that some academic is dissecting my entire law enforcement career. The written reprimands, suspensions, OPR investigations, *unsubstantiated* allegations of excessive force, and a few commendations for valor, all reduced to a single manila folder.

Dr. Alvarez's opening salvo sets the ground rules. "Agent Booker, I am Doctor Alvarez, the unit chief of the Behavioral Science Unit. My purpose here today is to determine your fitness for duty."

I interrupt her with, "What happened to Dr. Astler?"

"Went into private practice."

"He profiled the terrorists for us last year. Did an outstanding job."

"I know......The *Cairo* case." The disapproving inflection in her voice makes me cautious. Maybe she fell off a camel in Egypt during holiday but more likely she read the post op reports. I refuse to make it easy so I go into defense mode of basically guarding my goal line.

Alvarez grabs her designer pen and taps her note pad. "So, I hear you were involved in a deadly force incident yesterday."

"You heard right."

"Can you tell me what happened?"

"I provided a signed statement last night."

"I've read your statement, but want to hear it in your own words."

"Can I see my statement?"

Alvarez hesitates while she considers my request and finally hands me a copy of my FD 302.

I begin reading aloud *and* verbatim to include the preamble of, "Date: 2, February, Location: 12378 Euclid Avenue, Time..."

Alvarez interrupts me with, "I've been warned about you."

I smile at the good doctor and wonder, "So I come with a warning label like a hover board?"

The shrink smiles back and it is the first sign of her humanness. She throws her head back and seems to relax. She says, "You seem defensive."

"I am. My usual default is gratuitous flirting. My goal is for this meeting to end with you saying, '*You're an amazingly sane individual, in fact the sanest ever. Have a nice day.*' "

Dr. Linda laughs aloud and offers, "OK, let's dispense with my standard assessment procedure and go freestyle."

"My favorite style."

We spend the next 30 minutes simply bullshitting about life. I almost forget our location and more critically, the purpose of our meeting. If so inclined, Dr. Alvarez can put a severe crimp into my thrill-junky existence. I learn that my new bud was born in an El Paso Texas hospital one day *after* her mother crossed the border from Mexico. Though mom was in America illegally, baby Linda was a brand-new U.S. citizen. She excelled in school from day one and skipped a few grades in high school. The scholarship offers filled her mailbox and Linda chose The University of Texas at El Paso so she could remain home and help mom. Linda was homecoming queen, graduated with a 4.0, then breezed through graduate school earning a PhD. in Clinical Psychology.

"How'd you end up with the Bureau?" I ask.

"My mentor at UTEP conducted extensive research on serial killers and what makes them tick. His books are the gold standard used by law enforcement including the FBI. Doctor Fariha recently consulted with the Bureau on the techniques used by ISIS to recruit westerners. When Dr. Astler went into private practice Dr. Fariah recommended me."

"So we get the protégé, who in all probability is a lot better looking than Dr. Fariah." I chuckle. "A win, win."

Linda throws me a tight and controlled smile. The good doctor's access to my personnel file places me at a disadvantage. It includes my marital status, religion, psychological profile, blood type, childhood illnesses, and the fact that I grabbed Anita Polizzi's boob in fourth grade. She knows all about *me* so I decide to probe *her* lines. I begin a series of questions covering hobbies, favorite books, movies, and foods. My end game is her marital status and any disgusting fetishes. I culminate the mild interrogation with, "So does your husband *also* enjoy salsa dancing?"

She gives me a disapproving look and I understand that our *moment* just ended. She informs me that, "I'm not married but I *do* have a roommate."

In college, I had a roommate. His name was Bob Horovitz and he was a hairy, tough former Marine from Pittsburgh. We shared food, liquor, and once "dated" the same girl, whose nickname was Dirty Denise. But in today's world a roommate can be anything from a guy, gal, cat, llama, spirit, or even some inanimate object. So I ask, "Is that like a boyfriend?"

This last question seems to end the freestyle portion of the program. Dr. Alvarez ignores my inquiry, picks up my folder, and says, "I see that this is not your first shootout."

I'm back on defense and since I can't decide if this is a question, statement, or some counseling technique, I remain mum. After a full minute of awkward silence Dr. Linda follows up with, "You do realize that *most* law enforcement officers never un-holster a weapon during their entire career, yet you've been party to five incidents."

I do the math in my head and conclude that she's probably on the low end. During my deep cover days with the Mafia, I may have 'been *party*' to a few additional incidents that never made it to paper. Mob guys consider popping caps at each other a form of playtime, as long as nobody dies.

I enjoy bantering with a pretty girl as much as the next guy but this cat-and-mouse game has suddenly headed south and can only end badly for yours truly. Dr. Linda's leading questions are psycho bullshit so I tell her, "I've got a full day and never enjoyed verbal gymnastics. I understand that I require your blessing, so let's cut to the chase here."

"The chase?" She repeats with a tinge of condescension. "I am here to clinically determine your fitness for duty. *That* is the chase."

Dr. Linda is definitely Freudian fucking with me, so I stand and tell her, "I've been involved in a bunch of shootouts, because they shot first. Simple as that, so my motivation for un-holstering my weapon has *always* been to save my fucking ass. Goodbye."

As I'm exiting the room I *believe* Dr. Alvarez says, "My *roommate* is a super model and I am a stone bisexual. Would you enjoy watching us make love?"

Not really, but that would've been better than, "If you leave this room, you leave me no choice."

CHAPTER 14

"I wake up in the morning and I piss excellence."
Talladega Nights: The Ballad of Ricky Bobby

I pass Gia on my way back to the squad bay. She smiles and asks, "Did you meet with Doctor Alvarez yet?"

"Just left her." I say. "How about you?"

"It was a bit strange. She asked questions about my childhood. Wanted me to tell her all about the prejudice I've suffered growing up an Asian female in America."

"You don't seem very traumatized to me."

"I was born in Korea, but arrived in Zelienople, Pennsylvania, as an infant." Gia smiles and says. "I told Dr. Alvarez that I never felt any prejudice since my adopted parents are Italian and Swedish."

I chuckle and ask, "How'd that go for you?"

"Not well." Gia laughs. "She said something about me being in denial. Then inferred that my shooting Brenda had something to do with my ethnic confusion."

"A confused Korean-Italian-Swede. I refuse to touch that one myself."

Gia smiles and says, "When I disagreed with her she told me not to worry, that we were sisters. Then she babbled about how her mother entered the U.S. illegally and how she experienced the prejudice of being the daughter of an illegal alien."

"Pretty creepy." I observe. "I got a version of the Mexican momma saga."

"It gets creepier. We were finishing up, and she asked if I would date a Muslim."

"I thought you were *already* ethnically confused. So Alvarez adds Mohammed to the mix?"

"By this time, I've had enough so in my most serious voice, I tell her that, I'd *only* date a Muslim man, if he looked like Brad Pitt, was filthy rich on death's door, and bathed *occasionally*."

"She laugh?"

"Thought it was hysterical."

"Dr. Alvarez clear you for duty?"

Gia nods and adds, "Gave me a hug and as I was leaving she said, 'Good hunting.' "

"Let me get this straight Gia." I say. "You whack some girl in a shootout and the Bureau shrink wishes you *'good hunting.'* "

Gia chuckles and says, "A tad bit inappropriate."

"Well, welcome to the club."

"What club?"

"An exclusive secret FBI club." I whisper. "The only members are agents who shoot female teenage terrorists in the back."

Gia cocks her head and offers, "I'm honored."

"Later." I tell her then add, "Good hunting."

I arrive at my desk and am joined by Bruce who wonders, "How'd it go?"

"Not well. I'm a permanent office poge; wanna count paper clips with me?"

"You couldn't keep your sarcastic trap shut, could you!"

I protest, "Have you spoken with her. She's bat shit crazy."

My supervisor heads back to his office muttering, "You couldn't just *shut* up."

Maybe Bruce is right. I am a sarcastic pain in the ass and need to shut the fuck up sometimes. My Marine Corps Company Commander would sometimes counsel me, "Lieutenant Booker, you are an outstanding *combat* Marine but your garrison behavior is lacking."

I spend the rest of my day tying up loose ends. Vinny has lawyered up and refuses to talk. He'll eventually contract a case of verbal diarrhea when his attorney tallied the prison time associated with: attempted murder of federal agents, aiding and abetting a terrorist organization, conspiracy to commit mass murder, and general mopery. But his information will be worthless since *The Plain Dealer* has already plastered Vinny's photo on page one.

Sean stops by my desk and we compare notes on Dr. Alvarez's skull session. It seems that Fred's son survived the inquisition with no ethnic identity crisis and no mention of mom's border crossing. I tell him about Gia's skull session and we laugh aloud as I mimic Alvarez's adios of, "Good hunting."

We seem to have pushed through a rough patch in our relationship. My *'play dirty'* challenge last night caused Sean some ethical heartburn. When I graduated the FBI Academy *my* idealism lasted until some female fugitive pulled a derringer from her bra and pointed it at my head. I committed three mortal law enforcement sins: 1. Cuffed her in the front because she was female. 2. Didn't give Ms. Fugitive a complete pat-down because I didn't want to offend her, and 3. Didn't pistol whip her after I wrestled the gun away. From that moment in time, I adopted the mantra of, *'Always assume your enemy fights dirty.'*

I vaguely recall my conversation with Sean last night while knocking back shots of Croatian rot gut. I do remember challenging him with, "What the hell was going through your head when Brenda was running around the parking lot with a 45 cal?"

"I thought we could talk her into surrendering."

"Why would you think that? She was just about to murder 500 kids."

Sean gives this logic some thought and says, "In the church parking lot you told me that you were some old geezer and it may be time to retire. I didn't say anything, but I agreed. Then I watched how you handled the total chaos, how you put us in the best situation to survive. Your instincts and experience took over. You saw things clearly but I just saw craziness. Everything was a blur. I never even saw Brenda point the gun at me." He pauses and adds. "Now I think that maybe I'm the one who should hang it up."

There are times when saying the right thing at the right time can transform a life. You should choose your words and be serious, tactful and considerate, less you say something that can't be taken back. But the pearl of wisdom that escaped my drunken lips was, "Naw, don't do that. Your dad and I were *total* rookie fuck ups."

If I remember correctly through my Croatian induced fog, my '*total fuck ups*' confession seemed to work. It's also true that Fred and I *were* clueless baby agents.

It's 6PM and I've had enough fun for today. Time to go home and chase Lorri around the kitchen. I've resolved myself to be shackled to the desk until I can get a psychological do over with another Bureau shrink. It'll take some juice from my roommate, the Deputy Director (DD), and some fancy wordsmithing to get back in the game. I exit the JTTF office space and reach the elevator. The door slides open and standing inside the elevator is Doctor Linda Alvarez. Her smile is somewhat surprising given our recent past. I hesitate and she says, "I won't bite you John."

The two of us stand in an awkward silence as the elevator descends and I'm not about to make small talk. Linda says, "I'm sorry that we ended our session on a down note."

The normal response would be something along the lines of, I'm sorry too, blah, blah blah, but I'm actually speechless. Linda fills in the silence with, "Your team thinks that you walk on water."

I'm still not sure where this is going so I give a nod. She continues with, "Gwen was particularly effusive in her praise, and Sean and Gia paint you as a father figure."

I can't help myself and ask, "What about Tommy Shoulders?"

Linda chuckles and says, "He inferred that you may have a gender identity crisis."

"I'm *sure* he didn't use those words."

"Not exactly. It was something like, *'I think Booker screwed a unicorn in Bangkok.'*

Alvarez turns to me for a reply and I say, "I plead the fifth."

Now we're both laughing aloud and she says, "I spent about 20 minutes listening to a bunch of offensive Muslim jokes"

"Did he tell you the pimp joke and six goats?"

"Twice." Alvarez is still smiling and says. "And added one involving Bin laden and Mike Tyson. My unofficial diagnosis on Detective Shoulders is PPD."

"What's PPD?

"Paranoid Personality Disorder. A serious mental health condition in which the subject has a chronic mistrust of friends, strangers, and authority."

"That's pretty accurate," I chuckle.

She laughs and adds, "But I cleared your team for field duty."

The entire team?"

She repeats, "Yes, the entire team."

"Me too."

"You too."

The elevator doors open and as Dr. Linda Alvarez leaves she casually tosses out, "You ever get down to Quantico, come see me."

CHAPTER 15

"I hate it when the voices in my head go silent...I never know what they're planning."

Minneapolis – The Present

Gus Stevenson had a bad day. He flunked a math exam, received a DUI, and his Spanish girlfriend bid him *Adios*. Gus decided that college wasn't '*his thing*' so he quit, sold his car to pay the DUI legal bills, and spends his days surfing the net. He makes enough money stuffing envelopes inside his studio apartment to pay rent. A paternal grandmother stops by every week with groceries and some crumpled twenty dollar bills. Although raised Catholic, Gus hasn't been inside a church since his first communion.

A loner by nature, Gus enjoys the anonymous nature of chat rooms where his handle is *Grim Reaper*. It was subtle at first. No blood and guts or mention of beheadings. Two months of spirited debates on Ask.fm and he had cyber buddies who *got him*. Gus asked questions and every answer led him closer to the truth. America is a corrupt, warmongering nation that slaughters babies with bombs. *Ask.fm* is an anonymous website founded in Latvia in 2010, and quickly grew to more than 100 million users in 150 countries. Five more months of educational propaganda and Gus *belonged*. His life now had meaning and purpose. His web friends directed Gus to an app for

Android through Google Play called *Dawn of Glad Tidings*. It allows ISIS to communicate on the smart phone. Two months after that, Gus Stevenson went dark.

That's the time Gus received a steady flow of fluff depicting ISIS as a goodwill organization. Images of ISIS militants engaging with children, distributing food and performing other social services. A video featuring former German rapper-turned-ISIS-militant Denis Cuspert engaged in a snowball fight with fellow extremists, stating in German, "Now you see...here in Syria, we also can have fun!...That's jihad, jihad makes fun...and we have fun here with the children... Come on, we invite you to jihad!"

The German jihadist turned toward the camera and added in almost perfect English, "But if you *can't* make the trip, you can pledge allegiance and serve Allah in your own land."

Gus flipped from a dysfunctional American slacker to terrorist. ISIS whipped him up into a jihad frenzy by sending graphic military imagery. Images of shootings, crucifixions, beheadings, and mass executions, as well as images of individuals it claims as martyrs. Throughout the fall ISIS released a number of propaganda video posts explaining the "virtues of swords," "virtues of seeking martyrdom," and the benefit of "racing towards jihad."

By this time, Gus was begging to join the Crusade, and his jihadist sponsor provided the blueprint. How and where to purchase weapons to inflict maximum casualties followed by detailed instruction on soft targets. *'You must be ready to destroy many non-believers.'*

It was November 10 when the first serious snowfall hit Minnesota. Gus logged online and an advertisement caught his attention. Black Friday is two weeks away and promises $100 mini laptops and $145 thirty-six-inch flat-screens. It's the largest shopping day of the year with stores jammed by hordes of soccer moms and their spoiled kids battling one another for bargains.

The ad provides directions to the Mall of America in Bloomington with the addendum, *"THE LARGEST MALL IN AMERICA."*

CHAPTER 16

"I'm a nihilist. I don't believe in anything, not even nihilism."
The Anarchist Cookbook

I arrive at the Booker homestead and feast on a steak, baked beans, and diet Pepsi. My lovely bride and I are empty nesters since Nikki left for *The* Ohio State University. My daughter had the misfortune to inherit my caustic and irreverent sense of humor. Lorri often comments that, "She's *your* daughter," whenever Nikki does something totally inappropriate, like the time she asked Santa for a Taliban Barbie. Nikki is the love of my life and I smile whenever she enters the room. The feeling reminds me of a bottle of champagne being uncorked.

"How was work today?" Lorri asks.

"A bunch of paperwork about the shootout."

"Everything OK, John?" Lorri wonders.

"Yea, why do you ask?"

"Just wondering how the Bureau's taking two dead terrorists, one of which is a teenage girl from South Dakota?"

My wife is a Swede who came wired with the stereotypical logic and stoicism of that ethnic group. She's also a knockout so I frequently hear, "How'd she ever wind up with you?" And since I'm typecasting and generalizing, I am of Italian and English heritage, average height, muscular build, and hazel eyes. My hair, once jet black, is now littered with gray, but, I understand that gray hair is actually God's graffiti. I've always followed the philosophy of, *The world is filled with assholes who attempt to hide that condition from the rest of us.* So far, this has proven correct. My bride is a more trusting soul *except* when it comes to yours truly.

Lorri's concern has some validity. The FBI sometime eats their own and will cave to outside political pressure. So, the act of killing two terrorists in self-defense can somehow get distorted to fit the narrative of a few Fez heads protesting outside the FBI building. In the old Bureau, we had each other's back and understood the difference between good and evil. I have no idea how that absolute can become blurred by some maggot waiving a placard. I keep referring to the 'new' Bureau, but I suspect that every generation spews that identical tune, and that the *new* Bureau is the one that answered reveille the day *after* they joined.

"It was a good shoot." I tell my wife. "The *B* is on board."

Lorri shakes her head and I can't decide if her nod is in agreement or a *'bullshit!'*

We watch *Dancing with the Stars* (DWTS) and I'm rooting for this Czechoslovakian blonde with a great gluteus maximus muscle. Dirty little secret ladies; men watch shows like DWTS, lady gymnastics, and beach volleyball because we like athletic girls in skimpy outfits. That's the sole reason we sit on the couch and *pretend* to analyze the Tango with you.

I awake at 5:30 AM and head to the coffee pot. People are either day people or night people. It has something to do with biorhythms and is very difficult to change teams. I'm a morning guy and particularly enjoy my caffeine in the peaceful pre-dawn. Lorri joins me an hour later and we share a few moments catching up. It seems that her new supervisor is an arrogant dictator who will come and go like all boy wonders.

I commiserate with, "We have a buncha those types at the B. Call them Triple Ds."

"What's triple D?"

"Delegate, Deny, then Disappear."

Lorri's been through a slew of administrative hotshots who eventually discover that my competent and caring wife makes a difference in the lives of kids and leave her alone.

I rise and give my bride a kiss. "Love you sweetie." I say. "Remind little Adolph that your husband is armed, deranged, and dangerous."

I make my routine Starbucks visit and wait in line with the morning masses in route to work. Donnie Osmond works the room like a Pocono comedian tossing out asides ranging from sports scores to stock market tips. When I returned from Cairo I suggested a new Starbucks concoction called the double Jihad Camel Mocha, but the corporate types didn't think it suitable for their image. Donnie put up a valiant opposing view to no avail.

I tell him, "The usual," and Donnie wonders, "You feeling human today?"

"Wouldn't go that far." I say and ask. "How're you and the male fitness instructor doing?"

Donnie makes a face and tells me that, "He left me for a macho firefighter."

"It happens."

"It happens a lot to me."

"Maybe you need to give up on the manly types and go for an interior decorator, or hairdresser."

"You're such a homophobe, John." Donnie laughs and asks. "Have you ever gone the other way?"

He hands me my double mocha latte and as I turn to leave I say, "Only once, but it was with a unicorn in Bangkok." As I reach the parking lot, I think, that one *never* gets old.

I arrive at my desk and Peggy, our squad secretary, informs me, "Good morning John Booker, Bruce is waiting for you in the SAC's office."

Peggy would cuss like a drunken sailor compliments of Tourette's Syndrome which is a neurological condition that results in involuntary verbal ticks, but was cured during a tent revival when a roving preacher laid hands on her. She is smart, conscientious, and caring, which is rare among government employees. Peggy actually runs the place, when she's not singing in her church choir.

"Tell them I'm on my way."

Special Agent in Charge Mike Williams is old Bureau. He succeeded Jack Bell who retired and is now a fishing guide in the upper peninsula of Michigan. Williams is a former Marine whose nickname was "Iron Mike." One of these days, I'll ask him how he earned the moniker. SAC Williams bleeds FBI blue and has a reputation for supporting the troops. We'll see.

Jack Bell supported my shenanigans last year until I choked out my supervisor, called a Headquarters HBO "fat and sexually frustrated," and then accused my OPR investigators of being fascist turds. I may have been forgiven even those transgressions had I not been arrested for attempting to distribute 5 kilos of cocaine. But all ended well and Jack and I parted buds.

I find Bruce and Williams entrenched inside the throne room, which is my designation for the SAC's office. Williams points at an empty chair and we engage in small talk. These SES types rehearse rapport building in front of the mirror. We run the gamut from sports, music, and politics. Bruce informs us, "At Harvard, I played Lacrosse, the clarinet, and was president of the student body."

I attempt to one up my supervisor and say, "At Slippery Rock I played beer pong, bongo drums, and ran for Sgt. of Arms at the VFW." Williams gives a polite chuckle and informs me that, "The Deputy Director desires your presence."

I pretend to be clueless which is my specialty and say, "Why?"

"Your TDY orders don't specify." Williams explains. "But I spoke with Deputy Director Daniels. He would only confirm that it was a case of national significance."

Bruce asked, "Are you aware of why he is temporarily reassigning you?"

This is a loaded question. If I admit to Tony's *heads up*, then my chain of command in Cleveland will feel slighted.

"No idea," I lie.

Mike Williams informs me that, "You have three days to update your cases. Bruce will reassign them until you return."

Bruce can't help himself and sets another trap by asking, "And when will that be John?"

"No idea." I repeat coyly.

"Well don't even think about taking Gwen or Shoulders with you like last time." Bruce whines. "We're shorthanded and need them here."

I think, *that's exactly what I'll do,* but say, "Wouldn't think of it."

Now that we got the heavy lifting out of the way, Williams chuckles and says, "I've been informed that you pissed off the Bureau psychologist."

"Actually. I charmed the crap outta her," I explain. "Dr. Alvarez likes the dark, brooding, manly types."

"But Bruce tells me that she thinks you're more the Charley Manson type."

"Naw. I was just screwing with Bruce last night. Linda certified me without restriction or stipulations."

"Linda?" Williams repeats.

"She insisted I call her by her first name. Said it made her less threatening."

"You are such a bullshitter." Bruce laughs.

I rise and say, "That may be, but I've got work to do and this is turning into a meeting. I just timed out. Later."

On my way back to my desk I become inspired and think, *Not only will I steal Tommy and Gwen but also Gia and Sean.* I promised to keep an eye on Sean and Gia amuses the shit outta me. So take that, Harvard Boy.

CHAPTER 17

"We're gonna need a bigger boat."

Jaws (1977)

I find Agent 36 and Tommy Shoulders in the JTTF space. I ask them to, "Meet me at the Galleria." If Bruce observes us in some conspiratorial huddle, he'll know that I fibbed in the SAC's throne room. The three of us have been through hell and back last year. One member of our team had his finger amputated rather than tell the terrorist we were FBI. Special Agent Mohammed Asaki is a hero, and received the Bureau's top award for valor. Mo is currently the supervisor for the ISIS desk in Headquarters and proudly displays his hand, sans middle finger, to anyone who says, "Good morning."

Though we were only in Cairo for three days, we left a trail of bodies, money, and mayhem. But we eliminated a sleeper cell of terrorists attempting to purchase a nuclear suitcase bomb with North Korean monies. We were in enemy territory, seriously outnumbered, and operating off the federal grid. That's a combination that bonds people for life.

I grab two slices of pizza and a diet Pepsi and await Gwen and Tommy. Sgt. Tommy Shoulders is an interesting guy. He's smart, brave, and incorrigible. As a Cleveland narcotics detective, he modified the standard advice of rights form to, "You have the right to remain silent. But if you remain silent I'll just make up shit which will be used against you. Do you understand your rights maggot?"

They arrive at the Galleria food court and split up. Agent 36 proceeds to the Japanese kiosk while Tommy gets his usual fare of two super cheeseburgers, French fries, onion rings, and a milkshake. When everyone settles down I tell Tommy, "You keep eating that crap and you're gonna get fat."

Sgt. Shoulders laughs and admits, "I didn't make it to the gym today."

Gwen raises her eyebrows and says, "*Today?*"

Tommy nods and says, "Yea, and that makes 500 days in a row."

We all laugh and Tommy adds, "If God wanted me to touch my toes, he'd have put them on my knees."

I say, "Down to some business." I scoot my chair closer to the table. "Headquarters has their ass in some kinda uproar. Don't exactly know, but it could be something big."

"What the hell does that mean?" Shoulders asked. "You feds talk in circles."

Gwen tells him that, "We learn it at the FBI Academy."

"All I know is that my roomie wants to brief me on a case, *crucial to our national security.*" No one in our office has the details but Bruce made me promise on J. Edgar Hoover's grave that I won't involve you two."

Agent 36 feigns and injured look. "That's bullshit, Booker. We're a team, like The A Team, The Three Musketeers, and occasionally…. The Three Stooges."

"Not to worry. I'll refuse to do anything unless I can hand-pick my team."

"Can you do that?" Gwen asks.

"Whatta they gonna do to me? Shave my head and send me back to Cairo?"

Little do I know that in a few months, Cairo will seem like a Carnival Cruise.

Three days later I board the 7:10 AM flight from Cleveland to Reagan National Airport. I find Tony at the gate, which is rare in these post 9/11 days unless you have the FBI gold card. My former academy roommate is short of stature and well groomed. He is a former high school teacher and football coach from Pittsburgh. And just like the steel city, Tony's smart, tough, loyal, and loves his brick agents. Consequently, we field agents will go through hell and back for Tony Daniels.

We hug and Tony says, "Good to see you, roomie."

"It was either DC or Dothan, Alabama, investigating the Migratory Bird Act." I chuckle. "Tough choice."

"Do you ever get tired of being such a smart ass?"

"No."

I was raised by an Italian mother who didn't get the memo on proper childrearing. Sicilian women operate on guilt and fear. In an attempt to protect me from the cruel world, my mother warned me that every time I lied, the baby Jesus got diarrhea, she got me to eat calamari by claiming they were Italian onion rings, and that oil spots on roads were little kids who didn't hold their parents' hands when crossing the street. This strategy evidently molded me into a maladjusted smart ass.

We head toward FBI Headquarters through DC traffic. I gaze at the morass of cars inching along the highway and feel fortunate to be assigned in Cleveland. I'm all for diversity but doubt that I've eyeballed more than a dozen American-born citizens during the ride. There were turbans, dashikis, Puerto Rican bumper stickers, Albanian license plates, and I believe I saw a Somali pirate.

I comment to Tony, "You must feel like an ex-pat living here."

"Yea, but whenever I get home sick for America, I go to Pittsburgh for a reality check."

The Seat of Power, aka *The Obstruction Palace*, is situated at 935 Pennsylvania Avenue, NW Washington, D.C. The new Bureau has mass produced a generation of supervisors who obstruct rather than enable. I call them Boy Wonders because they dress well, speak in clichés, and feign compassion, but won't make a decision fearing the aftermath could be a career ending shit bomb which explodes in their face. Their favorite phrase when confronted with a decision is, I'll get back to you. They *never* do.

We park in the sub-basement and head to the executive suites on the fourth floor. I nod at a few Boy Wonders roaming the halls like zombies in search of HBOs (High Bureau Official) currently serving on career boards. I get no response.

I'm familiar with the Director's suite having spent several days here planning the Cairo operation. FBI Director Gary T. McKissock is a tall, lean former U.S. Attorney from the southern district of New York. He indicted forty-seven Wall Street types on a two-billion-dollar insider trading scam. The defendants bribed two prosecutors and a federal judge, so McKissock *indicted* them.

The scuttlebutt on our Director amongst Headquarters types is, *'He's a tight ass.'* But outside the beltway, the brick agents love the guy because he understands that the sole purpose of FBI HQ is to assist the field. McKissock once posed this insightful observation to his entire executive staff, "The FBI's mission is to put criminals behind bars. If Headquarters disappeared tomorrow, the field could *still* accomplish our mission. Think about that." Unfortunately, most of them *didn't*.

During the Cairo operation, the Director provided me a blank check to do my thing. He never questioned the body count and personally closed the case after a four-page post op memo and a wink and nod by Tony Daniels. A classic case of plausible deniability with the unspoken caveat of, *You really don't want to know.*

As we enter his office, McKissock rises and grabs my hand, "Agent Booker, I'm so glad you could make it."

I think, *'like I had a choice,'* but say, "No problem sir, how's your golf game?"

The Director smiles and says, "I try to shoot my age but end up shooting my weight."

Tony and I politely chuckle and McKissock offers. "It's been a few months since I've seen you John."

"At Fred Gregory's funeral."

McKissock's voice softens. "I'm sorry about the loss of your friend."

"Fred saved my ass in Cairo. He served our country with valour as both a Marine and FBI agent." I fill in a silence with, "His son, Sean, is a new agent with me in Cleveland."

McKissock nodded his head and told me, "I've read the reports on the fertilizer bomb case. His father would've been proud." The Director pauses and actually sighs. "The reason you're here today, John, is that you get results. You're not much on style points but these are unusual times."

I have no idea where this conversation is heading, but McKissock gets right to the point, "Our Intel analysts tell me that unless we stop the ISIS recruitment of lone wolf terrorist, America may turn into some third world nation."

It has been a very long time since John Booker was speechless.

CHAPTER 18

"82.7% of all statistics are made up on the spot."
                                                    Bob Songer

The Director reads from his notes, "The CIA estimates that thousands of westerners have joined ISIS within the last 3 years, with about 1700 being Americans. Westerners travel to Iraq and Syria, via Turkey, to join ISIS. The majority of these recruits come from France, England, Spain, and the United States. The U.S. may have started out slow but unfortunately, we're catching up fast."

"Isn't ISIS about to lose their caliphate in Syria and Iraq?"

"They are. ISIS is currently broadcasting that new recruits *not* travel to Raqqa."

"So we won and ISIS is on the run."

McKissock corrects me with, "Actually, this just worsens America's problem since ISIS is directing that recruits attack inside their *own* homeland."

It takes a few seconds for my brain to digest the implications. By losing their caliphate, ISIS creates *more* lone wolf terrorists on U.S. soil. I ask, "Can't we just start arresting them?"

"Two problems." Tony says. "First, free speech is protected and second, we simply can't identify them."

The Director clarifies. "ISIS can go fishing on public chat rooms and once they get someone hooked, they reel them in using encrypted communication. We are opening cases on lone wolves faster than we're closing them." McKissock checks his notes. "We're up to 2007 and counting. Instead of large, complex plots hatched by organized jihadist abroad, our new challenge is homegrown extremists who use the internet to self-radicalize. ISIS now operates the most sophisticated propaganda machine of any terrorist organization."

"How does this encryption work?"

"The term refers to messages masked in such a way that it's impossible to understand unless you have the correct key to decrypt it. Encryption puts the communications of criminals out of our reach and creates dark spaces. It allows terrorists a free zone to recruit, radicalize, plot, and plan."

I interrupt, "I never caught up with tech stuff Mr. Director. I only know that *hardware* is the only part of the computer that can be kicked."

Tony provides me a visual, "The ACLU rationalizes that encryption's like hiding a key to your house under the mat for the FBI, but a burglar can *also* find it. They feel that dark spaces already exist and we visit them every day. You have a dark place in your home where you can talk or you can meet in a park. So encryption is no big deal"

I nod and the Director continues. "Encryption has become a political football. Our agents are hindered by laws that prevent tracking people engaged in hateful speech unless there's a suspected crime. So, no matter how offensive expressing anti American views are, they are protected under the Constitution." He pauses and adds, "We can monitor communication on social media outlets but once they go encrypted, we need an electronic search warrant."

I comment that. "It's the usual liberal dribble that law enforcement will access private conversations just to bust some nickel bag weed commando or Henry the tax cheat. Excuse my language sir, but why can't those assholes in Congress get their shit together *before* another 9/11."

McKissock seems amused and says, "Because, those *assholes* lose all common sense when they read the latest public opinion poll which is *not* big on government surveillance."

I'm still trying to wrap my brain around this encryption thing. Let's say I wanna speak privately with some ISIS recruiter on Facebook. How do I go encrypted?"

The Director explains that, "Facebook recently introduced support for encryption on its social network. Users can now list their public key on their profile that others can use to contact them securely, and then Facebook will also send messages to users in an encrypted format if they opt in."

"Why won't Facebook cooperate with the FBI?" I wonder.

"Facebook, Apple, and other providers feel that by giving us access to encrypted conversations it could hurt law-abiding citizens. The bad guys could somehow hack into someone's savings account if they give us carte blanche."

"So pretty much anyone with even basic computer skills can go encrypted and be stealth."

"Unfortunately, yes, but that's just part of the problem."

Tony says. "The FBI is not equipped to deal with lone wolf terrorists."

McKissock clarifies. "By their very nature, lone wolves operate in a vacuum. Since we can't ID and track them electronically, we're totally dependent on informants. Lone wolves don't belong to an organization which we can infiltrate, they not part of a foreign nation and not exactly contributing members of society. So, lone wolfs are not on our criminal radar, and they are increasing in numbers."

"But." I challenge. "Most lone-wolf operations are not especially effective or destructive. As bad as the Boston Marathon Bombings was, the "brothers Grim" killed a total of only three people. Tragic yes, but not exactly a threat to our democracy."

Tony shakes his head and says, "The reality is that the toll of lone wolf terrorism can be severe. Each individual incident might not have a high body count, but if you track it over time the deaths add up, and will cause long-term effects."

"What kind of effects?"

"Paranoia, a bunker mentality, a sense that America is defenseless." McKissock pauses and looks me directly in the eye. "I'm sure you remember 9/11 John?"

"I do sir."

"Well then you remember the collective feeling of vulnerability America experienced."

"But we rallied, like we always do." I say. "We didn't experience another attack on our soil for over 12 years, until the Boston Marathon bombing."

McKissock softens his voice. "Just imagine if America suffered another incident like 9/11 or Boston *every* few days. Imagine the emotional toll on our daily lives; visualize empty malls, airplanes, football stadiums, and hotels. What would your comfort level be if your daughter heads off on spring break?" The FBI Director pauses and finishes our conversation with. "Because unless we can stop these lone wolves, that will be America's fate."

CHAPTER 19

"Imagine if there were no hypothetical situations."

The meeting ends on that down note and Tony and I go to lunch. He picks some Indian place on M Avenue that's heavy on the curry. My meeting with the FBI Director bummed me out. The United States is the last super power standing, yet we seem to be *constantly* teetering on the edge of some Armageddon. Our globe seems to be in a precarious period with psychotic despots everywhere. Iran even went nuclear, which is like giving your crazy drunk uncle the keys to a Lamborghini. The Iranians out-negotiated our ass and left Secretary of State Kerry at the table in his skivvies. We should have outsourced the negotiations to the Italian Mafia who understand the subtleties of the upper hand.

I'm confused since I can't figure out my role in this case. It seems to me that computer geeks, profilers, and Intel analysts are the correct mix for the lone wolf problem. I'm a brick agent who possesses none of those skills but I get the feeling that Tony and McKissock need someone to color outside the lines. That's my specialty.

After a cocktail of Sunda Kanji, which is made from fermenting rice and buried in mud pots, I tell Tony, "This shit is rank, but it's better than a Maraska."

Tony chuckles and asks, "OK, I'll bite, what's that?"

"Croatia's finest booze. You can either drink it or rub it on your hemorrhoids."

As we study the menus Tony says, "I come here about once a month. Try the Goga."

The waiter arrives and Tony orders the Goga. I request a well-done hamburger with a side of fries, but my roomie gives me a look and holds up two fingers. My Goga is actually pretty tasty. It reminds me of uncooked calamari.

Sometime during the meal, I ask my roommate directly, "What the hell do you want me to do with these lone wolfs?"

"Do what you do best."

"Annoy them?"

Tony chuckles and wonders aloud. "You ever think that we're getting too old for this shit?"

"Speak for yourself," I counter. "You're so old they discontinued your blood type."

Tony laughs aloud, then gets serious, "You have an unusual sense of humor John. I'm no psychiatrist but you view life different than the rest of us and you're a risk-taker, which makes you the person to take on this investigation. This isn't the conventional *arrest the bad guy*, case closed scenario, *and* that's why you're here."

"I know that's a compliment but for this particular Rubric's Cube, you need someone with a different skill set."

"Not really." Tony leans toward me. "A lone wolf terrorist is basically a common criminal. They may have a skewed religious ideology fueling their actions but it boils down to thugs trying to hurt people."

"I agree, but according to our intelligence these particular thugs are invisible and never ending." I look my roommate square in the eye and tell him that, "It can't be done."

"Why not?" Tony challenges.

"Because we can't ID them *before* they act, *because* they're growing in numbers, and, *because* our government is fucked up and cares more about some basketball player coming out of the closet than some wounded Marine."

"You'll have the resources of the entire FBI at your disposal."

"You seem to have no idea what we're facing," I tell Tony. "That fertilizer case we just wrapped up took us eighteen weeks of investigation, thirteen FBI personnel, and ended in a shootout with two dead, and they didn't use any encryption." I pause and ask the question, "Do you really think we can devote that manpower to similar cases with encrypted conversations?"

Tony nods his and says with conviction, "You proved with that case that we *can* deal with the lone wolf terrorist."

"But, the fertilizer group never went encrypted, they operated openly on Facebook and confided in an FBI snitch. We got lucky on that one but if there are potentially thousands of lone wolves communicating in the dark, we could never get ahead of that curve."

"Why?" Tony challenged. "The FBI has the best investigators, a world-class lab and cyber unit, the top profilers, and the most extensive database in the world. When we target an individual or group they will eventually go down."

I sip the Kanji and smile, "You sound like a fucking public service announcement. I agree that the FBI is the best investigative organization on earth, but, we're built like an RV and what we need is a motorcycle."

"Either the curry or the Kanji has reached critical mass on your brain."

"I love you roomie, but you need to come visit the troops in the trenches. You seem to have a bad case of ivory tower-osis. You get it by sitting on your ass at meetings all day."

"I worked the streets for years," Tony counters with an edge in his voice. "You constantly criticize authority figures. Even at the academy, you bitched and moaned anytime you disagreed with some instructor. Get over it John. We're *not* the enemy."

Although Tony's words sting, they have the ring of truth. Lorri is continually chiding me to stifle my mouth. Friends sometime smile at my asides and then ask the rhetorical question, "Do you always let shit go directly from your brain to your mouth."

"Touché," I reply. "I will attempt to insert a pause button between my brain and mouth."

Tony smiles and says, "Don't go too serious on me because that would be creepy."

"Not to worry."

I hold up my Indian drink concoction in a toast. Tony raises his glass and I say, "To the new John Booker." We touch glasses and I'm about to make some sarcastic racial aside about India, but hit the newly installed pause button. It works, but I understand that the button is only temporary.

I say, "Let's brainstorm this."

Tony asks, "Why a motorcycle?"

"When I was undercover with the mob, we could do things quickly. The FBI can't do *anything* quickly. We have to write up a proposal, discuss it with our supervisor, push it up the chain of command, have a buncha meetings, rework the proposal based on input, eventually ship it off to HQ where they discuss it and have meetings, then push it up their chain of command, all the while the field is answering inane questions from HQ boy wonders. *If* it gets approved, and that's a big *if*, we have more meetings to discuss manpower, budgets, and then schedule meetings with the US Attorney's office. They '*what if*' the proposal to death, schedule more meetings, and float it up their chain of command."

I look at Tony and ask, "How am I doing?"

Tony is amused and comments, "Your pause button didn't last long."

"Sorry, but, it's the truth and you *know* it's the truth. I can go on but basically the FBI is the Queen Elizabeth but we need a speedboat."

Tony counters with, "The Director will eliminate most of those roadblocks and you get to pick all the manpower you'll need."

"Not enough," I say and touch the side of my head. I announce, "I got it!"

"Got what?"

"The answer to this entire lone wolf problem."

Tony smiles and placates me with, "OK John, enlighten me."

"All we gotta do is get our FBI tech guys to make bombs look like prayer mats, then we flood the market with free ones." I raise my hands and finish with, "End of lone wolfs."

"Brilliant, John." Tony chuckles.

"I haven't thought this thing out yet, but just off the top of my brain, it'll be a major investment of manpower. This operation will require full time cyber staff, field agents, CIA and NSC staff TDY'd to the case, Intel analysts, surveillance squads, with aviation capabilities, our super SWAT guys, and our best profilers."

The Deputy Director offers, "Not a problem, John, and you'll be happy to hear that we have recently hired the best profiler in the business. She's smart, pretty, and has a world-class body."

"Let me guess," I interrupt. "Her name is Linda Alvarez."

CHAPTER 20

"I've been expecting you Mr. Bond."
The Spy Who Loved Me – 1977

Boston FBI office – February 14, 2011 – Two years prior to the Boston Marathon bombings.

FBI Special Agent Ray Smith reads his assigned lead. *'Interview Tamerlan Tsarnaev and determine possible ties to terrorist activities.'* This would not be an unusual lead post 9/11 had it not originated with Soviet Intelligence. The commies reported that Tamerlan had recently travelled to the Russian provinces of Dagestan and Chechnya where he spent ten months. While there, Tamerlan interacted with militant groups.

Smith is a former Marine and Oklahoma City detective with good instincts. Commonsense suggests that one does not travel halfway around the world and suddenly decide, *'Hey, wouldn't it be neat to get together with some terrorists and hang out.'* So Ray Smith ratchets up his bullshit antenna.

Background information contained in the lead indicate that in 2001, Tamerlan and his brother Dzhokhar moved to Dagestan, where their mother still had family. The boys were 14 and 7 years old at the time and they lived there for about six months before obtaining refugee status and resettling in Massachusetts.

Tamerlan was a competitive boxer for a club named Team Lowell. He attended Bunker Hill Community College in Boston before taking time off to focus on his boxing career. Tamerlan dreams of being selected for the US Olympic team and becoming a naturalized American like his brother. FBI Intel analysts checked social media and discovered that Tamerlan maintains a *YouTube* profile uploaded with 47 videos under the categories titled "*terrorists*" and "*Islam.*"

Smith investigative juices stew as he scans the file. There's something fishy going on here and at the *very* least it's your everyday pissed off Muslim. There's *also* the very real possibility that Tamerlan is going to commit jihad. But, the FBI agent knew that suspicion is a much lower standard than evidence and according to the current idiots running the executive branch, spewing *death to America,* is now considered some harmless form of youthful protest.

The Chechnyan lives in an inner-city area of Lowell, Massachusetts, among seedy shops peddling ethnic foods and cheap imported clothing. Smith raps on the door of Tamerlan's third floor apartment and his initial impression is *not good.* The boxer has an instant chip on his shoulder and seems impatient and annoyed to be questioned by the FBI. The smell of ancient cigarette smoke and the mellow undertones of men's room disinfectant permeates the room.

He's a big kid with unkempt black hair and a sleazy sneer. The apartment is your typical nuevo shithole popular with art history majors and junior jihadists. Tamerlan angrily denies meeting with terrorists, being radicalized, and he *even* denies that the Holocaust occurred. The FBI agent loses count of the lies and resists an urge to pistol whip Tamerlan.

The meeting ends minus the pistol whipping but it got close when Tamerlan demands that Smith leave. Although Agent Smith has been asked to leave numerous locations, it is the first time that a suspected terrorist had made the demand. Tamerlan's *exact* words were, "I am legally in America with constitutional rights and *you* will leave, now!"

Smith's frustration is rooted in the fact that Tamerlan is right! This greasy Muslim possesses a green card and receives food stamps, college tuition, free health care and an Obama cell phone. Smith leaves with a warning, "I'll be seeing you again Mr. Tsarnaev." As Smith exits the apartment building a man approaches him on the sidewalk. He's a middle-aged male of Middle-East extraction and appears nervous. Smith touches the comforting butt of his 9MM service pistol and says, "Can I help you?"

"No, but I can *help* you." The man's eyes are darting around the area. He speaks quickly, "I attend mosque with Tamerlan and he openly encourages jihad. I feel he will act upon his words."

"What's your name?" Smith asks, "I need to interview you someplace else."

The stranger shakes his head and quickly disappears down the street.

Agent Smith heads back to the office and directly into his supervisor's office. "This Tamerlan is bad news."

Supervisory Special Agent Peter Grimes says, "Talk to me."

"Tamerlan and his little brother, Dzhokhar, are up to something."

Grimes chuckles and says, "Can you be a little more specific?"

"Actually, no," Smith says seriously. "But I want you to open a case."

"A terrorist case?" Grimes asks. "We'll need something solid to open."

"At least a preliminary inquiry with a terrorist designation."

"No problem there, what's your PC?"

"We have probable cause with the Russian Intel report. In addition to that, we have the radical dialogue on YouTube."

Grimes interrupts with, "The Russians gave nothing specific, just rumors, and we can't exactly interview their sources to validate the info. The social media stuff is free speech, so we'll need something other than hearsay to take this anywhere."

"I got some inside info which'll provide plenty of leads and maybe even a snitch or two." Smith explains about the nervous man who approached him on the street. "This mystery guy witnessed Tamerlan's diatribes at the local mosque. So...," Smith concludes confidently, "We send a Muslim agent from another division into the mosque. Get him to record some of Tamerlan's hate speech, befriend him and get him talking his radical shit, find out who Tamerlan hangs with. I'll conduct surveillances during evening prayers and get tags of the people attending mosque, run their names. I'll bet we get some hits on terrorist sympathizers, and then wrap it all into an undercover operation."

The silence is Ray Smith's first clue that the Tamerlan matter just hit a speed bump. The next clue was Grimes shaking his bald head followed by the final nail in the investigative coffin, "We're not permitted to surveil mosques, interview people at or near mosques, *or* conduct undercover operations at or near mosques."

Smith gives an unsure chuckle and says, "You're fucking with me because I forgot my $5 for the coffee fund. Right?"

Grimes says, "You think I like this politically correct crap? We got sued in LA by the ACLU for violating the civil rights of Muslims. It was all bullshit, but the White House caved and now we can't be within 500 feet of *any* US mosque."

"But, statistics show that 80% of American mosques preach violent jihad and distribute violent literature to worshipers. So who we gonna surveil?" Smith sarcastically asks. "Lithuanian Catholics? Hell, they're a *real* threat to national security."

Grimes says. "You're preaching to the choir, Ray. Before this insane policy, the FBI launched dozens of successful sting operations against homegrown radicals inside mosques, and disrupted dozens of plots against innocent American citizens across the United States."

"Well, fuck the brass Pete. I'll do it on my own time. Keep it off the books until we get something solid."

"I'm not the enemy, but, this mosque thing is not gonna be the usual wink and nod if we get caught. The B will cut our nuts off. It's *not* worth *our* careers. End of story."

Smith can only mutter, "This is fucking wrong, Pete."

"I agree, so let's just *hope* that Tamerlan and his brother Dzhokhar don't go jihad."

But two years later, on April 15, 2013, two bombs went off near the finish line of the Boston Marathon, killing three spectators and wounding more than 260 other people. Four days later, after an intense manhunt that shut down the Boston area, police captured one of the bombing suspects, 19-year-old Dzhokhar Tsarnaev, whose older brother and fellow suspect, 26-year-old Tamerlan Tsarnaev, died following a shootout with law enforcement earlier that same day. Investigators later concluded that the Tsarnaevs, who spent part of their childhoods in the former Soviet republic of Kyrgyzstan but lived in the United States for about a decade prior to the bombings, planned and carried out the attack on their own and were not connected to any terrorist organizations. They were designated '*Lone Wolfs.*'

FOX News reported that, "*If only they* (the FBI), *were allowed to continue their investigation, perhaps the many innocent victims of the Boston Marathon bombings would not have lost their lives and limbs. The FBI was not even allowed to canvas Boston mosques until four days after the April 15 attacks. The FBI was further restricted by policy to check out the radical Boston mosque where the Muslim bombers worshiped, even though they were on the government's watch list. The Bureau didn't even contact mosque leaders for help in identifying their images after those images were captured on closed-circuit TV cameras and cell phone.*"

The news anchor stares intently at the camera and wonders, "Why didn't the Imam contact the FBI? Why don't these people of peace speak up when they hear people in their congregation espousing hate of the country they have adopted. Maybe it's because they see us as an opportunity to expand their caliphate and don't really care what happens to the infidels in their way who don't deserve to live. If church doors are open to anyone or anything, then mosques should be too. If Muslims have nothing to hide, then they should not object to being treated the same or equal to other religious organizations. And if our Federal agencies are going to protect us from attack, they have to adopt strong measures to root out these radicals and a plan to counter those who would commit atrocities against citizens of the United States."

Special Agent Ray Smith sits on his recliner at home. He sips his beer and says aloud to the television screen, "It's too fuckin' late for talk, you righteous assholes."

CHAPTER 21

"Believe nothing, no matter where you read it, or who said it, unless it agrees with your own reason and common sense."

Buddha

I catch the 4:47 return flight to Cleveland. It's the airline with the flight attendants who ad lib jokes during preflight instructions. Some may find their humor offensive or insensitive, but I find kindred spirits. The lovely Loretta Gould grabs the mic and encourages passengers to join their *'frequent near miss program.'* This aside gets a few scattered giggles. Loretta smiles and then reviews procedures should the plane have to ditch in water. She finishes with, "I do hope you have your bathing suits handy." This zinger gets some belly laughs and it occurs to me that if things go south with my FBI job I'll have career options with the airlines.

The meeting with Tony may have felt all warm and fuzzy but I still have no clue how to deal with lone wolf terrorists. Whenever my brain travels down this particular problem-solving road it hits a brick wall. FBI agents think in a linear way. A crime is planned or committed. We either prevent the crime or capture the criminal. In either case, you use standard investigative techniques. Conduct interviews, data checks, electronic or physical surveillance, snitches, undercover cops, and once I even used a psychic on a missing kid case. When the case is resolved, we move on to a different case. But in the lone wolf scenario, the case *never* ends. So, the question really becomes; can we *contain* the problem? Not likely unless Congress passes some laws to loosen the screws on encryption. We need to go *Eric Snowden* on their ass and data mine every e-mail, tweet, ham radio exchange, Facebook post, and hire some mind readers to boot.

The popularity of the rise in ISIS coincided with a technological shift that allows people to plug into terrorist propaganda anonymously online, rather than show up at meetings or rallies. That gives cover to potential lone wolf terrorists, who can become radicalized wearing pajamas in front of their computers. Before ISIS, investigators could focus on radicalized mosques and clerics to figure out those networks. But individual actors can be very difficult to thwart, even with the best intelligence.

The Goga is doing a rumba inside my stomach. I can actually smell the curry seeping from my pores. Thirty minutes till touchdown, and the lavatory is calling my name. I always felt that the Indian population was a mirthless group and now I know why. They're constantly in some stage of food poisoning from eating crap like Goga. I climb over a sleeping teenager and do a ballet twist into the aisle. I must have touched the sleeping prince because he jolts up and screams, "Hey man, watch it!"

The kid is big and probably plays linebacker on his high school football team. He's also a spoiled arrogant bully but someone has to be the adult here, so I say, "Sorry, didn't mean to wake you."

Bully boy confuses politeness with weakness and tells me, "Just don't let it happen again."

I count to five and head to the lavatory where I deposit 1 pound of Goga. If yellow crime scene tape were available, I'd place it across the bathroom door. I mentally cross India off my bucket list and head back to my seat. The kid has his eyes closed and his body is splayed over both our seats. There's no way I can contort myself back to my window seat without some contact with the bully boy, and my options narrow further when Loretta instructs us to "please return to your seats for landing." I tap bully boy on the shoulder and just as he's about to say something we'd both regret, I straddle him and place both hands on his chest. He makes a futile attempt to stand but I roughly shove him back in his seat. I glare into his vacant eyes and whisper, "You're about to enter a battle of wits unarmed, so shut the fuck up and stay stuck on stupid." He appears just bright enough to comprehend a legitimate threat and nods his head.

I arrive home at around 7:30 and somehow am feeling hungry. I can only surmise that the Goga drop on the airplane created stomach space. My wife suggests a late-night dinner at Lazzaras, which is a great place to go off our diets. Lots of bread, red gravy, cheese, and pasta topped off with the best tiramisu west of Sorrento.

We law enforcement officers sometimes get too insular in our thinking. Our problem is that we all think alike. I'm in a weird place inside my brain. Perhaps *frustrated* is a better description so I need some civilian perspective. Dirty little FBI secret is that agents discuss cases with wives, girlfriends, and sometimes both. It happens, and it can also include an occasional bartender.

But Tony's admonition of it's 'sensitive and crucial to our national security,' replays in my brain so I decide to back into the topic. During the main course of cannelloni and baccala I ask my bride if she's spoken with Nikki lately.

"She called me yesterday. Said she was thinking about changing her major to French, Art, or Astronomy."

I temporarily forget all about terrorists and observe. "That would be her *third* major in two years. The only unemployable majors she *hasn't* tried is Fermentation Science and Pop Culture."

Lorri puts things in perspective and rationalizes that, "Nikki's healthy, happy, and bright. Whatever she decides to do, it'll be fine."

I sip my Beam and concede, "You're right. When Nikki had the bird flu I could've cared less what she wanted to be. All I wanted was my baby to get better."

"Your terrorists did that to our daughter and I will *never* forgive them."

Lorri was referring to my last case when a sleeper cell of Egyptian terrorists teamed up with North Korea to wreak havoc with the U.S. They caused major blackouts, murdered the chief justice of the Supreme Court, hacked into our banking system, and introduced the avian (bird) flu. Unfortunately, my daughter was collateral damage. Having Lorri pissed at you, whether you're a soccer mom or psychotic terrorist, can be dangerous to one's health. Swedes seem measured and calm but if you piss them off, they can go Viking on your ass.

I've successfully maneuvered my lone wolf case into the conversation and say, "I'm just glad that Nikki has her head on straight." Lorri nods and I add, "Not like these American kids who get brainwashed and join ISIS."

"It's awful, John. What can they be thinking?"

"Well, whatta *you* think? You work with kids."

My wife has obviously given this issue some thought. She tells me that, "We seem to have lost an entire generation of children."

"How so."

"The family unit is broken." Lorri pauses, then picks up a head of steam. "Today's kids stare at screens all day, communicate in hash tags, and can't complete sentences. They feel unloved, disenfranchised, disillusioned, entitled, abandoned, and angry. They have no sense of right, wrong, reality, worth, or morals. They can't add, subtract, or divide, but can multiply like rabbits producing another generation of themselves, and then wonder why the world is so horrible."

I interrupt with, "You should've met this kid sitting next to me on the plane."

"What happened on the plane?"

"Just another lost youth in need of counseling."

Lorri smiles and asks me if I've heard of the 'Slender Man.'

I shrug my shoulders and she tells me, "The Slender Man is a viral internet myth. He's a paranormal creature who stalks, abducts, and traumatizes children. Slender Man supposedly controls people and communicates telepathically."

"What's the big deal?" I wonder. "Our generation had Ouija boards."

"Did you ever stab a friend to please the Ouija board?"

"Naw, but thirty years ago, we'd give each other wedgies."

"That is *so* you," Lori amused. "But a few years ago, two girls from Wisconsin believed Slender Man was real and they wanted to prove it by butchering their friend. At a sleepover Morgan Geyser and Anissa Weier stabbed her 19 times. They passed the knife back and forth between them as one held the victim down and the other stabbed her."

"That is unreal," I say. "How can these kids get so far off the reality track?"

Lorri looks me in the eye and says, "You just answered your own question about lone wolf terrorists."

"Really? I don't get it. What's the answer?"

"There *is* no answer."

CHAPTER 22

"We never really grow up; we only learn how to act in public."
Bryan White

"Starbucks is packed on this cold October morning in Cleveland. My adopted city has seen better days but is making a mini comeback. The theatre district is alive and well and the Flats is on the rebound. Toothless hookers on crack offering twenty-dollar blow jobs have been replaced by ladies of the evening in spandex. Prices have gone up and dental work has improved.

The gay barista is slinging his coffee and seems not to have a care in the world. In a strange sort of way, I look forward to our early morning bantering sessions. Donnie is smart, amusing, and irreverent. You really can't say that about too many people.

"Good morning, John. The usual?"

I nod and say, "Can I ask you a personal question, Donnie?"

He smiles mischievously and says, "About nine inches erect."

"I walked into that, didn't I?" We both laugh and I say. "You refer to yourself as 'the gay barista.' So you're evidently not a big fan of PC."

Donnie shakes his head, "I'm actually just confused why I came out of the closet. Was it claustrophobia or homophobia?"

I chuckle and say, "That kinda talk will get you fired in today's world. You'll end up pushing Slurpees at the 7-11."

"People are way too sensitive these days. We all need thicker skin." Donnie leans toward me and lowers his voice. "Last week, some guy told me that Starbucks should eliminate *black* coffee. Thought it was racist."

"You're shitting me, right?"

"I wish. He demanded we change it to, coffee *without* milk."

I observe that. "Being PC means *always* having to say you're sorry."

Donnie tells me that, "So, *gay barista* is actually kinda mild these days."

"Why's that?"

"The lesbians now want us faggots to call them vagitarians."

I grab my coffee and say, "Later."

My arrival at the JTTF office is met with major fanfare. Bruce desires the skinny on my meeting at the Seat of Power and the troops want an unsanitized version of the same thing. Since Bruce is my supervisor, I get to lie to him first.

He wastes no time getting to the heart of the matter, "So what's the case?"

"Can't tell you."

Bruce gives me a fuck you look and switches to his boss voice, "I've got the same clearance as you, and, I'm your supervisor."

I smile at my good friend and remind him, "Remember Matt Michaels?"

Supervisory Special Agent Matt Michaels was my previous supervisor who insisted on interjecting himself into the Cairo case. I begged, cajoled, and ultimately physically assaulted Matt but couldn't persuade his oversized ego to butt out. I may have failed but FBI Director McKissock succeeded and Michaels is currently selling real estate in Las Vegas.

"I'm not Matt Michaels," Bruce correctly observes.

I nod and tell him, "You're a lot bigger, brighter, and nicer. But McKissock kicked this up to a SCI sensitive case and ordered me to keep my trap shut."

Case information above Top Secret is classified as Sensitive Compartmentalized Information (SCI) and has additional controls on dissemination. In order to gain SCI Access, one would need to be specifically designated by the FBI Director and have a need to know, which is strictly enforced. These compartments of information are identified by code names and for this case I picked the name; Terrorist Under RaDar. If you put the emphasis on the intended letters, the working title is TURD. Tony immediately caught the implication but just shook his head and approved the designation.

Bruce is not taking his exclusion well and says, "That's bullshit!"

"Agreed." I say to pacify my friend. "But it's way above my pay grade, and," I add with a somber tone, "I'm just trying to keep *you* administratively pure." This is the same management hand job Bruce fed me a few days ago. SES types attend in-service training titled, *'How to make street agents feel warm and fuzzy while you fuck them.'* Bruce seems to be deciding if I'm fucking with him. I force an angelic smile, which resembles a botched facelift. He stands and declares, "I'll go see the SAC and get this shit squared away."

I maintain my look of pained concern and say, "You do that."

The second he's out of sight Agent 36 and Tommy Shoulders surround me. Gwen is already laughing. "What's up Doc?"

"Bruce is pissed that I can't discuss the case with him." I explain. "The Director classified it SCI and swore me to secrecy."

Tommy Shoulders has no idea what SCI means so he cuts to the chase, "Quit with the fed alphabet soup, what's the case?"

"We're going after the lone wolf terrorists."

Gwen says, "Tough nut to crack."

"A blinding flash of the obvious, Gwen. And I thought you were slipping. We need a sit down."

"Our usual place?" Gwen wonders.

I nod. "Let's scram before Bruce gets back and wants to have a *meeting*."

At the mention of the word *'meeting'* we all scrunch up our faces like we've been overdosed with cod liver oil. The Galleria is fairly empty at this time of the morning. The high glass ceiling and tiled floors make it an echo chamber. We find a table on the mezzanine and I fetch some coffee and bagels.

Gwen begins the cross examination given her Yale law degree. "Details, Booker. What went down in DC?"

I provide a summary of my conversation both with Director McKissock and Tony. I emphasize that, "Once lone wolfs go encrypted they become invisible and we'll have no heads up that a crime is being planned."

Tommy comments, "That's bullshit. So we have to *wait* until something bad happens, then we get to identify the bodies?"

Agent 36 adds, "And since they're lone wolves, they'll be no leads on co-conspirators or a criminal network we can take down. Law enforcement goes back to square one."

"Sadly, that's it in a nutshell," I sum up. "Ideas?"

Tommy declares, "I've been in this business for 27 years. Criminals can get away with shit for a while but they *all* eventually fuck up and go down."

Agent 36 puts the kibosh on the party and simply declares, "It can't be done."

"*Can't* is a strong word, Gwen." I challenge. "Where's the gal who kicked ass in Cairo?"

Agent 36 sighs and says, "Look John, I'm just being realistic. You may stop one out of five lone wolf attacks, but that's at *today's* numbers. The Bureau predicts these attacks will quadruple over the next five years and then quadruple again. We have our hands tied by politicians, our eyes blindfolded by technology, and our asses filled with the bullshit of policies, procedures, guidelines, and regulations." Gwen pauses and repeats solemnly, "It can't be done."

"It may be a *different* kind of inves, but I agree with Tommy. These lone wolves aren't rocket scientists, so we just need to figure out how to get *ahead* of the bastards."

Agent 36 points out that, there are 1.6 billion Muslims in the world and about 5% are radicalized. Five percent doesn't sound like much but do the math and we're dealing with 80 million people who wish to annihilate us. And," She emphasizes, "The *other* 95% hope they succeed."

I nod and says, "Maybe Gwen but first things first. We need information from experts. Once we know what we're up against, then we come up with the plan."

Gwen smiles and says, "No matter *what* we come up with, we'll have to work off the books."

"Why?"

"If we play it by the book, we'll need electronic search warrants, but by the time we identify subjects, obtain probable cause, get the warrant, have meetings, and get approvals, it'll be too late."

"Can't McKissock just assign the best FBI computer nerds to hack into these encrypted sites?" Tommy asks.

Gwen answers this one. "Not even the Director of the FBI can screw with the Constitution. It's up to us to bypass the due process and corrupt some cyber geek." Agent 36 pauses and muses, "Perhaps that's why they gave you the ticket, Booker. The Director *can't* operate off the books, but he knows that's where you live. Plausible deniability.'

"I have no problem leaving the reservation but we have to be careful who we invite to this black bag party."

Agent 36 reasons, "It's gonna take time to find someone that has those cyber skills *and* can keep their mouth shut, and we *don't* have time."

The reality pause is broken by Tommy, "Not a problem." He says with a crooked smile. "I got the person for the job, and, she *definitely* ain't a fed."

"She?" Agent 36 raises her eyebrows and asks, "Have you been programming her server?"

"Naw," said Tommy, defensive. "She's a computer genius who I arrested 25 years ago."

"Why?" I ask. "And, can we *trust* her?"

"Totally trustworthy," Tommy explains. "The short version is that Jun hacked into the police database and erased her arrest record."

"So the arrest was for hacking?"

"Nope. Jun was worried that a morals bust would hurt her job hunting, so she *disappeared her record.*" She actually plead to a bullshit misdemeanor charge of public indecency."

"I can't wait for this one?" Gwen laughs.

"Jun was a stripper who got caught up in an *alleged* prostitution sweep. The mayor needed the moral majority vote for re-election so he ordered Vice to raid topless joints. Just a bullshit show." Tommy pauses and adds, "Jun was just doing her job."

Dirty little FBI secret. Law enforcement officers do *not* like hassling prostitutes unless it involves sex slaves or kids. We view strippers and hookers as blue collar workers. They're like public servants and it's usually a win/win situation unless one of them has the clap.

"Are you saying *June* like the month?"

"No, *Jun* with no 'e,' like *run.*" Tommy explains that, "Jun is Chinese. She was 6 credits shy of her PhD in digital forensics cyber security when I snatched her from center stage. The stripping paid for her education."

"OK Tommy, I'm an open-minded guy. Are her cyber skills as good as her pole dancing?"

Tommy smiles and says, "The best on both. Jun was an exotic wet dream on the stage. Gigantic fake tits, long black silky hair, and a world-class ass. She was a feature act and only worked the best clubs. As far as the cyber stuff, Jun now owns a cyber security firm in New York. Does a lot of work with major international corporations to *prevent* getting hacked."

"So," Gwen wonders. "If she is so good, how'd she get caught?"

"She never got caught on the hacking," Tommy explains. "And that's where I'm leaving it."

I sum up the meeting with, "I don't have all the answers to this puzzle. We'll have to adapt and improvise, just like Cairo. In the meantime, Tommy, get in touch with Jun *today* and feel her out.... so to speak."

Tommy tells us, "Jun'll help us out."

Gwen challenges with, "How can you be so sure?"

"She owes me a big one."

"Indelicately put, but it's so you." I say, "We have an unlimited budget for this case. Get her on the first plane available and we'll make our pitch."

We gather our trash and head back to the office. Tommy laughs and asks, "What *do* Tehran and Hiroshima have in common?"

Gwen and I smile and repeat, "What *do* Teheran and Hiroshima have in common?"

"Nothing yet."

CHAPTER 23

"If men make war in slavish obedience to rules, they will fail."
General Ulysses S. Grant

Columbus Ohio - 2007

Abu Musa Nasar had difficulty understanding things like Twitter, Facebook, and even a TV remote. The 13-year-old recently emigrated from Pakistan and was behind the electronic curve of American teenagers.

Pakistan is the sixth most populous country in the world with an estimated population of 194 million. Pakistan will reach *fifth* position in terms of total population by 2047.

Abu's parents, Sosa and Jabar, left Punjab province following the 2006 floods that destroyed a significant proportion of agricultural output. They came to America because they were hungry, tired, and wanted a better life for their little Abu and daughter Faisan.

Pakistani authorities have ties to the leadership elements of ISIS who made Pakistan's tribal areas their home. The government wouldn't protect Jabar from having to pay these barbarians a monthly tithe, so it was time for a new beginning. Another concern was Abu's sudden interest with terrorist propaganda. He began mimicking their hatred, speaking of killing infidels and *'the near enemy.'* Jabar prayed to Allah that America would be a new beginning for their little boy.

A distant uncle in Ohio sponsored the Nasar family promising Jabar employment at his convenience store. They arrived with refugee status and their life savings totaling $1700. The bus trip from New York to Columbus Ohio was filled with hope as they transitioned from the inner-city chaos to the tranquility of Pennsylvania farms.

The Nassar family joined a local mosque and practiced ritual prayer, or salat, which is performed five times a day: at dawn, midday, afternoon, sunset, and evening. During the month of Ramadan they observed Sawm (fasted) from dawn to sunset.

He wished his son would fit in into the American culture and take advantage of a free society. Abu attended Tom Cullison middle school where he met friends of *all* religious beliefs, but his best friend was Musa Atwa. The two boys became inseparable friends. Atwa was born in Syria and frequently quoted passages from the Koran. At first Jabar welcomed Atwa into his home until the day the teenager quoted his favorite Koran verse, *'Fight them so that Allah may punish them at your hands. Kill the unbelievers, kill the infidel!'*

Jabar would have to keep his eye on this Atwa.

CHAPTER 24

"I forgot my mantra."
Woody Allen in Annie Hall

We need more information but the clock is ticking. As the U.S. plays catch up, our enemies are plotting to maim and kill innocent people. It's time to get back to the office and begin. I recall an old metaphor. Question: *"How do you eat an elephant?"* Answer: *"One bite at a time."*

It's time to take the first bite. As the group enters the JTTF space, Peggy informs me, "Bruce wants to see you ASAP. He seems agitated, again."

I like and respect Bruce Gombar. When Matt Michaels went *one flew over the cuckoo's nest*, Bruce took command of the task force and was an outstanding leader. With that said, he can be annoying and spend an hour discussing one minute worth of subject matter. Bruce minored in minutia at Harvard.

He begins our *meeting* with, "SAC Williams was personally briefed by the Director but won't discuss it. Not a word, not a hint, not even a grunt. He *did* advise me that McNulty, Shoulders, Olson, *and* Gregory are *immediately* assigned TDY to *your* little task force." Bruce pauses and semi whines, "And you looked me in the eye and *promised* that you wouldn't take Gwen and Tommy. But, you didn't stop there and took two *more* of my agents."

"Sorry, I lied."

Bruce is suddenly speechless. He looks at me with wide eyes and finally utters, "You *lied!*"

"You know I lie. I'm an undercover and that's what we do."

"But you're not undercover now."

I shrug and alibi with, "It's a bad habit, what can I say. You made the mistake of trusting me."

"You know John, sometimes I feel that you're *just* not a team player."

"Bruce, I apologize for taking 4 agents from the task force. I apologize for not confiding in you, and I apologize for being an asshole sometimes." My supervisor squints his eyes as if anticipating a punch line, but there is none. "You're a good FBI supervisor and I respect you."

Bruce says, "Thanks, John, but I *did* strongly recommend that the SAC reconsider assigning Olson and Gregory to you. They're first office agents and not ready for *your* type of operation."

"And *what* type is that?"

Bruce pauses, choosing his words carefully, "Fast and loose. These new agents need to learn the *FBI* way of doing things." Bruce concedes that, "Gwen and Shoulders are already lost causes."

"And what did Williams say?"

"He agreed with me."

"I don't think he has the juice to stop it."

"He agreed with me," Bruce clarifies. "*But* he can't countermand the Director of the FBI, so, you win again John."

I feel my blood pressure rising and say, "This isn't a game, Bruce. I need Olson and Gregory because they have the skill sets needed for this case. It's as simple as that."

Bruce nods and relents, "It would've been nice if we had this conversation *before* you lied."

He's right and I suddenly feel like shit. I stand up, and extend my hand toward Bruce. "I apologize. I *should* have trusted and confided in you."

Bruce stands and takes my hand. He asks, "So you'll reconsider taking Olson and Gregory?"

"I'll definitely give it some thought."

As I leave his office it dawns on me that I just lied to Bruce *again*. I also spent several precious hours in meetings. There are times when a second or third opinion is valuable but at *some* point, you need to confer with an expert, and that would be me.

I tell Peggy that I have a meeting if anyone's looking for me.

"*Everybody* looks for you, John Booker. Wanna tell me where or who?"

"I'm meeting with myself at Starbucks."

Peggy chuckles and says, "I got it John Booker, anybody asks, I'll tell them, '*you're incommunicado with a Caramel Macchiato.*' "

I love Peggy.

The traffic is light along I-71 South as I pass the Ford Casting Plant. The employee parking lot, once filled with cars, is now a crumbling empty wasteland with weeds sprouting through the concrete. Japanese steel and the American unions destroyed an entire industry that provided food and shelter for thousands of Ohioans. I call Gwen on her personal cell phone and ask her to, "Tell Gia, and Sean that effective immediately they're assigned to our task force. Tell them to pack their bags for a road trip to D.C." I pause and add. "You and Tommy too."

"How long?"

"Three days. And when we get back to Cleveland, we'll *have* our plan to deal with lone wolves."

"You're such an optimist, Booker. Where the hell are you?"

"I'm gonna be out of pocket for a few hours. Cover for me."

Donnie is surprised to see me at 1PM. My usual caffeine fix is with the early AM crowd. He asks, "You get arrested and fired again?"

After my arrest photo appeared on the front page of *The Plain Dealer*, I would sit at Starbucks and plot my defense. Donnie kept my coffee cup filled and reassured me that, *"things will work out."* And they did.

I smile and tell him, "I'm outta the dope business. I'm now selling red eye missiles to teenagers."

Donnie deadpans, "Teenagers are much more treacherous than dopers, John."

I grab a triple espresso and find the corner window table. When I was a Marine 2nd Lieutenant in Iraq, we relied on intelligence in making tactical decisions. So, the initial scribble on my legal pad is:

Gather Intel on lone wolves – profile them – who are they? What makes them tick? Can they be dissuaded? How? Disinformation campaign?

Begin master "watch" list/ deportation issues

Gather Intel on IT stuff like encryption, hacking, dark spaces, etc. Can we track thousands of conversations using key/red flag words or phrases? Can we follow up with Jun? How?

State department/Immigration - ID high risks/notifications upon leaving and entering U.S.

The role of informants/ how to develop snitches for this group? Where and who? mosques, schools.

Gather the manpower for the case. Intel analysts, cryptologists, forensic computer techs, full time liaison with CIA, NSC, Homeland Security, Defense, FBI profilers, Special Ops.

The beginnings of an investigative plan begin to flesh out, but I still can't resolve two major issues. How do we, legally or *illegally*, identify the lone wolves who go dark, and, *how* do we arrest them - legally or illegally? It occurs to me that we *need* to operate this train on two different tracks; *legal* and *illegal*.

I'm in a creative zone enhanced by a mega dose of caffeine and am feeling the onset of optimism, when two girls wearing Cleveland State University hoodies plop next to me and begin a loud conversation on *celibacy*. It's evidently the '*in*' thing, though Sandra isn't sold. Darlene argues that abstaining from sex can increase creativity and intelligence. Sandra counters with, "I'd rather lose 10 IQ points than give up oral sex." I totally agree with Sandra but remain mute.

I'm about to move to a different table when it dawns on me that this is an opportunity and not an interruption. Sandra and Darlene may be able to *shed* some light on the lone wolf problem.

"Excuse me girls." I get their attention, smile, and say. "I'd like to ask you guys a question."

They give me a strained smile and mutter "Uh huh" but *think* "Pervert alert!"

"Can I sit?"

Darlene, minus any enthusiasm, nods toward a chair. I realize that I'm on the *creepy* clock so I tell them that, "I'm a sociology professor at Case Western University doing research on the lone wolf problem."

I'm expecting a vacant stare and some comment on animal behavior but Sandra immediately offers, "Wow, brainless twits. Who'd want to blow themselves up for some creepy Arab guy?"

"Don't know," I reply. "That's what I'm trying to find out. What *would* make someone join a terrorist group like ISIS?"

Darlene bites her lip and observes, "Losers. They spend their days in chat rooms with screen names like *Vampire Chick*."

Sandra offers, "They're also loners. You can spot them a mile away."

This latest tidbit interests me since not one talking head expert has ever attempted a physical description of a lone wolf.

"*How* can you spot them?"

Sandra tells me that, "They dress weird. Dark clothes, too much makeup, off the geek rack at Wal-Mart, combat boots, and won't look you in the eye."

Not your most comprehensive profile, but interesting. I tell them that I have to leave and ask, "Anything else?"

Darlene looks at Sandra and disagrees, "I think that some of those Arab guys are kinda hot."

I shake my head in despair and make a final entry on my list: #7. *Pray.* I take a step then turn around and tell Darlene, "Sandra's right."

Both girls give me a quizzical look and I say. "Celibacy won't make you smarter, but it'll back your hormones up and you'll *eventually* implode."

CHAPTER 25

"If you're the smartest person in the room – you're in the wrong room."

Tommy and I head to Hopkins International Airport to meet the 7:50 direct flight from Kennedy. We badge our way to the gate area and I ask Tommy, "You said you arrested Jun 25 years ago. How old is Ms. Silicone chest?"

"Gotta be late forties, early fifties."

"Have you seen her lately?"

"Nope. We keep in touch by e-mail."

"Tell me about her life in the past few decades. Did she marry have kids, any health issues?"

"Jun is divorced from some NYU college professor, no kids but she moved a bunch of her family from China. Works 12 hour days, writes books on cyber hacking, earns big fees from major corporations to *prevent* hacking, and her only hobby is cooking."

"You tell her anything about the case?"

"Nothing specific but she's on board."

"You gonna tell me why she owes you?"

"Nope."

"We gonna be able to spot her?"

"Shouldn't be a problem. She's a gorgeous chink with big tits. Can't be too many of them on a plane."

I smile and tell Tommy that, "You evidently haven't been in New York City lately."

The first trickle of passengers deplanes and I'm looking for the *stripper* version of Jun. Silicone boobs, slender legs, long silky black hair, and a world-class ass. A few Asian women fit that description but I'm waiting on Tommy to make a move. The cop is scanning likely suspects and seems surprised when a chubby Asian woman with short gray hair approaches. She's wearing hiking boots, jeans, and a checkered flannel shirt. "My dear friend Thomas." she says while giving him a hug.

Tommy stares at the woman and tentatively asks, "Jun?"

I'm guessing cooking may *be* her *only* hobby since she has a Buddha-like body. As we walk along the airport corridors introductions are made and the unlikely pair reminisces with some raucous laughter. Jun may not be the exotic dancer anymore but she's full of joy with a tinge of caustic irreverence. I'm able to hear only bits and pieces of the conversation in the noisy terminal.

I piece together that when Jun was a teenager, her parents were sentenced to some Chinese gulag on trumped up charges. The government confiscated Jun's home and everything else of value. It got worse when Mom and dad *mysteriously* died in prison and the government accused Jun of espionage. Jun immigrated to the U.S. with a backpack and the equivalent of $47. She couldn't afford graduate school on a *GAP* paycheck but she *could* by providing an illusion. Customers who frequent high end gentlemen clubs may be astute businessmen, but become drooling idiots in the presence of strippers. These girls can conduct a net worth evaluation within 5 minutes of, *"Hi, my name is Mercedes, what's a handsome guy like you doing all alone?"* Over the next 14 years she danced naked, earned a PhD in forensic cyber security, and became a wealthy entrepreneur.

My eavesdropping uncovers no juicy tidbits on *why* this unlikely duo have such a strong bond. Tommy is short in stature, with a pot belly and Charles Bronson mug. He's smart but rough around the edges. Jun seems sophisticated, educated, and articulate. My *usual* default in these types of situations is a romantic relationship aka sex, but the jury is still out. Jun's English is perfect but I can detect the slightest lingering trace of her Chinese ancestry.

We've reserved a suite at the Courtyard Marriot. Jun's only accommodation request was a *kitchen*. No comment here but I may gain a pound or two during her stay. Gwen and Gia joins us at the hotel and we sip on coffee and brief Jun on the lone wolf problem. She's outraged that murderers can hide behind the veil of signals transmitted over public airways, but I'm still trying to gauge if she'll risk everything to stop it.

I conclude the brief with a warning, "I want to be perfectly clear about what's at stake. We're asking you to break a few federal laws. You have a lot to lose *including* your freedom."

Jun considers my words and looks at Tommy. She says, "I owe my dear friend Thomas much as I do my adopted country. It's a debt which I'm honored to repay."

Gwen wonders, "As a Chinese immigrant Jun, don't you feel any compassion or empathy toward Muslims?"

Jun explains, "I was attending university in Cleveland when Muslims destroyed the Twin Towers. They cancelled classes and I ran back to my apartment and turned on the TV. It sickened me to watch thousands of Muslims around the world celebrating the deaths of 3000 Americans."

I interrupt Jun and ask, "You said *Muslims* destroyed the Twin Towers, and not *radical* Muslims. So do you believe that *all* Muslims are radicals?"

"Allow me to ask *you* a question."

I nod and Jun inquires, "Can a *good* Muslim be a *good* American?"

"*Some* but not many."

"The operative word is *good*," Jun explains that, "If they are *good* Muslims then they can *never* be *good* Americans."

Gwen offers, "*Never* is an absolute."

"Some things *are* absolute." Jun clarifies, "Theologically, a *good* Muslim's allegiance is to Allah, the moon god of Arabia, and no other religion is accepted except Islam. Scripturally, a *good* Muslim's allegiance is to the Quran. Socially, a *good* Muslim's religion forbids him to make friends with Christians or Jews and they must submit to the mullahs, or spiritual leaders, who teach annihilation of Israel and America, the great Satan. Intellectually, a *good* Muslim cannot accept the American Constitution since it is based on Biblical principles and believes the Bible to be corrupt. Democracy and Islam can *never* co-exist since every Muslim government is either dictatorial or autocratic. So," Jun concludes, "Muslims obviously can *never* be both *good* Muslims and *good* Americans."

Gwen smiles and says, "I yield to logic and facts."

The group laughs and I tell Jun that, "Gwen has *rarely* yielded to anything, so what *can* be done about conversations that go encrypted?"

Jun asks the group, "Have you heard of Tor?"

The silence answers the question and Jun explains, "Tor is an anonymity network or a hidden service protocol."

Tommy interrupts Jun with, "You speaking English or Chinese?"

Jun smiles and apologizes, "Sorry but I spend my days with fellow signal geeks and we have our own language. In June 2014, when the government of Iraq blocked Twitter and Facebook as part of its response to the growing ISIS situation, Tor usage in that country exploded, according to Tor metrics data."

"So Tor is a way to communicate in secret."

Jun nods and tells us that, "Similar to a private club, and like that club, it *is* possible to gain access using the Tor hidden protocol." She pauses and adds the addendum, "But *very* difficult."

"Impossible or just difficult?" I wonder.

"We all remember Edward Snowden?"

"The NSA leaker currently imbibing Russian vodka and smelts."

"Well one of the things he leaked was the source code in one NSA program called XKeyscore, which showed that any user simply attempting to download Tor was automatically fingerprinted, essentially enabling the NSA to know the identity of millions of Tor users. But there's a difference between finding people who are on the Dark Web and revealing the nature of their intent."

"So," Gwen muses, "if we can get this XKeyscore program, we can track ISIS websites which recruit lone wolves."

"Yes but it won't be easy. NSA doesn't even acknowledge that XKeyscore exists, *but* if they did, they wouldn't share it with the FBI."

"Are you saying that the President couldn't order NSA to share XKeyscore with the FBI?"

Jun chuckles and reminds me that, "NSA will tell our President that no such program exists."

I wonder, "Is NSA the *only* agency with the program?"

"The word among Intel types is that the State Department also has XKeyscore."

I look at the group and ask, "Additional comments or ideas?"

Agent Olson raises her hand and says, "A question." Gia doesn't say much and at first blush seems a shy and tranquil soul. At the FBI academy, Gia required remedial training in firearms and defensive tactics, but I've come to recognize a confident tenacious individual. She tells Jun, "The FBI has begun a program where agents visit potential lone wolves and attempt to dissuade them."

Jun interrupts, "If they've already identified them as lone wolves, why not arrest them?"

Gwen picks up on the legal issues of that question, "Because they haven't broken any laws. Every FBI Division has computer undercover squads. For the most part they troll chat rooms for pedophiles who prey on children. They set up dates with the pervert and he's met by FBI SWAT teams. But since 9/11 agents monitor the social websites where terrorists recruit."

"And," Gia explains. "Once they identify someone on the brink of boarding an airplane to Turkey or buying weapons, the FBI visits them and *discusses* the bad things that can happen when you become a jihadist. The problem is that this *counseling* visit rarely works and only serves to alert the subject that they're on our radar. So instead of eliminating potential threats we're actually chasing these jihad recruits to encrypted sites where we lose them."

I observe, "It's difficult for two guys in Brooks Brothers suits to convince some mentally defective yahoo to get a job and join the Rotary Club."

Gia continues, "My questions is, since it's possible to intercept dark conversations, can we actually *block* the ISIS recruiter's transmission, so the recruit thinks they're talking to ISIS but it'll actually be one of us?"

Jun grasps the subtle implications and nods, "Very fiendish *and* .... doable. Get me that XKeyscore." Jun claps her hand and announces, "Well then, I'm hungry; let's get some lunch."

CHAPTER 26

"Great spirits have always encountered violent opposition
from mediocre minds."
– Albert Einstein

"So this is how the HBO's (High Bureau Officials) joyride?"

"It's how they measure the size of their bureaucratic dicks." I tell Tommy Shoulders.

The large SUV is roomy with options like video conferencing, collision avoidance system, camera's, bullet proof glass, and a refrigerator. The interior is as big as my college apartment at Slippery Rock College. We eventually got a fridge.

Agent 36 laughs and says, "That's what I like about you, Booker, it *always* boils down to a sexual organ." She turns her head toward the back seat and tells Gia, "Booker and Shoulders have potty mouths. You'll get used to it."

Gia Olson has been the subject of some good-natured jibes by the troops ever since she nailed Brenda in the back with a 40 cal. slug. SWAT Boy was especially complimentary giving her high fives and calling her Annie Oakley. He even attempted a chest bump but Gia sidestepped the effort.

But when SWAT Boy mentioned the possibility of Gia joining the SWAT team, Agent 36 went nuclear. She threatened, "Listen up testosterone man, Gia is now officially off limits to you and your Hitler youth group." She emphasized her point with the exclamation of, " Got it!" SWAT Boy nodded his head. He may be capable of 200 push-ups and 40 pull-ups, but Agent 36 is capable of going sexual harassment on his ass. Some men get excited by *Hustler* but S.W.A.T. Boy gets excited by the nomenclature of an MP5 machine gun. He spends work days alternating between the firing range and gym though I've never seen the guy sweat. It's a good gig. SWAT Boy's official title is Firearms coordinator. Our group is heading to the FBI mothership in D.C. The J. Edgar Hoover building is an eight-hour drive along the Pennsylvania Turnpike east toward Breezewood, then southbound I-70 into Maryland and Virginia. October weather in this part of the world can range anywhere from snowsuits to swimsuits. We're in luck today with a sunny 62 degree temperatures and spectacular fall-colored leaves floating to the ground. Dennis Hord requested a transfer to the white-collar squad after the fertilizer shoot out. He candidly admitted that, "I was a tax attorney before the Bureau and I've come to the conclusion that an audit *rarely* involves bombs and bullets."

Sean confesses that, "Bruce isn't happy with Gia and I going TDY." ("TDY" means Temporary Duty.)

I chuckle and say, "Don't sweat it, Sean. Bruce is actually a pretty good FBI supervisor. He misses the field but won't admit it, so he micromanages. It's a control thing; he'll get over it."

"He *strongly* suggested I turn down the assignment. Warned me that it could ruin my career, and...."

Sean hesitates and seems reluctant to finish his thought. I fill in the silence with, "We've got no secrets in this group."

Sean sighs and says, "Bruce wants me to be his snitch. He insisted I give him details on the case."

"You didn't tell him?"

"No way. I did tell him that I'd be fired if I divulged SCI material. I quoted CHAPTER and verse from the MIOG manual."

"How'd he take *that*?"

"Seemed surprised that I knew the regs so he backed off. Said if I kept him in the loop, he'd take care of me."

"What's the loop?"

"Didn't specify."

"What'd he promise you?" Gwen asks.

"A relief supervisor position, then he'd recommend me for management."

"Proves my point," I say. "His whole world revolves around titles, but let me tell you something, Sean." I pause and say seriously, "The only title that *really* matters in the FBI is *Special Agent.*"

"So what *did* you tell him?" Tommy wonders.

"Didn't say anything," Sean explains. "Just nodded my head. It was uncomfortable."

"Well, Sean," I announce, "you *are* going to be Bruce's bitch."

"I can't do that."

"Don't worry. We're just gonna fuck with Bruce for trying to flip you." I turn to Agent 36 seated next to me in the front seat. "Gwen, you majored in *Devious* at Yale, didn't you?"

Agent 36 flashes a conspiratorial smile and says, "Took 36 credits, A perfect 4.0."

"The closest I got to a 4.0 in college was my blood alcohol level."

Tommy Shoulders suggests, "Tell Bruce we're going back to Cairo?"

"Screams of being punked," I say. "It's gotta be both believable and screw with his head."

Gia chimes in and says, "I know. Tell him we're headed to Boston to investigate allegations that Muslim extremists have infiltrated the faculty at Ivy League schools."

I think about this for a second and announce to everyone, "That's actually *very* believable. These days the Ivy League is a sanctuary of radical feminists, communists, socialists, and circus midgets. Terrorists would be welcomed with open arms."

A small voice from the third row of seats mutters, "Thank you."

Being confined inside a small moving box for hours stimulates conversation. You can sleep, read, or contemplate life, but for five law enforcement officers shooting the shit is the usual default. Sean wonders, "Can I ask about Cairo, again. I know I'm being a pain, but according to you, what we learned at the Academy about Cairo was a sanitized version."

I think, *'You have no idea how sanitized,'* but say, "Ask away."

"How did you get Jabar to talk? You were in Cairo and he was a powerful imam there."

I say, *'We tased the shit out of Jabar, kidnapped him, repeatedly waterboarded his fat ass, until Agent 36 mangled his carotid artery.'* Not really, but I do say, "Everyone will talk if you can find what motivates them."

"So *what* motivated Jabar to betray his son, faith, and countrymen?"

I pause, attempting to provide some vanilla *and* believable explanations when Gia asks, "Did you torture him? That's what I would've done."

Gia is beginning to piss me off, *in* an affectionate way. I selected her for the task force because I recognized a kindred spirit beneath that veneer of sweetness and innocence. But I never realized the depth of her corruptibility. Since it's not the time or place to confide the *entire* Cairo story to Sean *or* Gia, I ask, "Did they teach you about interrogation techniques at the Academy?"

Sean volunteers, "The FBI can use only *approved* interrogation techniques with people engaged in terrorist activities or persons who have *knowledge* of terrorist activities."

"So there you go," I say, hoping to end this topic.

Sean challenges me with, "But you didn't answer the question. How did *you* motivate Jabar?"

It's time to go into deflection mode. "Why don't you tell *me* what interrogation techniques that are permitted?"

"You can use various coercive techniques such as threats, fear, pain, and debility."

"What the hell is debility?" Tommy asks.

"Things like sleep deprivation, shitty food, harsh language."

"That's bullshit, because you just described my enlistment in the army."

"But," Gia adds, "you can't strike, waterboard, or verbally ridicule them."

It's Agent 36, our resident attorney, who provides a legal standard, "The goal of any interrogation is to obtain usable and reliable information, in a lawful manner and in the least amount of time." Gwen pauses and adds, "The Detainee Treatment Act of 2005 provides uniform standards for interrogation, as well as prohibits cruel, inhuman, or degrading treatment or punishment of detainees, as interpreted through the United States Constitution."

"So basically," Tommy concludes, "you ain't allowed to do shit except discuss the weather."

"That sums it up, Tommy."

"So no waterboarding, punching, kicking, cursing, or stringing them up by their balls?" Gwen summarizes.

"Why so restrictive?" Gia wonders. "The FBI has documented evidence that when waterboarding was an approved interrogation technique, it produced information that saved thousands of lives."

I say, "In January, 2009, President Obama issued an executive order mandating that all government agencies conducting interrogations *must* follow the guidelines outlined in the U.S. Army Field Manual on Interrogation."

"Is that a good thing?"

"Not really. They're a bit outdated and don't apply to this age of terrorism."

"How outdated?" Sean wonders. "Fifty or a hundred years old?"

I end this particular topic with, "No, they were actually written in the 19th century."

CHAPTER 27

"Artificial intelligence is no match for natural stupidity."
Albert Einstein

We reach the puzzle palace and our group makes the trek from the sub-basement parking lot up the elevator to the fourth floor. The Boy Wonders roaming the halls seem intrigued by the strange gaggle of unescorted humans invading their space. A *few* even snap their eyeballs toward Agent 36's conspicuous boobs. Even though Gwen is sporting conservative courtroom business attire for the SOP visit, you can't camouflage perfect tits around men.

Tony awaits us in the Director's conference room. It's a case of *déjà vu* since this was our war room for the Cairo caper. My Academy roommate gives me a hug, shakes hands with Tommy, and hugs Gwen, which now constitutes a sexual assault in Federal buildings. Tony introduces himself to Sean and Gia with, "Congratulations on that fertilizer case, you both distinguished yourselves." He pauses and tells Sean, "Your father saved many lives."

"Thank you, sir."

The Deputy Director turns to Gia, smiles and says, "You did great work in Cleveland, Agent Olson."

Gia beams and softly says, "I appreciate that, sir."

Tony comments that. "You graduated the Academy barely six weeks ago and have already been involved in a deadly force incident. Now I *know* Agent Booker was on scene when you pulled that trigger."

Gia locks eyes with Tony and says, "Yes sir, he was *close* by."

Tony raises his eyebrows and asks, "Did Agent Booker contribute his many years of experience in such a dangerous situation to a new agent?"

Gia nods her head and says seriously, "Yes sir, his exact words were, '*Shoot that fuckin' bitch!*' "

Everyone is speechless until Tommy Shoulders fills in the silence with, "So she shot the bitch in the back."

We sit at an oblong conference table and Tony starts the brief with, "You know why you're here. Our goal is to degrade and hopefully eliminate the lone wolf terrorist in our nation. It won't be easy but you'll have the resources of the entire government at your disposal. John is assigned as case agent and based on his recommendations you'll be meeting with FBI cyber agents, State Department officials, CIA and FBI Intel analysts, Immigration, Homeland Security and ICE staff, and our entire FBI behavioural unit. Don't be shy and *don't* leave anything on the table. Questions?"

"Mr. Daniels," Tommy says, "I *have* a question."

Gwen and I share a look that says, '*This is not good.*'

Tony nods and Tommy asks, "What do you call a man who performs abortions on radical Muslim women?"

In unison Gwen and Gia say, "What *do* you call a man who performs abortions on radical Muslim women?"

Tommy chuckles and says, "A Crime Stopper."

Tony shakes his head, smiles, and says, "I'll be sure to tell that one at the next diversity forum." He informs us that, "The cyber folks will be here in 30 minutes. I'm down the hall if you need anything."

I tell Sean that he won't be joining us for the meetings.

"Why not?"

"I have a *special* assignment for you."

We have a brief discussion and Sean smiles then exits the conference room. I've arranged for Director McKissock to present Sean his dad's credentials and badge in a shadow box along with a posthumous Medal of Valour. Thumper willingly gave his life for the country he loved when he volunteered for the Marine Corps and the FBI. A medal and shadow box can never replace a father but Sean accepted the identical risk when he *also* took the oath to defend the Constitution.

Special Agent Bill Garrett is giving us the brief on computer stuff. The issue is *how* can we identify and monitor ISIS in the dark, *electronically* speaking.

"The Dark Web is not so much a place as it is a method of achieving a level of anonymity online. It refers to websites that mask the IP addresses of the servers on which they reside, making it impossible to know who or what is behind the site or sites."

He continues, "They don't show up on search engines like Google so, unless you know exactly how to reach them, they're effectively invisible. New evidence suggests that ISIS is using the Dark Web not only for propaganda but also recruiting."

Garrett is not your typical looking computer geek. He's a large rough looking guy with bushy eyebrows. He reminds me of a nose tackle with brains. Garrett explains, "We've found that a number of websites are raising funds for ISIS through bitcoin donations."

"BITCOINS?" Tommy repeats.

Special Agent Bobbie Geary picks up the brief, "BITCOINS is a new currency that was created in 2009. Transactions are made with no middle men – meaning, no banks. There are no fees and no need to give your real *name*. More merchants are beginning to accept them: You can buy webhosting services, pizza, or even manicures with BITCOINS."

"Why would ISIS deal in *BITCOINS?*"

Bobbie is the FBI Intel analyst that connected the electronic money transactions between the Cairo terrorist and North Korea.

Her outstanding work armed our President with concrete evidence of North Korea's involvement. The fat juvenile running N. Korea denied everything until an armada of American warships began doing lazy eights off their coast.

Bobbie's a brainy fox who hides her good looks with thick glasses, Cole Haan loafers, and a frizzy hippie hairdo. She explains that, "BITCOINS can be used to buy merchandise anonymously. In addition, international payments are easy and cheap because BITCOINS are not tied to any country or subject to regulation. And, people can send BITCOINS using mobile apps or their computers. It's similar to sending cash digitally."

"How can we stop that?" I wonder. "To defeat ISIS we must cut off their funding. Minus that, they can go on indefinitely."

"Unfortunately," Bobbie says, "This presents a major challenge for law enforcement, since we *have* the technology to intercept and track users on the Dark Web in a way that's effective against ISIS but..."

"....but," I finish her sentence, "that would violate a citizen's privacy."

Gwen adds sarcastically, "And we wouldn't want to do that."

Tommy mutters, "Fuck 'em."

Garrett asks me, "Heard you were a Marine?"

I think, *What an odd moment for that question*, but say, "A grunt officer, you?"

"Same, went in with General Boomer in the first Iraqi dust up."

I nod and tell him, "We'll have to sit down and swap some stories."

Garrett nods back and I turn to Bobbie and summarize, "You said that we *have* the technology to infiltrate these dark spaces, *if* we have a warrant?"

"Correct. We have the ability to do it, but *not* the authority."

"*Hypothetically* speaking, how can we do it?"

Garrett explains that, "We monitor websites of a few online communities which share information concerning the Dark Web.

About a year ago we lucked onto a closed Turkish forum used by hackers and discovered Tor."

"Tor?" Gia repeats.

Bobbie clarifies that, "Dark Web content *is* accessible only through this special software called Tor."

My interest peaks at the mention of *Tor*. Our Chinese computer gal, Jun, had briefed us on Tor, but I want to downplay any knowledge, which in my case, is not a stretch.

Garrett picks up the narrative with, "Tor's a package that encrypts a user's IP address and routes internet traffic through a series of volunteer servers around the world, called *onion* routing. Like the internet itself, Tor was a product of the military, originally designed by the Office of Naval Research to give sailors a secure means of communication."

"I assume that the FBI has some way to defeat this Tor?"

Garrett nods and says, "We *probably* can, but it's a moot issue *unless* we have probable cause for a warrant."

"What do you mean by *probably can?*"

"There's word in the cyber world that one or two government agencies have possession of a program called XKeyscore."

"What agencies?" I ask.

Garrett qualifies his reply with, "Just some inner agency scuttlebutt but rumors persist that NSA and State."

I'm beginning to like this Garrett guy. "I'd appreciate if you can remain for the brief with the State Department. They're bringing some cyber guy and I need a translator."

"Not a problem," Garrett answers with a sly smile.

I look at my watch and realize that State Department officials are due in fifteen minutes. I thank Bobbie and her staff for the brief and say, "We'll definitely be getting back to you."

The Intel folks stand and file out leaving Gwen, Tommy, Gia, and Bill. I need to take Garrett's ideological temperature and don't have much time. "Let's grab a cup," I tell Bill.

We stand by the coffee urn and await the State Department group. Garrett and I have a brief conversation about the Marine Corps. We hit all the high points of the brotherhood. Things that civilians could never understand, like the Yellow Brick Road, MREs, and liberty in Bangkok. Garrett was a platoon commander during the initial Gulf War and went back to Iraq with the Bureau on IT security matters. Like many other military and law enforcement types, Garrett loves our country, but the government has been irrational of late.

As we sip our coffee alone I tell Garrett that, "You *do* know that by the time we get PC for an electronic warrant, it's too late."

"Yep."

"And that the false argument of personal privacy trumping national security makes us extremely vulnerable to lone wolf attacks?"

"Yep."

I ask Garrett directly, "So, what's your *personal* take on this mess?"

"It's liberal bullshit that will get innocent Americans killed."

"I agree, Bill." I pause and measure my words. "You mentioned that State Department may have access to this XKeyscore."

"I did."

"And you seem to agree that innocent Americans are dying while we're mired in bureaucratic agency bullshit?"

"I do."

I place my hand on his shoulder and say, "I'm not asking you to do anything against your conscience, the law, or Bureau regulations, but I *would* like you to keep your eyes and ears open at this meeting and feel free to *probe the lines*, Marine."

"At your service," Garrett responds, beginning to sound like a co-conspirator.

Individuals drawn to the State Department are generally annoying nitpickers, and like to *discuss* things. They would have you believe that the Iranian Nuclear Deal was their shining historic moment, but their *real* accomplishments include the domestication of cats and the invention of group therapy. State Department officials like lite beer, (with lime added), but most prefer white wine or imported bottled water. They eat raw fish but like their beef rare. Sushi, tofu, and French food are standard fare at State Department dinners. The females generally have higher testosterone levels than their men.

It was also State Department officials that insisted Benghazi was a random reaction to some YouTube video. Being stuck on arrogant stupid is usually just annoying but when the bureaucrats denied desperate requests for reinforcements over a 13-hour period as the Benghazi consulate burned, this rises to accessory to murder. Keeping with standard government logic, the guilty were promoted and the dead forgotten.

The State Department gang enters the conference room, 20 minutes *fashionably* late. I can almost hear trumpets blaring somewhere off in the distance. Their point is a fiftyish lady with tree trunk legs and an attitude. Her two minions include a younger and shapelier version of the leader and a skinny emasculated guy with Buddy Holly glasses.

"I'm Ms. Crandle, the Under Secretary of State for Mid-East affairs." She turns to her posse and says, "This is Ms. Abdullah and Mr. Stein."

I shake hands with everyone and say, "This is Gwen, Tommy, Gia, and Bill. Gwen's nickname is Agent 36 because she has flawless large breasts, Tommy has anger management issues, Gia shot a teenager in the back a few weeks ago, and Bill whacked a few Iraqis in his day." I pause and turn back to Ms. Crandle and ask, "Do you guys have *first* names?"

Ms. Crandle actually smiles. She scans our group and offers, "I agree with your assessment of Gwen, I hope Tommy has taken his meds, we will sit *facing* Gia, and for Bill's information, Ms. Abdullah is *Egyptian*." She pauses and finishes with, "I'm Suzanne, and this is Houda and Stanley. How can we help you?"

I took notice that at the mention of Gwen's mammaries, Stanley snapped his head toward Agent 36 and his expression transformed into that of a teenager flipping through *Hustler* magazine. I also deduce that Stanley is their computer geek and Houdi is Crandle's handmaiden with some fancy official title.

Interesting, I think, and wonder how I can use Gwen's tits to our advantage. I provide the canned briefing. The State Department people nod at the appropriate time but maintain their creepy robotic stares.

Their particular piece of the lone wolf puzzle involves entry and exit into our country. I conclude with a simple question. "Why do we allow foreigners on the *watch* list, which include suspected terrorist, and individuals with known ties to radical groups, access to the US?"

Gwen adds, "Don't forget the American-born who radicalize on the internet, claim allegiance to Allah, then travel abroad to terrorists sponsored nations. When they return, we welcome them back with a *'have a nice day?'* "

Crandle gives Agent 36 a condescending smile and informs her that, "As you *may* know, the FBI is responsible for creating and maintaining the watch list. And, it's not a *stop* list, it's a *watch* list."

I nod and say, "Thank you for that subtle and irrelevant distinction, *but* the State Department can put the kibosh on anyone entering by alerting Customs and Immigration or refusing to issue a visa.'

Ms. Houdi asks a peculiar question. "Does your staff have top secret clearances?"

"It's required for members of the JTTF."

"Without getting into specifics, there are times when our Intel agencies *desire* that certain individuals, *with* terrorist ties, *be* granted access."

Gwen chuckles and tells Houdi, "Those cases are the entire reason the *'watch'* list exists *and* a great example of why it's broke. Americans are falsely assuming that our government is *watching* people on the list. *But* with our limited manpower the FBI is able to *watch* less than 1% of the thousands on the watch list who enter the U.S. every day."

I follow up with, "The bottom line is: *what's* the purpose of a watch list if nobody's *watching*? The State Department and Homeland

Security allow known and suspected terrorists with legitimate visas or passports into the U.S. daily."

Stanley informs us that, "There are actually *three* watch lists. They include the TIDE database, which has about 550,000 names; the FBI's terrorist watch list, which has about 400,000 names; and another list of about 14,000 people who are flagged for secondary screening at the nation's airports."

"But *only* the State Department has the authority to revoke a foreigner's visa and prevent access into the country," I say.

Gwen illustrates the point. "Umar Farouk Abdulmutallab, the suspected terrorist charged in the failed attempt to blow up Northwest Flight 253 over Detroit on Christmas, had a valid visa to enter the United States, even though he was listed in the TIDE database."

Gia adds, "And, none of the 9/11 attackers entered or tried to enter our country illegally. They arrived through 10 different airports and all but two of the hijackers were admitted for 6-month stays. Hanjour had a student visa and was admitted for a stay of two years, and Suqami sought and was admitted for a stay of only 20 days." She pauses and adds, "The 19 hijackers *legally* entered the United States a total of 33 times *before* 9/11, though we knew they had terrorist ties."

Rather than address the issue Ms. Crandle deflects with an old schoolyard tactic. "Part of the problem is *your* FBI. You seem *unable* to figure out how to add or remove suspected terrorists from the country's unified terrorist watch list. A 2016 audit of the watch list found that the list full of duplicate entries."

Two can hold their breath on the playground. "Well," I say. "*Our* former president appeared to have a terrorist '*hands off*' list that permits individuals with extremist ties to enter the country with the *State Department's* knowledge. And these bad guys *don't* have an FBI surveillance squad up their butt 24/7."

"That's ridiculous," Crandle counters.

"Is it?" I taunt. "The FBI has obtained DHS electronic mail exchange between U.S. Immigration and Customs Enforcement (ICE) and U.S.

Customs and Border Protection (CBP) asking whether to admit an individual with ties to various terrorist groups. The individual had scheduled an upcoming flight into the U.S. and *your* State Department ordered ICE to grant access."

The room goes silent and I realize that things have gone south with State. But, we'll need access to information that they alone possess to solve this lone wolf riddle, so I go for the schmooze. I smile at Ms. Crandle and offer my olive branch, "I apologize for getting us into an agency pissing match. We're all on the same team and I know you have a busy schedule. I just have a few technical questions and we can wrap up."

Crandle flashes me her practiced insincere smile. "The Secretary of State has asked that I provide you any and *all* assistance."

I return her plastic smile and ask, "Agent Garrett heads up cyber security for the Bureau and has some technical questions."

Garrett looks at me, raises his eyebrows and asks, "I do?"

"Yes, Bill." I stare at him. "You mentioned something about the State Department computer system and how it interfaces with Customs and Border Patrol at airports and border crossings."

Garrett repeats in the affirmative, "I *did*."

Crandle tells us, "Stanley is our cyber expert so if you have nothing left to discuss with Houdi and myself, we'll get back to work."

We all stand, shake hands, and lie about how we enjoyed meeting each other, blah, blah, blah. Once the ladies are gone I turn to Gwen and say, "Gia and I have a meeting with Tony. I'd like you to sit in with Bill and Stanley."

Agent 36 is my female clone and immediately understands her mission. She smiles seductively at Stanley and tells him, "I admire men with computer skills. Every time *I* try and search the web for lipstick, some porn site involving lesbian liaisons appears."

I recognize drool when I see it. The poor guy has no chance.

On our way to Tony's office Gia wonders, "What was that all about?"

I turn to the rookie agent and confide, "You're part of this team now. You proved yourself on the streets and seem to have your priorities straight. Simply put, you *understand* that our enemies fight dirty."

Gia shakes her head and asks, "We just met with the State Department. Are you saying that *they're* the enemy?"

"They may not be the enemy, but they *are* part of the problem." I pause trying to find the right words. "Let me ask you a question."

Gia nods and I ask, "We have Muslims burning our flags, screaming death to America, teaching the Koran in our schools, and voting Sharia law into several American cities. Do you see a trend?"

"It sickens me to see what's going on in our country, but doesn't the State Department *share* our goals?"

"No."

"No?"

"No, many of them are more concerned with protecting turf, promotions and the menu at State dinners. They don't give a shit about you or me and if you doubt what I'm saying just ask the families of those four Americans killed in Benghazi."

The South Korean/Italian/Swede raised by a FBI father takes a full moment to process this conversation. She looks me in the eye and says, "Got it."

Tony is on the phone when we enter the Deputy Director's suite. He waives us to chairs in front of the desk and it's evident that my roommate is pissed at someone.

"That's bullshit!" Tony says. "You tell your SAC that I could care less about that U.S. Attorney, I want that warrant approved by close of business today."

He slams the phone down and simmers for a few seconds. I've seen this version of the usually mild mannered *Tony* on a few occasions at new agent training. It frequently included pitchers of beer at The Board Room and heated discussions over his beloved Pittsburgh Steelers. He looks at me and says, "Get your team saddled up."

CHAPTER 28

"When did it change from… 'We the People,' to 'Screw the People'?"

"The U.S. Attorney in Minnesota ruled that we don't have probable cause for an electronic warrant."

Gia and I wait for the details and Tony spews them out. "We've got some nut in Minnesota, name of Gus Stevenson, telling his ex-girlfriend that she'll *'have* to notice him in a few days.' "

"That all?" I ask.

"The CART team in our Minneapolis office was tracking him on social media but a few months ago he electronically disappeared, they think he went dark, but before he did, Gus declared allegiance to Allah."

"What's the problem?"

"The U.S. Attorney feels that it's your standard angry white male rhetoric about wealth distribution and United States imperialism. No direct threats or specific targets, just rants, therefore no probable cause."

"What about the girlfriend?"

"Broke up with him about a year ago. Some e-mail contact at first then he dropped off the planet until a week ago when he called. He seemed different and spoke about how he'd finally amount to *something.*"

"What'd she mean by *different?*"

Tony scans his notes and says, "The guy is normally an angry hot head, and big into those violent video games with severed heads. Quit college last year, had a DUI, and dropped out of sight. His former girlfriend said he now seems calmer but programmed. Rambled on about how he found purpose in his life, how he finally feels part of *something*, and repeated how everyone will know his name."

I tell my roommate that, "Why are you so sure that this guy is ready to go bin Laden. We probably have a few thousand Gus Stevensons in the U.S. declaring allegiance to sand land. What makes this guy different?"

"Zacarias Moussaoui - the 20th hijacker."

"What's he got to do with our boy, Gus?"

"You *do* know that in August of 2001, a Minneapolis agent, Sam Garlow, told FBI HQ that he was *certain* Moussaoui was involved in an imminent terrorist airline hijacking plot. He requested a FISA (Foreign Intelligence Surveillance Act) warrant for Moussaoui's computer, but was denied by FBI HQ. One month later, 3000 Americans died needlessly. We arrested Moussaoui *after* the Twin Towers went down and found information on his computer that could've *prevented* the attack."

"How'd we fuck that one up so bad?"

"Because the Headquarter supervisor didn't trust the field. He was lazy and arrogant and refused to walk down the hall and get a FISA warrant. Told Agent Harlow that it wouldn't look good on the agent's career. Told him that no terrorist would hijack planes and the FBI had no Intel reports of an *imminent* attack. So Agent Harlow raised his voice and told the HQ supervisor that, *"I'm fuckin' giving you the Intel right now you obstructionist asshole."*

I shake my head and say, "This *is* called The Obstructionist Palace by the field for a good reason."

Tony concludes with, "And now we have another Minneapolis agent saying that Gus Stevenson is about to kill some more Americans and I took that call and, that is why I'm sending you to stop him."

"I'm on my way roomie."

Tony nods and says, "I have the Bureau plane standing by at Dulles. The JTTF supervisor, name of A. J. Perry, will meet you in Minnesota." He hands me a file marked, 'Stevenson, Gus - MN - JTTF.'

I tell Gia, "Go find Sean. Should be in the Directors office."

As soon as she leaves I tell my roommate, "All I'm gonna say is that unless we can get Congress to loosen up these bogus civil rights concerns, we'll *never* get ahead of lone wolves."

"We really don't have time for that conversation."

"Maybe not but we're just circle jerking ourselves *until* that happens." I pause and remember that, "Dr. Alvarez from the Behavioral Science Unit is due here in an hour to brief us on profiling lone wolves. I may need her in Minnesota to provide some clues on this guy. Can you divert her to Dulles?"

Tony smiles and says, "That actually sounds logical and work related, but knowing you as I do, there must be *some* ulterior motive."

"Need I remind the Deputy Director of our drunken debacle in DC at new agent training and your infatuation with some double-jointed college girl from NYU."

As I return to the conference room Bill Garrettt, Stanley from State, and Agent 36 are huddled at the conference table. Tommy is munching on donuts and sipping coffee. "Call Jun." I tell him.

"What do I tell her?"

"To pack a bag and stand by."

Gwen glances over and I give her the sign to wrap things up. She excuses herself and approaches me. I whisper, "We need that XKeyscore program, and access to the State Department computer site that interfaces with border crossings."

"Working on it but Stanley is a bureaucratic wuss and even *I* can't motivate him to locate his balls."

I approach Garrett and Stanley and inform them that, "We have a pressing matter on a case. Bill, you continue your meeting with Stan and call me later."

Stanley asks Gwen, "Are you leaving too?"

"Afraid so, Stan. But I'd *really* like to continue our conversation."

"I would *really* like that too, Agent McNulty."

"And remember," Gwen laying it on, "you promised to show me how to clean all those nasty viruses from my computer."

Stanley seems heartbroken as I steer Gwen into the hallway. She asks, "What's up Johnny?"

"We're going bye bye. I'll brief everyone on the plane."

Special Agent Bob Dupuis is a former Navy top gun. He is currently the FBI's aviation unit chief and its best pilot. Bob and co-pilot John Canley flew us into Cairo last year and thankfully flew us *out* of Cairo. He's tough and has a gallows humor typical of hot-shot flyers woofing in the ready room.

"Well if it isn't the famous G-Man Booker. Where we going this time....Tahiti, Bermuda, or another shithole like Cairo?"

"Nice to see you again, Bob. File a flight plan for Minneapolis."

"It's winter there."

"You must've aced the weather exam at flight school."

Bob chuckles and says, "What's our departure time?"

"Waiting on a few passengers. Shouldn't be too long." I pause and remember Jun, "We have to make a quick stop at Cleveland Hopkins."

"Winter there too."

"Can't put anything over on you. Where's Silent Johnny Canley?"

"My co-pilot is stocking up on coffee, soft drinks, and chow for our passengers. In case you didn't know, the FBI doesn't hire flight attendants."

"I may need a new career soon. Seems the airlines are hiring flying comedians and I'm a funny guy."

As Dupuis is disappearing into the cockpit he says, "You're frickin' hilarious, I caught your act in Cairo. You *killed*."

Thanksgiving is six days away and it wouldn't be the first major holiday that John Booker was absent from the family dinner table. But my undercover days are over and I made some heartfelt promises to be present henceforth.

I call Lorri and begin my repertoire of banter to deflect a Booker dereliction of family duty. "Hey hon, how you doing?"

"Doing good John, can't wait for you to get home. Nikki's bringing a friend from college for Thanksgiving. It's a guy."

"Oh, something serious?" I ask.

"Nikki seems smitten. Says she really wants you to meet Pedro. That you two have a lot in common."

"We might, since *Pedro* is probably an illegal alien and I can arrest him during the pumpkin pie portion of dinner."

"You are such a racist John. Pedro is a pre-med student from Kansas."

I'm reaching for the right segue to soften my upcoming absence at Thanksgiving so I say, "I heard a good joke hon. Ready?"

"No. Your jokes are tasteless and disgusting."

I ignore Lorri and ask, "What's the difference between your wife and your job?"

"I don't know and *don't* want to know."

"Well, after five years your job will *still* suck."

Lori forces a polite chuckle and tells me that, "You're stuck in the 10th grade locker room, John."

"Yea well, I mentioned the job thing because it *does* suck and I won't be home for Turkey Day."

The silence is my first clue that my spouse is not happy, but she's a Swede so her reply is measured. "Is it about what we discussed at Lazzaras?"

"Yes."

"Then I understand, John. Do good and call me when you can. Love you."

"Love you too. Make sure Pedro doesn't steal all our silverware." I say, but I'm talking to dead air.

John Canley arrives with sacks of fast foods and drinks. Canley is a former Air Force pilot who won the Silver Star in Afghanistan. He's tall, of some mixed ethnicity, and a man of few words. Canley was our co-pilot during the Cairo siege so I love the guy. He smiles, approaches, and wraps me in a bear hug, "Good to see you."

"That's a lot words for you, Silent John."

The big guy laughs and replies, "Probably," while disappearing inside the cockpit.

I notice a white passenger van approaching the plane. It's either a government vehicle or a lost nursing home outing. Tommy exits the van followed by Gwen, Sean, Gia, and the lovely Dr. Linda Alvarez. The Bureau's shrink is attired in spiked heels, and a thin, fur-trimmed leather jacket. As I offer my hand to assist her up the jets steep steps I comment, "A little overdressed for Minnesota in November."

Linda flashes me a million-dollar smile and says, "Well if it isn't Agent Booker. I must have missed the *change of plan* memo. I *thought* we were meeting at FBI Headquarters in Washington D.C., so I left my frozen tundra wardrobe at home."

Everyone laughs and I tell her, "Welcome to the field."

It's a 77-minute flight from Dulles to Cleveland Hopkins. Jun is awaiting us at the IX Jet Center located at the far end of Runway 32 L. Large, wet snowflakes float down to a wet tarmac as Tommy gathers Jun. She boards the jet and announces, "I missed lunch, any food on board?"

Tommy unpacks the food cartons and drinks. I conduct the brief as the plane reaches altitude as the group munches on tuna fish and chicken sandwiches in between sips of coffee and soda.

I finish my brief with, "Any comments or questions?"

Gwen gets right to the point with, "What's the plan?"

"Minneapolis agents are conducting twenty-four-hour surveillance on Gus, with the goal of getting PC to search his home. It'd be a lot easier if we get the FISA warrant for his computer, but if we can get inside his apartment we'll find *something*."

Our resident attorney Gwen informs me that, "Unless I'm missing something, being a loser does *not* constitute probable cause for a search warrant on his domicile. The burden is high and we've got squat. At this point, Gus is a loner, so no shady characters are visiting him, he has no criminal record, no history of drug use or sales." Gwen pauses and finishes with, "The bad guys may be visiting him alright but they're *not* using his front door, they're using the ether world."

Tommy wonders, "Why can't we just snatch this turd up and rattle his cage?"

"Because this guy is *already* radicalized and willing to give up his life for Allah. Not sure he'd rattle and why tip Gus off that we're on to him."

Tommy's about to say something that shouldn't be said aloud in mixed company so I give him the eye which translates to *shut the fuck up*. Agent 36 quickly picks up the narrative, "Can we encourage the girlfriend to patch things up and maybe Gus'll confide in her?"

"Minneapolis agents already tried to roll her, but she's petrified of this guy and her father is some hot-shot attorney who *requested* that the agents leave his property forthwith."

I look at Dr. Linda who is scanning Gus's file and say, "Can you provide us a psychological profile on Mr. Stevenson?"

Linda nods and begins with a *general* behavioral profile, "There are four types of control ISIS uses to radicalize: behavior control, information control, thought control, and emotional control. Self-radicalized Western recruits, like Gus, once indoctrinated are capable of independently conducting terrorist activities."

"Interesting but we need some *specific* insights into the mind of Gus Stevenson."

The shrink taps a folder and says, "Based on the limited information is this file, I'd say that Gus is disillusioned with his life and lacked purpose or a sense of belonging *until* ISIS *became* his family and provided him a new identity. He has low self-esteem and believes that killing infidels will make him a hero. His profile also indicates that he's addicted to violent video games which desensitizes him to actual pain and suffering to both himself and others."

Agent 36 wonders, "So killing innocent people or being riddled in a hail of police bullets is just another *play again* on his Game Boy."

Dr. Linda nods and responds with, "Exactly, Gwen."

Alvarez removed her leather coat and is seated *directly* across from me. I can't help but notice that her hem line has moved north of the Mason-Dixon line. We sit in a semicircle with the two baby agents positioned along the bulkhead. Alvarez is blessed with long muscular legs one of which she absentmindedly kicks slowly back and forth. The rocking motion has me hypnotized and becomes a distraction. OK, I do realize that some may find this reaction totally inappropriate given our subject matter and timing, but, men are wired this way.

Gia asks, "Do you see any indications that he may be *ready* to act on his rhetoric?"

"I do," Alvarez informs us. "We've all heard the term narcissist. Well, it originated in ancient Greece where the warrior Narcissus fell in love with his own reflection. Unable to pull away, he withered away and died."

Gwen interrupts with, "I once dated some wannabe actor who mounted a mirror on his bedroom ceiling."

Alvarez smiles and continues. "Some typical behaviors of a narcissist are fantasies of success, power, a deep need for admiration, and a lack of empathy for others. These behaviors have me worried."

"Why is that, Linda?" I ask.

"Because Gus emphasized to his girlfriend that he found purpose in his life, and finally feels part of *something*. That, combined with his last statement, present a *strong* indication that Gus Stevenson is *ready* to kill."

"I forgot his final statement." I say.

Dr. Alvarez locks eyes with me and says, "Gus Stevenson told his girlfriend that, '*everyone will know my name.*' "

The silence is creepy as the gravity of her words sink in so I ask, "Can we use any of this profile in our investigation?"

Alvarez gives my question some thought and says, "No lone wolf operates *totally* off the grid. Gus's anger evolved slowly into his self-radicalization by testing the waters with friends, family, and often with anonymous strangers in chat rooms. So," She concludes, "if you can identify one of these individuals whom Gus has shared his new ideology with, you *may* be able to stop him."

"I suppose we can put the full court press on the girlfriend but *if* I hear what you're saying, Dr. Alvarez, there are probably *others* who may know something if Gus has evil intentions."

"In all likelihood, yes."

I notice that Jun has been taking notes while listening intently. She asks, "Many of these lone wolfs have mental health problems so do they present a unique problem in profiling?"

Linda shakes her head. "Interestingly enough, no. Individuals with classic symptoms, such as psychosis, exhibit identical behavior patterns as those who radicalize on ideologies. They're both narcissists who have the need to test the waters before acting."

Sean says, "You lost me, Dr. Alvarez."

Linda smiles and explains, "Perhaps a few examples will help. Dylann Roof, who killed 9 African Americans at Bible study in Charleston, South Carolina, had a long struggle with mental health issues, and Maj. Nidal Malik Hasan, a Muslim Army psychiatrist, killed 13 people at Ft. Hood. Witnesses said Hasan shouted 'God is great' in Arabic before opening fire. Both Roof and Hasan gave plenty of indications that they were ticking bombs though Roof would be considered '*crazy*' by the public but Hasan thought to be radicalized by ideology."

"That's helpful," I say and turn toward Jun. In contrast to Linda, Jun is attired in an oversized turtleneck sweater, corduroy pants, and hiking boots. She looks like she's put on 10 pounds since her arrival. I ask her, "Any way we can intercept his messaging?"

Jun says, "Not if he's dark. We'd require the XKeyscore app. But perhaps I can interrupt his encryption abilities and force him to communicate in the open on social media."

"Worth a try. In the meantime, we'll reinterview the girlfriend, and get some leads on people who know Gus. Neighbors, family, former girlfriends, teachers, the works. There's got to be *somebody* in his life that he may have let something slip."

Tommy Shoulder is staring at me with the same pissed off look he had moments before he *accidently* whacked three terrorists. I nod his way and contemplate Plan B. This plan is not approved, condoned, or recommended in *any* FBI document.

CHAPTER 29

"Even if you are on the right track, you'll get run over if you just sit there."
Will Rogers

The SAT phone rings and Tommy informs me that it's, "Bill Garrett."

I'm hoping that Garrett has somehow conned or threatened Stanley from State to share the XKeyscore. He informs me that, "Stanley's demeanor changed a bit after Gwen left. Sulked and acted jilted. We bullshitted for an hour about life. It seems that Stan the Man is unlucky at love. Been through several relationships but the gals eventually dump him for some guy with NASCAR tickets. Stan was on the debate club at MIT and his hobbies now include entomology and jigsaw puzzles. After we became buds, I pulled a bluff."

"You were a Marine so I know you got some game."

"I dazzled him with some of the FBI cyber security abilities, we swapped the latest rumors on industry research, and then I casually mentioned the XKeyscore. Stanley innocently began discussing the program, so I let him roam until he realized he'd let the cat outta the bag."

"So he copped to State having the program?"

"He did." Garrett says and qualifies with, "But Stanley was *adamant* that he wasn't authorized to share. He's petrified of both Houdi and Crandle and made me promise I wouldn't tell anyone."

"I figured, but what's our chances down the road?"

"Not sure, *but* Stan wondered if Gwen would consider an invitation to dinner."

"What'd you tell him?"

Garrett chuckles and says, "Told him that Gwen is searching for a soulmate and she loves jigsaw puzzles and bugs."

"Perfect." I say and ask, "He give up computer access to our ports of entry?"

"He did. Said it was no big deal since it's known they control the lists and that Ms. Crandle ordered him to assist us."

"Final question. Can these codes be used to insert *wants and warrants* into their system?"

There is a silence that prompts me to ask, "You still there, Bill?"

Garrett finally answers with, "Yes, but *'as you know,'* we *don't* have the authorization to do so."

"I understand perfectly." I confirm and add, "And I'd *never* do that."

We say our goodbyes and I'm satisfied, for now, to get half a loaf of bread. No XKeyscore yet, but we're able to hack into the computers of those federal agencies that control our borders. We can now prevent many Muslims on the watch list from entering the U.S. I'm even tempted to include Arabs who watch the Al Jazeera TV network.

Some may believe that these actions constitute a temporary inconvenience to a *small* group, but they'd be wrong. It actually affects an enormous chunk of potential lone wolves. When you do the math on the number of individuals crossing our boarders, on a daily basis, with terrorist affiliations, expired visas, on watch lists, residing in sanctuary cities, or with avowed terrorist's leanings and sympathies, the numbers are significant.

But our culturally sensitive bureaucrats continue to admit them less some advocacy group scream *'racism'* and insist that *most* Muslims are law-abiding folks who only wish to contribute to the American dream. That's an insult to every thinking American and the most dishonest bullshit in the war on terrorism. Muslims *refuse* to assimilate into any of the countries that they infest like termites. Don't believe me? then talk to the British, French, or Spanish officials who've seceded large chunks of their country to Sharia law. Areas where police officers are forbidden to patrol and where Muslim courts have replaced sovereign law.

As Jun told us, "A *good* Muslim's allegiance is to Allah, and their spiritual leaders call for the annihilation of Israel and America. A *good* Muslim can never accept the American Constitution since it is based on Biblical principles. So Democracy and Islam can *never* co-exist and Muslims can *never* be both good Muslims and *good* Americans."

I rejoin the group who are engaged in several side bar conversations. I motion Agent 36 and Tommy Shoulders to the aft portion of the aircraft. "Gwen," I begin. "Stanley from State wants to jump your bones and you may have to take one for the team to get the XKeyscore."

Agent 36 smiles and says, "That's your problem, Booker, men actually *believe* women manipulate them with sex but it's actually the *possibility* of sex, because as Eve said to Adam, *'Take out the trash honey, and maybe you'll get some apple pie. Oh, and don't sweat the garden snake.'* "

Special Agent Anthony Joseph Perry, aka A.J., pulls his Bu ride up to the FBI jet as Bob Dupuis cuts the engines at the Minneapolis airport. Introductions are quickly made since the wind chill is somewhere approaching Siberia. Gwen and I jump into AJ's Bucar while the remainder of our group follow in another low bid white van.

After some small talk, I ask, "Surveillance doing any good?"

AJ says, "Stevenson rarely leaves his apartment. Occasional trip to the convenience store for cigarettes and beer. His only visitor is an elderly grandmother who lives close-by. Mother's dead, father's MIA, and no siblings. We're monitoring his social media but he either went cold turkey or encrypted."

Gwen asks, "The U.S. Attorney not budging?"

"Jay Sollis is a Democrat appointee who believes that law enforcement is the villain. He actually wrote a Law Journal article titled 'Civil Rights - Big Brother is Listening.' "

"Evidently, *not* on his watch. Any idea on targets?"

AJ nods and says, "The Minneapolis-St. Paul area has close to 4 million residents, with hundreds of schools, colleges, and universities. The number of soft targets is off the charts."

"Well, we better make an attempt to pick out the more obvious ones and develop a plan."

Gwen adds, "We also should be thinking about timing. Thanksgiving's in a few days. The most travelled time of the year." Agent 36 pauses and tells us that, "So we better wrap this case *before* Friday."

"Why's that?" I wonder.

"Because Friday is *Black* Friday. The *best* shopping day of the year and my Christmas list is long."

I observe, "It's also the most *crowded* shopping day of the year."

CHAPTER 30

"Demoralize the enemy from within by surprise, terror, and sabotage. This will be war in the future."

Adolf Hitler

The kitchen table is old and wobbly, crowded with two overflowing ashtrays, beer cans and the remnants of chicken wings. Gus Stevenson positions the Steyr M1912 fully automatic assault rifle inside a nylon tactical range backpack. Made in Israel, the Steyr has a 30-round magazine capable of firing 900 rounds per minute. He then places ten, fully loaded magazines into the outer pockets of the backpack for easy access. He sips his beer and picks up a Tec-9 machine pistol converted to fire on fully automatic. The Tec-9 is compact and easily concealed underneath a field jacket. He completes his preparations by placing seven additional 30 round magazines inside the many pockets of the military field jacket. Gus plans to begin at the food court and then run through the major department stores until he has no rounds left.

It has been a quiet Thanksgiving Day. Gus received an inspiring sendoff from his ISIS contact who promised the oft mentioned 72 virgins. As an informed convert to the Muslim faith, Gus was too embarrassed to inquire about the mechanics of *how* he'll get to meet the virgins. He also wondered if there were *really* 72 of them.

His daydreams are interrupted by a sharp rap on the door. Gus jumps with the guilty mind of someone intent on slaughtering innocent men, women and children in some 15 hours. Instead of a SWAT Team he hears the annoying voice of his grandmother screeching, "Gus, open up, it's Nana."

Gus hides the weapons inside a closet and realizes that his "Nana" will continue to pound on the door so he decides to make it quick. Nana is a pain in the ass. A tiny, 85-year-old nubby nuisance who has no life except church, bingo, and aggravating Gus. When Gus's mother died, the teenager moved into Nana's house until he finished high school. She would pray before meals, watch reruns of old sitcoms, and invoked a 10PM curfew on Gus, which he routinely ignored.

Nana pushes past him with two shopping bags saying, "I brought you some turkey, stuffing, mash potatoes, cranberry, and my famous pecan pie."

Gus usually has little patience with the old lady, but this *is* his last night on earth and he *is* hungry. So they sit at Gus's rickety, messy kitchen table and actually have a conversation. It strikes Gus ironic that his Nana has a framed print of *The Last Supper* on her kitchen wall. After the pecan pie Nana begins gathering dishes and says, "This was one of the most pleasant Thanksgiving dinners I've had in a long time. It's been lonely since your grandfather passed and I'm hoping we can get closer." Gus holds his tongue because his immediate reaction is, *I should kill this unbeliever in the name of Allah, then she'll die for something rather than live for nothing.*

Gus mutters, "Uh huh."

Nana smiles and tells Gus that, "I'll come by tomorrow and we'll have turkey sandwiches and finish off the pecan pie."

"Won't be here Nana."

"You're *always* here, Gus."

"I got some Christmas shopping."

"Almost forgot," Nana says, "tomorrow's Black Friday. Maybe I'll join you."

The impulse to kill his grandmother once again overwhelms Gus. Muhammad commands Muslims to fight against non-Muslims and speaks of their place in Hell. The Quran says that Allah hates non-Muslims to the extent that he will torment them for eternity in horrible ways. Allah creates infidels merely to fuel the fires of Hell. And so Gus will be a good Muslim and provide fuel for hell. He'll take his grandmother to the Mall where she'll join the infidels. Gus smiles and says, "Sounds good Nana, I'll call before I come by and get you."

Nana gives Gus a hug and tells him, "It's so good that we do things together. We're the only family we've got left."

As Gus is wrapped in his grandmothers embrace, he realizes that Nana will soon be in hell, while Gus is in Paradise fucking virgins.

CHAPTER 31

*"No, ma'am, we at the FBI do not have a sense of humor
that we're aware of."*
Men in Black -1977

It's been a tough week. Our meeting with the U.S. Attorney did not go well. It began with promise but quickly degenerated into some finger-pointing and name calling. Tommy *may* have muttered, *"You fuckin' liberal a-hole"* but I can't be sure. We *did* receive a legal lecture on the fourth amendment of the Constitution involving search and seizure.

U.S. Attorney Jay Sollis reminds us that, "What separates us from the remainder of the civilized world is *due process*. Every citizen has the expectation that the government can't just knock their door down, albeit an electronic one, minus probable cause." Sollis pauses and adds, "Of which you have *none*."

"Can you at least give us authority to place a GPS monitor on Gus's car?"

Sollis frowns at us. It's reminiscent of my Uncle Charley's expression who suffered with painful hemorrhoids. The U.S. Attorney is no longer listening to an opposing view and my guess is that Jay reads *Esquire* magazine, goes to a hair stylist, and slices his Snickers bar with a knife.

He informs us, "I will *not* consider *any* law enforcement intrusion into the life of Gus Stevenson. He is a U.S. citizen who has radical views. Need I remind you that this nation was *founded* on radical views. You allege Stevenson is communicating with ISIS but offer no evidence. You allege Stevenson has made anti-American comments, which his constitutional right of free speech, and it is *my* job to protect that right. The people of Minnesota have *nothing* to fear from Mr. Stevenson."

"So," I almost plead, "you're gonna just ignore our suspicion and hope things don't go to shit."

Sollis gives me the evil eye and comments, "You seem to be one of those hot-shot agents who see terrorists behind every bush?"

"No, but I *sure* do look, and," I glare back and tell Sollis, "I'm pretty good at spotting terrorists but I'm *really* an expert at spotting assholes."

The U.S. Attorney doesn't require a road map to my subtle insult. He stands and announces, "This meeting is over!"

When I realize that we're being booted out, I tell the U.S. Attorney that, "I just *hope* that you're right and I'm wrong because if it''s the other way around I'll be back and give you *plenty* of probable cause for a federal crime."

Sollis can't help himself and sarcastically asks, "And what would that be, Agent Booker?"

I look Sollis in the eye and say, "Assault on a federal employee."

As we are leaving the office Tommy Shoulders adds, "And that'd be you."

We get inside the car and I immediately grab my cell phone. I dial my roommate and inform him that, "The Director will soon be getting a call from the Attorney General."

Tony deadpans, "Who'd you piss off, John?"

"A federal prosecutor who thinks he's a defense attorney."

"How serious?"

"A low-level felony at best," I mutter. "I *may* have threatened him."

"*May* have," Tony challenges. "I know you, John, so cut the bullshit."

"OK," I relent. "But this U.S. Attorney has switched teams."

"That probably means Sollis wouldn't budge on the warrant."

"You're psychic."

My roommate segues into his Deputy Director's voice and gives me a verbal reprimand, "Sometimes, John, you go too far. Now I'll have to expend *my* time and energy explaining and apologizing for you. Someday, your mouth will write that proverbial check that your ass can't cash."

"When did you begin using clichés?" I chuckle. "It's beneath you."

A pause and then Tony alerts me to the fact that, "The Director's line is blinking. I wonder what he could *possibly* want."

"Wow, Sollis must've had the Director on speed dial, or maybe McKissock is looking to round out a golf foursome."

"Fuck you."

Tommy asks, "Tony pissed?"

"Naw, just wishing us a Happy Thanksgiving."

Tommy tilts his head and says, "Reminds me, probably should call my wife."

"You two doing OK?" A reference to Shoulders' ongoing marital hassles.

"My wife and I were happy for 20 years," he pauses, "and *then* we met."

We're down to the wire and not much has changed since our arrival in Minnesota. Surveillance produced squat, the girlfriend remained mute, interviews produced nothing, the U.S. Attorney wants me arrested, and Gia has diarrhea. Jun hacked into Gus's e-mail account but minus the XKeyscore, all we got is gibberish. Jun *did* use her cyber skills to determine that the encrypted communication originated in Syria and included a flurry of messages last night. We can assume that Gus was chatting with his ISIS contact but not much more.

Tommy and I got the eye on Gus's apartment and we're shooting the shit. Gwen and Sean are positioned down the street while Gia and AJ share the surveillance van one block away.

The neighborhood is seedy but quiet on this frigid Thanksgiving evening. A few people stroll by but most are watching football in food comas.

I tell Tommy that, "We've got to be careful on how we play this one. Sollis is watching this operation and he's no fan. We *can* play it fast and loose, but we can't rub his nose in it. If it don't look right, Sollis will refuse to prosecute Gus, but he just may prosecute *us*."

"Means we have to keep AJ out of the loop. How do we do that?"

"AJ's a good guy, but we don't have time to give him a loyalty test," I say and add, "I also don't need to put him in *our* jackpot."

"Yes, the guy has six kids and needs a paycheck."

"I'll handle it; you just cover my six."

I cue my mike and ask, "Gia, how you doing?"

"Hanging in, but my diarrhea may have morphed into inflammatory bowel disease. AJ got me a six pack of Kaopectate and I'm good for now."

"We got this covered. Have AJ take you back to the hotel and get some rest."

"I'm fine," Gia insists.

"Negative. Nothing much happening tonight and I'll need you healthy."

"10-4 John. Happy Thanksgiving, and, *good hunting*."

"And Good Hunting to you, Gia Olson."

Our team has been motoring nonstop today and it occurs to me that I haven't called Lorri and Nikki to wish them a Happy Turkey day.

My wife answers with, "John, is everything OK?"

"Fine, honey. Sorry I haven't called but we've been running. Happy Thanksgiving."

"Happy Thanksgiving, John. Have you had any turkey today?"

I chuckle and inform my wife, "No but I did grab a Colonel Sanders indigestion combo with the mash potatoes, coleslaw, corn, and stuffing. How's things at the Bookers'?"

"We're on the required timeout period between turkey and dessert." Lorri's voice lowers slightly and she says, "Pedro is so nice, John, and it could be serious."

I'd completely forgotten about Pedro but now I'm informed that this undocumented lothario has intentions on my Nikki. "How serious?" I ask.

"He gave her a friendship ring."

"Whatta we know about him, other than his future is limited to a landscaper or short order cook."

"You evidently don't recall our previous conversation when I informed you that Pedro is a pre-med student."

"Pre-med, huh?" I challenge. "His parents probably threw a graduation party when he got his GED."

The apartment door opens and out comes Nana. I inform my wife that, "We'll discuss this later, gotta go. Give Nikki my love and check this friendship ring. It's either fake or hot."

I *think* Lorri said, "Asshole." But I can't be sure.

I note the time of 1847 in my surveillance log. Gus's grandmother spent a total of 2 hours and 7 minutes visiting with her terrorist grandson. In conversations during the week we debated on whether to pitch Nana. Our background inves indicates that Norma Gustavson is a church-going widow with no arrests and a moderate case of scoliosis. She is *not* involved in terrorist activities and we doubt that Gus has made the pitch to convert her. Our dilemma comes with determining what, if any, useful information Norma may provide, and, *if* she'll alert Gus that the FBI is snooping around. The group was split. As always, Tommy wants to snatch Nana up and waterboard her. Not really, but he has mentioned, *'scaring the shit outta her.'* Sean, Gia, and AJ felt an interview risky, while Gwen and I feel that some good may come from a 'sit down.'

As the elderly lady walks slowly to her parked car, I realize that it's decision time. Perhaps a modified approach can shed some light minus alerting Gus. I cue the radio mike and announce, "Nanna is rolling."

Gwen immediately asks, "What's our move?"

"Follow her home and have a talk."

The silence is my indication that the group is not unanimous with my decision. I qualify with, "Gwen and I will make up some ruse for an interview. No mention of Gus."

"10-4 comes from the surveillance van and Gwen."

It's important in law enforcement to discuss the interview technique *before* the interview. One size does *not* fit all. You require a different approach for some psychotic hairy mob guy than a *Nana*. It's also important to limit the interviewers to two. More than two, it becomes an exercise in confusion and interruption. Then you fine-tune your strategy. For example, Gwen will add a feminine, less threatening, granddaughterly ambience as opposed to two grim guys.

I cue the mike and tell Gwen, "Tommy and I will take the eye. Once she gets back to her house, we'll wait ten and knock."

Nana resides in the Lowry Hill section of Minneapolis. All single-family ranch dwellings in need of minor repairs, paint, and landscaping. Tommy and I observe Nana angle her old Ford Escort onto a crumbling driveway and slowly climb the steps to the front door.

Gwen jumps into the back seat of my car and asks, "OK, Booker, so how do we play this?"

"Where's our profiler?"

"Linda is back at the hotel with the Chinese cyber stripper."

"Great visual," Tommy says, "Hey Gwen, just heard on the radio that the first female U.S. pilot is about to fly combat missions in Syria?"

Gwen frowns and says, "So what's the punch line?"

"No punch line, just that the mission was delayed."

"*Why* was the mission delayed?"

Tommy smirks and says, "She couldn't get the plane outta reverse."

Agent 36 punches Tommy in the arm, laughs, and says, "Good one."

I call Dr. Alvarez and say, "We decided on interviewing Nana. You've got her file now tell us what buttons to push."

A short pause before Linda opines, "Norma has a strong sense of right and wrong. She has traditional family values, respects law enforcement, and watches enough television to know we're at war with terrorism." Another pause. "But, if Gus commits a terrorist act, Nana will be the family member who tells the news media that she had no idea that her grandson could murder innocent people. She'll be quoted as saying, '*Gus is such a good boy.*' "

"Our bottom line is: how far can we push her about Gus, and is she likely to warn him?"

"Can't answer that. All I can do is provide some indicators. You're an intuitive guy, John, so follow your gut. I recommend you first establish rapport. Talk about the weather, bingo and church. Then ease into the topic of terrorism and gauge her reaction. Don't involve Gus in the equation unless the conversation veers that way naturally."

"That's it?" I ask.

"One last thing," Alvarez cautions. "If you *choose* to mention your suspicions of Gus, be sure that you don't paint him as a bad person."

"Why?"

"Because his Nana can *never* think of him that way."

"How *will* she think of him?"

"As her *grandson*, who may be confused or misguided, but *never* as evil."

I ask Linda to stay close to her phone and turn to Gwen in the back seat. "OK, you're at point. Knock on the door, smile, and badge Nana. Ask if we can come in. Lie if you have to but make yourself the all-American gal."

Gwen smirks and says, "So you want me to con some nice old lady." She pauses and adds, "I can *do* that."

Gwen taps on the door and a moment later, the porch light illuminates the porch. Mrs. Norma Gustavson stands a shade over 5 ft. but seems smaller by the scoliosis. She gives us a guarded smile and Gwen begins with, "Good evening Ms. Gustavson, my name is Gwen McNulty and this is John Booker. We're special agents of the FBI and we'd like to speak with you."

She says, "My God, what could the FBI want with me?"

Gwen smiles and assures her that, "You're fine Ma'am, nothing to do with you."

She directs us to a small living room. It reminds me of my grandparents' home, which always seemed dark by subdued colored carpets, wallpaper, and furniture. Gwen spends a few minutes bonding with Norma discussing the weather, Thanksgiving menus, and Catholicism. She follows Dr. Alvarez's script skillfully portraying us more as Peace Corps volunteers rather than gun-toting law officers. I give Agent 36 the eyebrow to nudge the conversation along. Gwen nods and a moment later says, "We're with the terrorism task force and interviewing people who may have seen or heard anything."

Nana's eyes widen and she blurts out, "Is there a terrorist nearby?"

We'd been doing OK but the sudden segue from church to terrorism leaves Nana speechless. I attempt to build a bridge and say, "No ma'am, just canvassing the neighborhood in different areas of Minneapolis."

She nods and offers, "It's terrible how these terrorists kill innocent people, but I don't know anything other than what I see on the news."

I jump in with, "Of course Norma. But sometimes we see or hear things that may not *seem* important, but are."

Nana looks puzzled so I clarify with, "For example, many young people are confused. They feel unloved and want to belong but they just drift looking for answers."

The old lady nods. "The answer is Jesus but this generation is too busy with their gadgets."

I'm hit with a blinding flash of the obvious. Nana has provided us with the perfect opening so I plow through and say. "Well, it's apparent that you can't help us so we'll get on our way. Hope we didn't take up too much of your time."

I rise but Agent 36 is frozen on the couch and giving me, *a look*, which asks, *"Why we leaving now asshole?"*

Nana rises and I shake her hand. I say, "Oh, almost forgot." I pause and look at my notes. "Our supervisor requires us to ask everyone a standard question. I already know that your answer is *'no'* but you know how bosses can be."

Nana smiles her understanding and I stare down at my pad, poise my pen and ask, "Do you know any males between the ages of 18 and 29, who are unemployed, spend considerable time on the internet, smoke, drink, may have had a recent breakup with a girlfriend, has few if any friends, no religious affiliation, seems angry, and spends most of his day alone?"

Nana gives my lengthy question some thought and I notice the sudden recognition in her eyes. "I do," she finally says. "My grandson Gus." Nana chuckles and adds, "But he's *definitely* not a terrorist."

We sit back down and readily agree with Nana that *her* grandson can't be a terrorist but couch our follow up questions under the heading, *'for informational purposes only.'*

Twenty minutes later, Gwen and I give Nana a hug with promises of getting together for dinner and church services. OK, I realize that we'll probably never see Nana again and we just conned a nice old lady, but, sometimes all's fair in love and war. We're almost out the door when a somewhat bizarre thought barges into my cranium. "You've been great ma'am, can we take a photo with you?"

Nana beams and says, "I'd be delighted."

We take about six shots on Gwen's cell phone camera alternating hugs with Nana.

Back in the car, Gwen tells me that, "You had me confused for a minute, Booker."

"You've got no trust in me, Gwen."

"No shit, Booker. I'd trust Mexican tapwater before you."

Tommy gets impatient with the banter and demands, "So you two done with all the bullshit and wanna tell me if Granny coughed up her loser grandson?"

"Not really," I say. "The poor lady had no idea of Gus being a bad person."

"So why all this silly talk?"

Agent 36 tells him, "You're such a caveman, Tommy. Always want the home run instead of three singles."

"Quit the baseball bullshit and tell me you didn't strike out."

Gwen explains how we conned Nana into talking about her grandson and added the photo op.

Tommy laughs. "Good shit. Now we got surveillance photos of the old bag but whatta we gonna do with them?"

I tell Tommy that, "Nana may have shed some light on time and location."

"I'm all ears."

"Nana and Gus are going shopping tomorrow morning."

"That's it?" Tommy wonders. "What am I missing?"

Gwen leans forward from the back seat and places her hand on Tommy's head. "Only that Nana saw a lot *bullets* on Gus's kitchen table during their Thanksgiving dinner."

CHAPTER 32

"Why are you pushing me?"
John Rambo, Rambo: First Blood (1982)

"TF one to niner six."

AJ responds with, "Go TF one."

"Get the next SO (Special Operations) shift on the subject's house and meet us at the nest."

The *nest* is my hotel room suite which is our default command post. It has a kitchen, living room and office area. We gather in a loose circle on chairs and couches. I even rouse up Gia from her sick room since tomorrow may require all hands-on deck. Dr. Linda looks striking even dressed down in a tight sweatsuit while Jun must have an endless supply of checkered wool shirts and hiking boots. Sean has been particularly quiet since we arrived but I have other things on my mind. Gia is holding her Kaopectate and looks queasy but engaged.

"Ok sports fans," I begin the brief. "We don't have much, *but* we have plenty to be concerned about."

I explain the visit with Nana and the bullets she observed on Gus's kitchen table. Questions from the group include: Q: What caliber? Answer: "We're lucky Nana could recognize a *bullet*." Q. What potential targets did they discuss? A: "No discussion on any location other than they're going shopping tomorrow." Q: Where? A:

"No idea. Gus is picking up Nana in the AM." Q: What time? A: "No specific time." Q. Why would Gus take his grandmother on a jihad?" A: "Good question but I haven't a clue."

This last item produces a somewhat heated debate. In the end, we are unable to determine any logical reason for tomorrow's shopping trip. Sean and Tommy conclude that Gus plans to jihad on a different day, but Gwen and I vote that the time is now and Nana is either a witness or collateral damage. Dr. Linda comments that Gus will strike *sooner* rather than later although she won't predict if it'll be tomorrow."

Jun has been rather quiet but offers and editorial aside, "It's now or never."

Tommy asks, "Why do you say that Jun?"

Jun smiles at her good friend and replies with, "Confucius said... *Before you embark on a journey of revenge, dig two graves.*"

We all take a few seconds to digest this byzantine remark. I gather that Confucius is being channeled through Jun and predicting that Gus will *off* his own Nana. How rude is that!

The meeting continues with some mild and some wild conjectures but basically all the meat is off the turkey. The group requires some shut-eye. I can recognize exhaustive babble when I hear it, so I sum up with, "Here's what we *know*. Gus had rounds on his table. Gus is going shopping tomorrow. Tomorrow is the busiest shopping day of the year, where large groups will gather. Gus was communicating with someone from Syria. Gus is sympathetic to radical Islam, and according to Dr. Alvarez, Gus fits the profile of a homegrown lone wolf terrorist."

The group is taking notes and nodding so I continue. "Here're the *unknowns* and assumptions. We have no idea of a target but given ISIS standard operating procedure, it'll be soft. The Syrian communication was *probably* with his ISIS recruiter, *and* the timing seems suspicious. This coupled with recent e-mails to his ex-girlfriend paint the picture that Gus *appears* ready to go jihad."

The gravity of my words seems to have left the group speechless, but not for long.

Agent 36 offers, "Based on the knowns, my hunch is that shoppers will be the likely target."

AJ says, "I checked locations and events scheduled for tomorrow which will have large gatherings. In addition to the hundreds of Malls and upscale shopping villages, we have The Holidazzle Parade, Peavy Plaza and The Holiday Market all open tomorrow. Other events with anticipated large gatherings are the European Market and the Winter Wonderland." AJ pauses then adds. "At least schools will be closed."

"We're fucked," Tommy editorializes. "Can't cover all these targets."

AJ provides the team a folder with five different photographs of Gus Stevenson. A one-year-old DMV, and four surveillance photos showing him from both profiles a full body shot and a facial close-up. Added to the file are three great photos of Nana with Gwen and I mugging it up in her living room. We all have shit-eating grins plastered on our faces, which now seem totally out of place. AJ tells us that, "Law enforcement agencies have copies of these photos. I've alerted police departments within 100 miles of here and every FBI agent in this division is on duty tomorrow. We'll cover every major event but we really *can't* cover every major event."

I tell the group, "So here's plan. We put manpower on Nana's home since Gus is heading her way. Two units on Gus's apartment, since it'll be a daylight surveillance and we don't wanna heat him up."

"Questions, suggestions, comments, or prayers?"

I ask Dr. Alvarez, "What's your take on *when* Gus will open up on a crowd?"

She raises her eyebrows and says, "I'm not sure what you mean."

"Let's say Gus runs into a sports stadium or a school. Would he immediately open up and start killing or wait a moment or two?"

"That's an excellent question." She pauses and says, "I believe that a sociopath like Gus will want to take in his surroundings. He'll need to work himself up into a fury to justify his actions and take time to look his intended targets in the eye. This intimate contact will provide him pleasure"

"Anything else?"

Dr. Linda's voice changes subtly, "The strategy of terrorism is to inflict the maximum amount of psychological damage. The best way to achieve that, is a *maximum* body count concentrating on women and children."

"Why women and children?" Gia asks.

"Because Americans have an overwhelming need to *protect* their women and children. We consider them off limits in *any* conflict, and images of dead and wounded kids and moms will put America in a traumatic shock."

I don't sleep well. Iraq seems to push its ugly recall button in times of trouble. Mr. IED revisited me and once again sent jagged hot shrapnel into 40 % of my torso. That shithole in the desert has turned into an early warning system that something bad is about to happen to yours truly. And unfortunately, that forewarning has been uncannily accurate.

Surveillance reports no movement during my nightmare. So far so good. We're scheduled to stage in the lobby at 06:45 with a loose plan. I'm up two hours before my alarm clock so I *coffee up*, grab a bagel, and head to the lobby. The alone time allows me to play with the many *"what ifs,"* since every military or law enforcement operation has land mines.

My reflections factor in that *something* is bothering Sean Gregory. You can recognize the subtle signs of discontent in the law enforcement family. Sean has been distant and distracted lately. It happens often in law enforcement but usually with older burnt out veterans. It *shouldn't* be happening to a brand-new agent. These should be the times of awe and wonderment. Sean confided to Gwen that he had nagging doubts about his chosen profession. Gia shooting Brenda in the back triggered some deep-seated beliefs. I had always thought that Sean

Gregory would have made a better social worker than FBI agent. His father, Fred, had no such reservations about shooting bad guys, or *gals*, in the back, front, *or* side. But Fred Gregory was a former combat Marine who viewed the world in terms of good or bad with no subtle shades of gray.

I'm evidently mumbling to myself as Tommy Shoulders approaches and asks, "You usually have bullshit sessions with yourself?"

"I talk to myself because sometimes I need expert advice."

Shoulders laughs and says, "That's what I like about you Booker, a modest fed is hard to find."

"Need your take on something."

Tommy nods and I ask, "What's up with Sean?"

"You noticed. Seems to have his head stuck up his ass."

"Well get it unplugged. I already had one heart to heart with the boy. I thought he got past his pacifist stage. We got lucky with Brenda but if we have to depend on the rabbit's foot again, just remember that it *didn't* work for the rabbit."

The team gathers in the lobby and its show time. AJ, Dr. Linda, Jun, and I head to the FBI field office to coordinate and communicate with the mobile units and local police. Gwen, Sean, and Gia will team up with Minneapolis agents in the field, while Tommy Shoulders will go it alone. There is a very good reason that Tommy is mobile, agile, and hostile, motoring around by his lonesome. He is our surveillance insurance but I hope we won't have to file a claim.

Terrorists, for the most part, attack soft targets. About 80% of *all* terrorist attacks are carried out at places without a security perimeter. Unfortunately, most of America is a soft target, including schools - nursery through college - sporting events, train and bus depots, malls, and contrary to the prevailing thought, our airports. Studies indicate that US airports are *no* safer than they were *before* the terrorist attacks on 9/11. They just *appear* safer.

I meet the Minneapolis brass, which includes the SAC (Special Agent in Charge) and *her* two ASACs. A female SAC was unheard of some fifteen years ago but now seems the norm. I've got no problem with female authority figures as long as they pay their dues and we don't lower the standards to reach down the career ladder. SAC Janelle Mann seems like an OK lawman, which, I believe, is the politically *incorrect* term. AJ provided the poop that she is a West Point grad who did two tours in Afghanistan. I'd bet that Janelle didn't take advantage of the *modified* push up allowed lady agents at our annual PT test.

We waste valuable time in *bureau babble*, which is a term I coined when agents meet for the first time and play a form of career Jeopardy. The categories include mutual friends in the 'B,' FBI Divisions you've worked. We *finally* reach the Ops Center. The operations centers in FBI field divisions are state of the art, but sometimes I feel that we are *too* dependent on electronic hardware and forget that crimes are solved by humans.

Supervisory Special Agent Jerry Yanello is the boss of the Center. He informs us that, "Neither target has left their residence. Police units within the Minneapolis St. Paul area assigned to sites with gatherings in excess of 500, report status quo. Multi agency Intel analysts report nothing on their radar."

I ask, "Did we shake the trees on snitches?"

Yanello nods, "Every agent and detective in the area contacted open sources with no joy."

I ask AJ, "Where's the coffee stash? It's gonna be a long day."

As I am mixing some cream and sugar into a Styrofoam cup, Yanello announces, "Gus is on the move."

CHAPTER 33

"Houston, we have a problem."

Tom Hanks - Apollo 13

At 0946: Gus exits his residence. I comment, "So far, so good."

At 1011: Gus *arrives* at Nana's residence. "So far, so good," I repeat.

At 1028: Gus and Nana depart residence. I smile and say, "I love it when a plan comes together."

At 1047: FBI surveillance *lose* Gus and Nana. My immediate reaction is, *"Shit!"*

There is a panicked stream of chatter on the radio as surveillance units attempt to find Gus and Nana. They *step* on each other's conversation until the SOG supervisor screams, "Quiet!" He waits a second and in a calm voice directs. "Unit 7 provide the last location observed."

"Westbound on 13th Street."

The supervisor barks orders, "Units 10, 17, and 9, bracket the area. Unit 12 head northbound on Delphi, Unit 17, eastbound on Snyder, and Unit 12, hit the gas pedal and haul ass a mile ahead of projected route. Unit 6, stand pat and make sure target doesn't double back on you. All other units saturate the area and find that car!"

I tell Yanello, "I requested air surveillance."

Yanello says, "We have two air units standing by at the airport. The ceiling is a solid 500 feet. This is Minnesota and weather severely limits air surveillance."

Gus is driving a beat-up, white, rusted 2009 Ford Taurus with a few dents and scrapes. A pretty nondescript target for surveillance units in this part of the world.

I ask, "What kinda area did we lose him in?"

Yanello explains that, "It's a main innercity thoroughfare with stores, restaurants, and shops. All foot traffic with no off-street parking. The surrounding area is being gentrified by young professionals. At 11 AM on Black Friday the area is probably elbow to asshole with shoppers."

Contrary to what the public believes, many targets evade FBI surveillance. It's a delicate ballet of not heating up a suspicious subject while also *not* losing them. Options range from bumper locking to aerial surveillance and every technique in-between. I had requested authority to place a GPS monitor on Gus's car but Mr. Sollis thought it unconstitutional. I asked the U.S. Attorney how long he'd been at the job. His reply was seven years to which I informed him that, "U.S. Attorneys and diapers should be changed often….and….for the same reason."

Sollis didn't find this aside at *all* witty and may have added it to my existing disciplinary tab. But since I'm inflicted with a case of serial insubordination, Tommy and I ignored Sollis's legal opinion and tagged Gus's car last night with a magnetic GPS unit. Technically we violated the 4th Amendment, but as Tommy so eloquently stated, "The Constitution's been raped lately by these liberal PC assholes. Fuck Sollis and fuck his legal opinion." Detective Shoulders has a way of getting to the crux of things.

I call Tommy on his cell phone and ask, "I hope you've got a signal?"

"Asshole just got on an interstate."

"Headed where."

"Southbound on Interstate 35."

"Standby, Tommy."

I grab Yanello and ask that he access an area map on the screen. It takes him less than 30 seconds until a Google map appears on the 6-foot screen, positioned above the console. "Where's Interstate 35?"

Yanello highlights the road and I ask, "Where was Gus last seen?"

I orient myself on the map and ask Tommy, "Any change?"

"Still on 35 but he's slowing down." A pause before Tommy announces, "Just went westbound on 35."

I turn to Yanello and muse, "If our boy is headed in this general direction, are there any targets of value?"

Yanello takes a moment to digest my question. "Can't think of anything." He turns to me and asks, "Did one of *your* units pick him up?"

"Tommy was in the area and believes he has the target."

Yanello gives me a nasty look and wonders, "Why the hell didn't he call it out on the radio!"

Since I have no logical reply I shrug and say, "Tommy's a local cop, he usually goes solo. It's probably a false alarm anyway."

Yanello informs me that we wasted precious minutes in the interim and begins barking directions on the radio sending several units to the area of westbound I-35."

I ask him, "Sure there aren't any targets of value in that area?"

"Nothing in that specific area."

I take a few steps away from the console and ask Tommy, "You still got a signal?"

"Yep, but it's getting weaker. Supposed to last 20 days but the wind chill here is nasty. The tech guy warned me about extreme cold."

"Let's keep an open cell line. Stay off the radio. Some units are headed your way so do what you gotta do but be aware that they're in the area and…....."

Tommy interrupts me with, "...Gus is moving to the far lane. Standby." About 30 seconds later Shoulders informs me, "Looks like he's taking the southbound ramp to I-494."

"Target vehicle may have taken the southbound I-494 ramp." I ask Yanello, "Where could he be heading?"

AJ looks at the map and states, "Looks like he's proceeding toward Bloomington."

"Is that a separate city?"

"Yes."

"Well," I say impatiently, "anything in Bloomington that presents a mass casualty target?"

AJ looks me squarely in the eye and says, "The Mall of America, which just happens to be the largest mall in the entire free world."

I tell Tommy in a calm voice to, "Take Gus down. He's headed to the Mall of America. Do *not* allow him to get inside that Mall!"

"Got it covered. He just turned into the Mall perimeter."

Yanello looks at me and asks, "Whatta you mean by '*take him down?*'"

I suddenly realize that I just ordered a preemptive strike on someone who is going shopping with his *Nana*. Although Tommy could interpret the word '*down*' in several ways, it's a safe bet that he'll shoot Gus in order to get him *down*. The FBI's deadly force policy clearly states that, "*Deadly force can only be used to protect the life of others or the law enforcement officer.*" And, since the U.S. Attorney has already determined that we lack probable cause to intercept his e-mails, it's a sure bet that he'd frown upon *assassination*.

Just as I'm about to amend my *suggestion* to Tommy, I am preempted by a loud profanity. "Fuck me!"

"What happened, Tommy?"

"I rear ended a FedEx truck."

"You OK?"

"Fine, but Gus will be parking his car in about two minutes."

Mall of America became the largest shopping mall in America when it opened in 1992. It has 42 million annual visitors, which is roughly eight times the population of the state of Minnesota. The Mall employs 13,000 during the peak season and 15,000 on Black Friday. Gus has stumbled upon what the military refers to as a *'Target rich environment.'*

No matter how many times you conduct training exercises, *shit happens* in the real world and you occasionally have to go off script. I actually have no idea of the standard FBI operating procedure for an active shooter in a mall, but it seems that AJ does. He directs all ground units to proceed to the Mall of America. It's decision time and my gut tells me that AJ is about to show our hand. He'll order an evacuation and then have FBI agents announce their presence, and clear each store. That's probably the smart move given the *book*, but my gut is screaming that, this time, the book is wrong.

I touch AJ's arm just as he cues the mike and tell him "Wait one." AJ looks at me and I lower my voice and say, "You're gonna spook him."

"What?"

"As soon as Gus sees law enforcement, he'll open up."

AJ counters that with, "He plans to open up *whether* he spots cops or not, and we risk giving him *time to kill.*"

My rationale is simple. I say, "If Gus sees an army of cops running through the mall, he may open up prematurely. A mass of humanity will be caught up in a crossfire, *but* if we can spot Gus *before* he decides to open up, then we avoid mass casualties."

Yanello immediately disputes my logic and counters with, "We're assuming too much. Chances are Gus will start firing while we're flapping our lips. We need to move!"

I explain. "The Bureau profiler believes Gus will wait, and I agree with Dr. Alvarez. Gus is in no rush and wants to look his victims in the eye. Timing *is* critical but we need to identify Gus first and then neutralize him in a contained area."

AJ's voice gets an edge to it. He says, "The FBI analyzed every mass casualty episode within the past twenty years. They concluded what tactical procedures worked and incidents when law enforcement fucked up and caused needless deaths. Then we took those lessons learned and trained hard so we could get it right the next time." AJ pauses and finishes with an emotional, "And you're asking me to say *'fuck the book.'* "

"Situations change, people change, tactics change, *and* Gus hasn't read our book."

"OK, Agent Booker," AJ relents. "Give me an alternative to our SOP, because I have to live with myself when we're counting bodies."

I place my hand on AJ's shoulder and say, "We'll get this done. Step one: We assign Gwen as commander on site. She'll establish a CP inside the mall security office and use the cameras to scan the mall. She has photos of Gus and his grandmother. Step 2: We'll have police officers secure the parking lot, Gus's car, and the outer mall perimeter. Step 3: FBI units will exit their vehicles, split into two man teams, stage at every mall entrance, and stand by for orders. No blue raid jackets or visible weapons. Step 4: We break the mall down into manageable grids and assign each team to secure their grid. Firing orders are to first identify Gus, and...."

".....And what?" AJ wonders.

"And, do what you gotta do."

CHAPTER 34

"Be not afraid of going slowly, be afraid only of standing still."
Chinese Proverb

When I was in eighth grade there was this bully by the name of Yon Yon. A somewhat psychotic, misguided South Philly youth who would beat me up on sight. "What'd I ever do to you?" was followed by a smack to my face. It stung but the embarrassment stung more. The fact that he was 16 and I a mere 13, didn't seem to deter or embarrass him. So, I hatched a plan. It was a simple scheme, but minus any FBI analysis of bully techniques, tactical training, or the counsel of profilers.

The next time Yon Yon approached me, I'd kick him in the nuts and run. I convinced myself that this strategy would work and even rehearsed a Yon Yon kick to the balls. But I was oblivious to the fact that my plan had serious flaws.

Two days later Yon Yon spotted me in St. Tommy's schoolyard and I almost smiled. He began his taunt of, "Hey shithead, come here so I can give you a smack."

I took several measured steps forward while staring at Yon Yon's testicles. As he drew his hand back, I cocked my right leg and kicked as hard as I could. Yon Yon stepped back and I missed, staggered a few steps, but somehow regained my balance. It was now time to execute the second part of my plan: the *getaway*. That also failed since Yon Yon was faster than me. So I received a severe ass whipping.

For some reason, I'm suddenly reminded of the Yon Yon episode as we are about to execute another one of my plans. But a failure this time can cost lives, lots of lives.

I cue the mike and advise all units that, "Agent McNulty is the onsite agent in charge. She will communicate with unit leaders. Keep radio traffic to a minimum."

So far so good. Gwen and I have an open cell line. She informs me that, "CP established, the locals have the perimeter and FBI personnel are staged and awaiting deployment."

"Good job Gwen," I say. "Do *not* notify the security guards on the floor about the situation. We don't need some minimum wage Gold's Gym cowboy doing his Dirty Harry imitation."

Gwen is working in tandem with the Security supervisor in charge of the shift. They begin the tedious process of dividing the Mall into grids. Mall of America has a gross area of 4,870,000 sq. ft. or 96.4 acres, enough to fit seven Yankee Stadiums inside. The mall is nearly symmetric, with a roughly rectangular floor plan. AJ informs me that there are 147 FBI agents standing by at the mall. Every agent is equipped with handi-talkies allowing the CP to issue general orders. Although I can't figure out the *exact* calculation of agents per square footage, I *can* visualize Yankee stadium. We have 73 two-man teams, plus a rover, which boils down to 10 teams per *one* Yankee stadium. That's manageable.

Agent 36 is a member in good standing with MENSA, the genius IQ club, so I'm confident that she'll organize this cluster fuck within ten minutes. Nine minutes later Gwen announces that, "All teams assigned. Stand by."

Gwen calmly broadcasts team assignments matching FBI unit numbers with mall location identifiers. "Units 7 and 9 assigned Mall grids 4, 5."

Gia is teamed with a Minnesota agent covering the eastern corridor while Sean and Tommy are assigned the central food court and two anchor stores below. I'm relieved that Sean is teamed with Tommy for two reasons. Maybe the veteran street cop can talk some sense into the baby agent and if he can't, then Sgt. Shoulders may keep him alive.

As the two enter the mall and head toward their sector, Tommy begins his mentoring process by tactfully asking Sean, "So what the fuck is up with you?" Shoulders evidently never attended the management seminar on employee compassion.

Sean shrugs and deflects with, "Don't know what you mean."

"Cut the bullshit." Tommy is pissed. "Spit it out."

When Sean realizes that his deflection mechanism isn't working he tells Tommy that, "Just wondering if I have this career thing right?"

"Why?"

Sean explains. "My dad and I are different. He was a tough Marine, state trooper, and won the medal of valor as an FBI agent. I don't know if I can be that."

"Then be yourself."

"Easy for you to say. You were at Cairo and been doing this for years."

Tommy sighs, "Sean, this Cairo thing was just another operation. Only difference is that it was an *away* game. You'll get your shot." He chuckles and finishes with, "So to speak."

Sean smiles but it lacks any enthusiasm. He says, "I'm really not sure I want it."

"Want it or not, it'll find you son."

Sean gives a weak concession smile and mutters, "I suppose you're right."

No one has any idea *how* wrong Sean Gregory could be.

I begin pacing, which alerts me that I've reached my expiration date in an office. I am a certified *thrill junky* who views enclosed settings as cages.

I ask Yanello, "How long will it take me to get to the Mall with lights and sirens?"

"Too long." He confides. "This thing is going down within the next five minutes. Traffic and distance puts you there *after......*" Yanello pauses and locks eyes with me. There's no need to finish his thought.

No one gives the kindly old lady and her grandson a second look. Gus realizes that Nana is providing him the perfect cover. They blend into the holiday shoppers and Gus actually maintains his patience when Nana patters into some store offering "*70% off.*"

It allows him the opportunity to scope out the nonbelievers who are cowardly, addicted to comfort, and lacking the sacrificial spirit. Jihadists believe that spirit can overcome material disadvantage, that victory belongs to the side with the stronger will. Gus smiles as the crowd shuffles along asshole to belly button. It is a mass of humanity and Gus visualizes his bullets ripping into the flesh of families carrying their packages and holding hands. He sits on a bench awaiting Nana's latest detour into the Hallmark Shoppe. A family of four is about to pass by when the boy stops and approaches Gus. He is about 7 years old and fits the Minnesota Nordic profile with blond hair and blue eyes. If Gus were to look at old family photos he would be looking into a mirror. The entire family, which includes mom, dad, and sister, also stop. Dad says, "Let's go Mark."

Mark ignores his father and asks Gus, "You a soldier?"

Gus is suddenly on guard and about to begin the slaughter with this twerp until he realizes that he is wearing a green Army field jacket. He smiles at the boy and says, "I am a soldier." But omits, '*In Allah's army.*'

Dad mutters, "Sorry." As he takes his son hand and walks along.

Tommy Shoulders and Sean Gregory repeatedly examine the photos of Gus and Nana as they eyeball the mass of humanity. Tommy observes that, "I wish Minnesota had more blacks, these people all resemble Disney characters."

Sean, being an African American, smiles and says, "Yep, all you white people look alike."

Nana rejoins Gus and says, "When you were just a toddler, your mom and I took you to this mall. You were in a stroller and we all had such a wonderful time. I thank God that we're able to do this again." She pauses and a tear forms on her cheek. She finishes with, "I love you so much Gus."

Gus is smiling but thinking, *'You will spend your eternity loving Allah, you old fool.'*

Agent 36 is working the video surveillance system, which includes a bank of monitors that cover different sectors of the mall. Multiple cameras alternately flash images onto the monitors in a chaotic symphony of humanity. Whenever Gwen or the shift supervisor find a likely target they push the zoom lens for close ups. A few false alarms and many *not even close*.

Gus has seen enough. His ISIS recruiter gently reminded Gus on several occasions to, *"Remember your destiny. Do not become distracted with earthly concerns. Allah awaits you as his martyr and son."*

He absentmindedly touches his Tec-9 machine pistol positioned inside his field jacket and looped around his left shoulder. It's been converted to fire on fully automatic and will be Gus' opening salvo. He plans to spray the food court, then rush to the balcony and fire down below on the mass of humanity. When he expends his Tec-9 ammo, then he'll open his nylon backpack and unleash the Steyr M912 fully automatic assault rifle on the infidels inside the anchor store. That was as far as his plan went except for the 72 virgins who awaited Gus in paradise.

CHAPTER 35

"Say 'hello' to my little friend!"
Scarface (1983)

I'm having issues. They involve feelings of helplessness and vulnerability. Dr. Linda would probably diagnose me with some trendy disorder but basically I'm an adrenaline junkie in withdrawal. My brain is trying to process the mall scene from the safety of the FBI office. It's not possible due to the many unknowns, but the one constant is, *'I ain't there!'* Gus and Nana are currently strolling around that fucking mall, and I'm drinking coffee. When you think about mall pairings, an elderly lady and young man is *not* that common. There are plenty of teenagers, families, and couples. So my brain is flashing an alert of, *'Why haven't they spotted them yet!'*

Gwen is also experiencing some anxiety issues of her own. There's the steady mental *tick, tick, tick* of an imaginary clock in her head, and it's getting louder. Agent 36 stares intently at the monitors anticipating the carnage at any moment. She completes her scan of the center west portion of the mall and redirects her gaze to the cameras covering the food court. As each second passes, Agent 36 is fully aware that they are on borrowed time. Seventeen minutes have elapsed since Gus arrived and Agent 36 understands that this game has gone into overtime. First team that scores will win.

There's a sad irony that the Stery M912 is an Israeli-made and -manufactured weapon. Gus has no idea of the weapon's origins but he *does* know that when fired on auto, it's a kick ass killing machine. But first, the Tech 9 machine pistol.

Gus turns to his Nana and says, "I'm hungry, let's go to the food court."

Nana smiles and says, "I'm in the mood for a Cinnabon."

The two follow the sign which directs them to the escalator leading to the food court.

Unlike Gia, Sean qualified expert on the tactical pistol course at the FBI Academy. He did *not* require remedial training in defensive tactics, academics, *or* firearms. But, that was with paper targets. There have been many law enforcement officers who excel at the training academy but don't possess the mind set for the streets. Tommy Shoulders reaches the escalator and says, "We'll do the food court, then head to an anchor store."

Gwen identifies a possible. Looks like a younger male and an older woman. She zooms the camera lens toward the pair and the older lady turns and faces the camera. It is the woman she interviewed some 13 hours ago in her living room. Agent 36 quickly checks her assignment sheet and smiles. Tommy Shoulder and Sean Gregory are patrolling that sector.

"CP to unit 13, com'on Tommy, answer up."

Shoulders recognizes Gwen's voice calling his name in the earpiece. "Go."

"We got a positive ID. Two subjects heading toward the food court."

"We're a minute away."

"Will keep you updated on their position. They're just getting off the escalator."

Tommy turns to Sean and says, "Let's rock and roll. Our boy is at the food court."

The two agents do a fast walk up the escalator, bobbing and weaving through the shoppers. The food court is especially crowded with hungry holiday shoppers. Crooked lines with people shuffling their feet wait patiently to order food. The usual walkways separating tables from the food kiosks are packed with humanity. Tommy scans the area and recognizes that mall food courts present the perfect killing zone. They are generally oblong shaped areas with one way in and *one* way out. If they can't stop Gus before he pulls the trigger this could result in a bloody massacre of epic proportions.

Gwen keeps the camera focused on Gus and tells Tommy, "As you enter the area make a left. Subject is stalled in front of The Chinese Wok Shack. Hurry, he seems to be opening his coat."

Tommy scans the outsized neon signs mounted above the kiosks identifying their brand and spots The Chinese Wok Shack. It's about thirty yards away but the path is blocked by a throng of humanity. Tommy grabs Sean and points him toward the right side of the food court, "I'll go straight at him, you circle around."

Tommy looks Sean in the eye and doesn't like what he sees. It's fear. His observation is confirmed when Sean asks, "Whatta I do when I see him."

The veteran detective thinks, *'We don't have time for this shit,"* but says, "If he has anything in his hand *other* than an egg roll, *shoot* him." Then adds. "*Many* times. Now GO!"

As Tommy is pushing and shoving his way toward the Wok, Gwen informs him that, "I lost Gus. Last seen in the vicinity of the Chinese Wok place."

"We'll find him." Tommy says as he grabs the butt of his 9MM Smith & Wesson.

Sean is having better luck maneuvering through the north side of the food court. He reaches a point some thirty feet past the Chinese Wok kiosk and cuts 90 degrees through the tables heading toward Gus's last known position.

Gus has decided that the time has come for jihad. He selects his initial targets, which consists of a table full of children and moms. The play group generally meets at a local park or a home, but chose The Mall of America for their Friday playday. Gus is working himself into a frenzy as the toddlers giggle and run around the table while their moms yap about their miserable lives. It will be his gift to Allah to end their unbelieving, ostentatious lives. Gus mouths the Koran 3:56 *"As to those who reject faith, I will punish them with terrible agony in this world and in the Hereafter, nor will they have anyone to help."*

Tommy has his weapon drawn and is pushing and shoving his way through the crowd. Sean has yet to touch his weapon which remains holstered at his side. Gus reaches for the butt of the Tech 9 and decides that his holier than thou Nana will be the first to die. Gus shouts the Koran verse 21:93, *"And kill the Christians and Jews wherever you find them!"*

Nana looks at her grandson and asks, "Did you say something, Gus?"

Gus points his Tech 9 at his Nana's head and pulls the trigger.

It takes a full five seconds before the mass of people recognize the sound of gunfire. Sean reaches the playgroup table and hears the distinctive retort of gunfire. Any agent who completes training at the FBI Academy will instantly recognizes this sound. New agent trainees fire over five thousand rounds before graduating.

Tommy also recognizes gunfire and observes as the civilians react in stages. Some hit the ground, some run, and some freeze in place. *All* of these actions make it more difficult to reach Gus and stop the slaughter. Sean is no more than twenty feet from Gus and assesses the situation. The gunman is leaning over a fallen elderly victim who lays motionless and bleeding on the floor. He is saying something that Sean can't hear. Sean pulls his FBI Glock 40 cal. pistol from his holster and assumes the Weaver position while aiming the weapon center mass at Gus. Tommy arrives and *also* sizes up the scene. Gus has whacked his Nana and is raising his weapon toward a group of kids at a nearby table.

Sean and Gus face each other. Their eyes meet for a split second before Sean commands Gus, "FBI, Drop the weapon!"

Gus disregards this *suggestion* and fires a burst of 9MM rounds in the direction of Sean. The weapon recoils upward and to the right as bullets indiscriminately spray the food court. Sean is spun backward as several rounds hit his leg, chest, and graze his head. Lindsey, a six-year-old, Michael, age five, and his mom Tiffany are also hit with the initial burst. Gus regains control of his weapon and aims the Tech 9 at the remaining children who are frozen in place. His finger begins to pull the 7.7 pounds of pressure required to fire the assault weapon just as a bullet enters the back of his head. It exits along with his left eyeball as Gus crumples to the floor. Detective Tommy Shoulders runs toward gunman who lay on the cold tile and notices that the Tech 9 is still attached by its sling to Gus. As he leans over the body, Gus slowly moves his head in an attempt to observe his carnage. Shoulders grabs Gus's hair and roughly twists it toward him so their faces are now inches apart. He whispers to Gus, "Asshole" and puts two additional slugs in his head. Tommy later tells me that he wanted to send Gus off to Paradise with a personal message to Allah.

CHAPTER 36

"Life isn't about waiting for the storm to pass...
it's learning to dance in the rain."

Vivian Greene

AJ and I are going lights and siren to Methodist Hospital. The initial reports are three dead and two wounded. Nana lay dead on the dirty food court floor with a look of bewilderment frozen on her face. It asked, *'How can you do this, Gus?'*

Five-year-old Michael Torenson and his 29-year-old mom Tiffany were killed instantly. Six-year-old Lindsey Rosen is listed in serious but stable condition, and FBI Special Agent Sean Gregory is critical and clinging to life.

Gwen provides updates on the phone that the Mall of America is one big cluster fuck. Agent 36 is attempting an orderly evacuation but human beings will usually default to, *'every man for himself.'* FBI agents conduct interviews with food court witnesses. Police officers direct the exodus requiring shoppers to pass checkpoints with their hands raised over their heads. Unfortunately, this process has been all too common since the advent of mass shooting incidents. The rationale is to ensure that Gus is the lone gunman. Although Gus proves to be the lone shooter, there are plenty of *other* criminals at the mall. The monitored evacuation produced two fugitives, forty-seven outstanding warrants, and confiscation of 113 weapons as well as 13 spontaneous confessions of shoplifting. I later recommend that law enforcement conduct mall evacuations as standard sting operations.

We arrive and badge our way to the surgery unit where our badges no longer work. A 100-pound nurse bluntly informs us that we are to sit in the assigned waiting room *until* someone provides information *'at the appropriate time.'* After 5 minutes, I consider it the appropriate time and find a doctor roaming the hall. He tells me, "Your friend is in respiratory distress. He is apnoeic and requires tracheal intubation. We suspect damage to the chest and lung wall so we must drain the blood before we can proceed."

I look at the doctor and ask directly, "Is he going to live?"

"He's young and fit so we have good intravenous access. The surgery consists of stopping the rapid hemorrhages. If we can do that, his chances improve." The young physician pauses and finishes with, "Bottom line is, I can't tell you if your friend will live or die."

I say, "Thank you." But think, *'For nothing.'*

My cell phone is chirping nonstop. Tony Daniels wants a brief for the Director, the Minneapolis SAC wants a brief for the news media, and somehow Christian Mingle wants a brief concerning my availability. I dial my roommate's cell and he seems animated. "Talk to me, John."

My brief is *actually* brief and to the point. "Tell the Director that his agents performed heroically and although we have a body count, it could've been much, much worse." I provide as many details as I can recall, including the prognosis for Special Agent Gregory, *'don't know if he'll live or die.'*

When Tony presses me for details, I refer him to the Minnesota SAC, Janelle Mann. "She'll have a more complete post op." I suppose I should get to the mall but Gwen has that covered. I turn to AJ and tell him, "Go take care of your people, I'll be here for a while."

My last medical update was some 4 hours ago when my skinny nurse buddy informed me, "The surgeons stemmed the internal bleeding in the chest cavity. A team of neurosurgeons are now working on his head wound."

I make some calls to pass the time. Lorri is both relieved and sympathetic. She knew I was in the state of Minnesota and when *breaking news* of a shootout in Bloomington interrupted a Rachael Ray recipe, it *had* to be her hubby. She tells me that the talking heads are blathering opinions to determine if it's terrorist related. They'll find out soon enough due to their many sources working at hospitals, police departments, and EMS. Tony contacted Sean's mom and she's on her way to the hospital. Agent 36 tells me that the mall is cleared. Tommy Shoulders calls and seems agitated. "Some fuckin' junior G-men want to interview me about the shootout."

Not knowing the specific details of the shooting, it's best to postpone any official interview since Tommy is not nuanced in Fed speak. Bureaucrats frown upon glib pronouncements like '*I put three in the asshole's head.*' I instruct Tommy, "Don't say one word. Just tell the agents that you're upset, you'll write a complete report, but in the meantime, you need to see the Bureau psychologist." Tommy is not happy about having to act *upset* since he's been involved in *nine* shootouts and is happy and proud to provide *every* gory detail over a beer. "I'm at the surgery waiting room at Methodist Hospital. Get over here now and no statements!"

Tommy arrives in fifty minutes and provides the uncensored version of the mall shootout. It was textbook proper until the, *"two in the head."* Although I agree with Tommy's memo to Allah, shooting a helpless and *wounded* subject doesn't pass our deadly force policy. Maybe in the Ugandan FBI.

"You really need to rein in that urge to ventilate terrorists who are about to die anyway." A reference to Shoulder's Cairo trifecta where he shot three wounded terrorists who lay on a dirty Apartment floor. Of course, I am guilty of shooting the fourth unarmed jihadist, in surrender mode, so I really can't pass judgment.

I ask, "How many witnesses?"

"Anywhere between two or five hundred." Tommy casually answers. "But most were either running, hiding, or crapping their pants."

We agree that they'll be a *few* eyewitnesses who observed Tommy's summary execution so we write a statement that basically claims self-defense. A stretch, but many law enforcement officers stretch the truth in official reports. It's almost required in this day and age when cops are indicted for defending themselves. Then there were four Marines who were punished for pissing on some dead Al-Qaida terrorists. Should've been given medals instead of a shitload of aggravation. I never got the rationale on that one.

The statement claims that Tommy approached the shooter to assure he was neutralized….. 'As Detective Shoulders bent down to separate the subject from his weapon, said subject attempted to grab his Tech 9 automatic pistol. Fearing that subject was an imminent threat to many civilians, Det. Shoulders neutralized subject."

The wording is taken *directly* from our deadly force policy and I include the word, *neutralize'* since bureaucrats love nonjudgmental words in lieu of *whacked, slayed* or *wasted.*

Once we administratively *tidy up* Tommy's involvement in the great mall shootout I ask the street cop, "What the fuck happened with Sean?"

Tommy shakes his head and says, "You want the bottom line?"

I nod and Tommy says, "Sean froze, *again*, and got himself *and* innocent civilians hurt."

"That's pretty extreme, even for you."

Shoulders describes the five minutes preceding the shootout. "I looked in his eyes and *knew* he couldn't pull the trigger. I *knew* that those civilians needed someone who didn't give a shit about some shooting policy, I *told* him if Gus had a weapon to shoot the asshole and fuck any warning. But he was never gonna pull that trigger because his brain ain't wired that way. End of story!"

It's dark outside when a doctor wearing blood stained blue scrubs approaches us, "Your friend is in post op recovery."

"How'd it go?"

"Ninety percent of all gunshot wounds to the head are fatal." The doctor pauses and asks. "You've heard of Traumatic Brain Injury (TBI)."

I nod. "Yes, I've served in Iraq."

"Well, as the bullet travels from the cranium through tissues, it causes laceration and also produces multiple, high-energy fragmentation to the brain parenchyma. These fragmentations result from both shattered skull bone and bullet's pieces, which leads to more injury."

I interrupt with, "Just give me the bottom line, Doc."

"He'll probably live but we can't predict any quality of life. He...."

"....Whoa." Tommy interrupts. "Is that double-talk for Sean's gonna be a vegetable?"

The doctor measures his words. "That's a possibility, but it's also possible that he'll regain *total* motor, neurological, and sensory abilities."

A few seconds pass as I process the possibilities. "Thanks Doc, can I see him?"

"Not at this time. He's in recovery unit in a medically induced coma."

We spend the next few days in Minneapolis tying up loose ends and monitoring Sean's condition. He's stable although still in a medically induced coma. We meet daily at the FBI office for post op briefs. Tommy slings his rehearsed fable to an official shooting team and it passes muster. But this is with the FBI home team and *not* the Justice Department, which in this district. is headed by Jay Sollis.

Five-year-old Michael Torenson and his 29-year-old mom Tiffany have funerals, six-year-old Lindsey Rosen's condition is upgraded to good, and Gia's diarrhea is all but gone.

SAC Janelle Mann pulls me aside and quietly says, "You didn't hear this from me." I nod and she continues. "We *may* have a problem.

It *seems* that the US Attorney for Minnesota has *'questions'* concerning Gus's death. It *seems* that several eyewitnesses at the food court provided statements that contradict Tommy's sworn statement. It *seems* that Sollis is convening a grand jury to *'get to the bottom of this situation.'* "

I thank Janelle and head directly to see Jay Sollis. The U.S. Attorney's secretary asks the question and I answer with, "No, I don't have an appointment, but, tell Mr. Sollis that John Booker is here to return the warrant he never approved." She raises her eyebrows so I clarify, "He'll understand."

It turns out that Mr. Sollis, indeed, desires a conversation. He opens his door and waives me inside. As I enter his office Sollis immediately retreats behind his massive desk. He is in a protective womb surrounded by the imageries of his power which include flags, plaques, and photos with two past presidents. It's a calculated move but I'm not in any mood to be impressed. He points to a chair but I shove aside some papers and sit my ass down on his desk. This seems to confuse the U.S. Attorney who is accustomed to subservient subjects within his kingdom.

I begin, "You want a grand jury on the mall shootout?"

"That's correct Agent Booker." Sollis now assuming a comfortable official mode. "There seems to be several eyewitnesses who dispute Officer Shoulders account."

"Is that so?" I mumble. "Well, allow me to enlighten you regarding your eyewitnesses." I slide myself closer to Sollis and violate his personal comfort zone. This is a rare affront for the top law man in Minnesota.

Sollis knows something's up. He gives me an anxious smirk, but says, "I can't wait."

I grin back and casually remove a micro cassette tape recorder from my pocket. I hit *play* and it takes a few seconds for Sollis to recognize the conversation we had just a few days ago in this very office. Shoulders and I were basically begging Sollis to approve *some* investigative tool to prevent Gus Stevenson from killing innocent civilians. The U.S.

Attorney's words hang in the room like an unexploded grenade. He proclaims, "I will *not* consider *any* law enforcement intrusion into the life of Gus Stevenson. He is a U.S. citizen, who may have radical views and may even be communicating with ISIS, *but,* he has a constitutional right of free speech, and it is *my* job to protect that right. The people of Minnesota have *nothing* to fear from Mr. Stevenson."

I hit the *Pause* button and silently stare at the U.S. Attorney. Jay is processing the threat level and looking for outs. It's similar to those video games that require some immediate remedial action to avoid the ballistic missile to the forehead. Any hope of elected office or a judgeship is toast if this tape becomes public. Hell, the guy will be lucky if he isn't sued, disbarred, and ends up teaching intro to criminal justice at the local community college.

Sollis fires a final salvo to maintain a shred of his authority, "That tape was illegally recorded. *You* can now be indicted."

People with unlimited power eventually come to believe that their pronouncements, whether true or not, will remain unchallenged. It usually works, but only if you have some bullets left in your gun. I correct the U.S. Attorney with, "We *both* know that there was *one* consenting party as required by federal law."

Sollis reluctantly concedes the point, "OK, Agent Booker, I will cancel the grand jury in exchange for that tape."

I inform Mr. Sollis, "Don't think so, this tape is my insurance."

The U.S. Attorney of Minnesota nods and slowly rises. He leaves the protection of his desk, offers me his hand, and says, "I seem to have lost my Queen and find myself checkmated."

I smile and take his hand, "Agreed, and to mix metaphors, you should just *tap out* so we can both get on with our lives."

Sollis returns the smile and tells me that, "I realize you think me some ideological extremist who *always* sides with the bad guys. I grew up supporting the civil rights movement, affirmative action, Roe versus Wade, and free speech. I've seen too many cases of law enforcement tramping all over our constitution so law school seemed the logical step to effect social change."

"How'd you get sidetracked into the prosecution end? You seem better suited for defense."

"I may have been wrong about Gus Stephenson but *someone* needs to ensure that *every* citizen is afforded the protections our forefathers intended. This job provides me that opportunity."

"Well, Mr. Sollis, I can't say that it was *good* meeting you, but I *can* say that I'm glad we had this talk." As a sign of good faith, I hand him the tape and exit with, "This one's on the house from one hard-headed asshole to another."

I return to the FBI office and inform Special Agent in Charge Mann that, "Mr. Sollis has reconsidered the grand jury."

She seems surprised and tells me, "That is *highly* unusual. Mr. Sollis rarely, if *ever*, changes his mind. Believe me, I've tried. How'd you do it?"

"I made him an offer he couldn't refuse."

CHAPTER 37

"You can't make this shit up."

Anonymous

Fort Bragg, North Carolina - 1991

FBI agents Bob Hayes and Gordan Batcheller head up I-40 toward Fort Bragg, North Carolina.

Batcheller closes a folder and comments that, "This narrative don't add up."

Hayes shakes his head. "Probably some mix-up with Muslim names. They all seem to be named Mohammed or Ali."

The two agents from the Charlotte Division are assigned to interview a former Egyptian Army Major who is *now* an active duty Staff Sergeant in the United States Army. Ali-Mohammed was a member of the elite Special Forces unit assigned to the John F. Kennedy Special Warfare School at Fort Bragg. Something *just* didn't seem to jive with this fairytale.

Batcheller felt that, "The CIA has their sleazy hands all over this one,"

"Yea, but when I contacted them, it was their usual bullshit of, *"We'll check it out and get back to you boys at the FBI.'"*

"That was four months ago."

The two FBI agents chuckle since the CIA had *never* gotten back to the FBI. Imagine two prom queens with only one prom. Hayes asks, "Do the timeframes add up?"

Batcheller re-opens the file and reads aloud, "Ali Abdelseoud Mohamed, born in Egypt in 1952. Mohammed joined the Egyptian Army in 1971 and rose to the rank of Major in the Special Forces. In 1981, the Egyptian Army sent Mohamed to Fort Bragg for 4 months training with the U.S. Special Forces. Working alongside Green Berets, he learned unconventional warfare, counterinsurgency operations, and how to command elite soldiers on difficult missions. After that, he returned to Egypt and served in the Egyptian Army until 1983, when he left to work as a counterterrorism expert for Egypt Air...." Batcheller pauses, turns a page. ".....In 1984, he received two Bachelor's degrees from the University of Alexandria, and a 1986 master's degree from the Egyptian Military Academy in International Relations."

"So," Hayes interrupts, "how and *why* in hell would he *return* to Bragg as a *Sergeant*?"

"That'll be one of my first questions," Batcheller says. "Sometime after his master's degree, Mohamed drops off the face of the earth, but word is, he went covert with the CIA. Four years later he reappears back at Special Ops with the US Army."

Hayes adds, "He disappeared just about the time the CIA stepped up its operations against Muslim militants. Terrorists had bombed the American Embassy and Marine barracks in Lebanon in 1983. In March 1984, terrorists linked to Iran-backed Hezbollah kidnapped William F. Buckley, the CIA station chief in Beirut."

"So," Batcheller says, "let's assume for purposes of this interview that Sergeant Mohammed either contacted the CIA on his own initiative or on instructions from Egyptian Islamic Jihad to penetrate CIA operations."

"I vote on the latter."

"Then," Batcheller concludes, "we are about to interview a double agent."

"Would appear so."

"Who'd you talk to?"

"A Major Mike Arnold. He's the XO and asked a lot of questions."

"What'd you tell him?"

"The usual bullshit, 'Routine interview, not a suspect, may be able to help us in an investigative matter....' "

The two agents arrive at the JFK Special Warfare School and present their credentials to the duty NCO. After a brief moment, Major Arnold appears and says, "Let's go to my office."

As they walk down the hallway to Arnold's office, Batcheller whispers, "Something ain't right."

Major Arnold closes the door and informs the two FBI agents, "Sgt. Mohammed has disappeared."

It takes twelve years for the FBI to fully unravel the complex saga of Army Sergeant Ali Abdelseoud Mohamed. All roads led to the CIA but they had set up their usual roadblock of gibberish.

The narrative *finally* emerges and it's a total US Intel fuck up. Mohammed was forced out of the Egyptian Special Forces as an intelligence officer for his Islamic extremist inclinations. They correctly suspected that Major Mohammed was a plant of the extreme group known as the Egyptian Islamic Jihad (EIJ). Not to be dissuaded by this turn of events, the EIJ instructs Mohammed to penetrate CIA operations. This may sound a somewhat complex effort filled with extensive vetting but Mohamed simply volunteers his services to the CIA. During the initial brief, Mohammed casually mentions some friends who are on the rogue's gallery of worldwide terrorists. The CIA believed they hit the covert jackpot and provide Mohammed fancy cars, plush accommodations, and an unlimited expense account. While employed by the CIA, Mohamed plans *every* aspect of the first *World* Trade Center bombing plot in New York. The evidence for Mohamed's role in the 1993 bombing is substantial.

Still unaware of Mohammed's role as a double agent the CIA tasks Mohamed to travel to Germany and establish contact with the Hezbollah. A few weeks later the CIA discovered that Mohammed confided to Hezbollah operatives that he was a CIA agent. So, they quickly deem him untrustworthy and cuts ties. Assuming Mohammed may try to reenter the United States, the CIA place Mohamed on the State Department *Watch List*, which *should* prevent him from obtaining a visa. But the American Embassy in Cairo issues him a visa because of confusion in the spelling of his name. There are many different ways to transliterate the Arabic name Mohamed into English.

Sometime in late 2000, Mohammed lands at JFK airport in NYC. The Customs Agent notices a red flag next to Mohammed's name and requests a supervisor. The retired NYPD detective smells something rancid and says, "We got some towel head who's on the Watch List." The frustrated supervisor recently had his ass chewed for delaying an individual on the List who was some diplomat's cousin. The asshole missed some official dinner at the UN and the fallout almost caused an international incident. "So," the supervisor says, "unless this guy's got an RPG hid up his asshole, we gotta waive him through."

In 2003, the 9/11 Commission's final report concludes the men responsible for masterminding the September 11, 2001, attack that killed over 3000 Americans were Ramzi Yousef and Sgt. Ali Abdelseoud Mohamed. The report also recommended that the *Watch List* be either eliminated or enforced.

Neither of these recommendations has ever been implemented.

CHAPTER 38

*"Optimism is going after Moby Dick in a rowboat
with a jar of tartar sauce."*

Zig Ziglar

Special Agents Bob Dupuis and silent John Canley have the plane gassed and ready for take-off. We fill in the blanks concerning events not covered by the news media. Bob just shakes his head and tells me that, "We're lucky you kept the body count to three." And adds, "But with you, there's always *some* bodies to count." Silent John smiles, punches my arm and says, "Good shit."

Sean is now in stable but guarded condition and seems to be improving. He has regained some verbal and motor skills, which leaves the medical people cautiously optimistic for a full recovery.

I tell everyone to take three days off and meet in the Cleveland office on Monday. Jun heads back to New York to check on her business, Dr. Alvarez returns to DC, and Gia visits her parents in Zelienople, Pennsylvania. Tommy and I remain in Cleveland to gather ourselves for the next phase of the lone wolf problem. The Minnesota affair seems proof positive that we can *never* resolve the issue under the current rules of engagement (ROE). It took a major effort of manpower, time, and resources to take out *one* lone wolf. Along the way, innocent people were killed and wounded and we were obstructed by the very people who could make our job easier.

While *we* were running around the Mall of America *ISIS* recruited twenty lone wolves who are currently planning similar attacks. I conclude that our kinder and gentler government will *never* confront the problem until body bags fill morgues in U.S. cities. And even then, they'll be some legislative bleeding heart assholes who'll want to find jobs for the disenfranchised terrorist, rather than kill them. So, it may be time to play *Dirty* once again.

Lorri and I decide to visit Nikki at Ohio State during my downtime. My daughter is the love of my life. You can have many wives in a lifetime, but children are forever. We make the two-hour drive to Columbus and find her dorm at 196 West 11th Ave. Morrison Tower is a single-gender floor dormitory with optional *mixed* gender floors. That mixed option was *not* available for *my* daughter as I wrote the check for room and board. When I attended Slippery Rock State College *all* dorms were designated single gender though there were many *unofficial* gender mixings. But that was then and with some *other* father's daughter. Since I was once a horny young male filled with overflowing testosterone, I'm not at all reassured by these imaginary dorm barriers. But, I rationalize that Nikki will do the right thing, whatever that is, in these confusing social times.

We take a stroll around the campus as Nikki points to class room buildings where she studies English Lit, Poly Sci, and US History. I'm surprised to learn that there are 58,322 students enrolled just at the main campus, which covers over 1765 acres. It suddenly strikes me that Ohio State is a soft target, very similar to The Mall of America. But I rationalize that there are thousands of soft targets and Ohio State is off the terrorist beaten path.

Nikki suggests lunch at *GOOEYZ*, located in the South Campus Gateway, which specializes in grilled cheese sandwiches. *GOOEYZ* loads their grilled sandwiches with meat, veggies, and surrounds it all in a blanket of gooey cheese. Lorri and Nikki seem to be very amused as I struggle with the sandwich. Strings of gooey cheese hang from my lip after each bite, and they take turns pointing at my chin and chuckling. We catch up and discuss things like grades, professors, roommates, and somehow Nikki slips *Pedro* into the mix. I'd almost forgotten about the future physician aka short order cook who probably stole our silverware during my absence on Thanksgiving. My hope had been that Pedro had long since gone the way of the hula hoop.

My hopes are dashed when Nikki casually mentions that, "Pedro is on his way here Pops, he's dying to meet you."

My initial thought is, *He may get his wish,* but I say, "Can't wait to meet him."

But Nikki knows her dad and pleads, "Be nice, Pops."

"I'm *always* nice." I say with little conviction.

Lorri comments, "I'm rolling my eyes out loud."

Doctor Pedro arrives and first impressions are good. The kid is actually wearing a sports coat, has no facial hair, obvious tattoos, or body piercings, and a high and tight haircut. Nikki later tells me that Pedro was petrified to meet me given her description of her father as a, *'Marine killing machine who spent 8 years undercover as an FBI agent with psychotic Mafia guys.'* Though true, it seems a bit theatrical. Pedro passes the pre-test, which consists of rapid questions attempting to trip him up. No signs of deception but that can be chalked up to cultural irregularities given he's a first generation beaner from Kansas.

Pedro's father is a neurosurgeon and his mom an oncologist, hence Pedro's pre-med major at Ohio State. OK, so I end up liking the kid but I won't let him off the intimidation hook for now. On the ride back to Cleveland Lorri wonders, "What'd you think of Pedro?"

I understand that anything I say, *'can, and will be, held against me'* by the Booker women, so I tell the truth. "I liked the wetback."

Lorri smiles and nods. We drive along in a content silence pleased that our daughter seems happy, healthy and excited with her life. There are many distinct categories of *silence* in relationships. They include: *'nothing much in common,'* or, *I'm pissed,'* but the *greatest* silence in a relationship can be classified as *'peace and love, no words required.'*

Somewhere near the Medina exit Lorri asks if I'd *like* to discuss the Mall of America shooting. Her stoic Swedish DNA prevents head-on conversational collisions. Were my wife of Italian descent she'd insist, *'So give me all the gory details, and don't leave anything out.'*

"It could've been a lot worse." I say and explain how Gwen took charge on scene and how Tommy killed the terrorist. My wife knows that Sean was critically wounded and though I trust my bride, I'm reluctant to paint him with a negative brush. "All in all." I sum up. "The FBI done good but one dead jihadist in Minnesota doesn't solve anything."

"You're talking about the ongoing recruitment of lone wolf terrorist?"

"It's a losing battle." I say my voice filled with defeat.

My words hang inside the car for a full moment. It's pitch dark outside on a moonless frigid evening and the only sound is the tires on the highway. Lorri half turns in the passenger seat to face me. She breaks the silence with, "You can do this John. I know you and I know that you're not a quitter. People are depending on you. You'll figure something out." My wife pauses and concludes with, "You *always* do."

CHAPTER 39

*"If everything seems to be going well, you have
obviously overlooked something."*

Murphy's Law

I arrive at the FBI office bright and early on Monday. It's still two hours before sunrise and the night duty agent wonders, "Insomnia?"

"Naw, I OD'd on gooey cheese so I'm afflicted with mild indigestion and severe flatulence. I'd keep your distance."

Special Agent Joanne Overall smiles and offers. "You are *such* an asshole Booker."

The mental health break put some things in perspective. We've done our due diligence and it's time to kick some terrorist butt. I refill my coffee cup and grab a yellow legal pad. My purpose is to provide the broad strokes of the puzzle. Our team will supply the specifics because they're smart, creative, and mission oriented. It will be my job to deliver the tools and keep the bureaucrats from fucking it up. I once had a boss who summed up his management style by telling me, *'I didn't say it was your fault, I said I was blaming you.'* And the public wonders how we choose our leaders.

A secondary goal is to keep my team from being indicted. I've made the decision that if we *do* get jammed up, it'll be *my* ass hanging on OPR's trophy wall. I'll swear on a stack of bibles that I assured my team we had legal authority to do all of those illegal things we are about to do. I'm not too happy about exposing myself to a 10 spot at Lewisburg Federal Prison, but, our country is teetering between anarchy, paranoia and insanity. So I feel that God or some higher being has put me in a position to do *something*. I suspect that Hitler had the same rationalization but immediately dismiss that logic as faulty.

My 'To Do' list is straightforward.

Make the Watch list a STOP list. *HOW*? Jun inserts bogus wants and warrants into the State Department computers.

Interrupt ISIS recruitments. ISIS spews out 90,000 messages every day. *HOW*? Jun intercepts and substitutes a *different* type of message.

Monitor encrypted sites minus a warrant - disrupt radicals *before* they act. *HOW*? Gwen gets XKeyscore from Stanley, then Jun hacks into encrypted communication.

Disrupt and reduce ISIS finances. *HOW*? Jun skims money from major ISIS donors and interrupts BITCOINS' abilities to fund terrorism.

Develop Human Intelligence (HUMINT). Snitches, rats, sources, informants. The lifeblood of law enforcement is confidential informants.

Amend FBI policy prohibiting surveillance on U.S. mosques. *HOW*? With fictitious Intel reports identifying U.S. mosques planning terrorist activities.

I'm actually the expert on writing fictitious official reports so I'll take the lead on this one. As my daughter Nikki would probably utter on this mosque restriction, "Duh." And she'd be right since the conspirators behind the 1993 World Trade Center planned their attack in *mosques, and* subsequent *mosque* investigations led to the arrest and the conviction of militant Sheikh Omar Abdel-Rahman, who hoped to launch attacks in the transit system. And *finally*, there's my own unscientific analysis, that sleazy looking guys in fancy flip flops who are up to no good hang around mosques.

But critics often argue that mosque surveillance violates Muslims' civil rights. My first reaction is that *innocent* Muslims have nothing to fear. My second reaction is "Fuck them!" We're the FBI and will make the investigative decisions on who and where we surveil.

First to arrive is Gia who informs me that all is well in Zelienople, Pennsylvania, and that she is now engaged to Cleveland FBI agent Pat Cloutier. I had no idea that they were even dating and fault Agent 36, who is my gossip Intel officer. Pat's a good guy so I congratulate her but warn, "I thought Pat was a Browns fan."

"He is," Gia says, "but he signed a pre-nup to root for the Steelers as long as we're married." Only a die-hard Steelers fan would understand.

Agent 36 is next up and tells us that she spent a relaxing few days catching up on her reading and vodka drinking. She spent Saturday evening at the Barking Goose, which is an old-style hippie joint with great music. I'd introduced Gwen to the Goose during the Cairo case using the location for clandestine meetings while I was *persona non grata* with the FBI. She now frequents the joint and hauled Ray Kopka to the Goose for some good jazz and a few Comas. A Coma is a mysterious concoction that will render any fit individual comatose. The retired police captain and hero of Cairo proclaimed the drink unfit for human consumption, *but* suitable for Cleveland cops.

Tommy Shoulders arrives with a black eye. He warns us, "Don't ask."

Gwen immediately responds with, "What happened?"

"Tripped over my dog's tug toy and found the bathroom door knob."

Gwen laughs and says, "You *really* need to work on that story."

I wait for everyone to get settled, grab coffee, check their e-mail, and shoot the shit. Gia makes a general engagement announcement and Agent 36 swears that she had no advance '*heads up.*' Office settings have *no* secrets. And, FBI agents pride themselves in recognizing any subtle romantic cues between employees. Gia and Pat had met, dated and moved onto engagement status under the radar.

Bruce wanders into the squad area and welcomes the crew back with congratulations. Our supervisor flew out to Minnesota over the weekend to check on Sean's progress and reports, "He's a tough kid. Doctors expect a full recovery."

"What's the time frame for his return to work?"

Bruce shakes his head and offers, "That's a somewhat touchy issue."

"Why's that?" Gia asks.

"Sean didn't seem too eager to return. Said he'd have to give it some serious thought." Bruce hesitates and adds, "It's too early to be discussing this stuff anyway. He's been through a lot."

There's an awkward silence in the room until Tommy says what's on everyone's mind, "Sean's a good kid alright, but maybe law enforcement's not for him."

This candid verdict takes the air out of the room and Bruce informs us that the SAC desires our presence at 10:00. "Wants to personally thank you for representing the Cleveland Division with distinction and valor."

Bruce leaves and I direct the group into the JTTF conference room. I ask Tommy if he's been cleared for duty following the deadly force incident at The Mall of America.

Tommy nods and casually says, "Nailed the test."

Gwen demands, "I want details since you're a *very* disturbed individual and should be in an institution."

Tommy chuckles, "I got cleared on the plane. Dr. Alvarez was drinking a beer and asked me three questions."

"I'll bite," Gwen says, "what were the three questions?"

"Question 1) was, '*Do you love your mother?*' Question 2) was, '*Do you often dream of demons?*' and Question 3) was, '*Do you feel any remorse over killing someone in the line of duty?*' "

"And your answers?" Agent 36 prompts.

"Yes, Yes, and *fuck no.*" Tommy laughs and adds, "The good doctor told me that I was *completely* sane."

"And I thought Dr. Linda was the adult in this group."

"I corrupted her," Tommy informs us. "I even told her a racially tactless joke involving her line of business. She laughed her ass off."

Gwen can't help herself. "I *really* need to hear that one."

Tommy gets serious. "What do you call a Muslim shrink?"

Agent 36 and Gia repeat, "I don't know. What *do* you call a Muslim shrink?"

Tommy pauses and says, "A terrorpist."

We laugh and this encourages Shoulders to say, "Also told her that I hear voices in my head."

Gwen bites and asks, "How'd she handle that one?"

"Asked if that's a bad thing, so I said, '*only when the voices in my head go silent, because I never know what they're planning.'* "

Dr. Linda *later* informed me that although Sgt. Shoulders has multiple psychological issues he is *eminently* competent for law enforcement. My thought exactly. I take a sip of my coffee and tell the group, "It's time we get moving on this lone wolf problem."

Tommy counters with, "We haven't exactly been sitting on our asses. Our little group just saved a few hundred lives in Minnesota."

"I agree, Tommy. Minnesota could've been a lot worse, but it accomplished *nothing*. Because within the next 60 minutes, ten Americans will begin the process of being radicalized by ISIS. And, we don't have the manpower, resources, or time, given the current rules, to stop them from slaughtering innocent Americans."

Our discussion is brief. We've already had this dialogue too many times over the past few weeks. I caution everyone that our investigative plan is *NOT* to be discussed or shared outside this room.

I continue with a brief statement aimed at reducing this get together to ten minutes or less by answering anticipated questions. "I'll give you assignments. You can accomplish your mission in *any* manner you choose. Adapt, improvise, and overcome. If you want my help, just ask. If you require anything, just ask. If you need clarification, just ask. *But,* you're in this room because your self-starters, can work independently, and don't require any hand-holding. You can team up, work alone, travel, or request funds. Just *accomplish* the mission."

As I scan the team everyone seems on board with a few head nods and absent any blank stares.

"OK," I say, and look at Agent 36. "Gwen, get the XKeyscore from Stanley at State. We need access to encrypted sites."

Gwen replies with, "On it."

"Tommy. Have Jun review the Watch List and begin inserting *'wants and warrants'* into the State Departments database. Start with the more dangerous assholes, then work your way down the list until *every* questionable towel head attempting to enter our country at *every* port of entry is detained, arrested, deported, extradited, or prevented from entering. It'll take our bureaucracy years to square away the mess we'll create, but in the meantime, we essentially construct an electronic wall at every border crossing and airport." I pause and add the addendum. "Also have her deal with the thousands of assholes whose visas have expired and get them gone!"

Tommy mutters, "No problem."

I continue. "We *also* need Jun to begin the defunding of ISIS. While she's working on the watch list you need to get with our FBI financial analyst folks. They've already identified the key terrorist financiers in countries which sponsor terrorism. Our Intel folks estimate that ISIS has a net worth in excess of $2 billion. Its assets are larger than the sovereign wealth funds of nations like Nigeria, Panama, and Vietnam. Jun needs to hack into these accounts and begin moving money."

"Where to?" Tommy asks.

"When she's ready to hit *Send,* I'll have electronic routing instructions for her."

I look at Gia, "Contact Bill Garrett at HQ. He's been busy tracking cases of *every* Field Division's cyber program. At last count, the FBI is monitoring 1300 conversations on some form of open social media.

Director McKissock's been warning Congressional committees that we have cases in *all* 50 states, but unless they change the law and allow us to go dark, minus a warrant, lone wolves will kill innocent Americans."

"But," Tommy says, "those assholes won't do the right thing."

I smile and say, "Exactly, and that's why we *will*. Gia, have Garrett *immediately* provide us IP addresses of any potential ISIS recruits suspected of going dark. At that point, *if* Gwen has accomplished *her* mission, we'll have the XKeyscore and be able to track the more dangerous lone wolves on encrypted sites without the hassle of obtaining warrants. Then we can *prevent* attacks rather than *witness* attacks."

"10-4," is Gia's simple reply.

"I'll handle the mosque policy fiasco by creating bogus informant reports indicating increased efforts at recruitment, funding, and planning of terrorist acts at mosques."

Gwen says, "That will be hard to ignore, even for politicians with no souls."

"They may not have hearts and souls but they *are* bastards with survival instincts. Most of them are up for re-election and won't get on the wrong side of this issue."

Agent 36 brings us back to reality. "Bout time considering our former Commander-in-Chief would rather attend funerals of six-year-old girls than offend our sworn enemy which *are* radical *Muslims*." A pause and add, "Emphasis on the *Muslims*."

"I also got a few devious cards to play." I look at my small group and conclude with, "Questions or Comments?"

Tommy shakes his head and observes, "Seems like we're reduced to paper pushers now. We do our best work in the field."

"I promise you that once we get rolling, they'll be *plenty* of brick time." I finish with, "Anything else?

Agent 36 tells Gia, "Congrats on your engagement to Patrick, and as an engagement gift, I'm taking you to my salon in Parma. We'll get the works. Pedicures, massage, aroma therapy, and Benny the Beautician will fix you up with a stylish new do."

Gia smiles and says, "Sounds good. People always tell me that I have this beautiful, straight silky hair, but, to be honest, I'm tired of it."

I interrupt the beauty consult with, "You two done?"

Gwen eyeballs me for a few seconds and announces, "Know something Booker, you could use a *Benny* razor cut and some color. A little grey at the temple, frizzy split ends, and a slight cowlick."

I thank Agent 36 for her beauty consult and tell the group that, "Our last topic is the need for snitches. History is bound to repeat itself unless we get our act together. Cyber Intel is important and we seem to have that covered with Jun but we'll need *human* intelligence. The attacks on 9/11 succeeded in large part because President Clinton drastically cut the budget of HUMINT (Human Intelligence)."

"Some commission determined that the 9/11 attacks and failure to find WMDs in Iraq were directly related to our lack of human assets," Gwen says. "We relied too much on imagery and signal Intel (SIGMINT). "In 1991 Saddsam Hussein marched 300,000 troops south from Iraq down the middle of Saudi Arabia into Kuwait, and not *one* of our million dollar satellites caught it. We also gather Intel using assets such as satellite imagery and thermal energy detection devices, known as MASINT. However, *none* of this information is complete *without* a person on the ground able to see with human eyes what is impossible for satellites to see."

Tommy comments that, "You fed agencies act like jealous horny teenagers. The CIA don't talk to the NSA who won't share information with the FBI. And," Tommy winds down, "the FBI don't even talk to each other."

"Unfortunately, true. After 9/11, the CIA promised President Bush that they'd share information with the FBI. They just haven't told the FBI yet." A few polite chuckles and I continue. "This jealousy and mistrust created US Intel agencies, like the FBI, CIA, NSA, and DIA each with a piece of the 9/11 information pie. Together we had a *complete* picture of threats but separately did not have enough information to act upon such threats. The missing element was effective management at the top."

Gwen agrees that, "Action officers should have demanded that *all* government agencies share intel, but they were too concerned with guarding their turf."

I say, "You recruited a ton of snitches in your day, Tommy."

"I did."

"And what motivates a person to inform on another person?"

"Could be revenge, working off a charge, eliminating the competition, or moola."

"What's the strongest pull?"

"Money, but when I was working for the Cleveland PD, the city had no money."

"What would have happened if you had unlimited money?"

"Then we would have had a shitload of snitches and made a shitload of cases."

"I'll take care of the money and we'll get a shitload of cases, which we refer to our field offices." I ask, "Any other business?"

Tommy says, "Yes, what's the fastest way to break up a bingo game in Syria?"

Gwen and Gia repeat, "What *is* the fastest way to break up a bingo game in Syria?"

"You shout out, B-52."

CHAPTER 40

"I was going to the worst place on earth, and I didn't even know it yet."
Apocalypse Now

Peggy finds me at my desk. "The SAC wants to see you ASAP."

"Thought he wanted to see the whole team at 10?"

"I'm just the messenger, John Booker, Mr. Williams's exact words were, '*Have Booker come see me please.*' "Peggy adds, "Mr. Williams *always* says, '*please*' and '*thank you.*' "

Our squad secretary is a rotund, church-going, elderly black lady who risked both her career *and* freedom during the Cairo case. Peggy slipped me "Sensitive Compartmented Information" (SCI) access codes when I was a suspended FBI agent. It was an act both patriotism and bravery since it proved to be the missing piece of the Cairo terrorist puzzle. I love and respect our squad secretary but miss the Tourette days when Peggy cussed like a drunken sailor. She has since been cured in a Revival tent when a minister, '*laid hands*' on her and drove Mr. Tourette away. It seems to be the Catholic equivalent of confession.

"Hope you're not in trouble again, John Booker?" Peggy chuckles.

I laugh but say, "I never know, Peggy."

And it's the truth. Dirty little FBI secret. Hard-charging agents operate on the edge of the institutional divide. They push the envelope in a highly regulated environment and either get results or heartburn.

Alpha agents tend to be rule benders and considered career *'shit bombs'* waiting to explode in the faces of our superiors. So when we get the call up to the front office, it's even money between an *'attaboy'* and a scolding.

I find the SAC in his throne room. Mike Williams is an old-school boss who understands that our basic mission is to put bad people in jail. He'll ignore some agent improvisation if done for the good of the case. As I enter his office, Williams rises and smiles. I breathe a sigh of relief sensing this is an *'attaboy.'*

"Great job on the Minnesota case."

"Thanks boss, but there shouldn't have had *any* victims."

Williams shakes his head and agrees, "My heart goes out to the families." The SAC pauses and adds, "But your team saved many, many other heartaches. It's sad to rationalize it that way, but in this day and age of mass shootings, it's a reality."

We spend a few minutes shooting the shit about trivial matters like sports, family, and Bureau gossip. Williams observes that, "There seems to be a recent epidemic of breast enhancements in the B."

I chuckle and ask, "Have you noticed that Miss Martha Wiseman, the previously flat-chested squad nine secretary, seems to have grown beach balls?"

Williams laughs and says, "Hard *not* to notice. I won't look her way during office meetings." The SAC puts on his game face and says, "Know you're busy but I want you to sit in on a conference call with the SAC of the Cincinnati Division. It may have some relevance to your lone wolf investigation."

Williams and I move to his conference table and sit facing a device that resembles a large tarantula but is actually a conference call gadget. I'm introduced to SAC Rose Egan who is an Ohio native. We make some small talk about the annual drubbing of the Browns by the Bengals before Rose gets down to business.

She says, "The Cincinnati Division covers 48 of Ohio's 88 counties, while the Cleveland Division handles the remaining 40 of the Buckeye State." Egan takes a few moments discussing the lone wolf problem in general then gets specific to Ohio, "The threat of homegrown terrorists in Ohio is surprising. People in the Midwest don't realize that violent extremists are here and increasing at an alarming rate."

She provides several examples including Nuradin Abdi, who was convicted in 2007 of planning to blow up an Ohio shopping mall. Then there is Iyman Faris, convicted in 2003 of planning to blow up the Brooklyn Bridge, and Christopher Paul, who was convicted in 2008 of conspiring to use explosives against targets in the U.S. and Europe.

"All three terrorists worshiped and socialized at this small mosque in Columbus Ohio, the Omari Mosad. They were also part of a larger group of jihadists and extremists who also frequented that mosque. The FBI is currently investigating reports of links to that same mosque by Muslim-convert Abdulhakim Muhammad who allegedly shot and killed one soldier and critically wounded another in a drive-by attack on a Little Rock, Arkansas, recruiting station."

"It seems more than coincidence," I observe.

"According to sources, Muhammad attended the mosque from 2006 to 2007 when he resided in Columbus. It's unclear what, if any, links he had to the individuals already convicted. All of the above individuals informed authorities that they acted alone in the name of Allah." She pauses and adds, "Your recent Minnesota case is proof that homegrown terrorists are not confined to the New York cities."

Williams agrees, "Bloomington, Minnesota, was not considered a terrorist hot bed."

"I'm not sure the general public quite gets the gravity of it," Egan continues. "In late February we arrested two individuals from Ohio. Christopher Lee Cornell, of Cincinnati, on charges he planned to attack the U.S. Capitol, and Abdirahman Sheik Mohamud, 23, of Columbus, accused of planning to attack a military base. Mohamud had trained at a terrorist camp in Syria." The Cincinnati SAC sighs and adds, "It seems like once we get one guy, another guy pops up high on the radar. We just keep moving from one to the next."

Egan spends a few minutes discussing research conducted at the University of Dayton, Ohio, which concludes that, *trying to detect homegrown lone wolves before they act is a nightmare for national security.*

My immediate reaction is to say, *'No shit, Sherlock,'* but I hold my tongue. A quick confession here. I have a terminal case of anti-authority syndrome. My affliction began as third grader when our nun told us that the devil can crawl inside our body and possess us. It dawned on me, then and there, that the person leading the way is often attempting a con job.

I challenge SAC Egan, "I agree with what you're saying ma'am but *you* SES types." I pause and attempt to soften my rhetoric. I fail and finish with, "Need to *demand* these politicians do the right thing and use your position for something *other* than attending office retreats in the Poconos."

The ensuing silence isn't very comfortable. I imagine that SACs rarely entertain verbal reprimands from brick agents. She gathers herself and says, "I take it that you're referring to our restrictions in surveilling mosque and the encryption issue."

"You'd be right. These lone wolves begin their radicalization on open internet or Twitter forums where we can track their journey. But, then they go encrypted and our elected representatives are more concerned about protecting the privacy rights of terrorists than preventing bullets from entering the cranium of some six-year-old kid at The Mall of America. You SACs have a powerful voice in your community. You're constantly meeting with legislators so put the arm on them." I pause and lighten up with, "You gotta ask yourself the question, *'What would J. Edgar do?'* "

There's some polite chuckles before the two SACs begin a civil discussion that basically sounds like a philosophical discussion between two drunk 19-year-olds at some college bar. It's almost as if they can't utter the words that the *system is broken.* Both seem to agree that law enforcement's hands are tied but neither comes to the logical epiphany that they're part of this dysfunctional bureaucracy.

Their conversation becomes background noise until the Cincinnati SAC wraps up with a naïve, "So it's more important than ever for us to get cooperation from the public and *hope* that family and friends are able to recognize changes in behavior, adopting of radical views, and support for terrorist groups and acts."

I think, *'That is a load of gullible bullshit,'* but ask, "So I'm sure you have that mosque under surveillance?" Since I already knew the answer to this rhetorical question, I am merely being a shit.

The Cincinnati SAC goes passive-aggressive and says, "As you are aware, *John,* current FBI policy forbids the surveillance of mosque minus approval from the Special Oversight committee at Justice, and we haven't met their probable cause threshold yet."

Two can play at this verbal masturbation game so I ask quite innocently, "And what exactly *is* that threshold for this committee?"

We both know that the committee is some stealth group operating somewhere at the Justice Department with *no* written standards or guidelines. Their names are classified but the scuttlebutt is that the group includes prominent Muslim religious leaders, members of CAIR, the ACLU, and two Muslim Assistant United States attorneys. The deck is stacked and the Vegas odds of an *'Approved"* is 1000 to 1.

It's Mike Williams who comes to Angela's assistance. I temporarily forgot that they are SAC lodge brothers. "The threshold is high." He pauses and adds, "*Too* high, but that's our rules of engagement and we'll abide by them."

I think, *'You do that'* but say, "I agree."

SAC Williams wraps up the conversation with, "We'll shake our informant trees here Rose and get back to you."

I add a half-hearted, "Nice speaking with you ma'am."

No response but just as Williams is hitting the *Off* button on the electronic tarantula, SAC Egan says, "One last item. A source of unknown reliability has provided vague Intel that Ohio State University is on some lone wolf's radar. I'd ask that the Cleveland Division put out feelers to their informants since we share that territory."

We bid farewell to SAC Egan and as I turn to leave Williams asks me, "Doesn't your daughter go to Ohio State?"

CHAPTER 41

"Hey, at least I won't have to lie to you anymore."

All That Jazz (1979)

"You got a call on line two."

"Booker," I say.

"Dick Vercauteran from the LA office."

"I hope you didn't call Cleveland in January to inform me that the LA temperature is a balmy 72."

Vercauteran laughs and says, "*Actually* it's a balmy 77 degrees, but that's not why I called." A pause, then, "Heard you're looking at this lone wolf problem."

"You heard right, Dick. I'm looking hard but my vision is muddy. It's a tough nut to crack given our restrictions."

I figure that Vercauteran may *not* want to hear about working this problem *off the books*, so I play it safe and ask, "How can I help you?"

"I'm working a case in San Bernardino."

Agent Vercauteran provides a case brief involving a married couple who may have radicalized. Syed Rizwan Farook, age 28, was born in Pakistan while Tashfeen Malik, age 27, was born in the United States. The wife entered the country from Pakistan on July 27, 2014 using a K-1 visa, a 90-day visa for people planning to marry Americans. The K-1 visa application process focuses on whether or not the applicants know each other and have a personal relationship, and does *not* ask about jihadist support. One month after Malik entered the United States, she married Farook."

I interrupt the brief with, "I'm sure this isn't a love story."

"You're right." Vercauteran laughs. "The CIA just gave us a heads-up that Farook has been communicating with terrorists both domestically and internationally. Our cyber guys confirmed that both Farook and Malik pledged allegiance to ISIS leader Abu Bakr al-Baghdadi on Facebook using an account with different names. A month ago, their Facebook posts stopped."

"Sounds like this couple went to encrypted communication."

"Would appear," Vercauteran says. "I can't get approval for anything *other* than drive by surveillance. But what I *need* is authority to monitor their electronic communications."

"Let me guess," I say. "Not enough probable cause."

Vercauteran chuckles. "I heard you were a smart guy. The U.S. Attorney determined that none of the interactions were *'substantial'* enough to merit a warrant."

"I really love these guys and their aversion to risk. They use words like *substantial* to deflect any push back because they're fuckin' cowards."

"Any suggestions?"

"Look Dick, I don't know you from the man in the moon but I'll give it to you brick agent to brick agent." I search my brain for words that will not paint me as some crazy rogue agent. "If you're ready to accept the consequences Dick, then do what you gotta do." Not exactly a revelation but it conveys the message.

Special Agent Vercauteran mutters some solidarity bullshit but evidently wasn't prepared to lose his job, pension, and risk prison time. You can't blame him. Because on Wednesday, December 2, 2015, Farook and Malik killed 14 people and injured 22 others at the Inland Regional Center in San Bernardino. I am not faulting Vercauteran but rather a system that forces good people to make impossible choices.

The facts all trickled out *after* one of the deadliest terrorist attack on American soil since 9/11.

The press had a field day criticizing the competency of the FBI's security infrastructure in tracking "lone wolf" terrorist plots. But that's a cop out. It's like having the answers prior to an exam and still flunking. The attackers discussed jihad privately online before the shooting but the trail they left was so small-scale as to be negligible, and was undetected by authorities until *after* the fact. But what the press and public *don't* know is that Special Agent Dick Vercauteran *wanted* to stop the killers *before* they shot up a Christmas party but was stymied by the home team.

Attorney General Loretta Lynch described this incident as an *"inspired-terrorist model."* This slogan is evidently some new Justice Department expression meant to confuse we FBI agents assigned to fight terrorism. I haven't the slightest idea what the hell it means. Ms. Lynch proclaims that lone wolf terrorists are becoming much more common and poses a significant challenge to the security community. "It is almost *impossible* to detect individuals in such cases." Lynch offers this *blinding flash of the obvious* and then repeats the call to report any suspicious behavior to law enforcement.

FBI director McKissock asserted that ISIS may have motivated the attacks but felt that Farook and Milak were likely radicalized *before* coming to the United States and prior to meeting one another. A spokesperson for the White House believed the attack was an act of workplace violence, and *not* terrorist related. You can't make this shit up.

And *all* the preceding double speak babble mouthed by our bureaucrats is *why* we are getting our asses handed to us by terrorists. We're fucking doomed!

CHAPTER 42

"You guys up for a toga party?.....TOGA!"
National Lampoon's Animal House (1978)

Agent 36 enters the Reagan International Airport terminal and immediately dials my cell phone. "OK Booker, I'm headed to my meeting with Stanley from State, but I'm not a happy camper."

"You're not supposed to be happy, Gwen." I chuckle. "You work for the government."

"I feel like the Bureau hooker."

"Quit the complaining, you're on a mission from God, just like the Blues Brothers."

"Fuck you."

"Maybe later, but *first* there's Stanley from State."

Agent 36 chuckles and tells me, "You are such an asshole Booker, but you make me laugh. Stanley reminds me of one of those creepy pedophiles who hang around middle schools. He's been calling me three times a day ever since I set this *meeting* up."

"What's the big deal? You're on the phone all the time with your Zumba posse."

"I can explain this to you but I *can't* make you understand. Shooting terrorists in Cairo and whacking Bruno in Euclid, Ohio, was fun. Spending a day with Stanley constitutes torture."

"You're overthinking this thing," I tell her. "Stanley from State is no match for Special Agent Gwen McNulty. You're smarter, more devious, *and* a better shot. Besides you don't have to *actually* do anything." I pause and add, "Well, maybe a quick blow job."

Agent 36 is now laughing aloud and tells me that, "You need help Booker."

"You're not the first person to suggest that." I pause and ask, "What's the plan?"

"It's not very complicated. Stanley's smart but he's a man, and *all* men are simple one cell organisms so Stanley *may* get the sizzle but, his lips will never touch the steak."

"I refuse to comment on what you just said. Call me when you have the XKeyscore."

"It'll probably be late. I'm meeting him at the State Department for a tour and an update on Port of Entry issues. Then he's taking me to dinner and, get this," Gwen pauses and begins chuckling, "Stanley attempted some geek flirting and told me that he'd *like to probe* my *port of entry*. If that asshole touches me, I will dropkick his State Department testicles into his IT weak chin."

"These violent tendencies *could* be the reason you don't have a boyfriend. Stanley may not be Prince Charming but remember what Shakespeare wrote in *A Midsummer's Night's Dream*."

"Don't you *dare* quote Shakespeare, Booker, that would be too weird."

I ignore her protest and say, '*Love looks not with the eyes... but with the mind, and, therefore cupid.....is painted* blind.' The call is terminated. Must be a weak cell signal inside the terminal.

I hit the access code and enter a 20- by 30-foot room. Tommy Shoulders is sitting side by side with Jun and surrounded by computer screens, CPUs, servers, towers, motherboards, keyboards, and wires. Jun made some kind of passing reference to Hillary's e-mail scandal with the addendum of, "Our set up is *much* more secure but also *much* more *illegal*." I take no solace in that legal opinion but I can always plea stupid. It worked for our former Secretary of State.

I insisted on this room with access *strictly* limited to members of the task force. We call it the *mush room* since it's windowless, dark, and dank, thus perfect for growing mushrooms. No janitorial service, no curious supervisors, or flirtatious secretaries are permitted to cross the threshold. The SAC wasn't too happy about being excluded from part of his kingdom, but it's for his own protection. Mike Williams shouldn't be complicit in what we plan to do in this room. We'll leave brown poop tracks on the underwear of the Attorney General's Guidelines and totally *soil* the FBI's Manual of Policies and Procedures. And the fourth amendment of the constitution is *really* in danger of a bad case of diarrhea.

We'd discussed the pros and cons of Jun's presence at the FBI office and concluded that the location offers equipment security in addition to vast government resources. Before we said our goodbyes in DC, Jun handed me a lengthy list of needed equipment. Tony Dennis s rushed the order and crates arrived over the next few days filled with wires, cartons and screens. The Chinese computer guru doesn't suffer fools lightly. She personally unpacked and inspected each crate making unintelligible sounds of displeasure. One of the eight crates contained damaged items, two with missing items, and one box was filled plastic plants destined for our Miami office.

Jun shakes her head in disgust and declares, "I'd fire them if they worked for me."

"And why is that?"

"Your bureaucracy is wasting their most precious commodity." Jun says, "Its employees. Your workforce lacks initiative and inspiration because management discourages self-starters. I see workers who are not permitted to *invest* in their work product, so, they are forced to care *more* about their job than their *purpose*."

"I never thought of it that way. That's an interesting take on the bureaucracy."

"*Sad* actually." Jun clarifies, "Buddha said, 'Each morning we are born again. What we do today is what matters most.' "

I look at Jun and say, "Well let's put our Buddha bellies on and get born."

Jun's evidently been busy while we were shopping jihadists at The Mall of America. I *thought* I knew the basics of how we keep terrorists from crossing our boarders, but Jun fills in plenty of my missing blanks. She begins the seminar with an editorial aside, "Our elected officials blindly cast their votes along party lines. They seem more concerned with *not* offending anyone!"

"Sad but true Jun, they're ideological whores who sell their votes to lobbyists."

"*Unfortunately*, their sexual penchants affect our national security. The FBI and the remainder of the intelligence community use certain standards to place individuals on the consolidated terrorist *watch* list." Jun picks up a sheet of paper and informs us that, "These are the *exact* words listed in the HSEC Presidential Directive-6, which states: '*The watch list is to contain information about individuals known or suspected to be, or have been engaged, in conduct, in preparation, aid, or related to terrorism.*' "

Tommy interjects with a question. "So this is a good thing, isn't it?"

"I wish it so Thomas, but the *watch* list is often confused with the *no-fly* list. People assume they're the same."

June takes a moment to explain that in mid-December 2001, two lists were created: the *No Fly List* of 594 people to be *denied* air transport, and the *Selectee* list of 365 people who were to be more carefully searched at airports. By 2002, the two lists combined into the *No-Fly* list and had over a thousand names. By April 2005, the list contained 70,000 names of people who are *not* permitted to board a commercial aircraft for travel in or out of the United States. The list has also been used to divert aircraft flying into U.S. airspace. The number of people on the list rises and falls according to threat and intelligence reporting. There were 10,000 names on the list in 2011 and 67,000 in 2016.

I add, "So, at least we *won't* have to deal with those 67,000 people provided Homeland Security does *its* job at our Port of Entries."

"Correct." Jun says but adds, "Hopefully."

Tommy asks, "How about individuals in the system who share the exact or similar name of another person on the list?"

"As of November 2015, 30,000 people complained that their names were matched to a name on the list via the name-matching software used by airlines. Individuals can be added to the list based on reasonable suspicion, so inclusion does not *automatically* prohibit an individual from being issued a visa or entry into the United States. In fact, embassy staff will generally accept *any* excuse and stamp their visa."

Tommy comments, "And that's why our country is filled with guys named Mohammed with crooked teeth, smelly breath, and attitude."

I say, "So all we're *really* doing is making the public feel all warm and fuzzy while terrorists are sipping Starbucks at JFK Airport."

"Unfortunately, John," Jun agrees. "The Watch List is actually a meaningless paper placebo. Back in August 2015, the Inspector General did an investigation of the Department of Homeland Security. Remember, these employees constitute the first line of defense in our war on terrorism. The IG found 72 individuals that were on the terrorist watch list *working* at the Department of Homeland Security."

"Fuck me," Tommy editorializes.

"The HSEC director had to resign because of that." Jun adds, "The current *Watch List*, as of this morning, includes 860,000 individuals worldwide."

"That sounds like an insurmountable number to deal with Jun."

Jun smiles and informs us that, "Normally, but I can devise programs which makes it *quite* manageable. I'll explain, but first let me provide some background. In a very real sense, Foreign Service officers are America's *other* border patrol. They determine who is allowed into the country. Of 48 terrorists who have attacked America in the last twenty-one years, 41 had at some point been approved for a visa by an American consulate overseas. There are times when the visa-processing system will quickly identify the terrorist applicant and prevent him from getting a visa, but the mere fact that so many terrorists make it through certainly suggests that there are significant problems in the system."

"Like what?"

"Undesirables on watch list, with criminal records, known or suspected terrorists, sympathizers, financial supporters, and those who communicate with ISIS recruiters. I can have them arrested, deported, detained indefinitely, or shuffled endlessly between court jurisdictions for years."

"So basically," I sum up, "the U.S. has open borders. We just *pretend* that the screening process is working. What's the answer, Jun?"

"The State Department has input *every* name on the watch list into government computers at our port of entries as well as all State Department embassies worldwide. Our embassies generally grant VISA's to *any* foreigner who wishes to visit the US. So we must first *deny* visas to *everyone* on the watch list *before* they travel *and* second*ly* *block* those from clearing customs once they *arrive* at points of entry."

"I'm all ears on this Jun," I say. "But how?"

"Easy. I simply input *'Denied Entry'* on any watch list designee seeking visas from our embassies."

Tommy can't help himself and asks, "Can you do that?"

"Yes, Thomas." Jun laughs. "With a simple tap of a computer key. This will take care of a significant number on that list *before* they ever reach our border."

I'm not *totally* following the computer machinations so I say, "Let me get this straight. Mohammed from Turkey is on the watch list. He wants to attend his cousin's wedding in Indiana. He goes to the U.S. embassy and applies for a visa. The embassy employee conducts a routine check. Normally just being on the watch list wouldn't preclude

Mohammed from getting his visa, but, now there's an official STOP and an order to deny Mohammed his visa."

"You got it," Jun says.

"Wouldn't the embassy look into the reason Mohammed's being denied since Mohammed is making a stink that he's missing his cousin Abdullah's wedding?"

"Embassy employees do *not* have access to the original Intel data bases, nor do they have the authority to change the denial. U.S. Intel agencies are basically telling the State Department that Mohammed presents a threat to U.S. citizens."

"Yea," Tommy says. "But what happens if he comes back in two months and State requests an update on Mohammed's status?"

"I simply type the word *'Indefinite'* into every Mohammed's file on the Watch List."

"Brilliant," I comment. "But how do we handle all those individuals on the watch list who *don't* require visas and land at our airports every day?"

"No problem. I'll enter a variety of STOPS such as, *'wants, warrants, denied entry, fugitive, upgraded to the no-fly list, pandemic disease threat,* and *any other* prohibitive reason I can invent that will deny entry into the United States."

"I've been in the government for a long time," I say. "And these thousands of *Watch List* people will raise hell. They'll be calling Congressmen, embassies, business associates, *and* the press. Our wussy government will cave and demand investigations into the computer system and wonder why fine upstanding foreigners are *suddenly* being persecuted."

Jun actually laughs. "This is the beauty of a government so large, unmanageable, and compartmentalized. We can use these weaknesses for our own good." Jun continues, "Even though the numbers are big, the FBI along with other Intel groups have prioritized the security threat posed by each person on the watch list. So, I'll begin with the most dangerous and continue down the list."

I suddenly understand the ironic karma of this cluster fuck. "And, each agency has the authority to unilaterally add names to that list. So even *if* some official demands that a STOP designation be removed, *only* the agency that originally placed the designation can remove it."

Jun smiles and adds, "*And* that could take months if not years."

There is a silence in the sterile room as I process the byzantine, yet simple plan, to settle inside our brain. Tommy and I are in the presence of a *fucking* genius.

I ask Jun, "How long will it take you to handle the *Watch List?*"

"Not long. It's simple inputting. I showed Thomas how to do it."

Tommy nods and says, "I got this shit down."

"What about immigrants who arrived in the U.S. with an authorized visa and never got it renewed?"

Jun says, "Yes, an estimated 40 percent of all illegal immigrants fit that category. Hard to believe but INS *never* devised a tracking system so we have about 5 million illegal immigrants with no idea where they are *or* what they're doing."

"But most of those are Mexicans, must be very few Muslims."

"Less than 5%." Jun says. "I have the list of every expired visa. When they filled out their visa application it included a ton of biographical data to include religion, POB, and country of origin. So we will play God and allow the Mexicans and Guatemalans the privilege of an extended stay. Unfortunately, Muslims will not be granted that luxury."

I comment, "Here's the problem, Jun. Our previous President didn't enforce immigration laws so until the current administration changes the law, even if law enforcement grabs them, they'll just be waived on with a, '*have a nice day.*' "

Jun chuckles, "Not if I input contagious diseases, psychiatric conditions, and INTERPOL warrants, with a variety of charges that can't be ignored," Jun sighs. "Look, this may not be airtight but I will guarantee you that we will create complete chaos and at the very least we'll begin to identify these lost souls."

I nod agreement and note, "You're doing a fantastic job, Jun."

"And it's made me hungry. Can I get some Chinese delivered to this fortress?"

"I'll handle that as soon as I make a call. Be back in little while."

I head to my desk and order five General Tso chickens with sides of egg rolls and egg duck soup. The FBI has hundreds of foolish internal policies and guidelines. One doozy requires agents to have no more than 50 paper clips in our desk. We probably lead *all* government agencies in triviality, which is quite an accomplishment *since* the Congressional Research Service cannot even count the current number of federal rules and procedures. Most are merely aggravating obstacles but this *particular* policy has resulted in the death of innocent Americans. I will either change this policy or get fired trying.

Since October 2011, mosques have been *off-limits* to FBI agents. No surveillance or undercover sting operations without high-level approval from a special oversight body at the Justice Department dubbed the *Sensitive Operations Review Committee.*

I call Tony to probe the lines. The Assistant Director needs to confirm or deny some Bureau scuttlebutt that's been lingering like a chili fart. "Hey roomie, got a question. Who makes up the Sensitive Operations Committee, and how do they decide requests?"

The Deputy Director of the FBI sheepishly replies that, "Nobody knows. The names of the chairman, members, and staff are kept secret."

"You mean to tell me that *nobody* at the FBI has input?"

"Nope." Tony explains that, "The panel was set up by President Obama under pressure from Islamist groups *after* we began busting terrorist plots at mosques. six years ago, our LA agents had PC that some members of a mosque near Compton were preaching jihad. They were about to send a 137 (snitch) inside, when the Council on American-Islamic Relations (CAIR) sued the FBI for *allegedly* violating the civil rights of Muslims in Los Angeles. Three months later this Sensitive Operation panel formed, and word is that Muslims *now* decide who the FBI can investigate."

"Why the fuck do we cave anytime some fringe group gets their diaper heads in an uproar and create some phony controversy?"

"We've lost our backbone." Tony adds, "Because, *before* mosques were placed off limits, the FBI conducted hundreds of successful sting operations against homegrown jihadists *inside* mosques, *and*, disrupted dozens of plots against the homeland."

"The word among us brick agents is that we could've prevented the Boston Marathon bombings if not for this restriction. Any truth to that?"

Tony is silent, which tells me that I hit a nerve. He confides, "We probably *could've* stopped it. Tamerlan Tsarnaev, one of the Muslim Boston bombers, made regular extremist outbursts during worship *before* he planted the pressure cookers, yet because the mosque wasn't monitored, red flags didn't go off inside the FBI about his increasing radicalization."

"So the victims of the Boston Marathon bombings may not have lost their lives and limbs had we been able to surveil that mosque."

"Unfortunately, yes, there was a Boston agent name of Ray Smith who had strong leads, which led back to Tamerlan's mosque. His information indicated that the brothers were radicalizing and using the mosque to sound off on jihad. But the story gets worse, John."

"How so?"

"Justice Department denied FBI requests to canvass Boston mosques until four days *after* the April 15 marathon attacks, and, even then they *refused* the FBI access to the radical Boston mosque where the Muslim bombers worshipped."

"Un-fuckin-believable. This is *after* 240 Americans lay bleeding on the streets of Boston! I pause to lower my blood pressure and ask, "Can't McKissock do anything?"

"McKissock met with the President and *demanded* he lift this mosque restriction. Provided him independent surveys which revealed that some 40% of American mosques preach violent jihad or distribute violent literature to worshippers."

"I suppose this Boston Marathon shit's all hush, hush because if the public knew their government could've stopped it, they'd have a hernia."

"Strictly *need to know*. If the story gets leaked the embarrassment would politically damage the Administration, and all roads lead back to the FBI. At which point the President will make our lives unbearable."

"My prostrate is enlarged so I feel a *leak* coming on."

Tony threatens me with, "Don't even *think* about contacting anyone *outside* the Bureau. I can hear your devious brain working, and it's *my* ass if word gets out that the Boston Marathon bombings could've been prevented. The only Bureau people privy to that info were myself, 4 Assistant Directors (AD), and 7 Deputy Assistant Directors (DAD). So, all roads lead back to us."

"Was DAD Maulbit at that meeting?"

Tony laughs, "Walt led the charge on supporting the President's policy. It seems Walt's angling for some appointment at the State Department and wants the President to know he's a loyal fan."

"Please don't tell me that a FBI Deputy Assistant Director is *actually* against mosque surveillance?"

"Hard to believe and get this; someone at the meeting mentioned *radical* Islamic terrorists. Walt corrected him saying that Islam is *not* radical and insisted we refer to them as radical terrorists."

Chicken Shit Walt Maulbit, as he is *not* affectionately known to the troops, is the Deputy Assistant Director who fucked me on my last undercover case. Walt somehow blamed *me* when some Guido was discovered fermenting the land fill in Staten Island. I *may* have had some prior knowledge of the hit, but, hey, that's one less asshole in the pepperoni gene pool. Walt closed the case and sent my ass back to the office. Ironically, *Chicken Shit* Walt unknowingly saved New York City by fucking me. I still don't like the man.

"So let me get this straight. Our President assures the public that tracking their every phone call will *stop* terrorists, and yet the asshole won't let us snoop in mosques where the terrorists actually *are*."

"Defies logic John. Remember Rashid Baz?"

"Doesn't ring a bell."

"Rashid was the Palestinian immigrant known as *'The Brooklyn Bridge Shooter.'* In 1994, Baz attended a service at the Islamic Mosque of Bay Ridge in Brooklyn where he heard a fiery sermon calling for revenge on Jews for an incident that had recently occurred in Hebron. Baz left the mosque intent on killing Jews. He opened fire, killing anyone that *resembled* a Jew. A witness later testified that Baz was enraged after the speech, determined to act. To this day, the imam of that mosque has never been held accountable."

"Defies logic."

"Yea, why *exclude* the jihad factories which *happens* to be where homegrown terrorists are radicalized."

"Political correctness gone mad. Even Agent 36 is working on her potty mouth. Told some guy at a club that he was a horrible dancer. The guy got all shitty, saying Gwen was insensitive."

Tony asks, "She tell him to fuck off?"

"She didn't. She apologized for her comment and said, *Sorry, maybe you're just overly Caucasian.*"

Tony laughs and changes the subject. "How's the case going?"

"Promising but it never moves fast enough for me. In fact, I gotta go."

"OK, but *remember* that our discussion is *just* between us roomies. Don't even *think* about leaking the Boston Marathon stuff to the press or some legislator. That would be the end of both of us. Promise?"

"Promise." I say.

"Why don't I believe you?"

"That *really* hurts roomie, after all we've been through. I'm insulted." I make a dramatic pause for effect. "I would *never* stoop so low to go outside the B and contact the media." Another pause and I end the conversation with, "Give Nancy a hug."

I hang up and immediately grab my electronic rolodex. I scroll down to Florence Kuhns who just happens to be an esteemed member of the fifth estate. For those of you don't know, that particular estate is the *Press*.

CHAPTER 43

"We declared war on terror, it's not even a noun, so; good luck."
John Stewart

Leaking information to a member of the press goes against my DNA, *but*, sometimes you have to hold your nose and perform a public service. My plan is similar to a General Patton pincer movement.

I'll start with a frontal attack by spreading a load of mosque manure and build the case to overturn the President's restriction. This requires counterfeiting a series of reliable informant reports which link mosques to planned terrorist acts. Since bureaucrats often play *cover up* with far less prickly issues, I'll need a second front. Someone with enough pinch power to remind Washington that the mosque policy made possible the Boston Marathon bombings. Florence Kuhns is the perfect candidate and will be able to shield Tony, but *not* Chicken Shit Walt.

Midterm elections are looming and the Democrats are hoping to gain control of both Houses. That hope will vanish if the public discovers that the mosque policy resulted in the death and maiming of women and children.

I pick up the phone and dial my good friend at the Cleveland *Plain Dealer*. Florence covers the political beat and was front and center when Cleveland hosted the Republican National Convention in 2016.

Flo has a *rep* as a straight shooting investigative reporter who has several political hides mounted on her wall. She will be very hard to ignore.

I experience only *slight* guilt pangs about throwing Deputy Assistant Director Walt Maulbit under the bus, but *hey*, it's payback time. Flo will lay out the entire Boston Marathon debacle and finger *Chicken Shit* Walt as the architect. The Senate will haul Walt before a committee hearing where the DAD will crap his bureaucratic pants. Then Chicken Shit will sing like a birdie because he's a coward. Tony is off the hook, Chicken Shit takes the hit, and, most importantly, the mosque policy is over turned. Sometimes I amaze even myself.

I gather up two large plastic bags filled with Chinese victuals at the receptionist console and head back to our cloistered room dubbed *The Mush Room*. Jun comments, "About time."

"Tommy, call Gia and tell her that chow's on."

A moment later Gia appears and I ask if she likes Chinese food. She smiles and informs us, "Good thing I was adopted because I'm allergic to rice."

"I keep forgetting your 100% Korean," Tommy says seriously.

"Me too, my adopted parents are Italian and Swedish so my food tastes run to rigatoni and Swedish meatballs. But I do like fortune cookies." Gia continues, "Been on the phone with Bill Garrett. He sent us 17 cases of individuals who *had* been spewing ISIS propaganda, and then suddenly went dark."

'That's 17 ticking bombs waiting to explode."

Gia reads from her notes. "ISIS's most successful venture is an app called *The Dawn of Glad Tidings*, or just *Dawn*. The app helps ISIS get pre-approved hash tags trending on Facebook and then amplifies its message. ISIS's presence on Instagram is more informal. Users often post pro-ISIS images as opposed to video clips disseminated by the group's official channels."

I look at Jun and ask? "Can you intercept their recruitment messages on the open web *and* substitute something horrible?"

Jun gives a sarcastic chuckle. "Not a problem interrupting ISIS signals but what do we replace their message with? The most *logical* message to frighten potential ISIS recruits would be to promise a miserable existence of eating goat poop followed by a bloody, torturous death. But, that's the *exact* propaganda that excites *these* idiots."

"What are the Europeans doing?"

"France's Stop-Djihadisme (Stop Jihad) campaign went online just three weeks after 17 people were killed in terror attacks carried out by radicalized French citizens, connected to ISIS. The French *allow* the ISIS message to reach their citizens but provide a *counter*argument. A French video warns potential recruits that, *'You'll discover hell on earth and die far from home. In reality, you'll be an accomplice in the massacre of civilians.'* "

Agent 36 chuckles and says, "That message is having the *opposite* effect. It romanticizes ISIS soldiers as crusaders."

I say, "Our own State Department couldn't even get original and copied the French with a Disney sounding campaign called '*Think Again, Turn Away,'* and YouTube videos *with titles such as* 'ISIS Kills Muslims,' and, 'Young People Fooled by ISIS,' *and* 'ISIS Leaves only Tears & Rubble.' "

"And some wonder why we are losing this war." Jun declares sarcastically, "I'm famished, let's eat while we talk."

We pass the cardboard food cartons around and take a break. The group feasts on General Tso's chicken and sides of egg rolls, and slurp egg duck soup while debating the perfect message to discourage ISIS recruiting efforts. Gia cues up an ISIS recruiting video showing a collection of bombings, executions, kidnappings, and beheadings. As one roadside bomb blasts a vehicle into the sky, two men in the background of the video chuckle.

The group argues back and forth on the *right* message which may deter some kid from Toledo from going jihad on his neighbors.

Tommy offers, "Just tell them that they'll have to clean their bunker, take out the trash, and have a strict 9PM curfew."

Jun says, "Be serious Thomas."

"I am," Tommy protests.

Forty minutes later, I observe, "We have some of the most depraved minds *right* here in this room and not *one* of us can solve this riddle. I'll give Dr. Linda a call."

Tommy adds, "She's just fucked up enough to figure this out."

"In the meantime, Jun get going on disrupting ISIS's income. Tommy, keep papering the Watch List folks with warrants. Gia, gear up on these 17 cowboys who went dark. Put the JTTFs on notice in the affected Divisions."

"You seem sure that Gwen is going to separate Stanley from his XKeyscore."

"Stanley's got *no* chance." I say and then remember to ask Jun. "Can you do anything about this sanctuary city thing. They deported Kate Steinle's killer five times but Juan Sanchez just strolled back to San Francisco where he had safe haven. The mayors and police departments ignore our immigration laws"

Jun deadpans, "Sounds a lot like us."

"Touché'," I concede. "But at least we have God and country on our side."

Jun says, "The federal government is attempting to hold up funds but the courts will tie up this catch and release program for years."

"That's a dead end. Our executive branch seems to care more about Mr. Sanchez as a potential partisan voter than Kate Steinle."

Jun says, "I'll give the sanctuary city issue some thought. One problem is these illegals with rap sheets generally don't have a Visa, driving license, SS card, or passport, so we have to find them first."

Tommy counters, "That won't be hard. These assholes leave an *extensive* paper trail. Kate's killer had five arrests logged into local police departments, the INS, and Customs database when they deported him, and the FBI NCIC when the locals checked for wants and warrants."

"So, the locals can find them but aren't really looking."

"The San Francisco PD actually *had* Sanchez in custody on a drug charge with a federal INS hold, but they released him rather than pick up the phone and say, *come and get him.* So even if we input INS violations into NCIC, the sanctuary cities will look the other way. Liberals will *not* arrest or detain illegal aliens on *any* immigration beef."

I sum up with, "So let's ask ourselves, *'what would motivate some bleeding-heart mayor to enforce the immigration laws.'* "

My rhetorical question hangs in the air until Gia grabs a fortune cookie, cracks it open, and unfolds the paper. She says, 'One path leads to heaven, one path leads to hell.'

CHAPTER 44

"Frankly my Dear, I don't give a damn."
Clark Gable, Gone with the Wind

My caller ID indicates Agent 36. Even though Gwen is armed and dangerous, I worry about my good friend and fellow crime fighter. We hadn't spoken since yesterday when Gwen arrived at Reagan International and was on her way to the State Department. Innocent enough, except that her office meetings were to be followed by a romantic dinner with Stanley. I really didn't believe Agent 36 would trade sexual favors for the XKeyscore, but I do believe that Gwen may dry hump the idiot. No harm, no foul with a little innocent dry humping that could save American lives.

"Booker, you asshole," Agent 36 begins the conversation. "This horny teenage plan of yours was doomed from the get go. How could you expect a high-ranking government official to risk his career, reputation, and freedom for a piece of ass?"

"Because you're not just any piece of ass, but you're right." I offer sarcastically, "Normally that would be highly unusual. Just ask Presidents Clinton, Kennedy, Eisenhower, Johnson, half of Congress, and Henry from the Commerce Department's mailroom."

"You're a funny guy but I took four showers last night." She repeats. "Four!"

"Look Gwen, spare me the sordid details. Did you get the XKeyscore?"

"Is the Pope German?"

"They use to be all Italian but I knew you'd score."

"Bad choice of words Booker."

I laugh and say, "Get it back here ASAP. We have 17 potential lone wolfs who just went dark."

"On my way Booker, but you will pay for this."

"She got it." I announce to the room.

Tommy asks, "Did she have to fuck him?"

"You have always been very direct, Thomas," Jun scolds and then asks me. "Well, did she?"

"I doubt it, but she did mention that she took four showers this morning."

Gia laughs and ends our speculation with "TMI."

Jun calls the group over to her computer screen. "I've begun Operation SAT."

"Are you going to give the terrorists college entrance exams?" I ask.

"It stands for **Stop All Terrorist**. Look at this." Jun points to the name *Jiadi Mostafa*. She explains that, "Mr. Mostafa's suspected of providing material support to terrorists. Our government uses the word, *suspected* very liberally because Mostafa is *actually* a part of a terrorist cell in Los Angeles. He's been on our Watch List for the past six years and about to land at LAX from Syria. *Normally* he's waived through customs but today will be different." Jun pecks away at her keyboard, leans back, and asks, "Notice anything?"

Gia says, "Hard not to notice those big red block letters, *DENY ADMISSION – COMMUNICABLE DISEASE – TUBERCULOSIS*."

Jun chuckles and says, "Mr. Mustafa is about to go into quarantine and be returned to Turkey on a nonstop flight."

Tommy wonders, "What happens when he gets back to Ankara and has some doctor certify he don't have TB?"

"The Turkish government can certify he's Allah reincarnated, but only the originating authority can remove the denial of admission."

"And who would that be?" Gia wonders.

"The Centers for Disease Control, our CDC in Atlanta. But I've already hacked into their mainframe and placed a *permanent status* in Mustafa's file." Jun looks at me and says, "We really should tighten up our government mainframes. I would wager that some kid living in his parent's basement can hack into the CDC."

Tommy adds, "Jun has me inputting a list of things into the State Department computers that'll prevent these *Watch List* idiots from crossing our borders."

Gia wonders, "What kinda things?"

Tommy picks up a piece of paper and reads, "Mental Disorders like Bipolar, Opposition Defiant Disorder, Schizophrenia, and PTSD. We can make them drug dealers, people without vaccinations, prostitutes, drug addicts, child molesters, pedophiles, or paper them with a variety of convictions for murder, kidnapping, weapon sales, and twenty other felonies. I can mix and match, or give them syphilis, avian bird flu, bubonic plague or irritable bowel syndrome." Tommy pauses and adds, "I feel like God."

"The Devil is more in character."

I ask Jun, "Do you have a handle on interrupting the flow of ISIS cash?"

"It'll take me a good week to do my thing."

'OK." I tell the team. "I gotta make a few phone calls then I'm headed to DC. Got meetings with Bill Garrett, Tony, and I'll stop by Quantico to pick Dr. Linda's brain on our ISIS message problem."

Tommy smiles and says, "You just gonna pick her *brain*?"

"Whatta you talking about?"

"You two have been eye fucking each other."

"What the hell does that mean?"

"You know what that means. *'Take the moustache ride,' 'eat the pink taco,' 'the horizontal hula,' 'make whoopee,'* and, my personal favorite, *'get some stanky.'* "

"You are a seriously disturbed individual Sgt. Shoulders."

"Thank you."

Gia has this shit eating grin on her delicate Asian mug so I ask, "What?"

She offers, "I don't know if I should say this."

Tommy goads her. "Give it up girl."

"OK," Gia relents. "Linda has a *thing* for you. I noticed it on the plane when she positioned her skirt somewhere near her belly button. Be careful John, she's smarter and more devious than you."

"Everybody's a fuckin' comedian."

As I am leaving the room, Gia gets the last word, "Good Hunting."

Back at my desk I dial Florence Kuhns. "Well if it isn't my *favorite* crime fighter."

"You say that to all the boys in blue."

Florence laughs and confesses, "I do, and that's how I get my exclusives."

"Speaking of scoops, how would you like to enlighten the public on how the Boston Marathon bombing could've been prevented?"

"That's the stuff of Pulitzers. Talk to me."

"Well get ready to write your acceptance speech."

A half an hour later and I'm at Burke Lakefront Airport harassing Bob Dupuis and *Silent* John Canley. "I need to get to the Seat of Power, boys."

Dupuis wonders, "How does a hump GS 13 agent rate a private government ride. I know you kicked ass in Cairo, but the B's big on '*whatta you done for me lately?*' "

"Working on the lone wolf problem."

"That's a big nut to crack."

Silent John adds, "A *very* big nut."

CHAPTER 45

"I will look for you, I will find you, and, I will kill you."
Liam Neeson Taken

Columbus Ohio – 2013

Abu Musa Nasar works at his father's convenience store but lately has been missing work. He has problems interacting with non-Muslim customers. Abu attempts to preach the Quran but the clientele in the ghetto of East Cleveland want their wine, cigarettes, and Lotto tickets. Several of them have argued with Abu and a few have even uttered racial slurs like, *'Quit your sand nigger jive muthafucker.'* The store has been robbed twice within the past 9 months and Abu implores his father that they protect themselves with a gun.

Jabar attempts to explain that a gun will only lead to more violence and tells his son, "Allah has proclaimed, *'When you find peace within yourself, you become the person who can live at peace with others.'*

Abu counters with, "It is written in verse 5:35 of the Holy Koran, *'To crucify or amputate the hands and feet of those who make against Allah and Muhammed.'* "

The Nasars practice certain tenants of their Muslim faith such as Sawm (fasting) from dawn to sunset during the month of Ramadan.

They recite evening prayers, read from the Quran, but have lately avoided the local mosque. There is constant talk about slaying unbelievers, which in America are now his friends and neighbors.

Abu Jabar chastises his son and attempts to explain that hate is not an answer to people with different views. He forbade Abu from seeing Atwa but his son spat at the ground and said, "You are weak, my father, and fight Allah's message. The Koran has decreed that those who fight Allah and his messenger will be put to death or suffer the torture of the cross."

It got worse, much worse. Abu was arrested for dousing a dog with gasoline before throwing a match on the helpless animal. He had no excuse except that the Koran considers dogs unclean. Abu was lucky since he was three weeks shy of his 18th birthday and still considered a juvenile. The court levied a $4000 fine and ordered a psychological evaluation as a condition of his probation.

The court psychiatrist's report was thick and filled with terms like *sociopath, anti-social, lack of empathy, abnormal moral conduct,* and *inability to conform with the norms of the society.*

"Mr. and Mrs. Nasar," Dr. Beth Barton began, "your son is a disturbed individual. He seems unable to control his behavior and lacks empathy towards others."

"Excuse me Doctor," Jabar interrupts. "But these words have no meaning to us."

Dr. Barton sighs and says, "Abu is sick."

"But he seems healthy."

Dr. Barton smiles compassionately. "He's not *physically* ill Mr. Nasar. Abu is *mentally* sick. He has been radicalized with an ideology that preaches murder and given his mental state, Abu is capable of genocide in the name of Allah." Beth leans forward and asks, "Do you understand me?"

"Can you give him a pill and make him better?"

"Abu is a sociopath. This means that he is unable to control his behavior. He has no feelings or concern for others and when faced with people he considers nonbelievers will resort to threats, verbal abuse, and eventually violence."

"Abu is my only child and we will take care of him."

"I'm going to recommend a period of evaluation in a state center."

"But I do not wish my son inside a state center."

"It'll just be temporary," Dr. Barton says softly. "Until he gets better."

Dr. Beth Barton recommends to the court that Abu Nasar be involuntarily committed for an indeterminate period of time for evaluation and treatment to the OSU Harding Psychiatric Hospital in Columbus, Ohio. The Court accepts Dr. Barton's recommendation but the Council on American-Islam Relations (CAIR) immediately files suit charging the State of Ohio of violating Abu Nasar's constitutional rights under the Fourth Amendment. The fact that Abu is not a U.S. citizen matters not.

Abu sits in *lock down* inside the secure ward at the Harding Psychiatric Hospital while court proceedings occur several miles away. In the three days of his stay, Abu has physically attacked several attendants, patients, and attempted to bite the ear off of the treating physician.

Dr. Barton leaves the courthouse and shakes her head. She says, "Our American justice system just released a ticking time bomb. And the sad part is that the Harding Psychiatric Center could have helped Abu."

Abu *leaves* the Harding Psychiatric Hospital located on the Ohio State University campus. He accompanies his parents to their car and notices hundreds of college students as they rush between classes. Abu is fighting a strong desire to kill these nonbelieving infidels, but for now, he will go to his mosque and seek guidance.

CHAPTER 46

"Do I look like someone who cares what God thinks?"
Hellraiser (1987)

The SOP or Seat of Power gives me the creeps. It reminds me of those Halloween straw mazes where kids get lost and begin weeping. Its official title is *The J. Edgar Hoover Building* but our former Director *unofficially* christened HQ as *The Seat of Power* (SOP). We brick agents immediately rechristened it *The Obstruction Palace* and sometimes *The Puzzle Palace*. The designation depends on your mood after being *either* obstructed or confused when struggling to get something approved. Decisions use to be based strictly on our mission which is to put bad people in jail. But somehow we lost our moral compass and the Justice Department became a political arm of the executive branch.

When Eric Holder was Attorney General, he ripped the blindfold off Lady Justice and shoved her scales of impartiality right up our ass. Eric the *Red,* as I dubbed him, committed perjury under oath on The Fast and Furious case, perjury under oath on James Rosen warrant case, and blamed every police officer for defending themselves two minutes after a shooting occurred. So much for gathering all the facts *prior* to reaching a decision. After being presented with evidence of his perjury, the Attorney General of the United States, stated something to the effect that, *"I misremembered."*

Then there was the Benghazi lies, and who can forget Hillary's e-mail felonies. OJ Simpson at least had Karma bite his balls but Holder is on the lecture circuit at $25,000 a syllable and Hillary is in perpetual yoga class counting her money.

I find Bill Garrett and we head to the B cafeteria. This place is similar to your high school lunch room where students sit at segregated tables. The jocks, theatre group, nerds, and I suppose in today's world, a transgender table would exist. At the FBI cafeteria, seating is by rank, then by Sections such as Organized Crime or Kidnapping, and then it segregates down to agents versus support staff. India has a much less complex caste system.

"So we got 17 potential lone wolves who went dark," I say.

"That'd be my guess. They were spouting some pretty violent jihad crap before they disappeared from social media. Most were monitoring ISIS web sites and got into heavy conversations with suspected ISIS recruiters in chat rooms. Then they vanished"

"*Sounds* like encryption since you don't usually get whipped up into a frenzy and suddenly go cold." I laugh and add, "Sorta like making out with a girl. A few kisses, then the tongue, a grope, hand *inside* the bra, blouse in the back seat, and at that point, no guy I know will say, '*See you, gotta get to the library before it closes.*' "

Garrett laughs and agrees, "Definitely went dark." He pauses and lowers his voice. "How're you doing on getting that restriction lifted? Where we can monitor them on encrypted sites minus a warrant."

Bill is fishing so I provide a vanilla sound bite of, "You know how that goes. The House *and* Senate would have to pass a bill and then the President has to sign it. Given the current voting along party lines, I'm not holding my breath."

Bill nods and says, "Understood."

"Give me a quick rundown on your decision process for identifying likely jihadist?"

"I'm personally in touch with all 57 Field Divisions as well as our LEGATS (Legal Attachés) abroad. McKissock has ordered dedicated personnel in *all* offices to monitor social media. I provided them a guide on certain *tripwire* words or phrases that would warrant more constant monitoring. The threat level ranges from 1 to 5. As soon as a subject reaches level 5, then fails to communicate consistent with their pattern, we assume they went encrypted and I alert Gia."

"What happens when they're talking serious jihad but *don't* go dark?"

"Freedom of speech," Garrett offers. "But our Director has allowed us some leeway. As you know a *conspiracy* consists of two or more people who get together and agree to break the law."

"Yes." I interrupt, "But speech alone is not enough for us to act. They must commit an *overt* act in *furtherance* of the conspiracy."

"McKissock and our Legal Division decided that conversation involving violence, even though not specific to a person or place, constitutes an agreement, and any conversation *after* that constitutes the *overt* act."

"Not following you, Bill."

"OK, say you and I are chatting on a web forum, posting some vile stuff mentioning beheadings, infidels should die, the usual rhetoric. That speech will *now* constitute the *agreement* to do violence, which is *not* a crime. But, the next time you turn on your computer and engage in similar talk, that constitutes the *overt* act, and we can then arrest them on conspiracy to commit terrorist related violence."

"What if I'm *not* chatting with you but just posting shit."

"The FBI Legal Office determined that much like narcotic violations, there's an *assumption* of a co-conspirator, or an unindicted co-conspirator, since narcotic sales cannot operate in a vacuum."

"Fuckin' brilliant, and about time we got off our politically correct asses. Whatta you do with level 5s who cross the overt line in the sand?"

"Send out the SWAT Team with both arrest and search warrants. They've been finding weapons, explosives, drugs, and stolen property, which just adds charges. Our Legal people feel that our search and arrest warrants will be constitutionally challenged but it'll take years for the courts to figure this out and in the meantime, these idiots will be off the streets or deported."

I thank Bill and as I'm leaving he asks, "Ever get the XKeyscore from State?"

I give my Marine brother a sinister grin and say, "Now we *both* know, that would be against the law."

Tony is next on my list and I intend to make it short and sweet. I still have the 40-mile drive to Quantico for my meeting with Dr. Linda. I love Tony Dennis and refuse to place him in legal jeopardy by sharing my unlawful activities. And the truth of the matter is that the Deputy Director can't use that position to advance our vigilantism. And finally, it's my choice to work off the books and *not* Tony's.

"Well, roomie here's the brief," I say. "Our little task force is working hard on several fronts. I just met with Bill Garrett and he's tracking potential lone wolves on social media."

Tony tells me, "I'm up on that issue. Seems like ten of our field divisions have executed warrants and made 27 arrests. The liberals are screaming foul but the majority of Americans support the effort. The threat of terrorist acts is now the number one concern of the American public."

"Seems like a good time to piss off liberals. I'm sure that the ACLU is having heart palpitations."

After a few awkward seconds of silence Tony says, "You gonna brief me or what."

I mentally run down our efforts to date and realize that *all* of them are illegal, immoral, or disgusting. There's Jun inserting bogus Stops and Detains, then we have Gwen's sexual blackmail of a high-ranking State Department official, then back to Jun who is about to steal millions of dollars, and finally, my leaking top secret and embarrassing Bureau information to a member of the Press. "So I tell the Deputy Director of the FBI, "Nothing to report, but we're making progress."

"Quit the bullshit, John." Tony suddenly serious. "The Director will hand me my ass if my report consists of, *'we're making progress.'* Give me some details."

I stand and tell my roommate, "You're gonna have to trust me roomie, just like Cairo."

"You pulling that plausible deniability crap."

"Yes." And on that note, I leave the Seat of Power.

The FBI Academy is located deep within the womb of Marine Corps Base, (MCB), Quantico, Virginia. As a former Marine I get a *woody* every time I clear the gate. It's not exactly a sexual experience but rather a sense of pride, joy, and belonging. Only a former Marine will know what I'm talking about. It's now 3:00 PM and my intention is to make it back to Cleveland sometime today. Bob Dupuis and Silent John are standing by at Reagan International.

The Behavioral Science Unit is the FBI's glamour group. There have been more movies and books written about our profilers than all the Pretty Boy Floyd stuff put together. The new unit chief is Dr. Linda Alvarez and the word amongst the rank-and-file is somewhat mixed. She gets above average grades for energy, and a *high* hem line, but some of the more conservative staff feel she's *quirky* and *not* being FBI enough.

I never understood the argument that someone has to live up to a preconceived image. In law enforcement, I'll take free thinking and creative over predictable. Too many FBI agents are linear thinkers, which places blinders on their brain. If your son is kidnapped give me Dirty Harry any day. So Linda's rep as *not being FBI enough* rings hollow in my ear. But it's my duty to check out the adjustable hem line prior to a final vote. The Behavioral Science Unit is purposely situated in the sub-basement. There are no outside windows in keeping with their mysterious activities of dissecting brains and predicting behavior. There've been unconfirmed rumors of agents going down the steps and *never* making the return trip.

I tell her secretary, "Dr. Alvarez is expecting me so I'll just go in unannounced."

"Dr. Alvarez may be engaged sir and I'll have to check."

FBI personnel acting as palace guards to supervisory staff are *very* territorial. Access is granted after a vetting system that can sometimes rival interrogation at a Russian gulag.

I head toward the inner door as Donna, a prim middle-aged FBI lady, dressed in a conservative dress and two inch heels, rises from her chair and sprints in my direction. Donna proves surprisingly fast so I have to shift to second gear. I open the door and observe a perfectly naked Dr. Alvarez. Not really, but one can hope.

A fully clothed Linda smiles when she recognizes me just as the palace guard catches up. Donna apologizes, "Sorry Dr. Alvarez, but he wouldn't listen."

Linda laughs aloud and says, "It's OK, Donna, Special Agent John Booker has a mental disorder known as ODD or Oppositional Defiant Disorder. Its symptoms include anger, bipolar behavior, and being argumentative. For certain individuals, such as Agent Booker, ODD is incurable, so we must pacify and humor him." Dr. Alvarez says, "Been expecting you John," which is Donna's clue that I am not dangerous. The secretary gives me a nervous smile and exits with, "I'll be working late Dr. Alvarez, just in case you need me."

Dr. Linda surprises me with a hug. It registers somewhere between an elderly aunt and soft porn on the intimacy meter. I notice that it isn't one of those *bend at the waist* hugs that separate midsections. She directs me to a couch and asks if I'd like coffee or a soft drink. "Coffee please, black."

Linda passes the drink order to Donna and sits at the opposite end of the sofa. She says, "Minnesota was a textbook case on critical decision-making."

"You provided the profile that Gus would wait until he looked his victims in the eye."

"I only reinforced what you *already* knew John. Remember, you *called* me and felt Gus would need time to personalize his act. I only agreed with your opinion."

I recall the scene in the OPS Center when I argued with the Minnesota agents that Gus wouldn't open up. My rationale was that if we charged into the crowded mall, we'd lose the element of surprise, and the body count would be horrendous.

Linda adds, "You're comfortable in your own skin like most natural leaders. You weighed risk vs. reward and made some very hard decisions." She pauses and adds, "Decisions that determined who lived and who died."

I mumble some thanks but after our hug/grope, I'm off my guard. I'll admit to being somewhat infatuated with our Bureau shrink. A combination of beauty, brains, and body *always* leave me intrigued. My being married has nothing to do with this equation and any man who claims otherwise is downright dishonest. I notice that Dr. Alvarez just crossed her long, muscular, tanned legs and begins that involuntary foot kick that had me hypnotized on the airplane. As opposed to her matronly secretary, Dr. Linda sports 4-inch stiletto stripper trainee shoes. No wonder some leftovers from the Hoover days find her *not Bureau enough.*

We make small talk and I notice that it's 4:17 PM. I do some beer math and estimate and hour with Linda, two-hour DC traffic, 45 minute pre-flight checks, and an hour thirty-five-minute flight to Cleveland. This will place me home just shy of midnight, so I better get this confab moving along.

"We'd discussed this propaganda problem," I begin. "How do we counter the appeal of ISIS? For all its brutality, young people continue to make the journey to Syria and Iraq to join its ranks."

Dr. Alvarez measures her words. "The simple answer is that we must *replace* or offer an alternative. The difficult part is, *what* will that alternative be?"

"That's why I'm here, Linda. Talk to me."

"There are powerful cultural forces behind the appeal of ISIS. Individuals drawn to ISIS feel a deep dissatisfaction with society and find in ISIS, adventure, camaraderie and a sense of belonging."

"I still don't get it."

"Well most attempts to dissuade young people from joining ISIS focus on the negative – the violence, savagery, and repression. This is faulty logic. Can I ask you a personal question?"

I smile and say, "Ask away."

"Why did you join the Marine Corps?"

I can recognize a trick question when I hear one, so I go into a goal line stand. I begin tentatively with, "The Marine Corps is a brotherhood and….." I pause realizing that Dr. Alvarez had psychologically trapped me. "OK," I concede. "Point made. I joined the Marines for the identical reasons that people join ISIS. Adventure, camaraderie, danger, and a sense of belonging."

"So we need to answer the question, *'when you made up your mind to enlist, what would have stopped you?'* "

"Your analogy is creepy, but true. When I made up my mind to enlist, people tried to talk me outta it by describing boot camp as mental and physical torture. They said the food was bad, the living conditions poor, and I'd end up in a body bag in the sandbox and never see my family again."

"And?" Dr. Linda presses.

"And," I say. "It only made me want to join *more*."

"Why did you ignore those dire warnings? What thought process forced your heart to override your brain?"

"I had to see for myself and if I *didn't* join the Marines, it would be a major, hole in my life."

"Do you see ISIS as a terrorist cult?"

"Sort of."

"How about the Marine Corps?"

"Not even close," I protest. "Marines don't behead and burn innocent civilians. We don't kill people for their religious beliefs or rape children. We're the good guys and America is lucky to have the Corps."

Linda gives me the same stare that Sister Alberta Marie conveyed when I spouted something irrational. I say, "This may sound weird but what *attracted* me to the Marine Corps was old John Wayne war movies like the *Sands of Iwo Jima*, putting on those Marine dress blues, going on liberty in some foreign ports with buddies, and..." I concede, "fighting in a war and killing bad guys."

Linda maintains her nun-like incredible stare. "OK," I concede, "it may not make sense to *you* but it's what *I* believe."

"Listening to yourself today, does it sound rational or make sense?"

"No, but strangely enough, I'd do it again."

"What was it that motivated you to raise your right hand and take an oath to die for an ideal, and couldn't ISIS be considered a similar ideal?"

"I *think* I see where you're going with this. A lot of boys dream of being a Marine, but relatively *few* actually enlist. So somewhere between *wanting* to do it and *really* doing it, something changes their mind."

"Exactly," Linda says excitedly. "If we can discover that *something*, we're in business. So, you went to Marine basic training where you were harassed, sleep deprived, insulted, degraded, and trivialized. Did that strengthen or weaken your commitment to the cause?"

"It strengthened it and further motivated me. The conditions may be similar to ISIS but our *causes* are different. It's a classic case of good versus evil."

"Who gets to decide which one is good?"

"OK," I relent. "So both ISIS and the Marine Corps radicalize their troops, but the question should be, *'What will change hearts and minds?'* " I add, "And, how do we keep that person from acting on his John Wayne movie?"

"Very good Agent Booker." Linda smiles. "We have to disrupt that process and replace it with something else. We tend to think of ISIS soldiers as crazy because of the barbaric acts that they do. We assume that can be explained via the pathology of those people, but trying to explain terrorism as mental illness is *misleading*."

"Because it's ideologically based?" I ask.

"Not really. ISIS is basically a political cult using religion and a perversion of Islam as the shield. It's a systematic effort to create an army of basically tranced-out followers. A case in point was the beheading of U.S. journalists James Foley and Steven Sotloff. Rather than discourage recruitment, dozens of men and women from places like Illinois and Idaho left their homes to join ISIS."

"This has been a fascinating Physc 101 lecture, but I need *answers*. What's the *alternative* message to discourage ISIS recruitment?"

She offers, "Our goal is to intercept ISIS propaganda and replace it, *before* it prompts people to act."

"That sums it up."

"Did you see the movie *Wag the Dog?*"

"No."

"Great flick with De Nero and Dustin Hoffman. It's the perfect example on ISIS use of the media to create their reality. The plot involves some political hack who wants to influence a presidential election. The current president is a certain loser until a Hollywood film producer constructs a bogus diversionary war with Albania."

"You lost me."

Dr. Linda's leg is now in full unconscious kick mode, which ratchets up her hem line with each thrust. She says, "They duped the public in believing America was at war and the President was doing a great job in preventing an Albanian victory."

"How?"

"By controlling the images on television. The Hollywood producer, played by Dustin Hoffman, cut old stock war footage with the President soothing fears and describing overwhelming American victories. This made the electorate fall back in love with him and got him re-elected."

"That sounds like a stretch in suspending belief."

"This *was* before mass social media but your reality is *already* shaped by the media. Nations like North Korea with total control of media can make their citizens believe that the world is flat and their short fat dictator is Brad Pitt."

After a few seconds, I say almost to myself, "Have we solved anything here?"

Linda smiles and says, "Yes, to sum it all up. We need to *wag the dog* and provide ISIS recruits an alternative. Now, you *will* take your teacher to her favorite restaurant where we will continue this class."

I want to say the right thing, which is, *"Can't do that', 'planes waiting,' 'wife's expecting me,' 'got a ton of work,' 'an early morning,'* and finish off with *'thanks but no thanks'* but what comes out of my mouth is, "Yes teacher, and your student's been a bad, *bad* boy."

CHAPTER 47

"Never go to a doctor whose office plants have died."

Erma Bombeck

"How many?"

"Under a hundred, but increasing."

"Well, let's keep up with it," Doctor Goodrich says. "When it hits the century mark, we'll have to go public."

John Goodrich M.D. is associate director for the U.S. Food and Drug Administration (FDA). He is having a telephone conversation with Dr. Bob Dickerson from the Centers for Disease Control (CDC). The topic is a mild outbreak of Salmonella and Ecolab, a common bacterial infection that humans contract via food contamination.

Under the Federal Food, Drug, and Cosmetic Act of 1906, the U.S. Food and Drug Administration has the authority to ensure that animal feed is properly labelled, is safe for its intended use, and produces no human health hazards when fed to food-producing animals.

Goodrich wonders, "Any idea of where the contamination entered the cycle?"

"None," Dickerson confesses. "Since animal feed is the beginning of the food safety chain."

Goodrich warns, "Food-producing animals like cattle, chickens, pigs, and turkeys are the major reservoirs for many of these organisms.

And, animal feed is frequently contaminated with non-Typhus serotypes of *Salmonella enteric*....."

".....Yes, John," Dickerson interrupts. "I *know* that it can lead to infection and colonization of food animals. I *know* that these bacteria can then contaminate animal carcasses at slaughter or cross-contaminate other food items." Dickerson pauses and say mostly to himself, "I *know*."

An awkward silence is broken by Goodrich who asks, "Terrorist attacks in the food supply chain would be difficult to distinguish from natural events, considering the large variety of human food borne illnesses coupled with crop and livestock diseases. Any signs of terrorism?"

"Absolutely not," Dickerson says firmly. "Terrorists would require access to the best scientific minds on earth. Our Middle East enemies are fifty years away from developing the masking agents required to make this outbreak appear an act of nature."

Goodrich pushes with, "But couldn't our enemies introduce more primitive poisons?"

"They could." Dickinson explains. "But we've run exhaustive tests and there has been *no* evidence of biological or radio-nuclear agents. We even checked for the less obvious naturally-occurring toxic chemicals such as ricin."

"Well it's probably just your run of the mill contaminated food incident." Goodrich muses. "Generating a bunch of stomach aches, some hospitalizations and a few senior citizens' deaths."

Dickerson reluctantly agrees. "It usually plays out that way."

Goodrich says, "Look Bob, *we* know that tracing contamination to its original source is almost impossible, but the public still believes that we're batting 100% on these types of cases."

"None of that will matter if bacterial enteric pathogens are the cause of this food contamination outbreak."

"Maybe I should call the White House," The FDA associate director says. "Just to give them a *heads up*."

Dr. Bob Dickerson emits a cynical chuckle and says, "A *cover your ass* move, John. It's beneath someone of your stature *and* an exercise in political futility. Because if this outbreak is *not* your run of the mill incident, then thousands upon thousands of American men, women, and children will die, there'll be widespread panic and civil unrest, our economy will be obliterated, and there's *nothing* we can do to prevent it."

CHAPTER 48

"With sufficient thrust, pigs fly just fine."
Merlin......The TV Show

Since the two FBI pilots are based in the DC area my unplanned dinner will allow them to sleep in their own bed. I call Bob Dupuis and say, "Good news Bobby, you and Silent John can stand down for the night. My meetings are running late and I'll just bunk in at the Academy."

My brain justifies this escapade of food and alcohol as work related but my Catholic heart knows the truth. The Bureau shrink is a fox and I am a *hound*. We all must eventually accept our lot in life.

Dupuis was a Marine pilot who flew combat missions during the Gulf Wars. He immediately smells my bullshit and says, "So your meeting with Dr. Alvarez is *still* going on, and it may continue for a while?" Bob's inquiry was actually the statement, '*You really don't expect me to buy that lame excuse.*'

I double down with, "Yea, some of the profilers on her staff feel they can solve this message problem. We got a head of steam and I don't wanna stop."

Telling lies to FBI agents is fraught with risk. We're trained to detect deception at the Academy and fine tune our trade on an endless supply of suspects who begin every sentence with, '*Wasn't me.*' '*Didn't do it,' 'I was in the bathroom.'* But my many years telling lies undercover makes me a convincing fibber. I add, "Good of the case."

He ignores my phony alibi and tells me, "All I'll say is, be careful."

"I'm at a meeting Bob, not landing on Iwo Jima. Why do I need to be careful?"

Dupuis chuckles. "Because our Bu shrink has her eye on you and I've seen that *eye* on liberty in Olongopo."

"You comparing Doctor Linda Alvarez with a Philippine hooker?"

"Not really, but I am comparing *you* to a 21-year-old Marine on liberty." Dupuis answers and baits me with. "You gonna be able to get some chow?"

"Not a problem. We'll probably just grab something at the cafeteria."

"Good chow there, and, I heard that *tonight* they're featuring *Mexican*." A reference to Dr. Alvarez's ethnic roots.

I laugh and end our conversation with, "You're a racist a-hole. Meet me at the airport at 0700."

Most individuals will make some major assumptions on what happens next, but I'm a married man, albeit an inveterate flirt. There may have been some kissy face and perhaps a foot massage, but there's a line in the sand that I won't cross no matter how many margaritas I down. With that said, I recall leaving the FBI Academy and following Dr. Alvarez to her favorite Mexican restaurant, *Jose's Diner and Live Bait.*

There were several tequila shots, which preceded a series of margaritas dubbed The Classic Margarita, Lover's Margarita, Martini Margarita Cuervo, and I believe two or three potent Cazadores Reposada Margaritas served with tequila, Baileys, and lemon vodka. There were some clumsy attempts at using the red restaurant napkins as a cape for mock bull fights, and a *vague* recollection of my singing debut with a roving Mariachi band who visited our table. Olé! Thankfully Linda's condo is only two blocks away, so we leave our cars at Jose's, and do a combination walk/stagger while repeatedly singing the chorus from *LaBamba*.

We arrive at one of those upscale condo complexes with an abundance of marble, plants, and glass. Her place is eclectically decorated with a Mediterranean, Mexican motif. I *may* have suggested a nightcap of brandy, which, in case you're wondering, *doesn't* mix well with margaritas. Dr. Linda sits next to me on the couch and plays with the back of my neck. *Innocent enough*, I think as my meat puppet begins to awaken. Then she removes her shoes and says, "John, my feet are killing me, can you rub them?" And without waiting for a reply, she reclines and hoists her lovely tootsies onto my lap. I can't help but notice that her skirt has somehow shrunk exposing red lace thong panties, which appear moist in the crotch area. That last observation may have been just wishful thinking.

Dr. Linda must have sonar because her feet score a direct hit on my now fully engorged meat puppet. My fogged brain rationalizes this innocent accident, *until* her feet begin to massage *my* Johnson as I *massage* her feet. During these gyrations Linda *may* have raised her right foot and inserted her big toe in my mouth, but I can't be sure it happened or, if it did, was intentional. During this entire erotic episode, I recall repeatedly singing the refrain from *LaBamba*...... *"Baddada Bamaba, Badadda Bamba."* Which in case you're wondering, is made more difficult with a big toe in your mouth.

I awake at Dr. Linda's Old Town Alexandria condo, on the *couch*, at 0711 and break the land speed record to Reagan International Airport. I'm an hour and half late with the residual effects from one too many margaritas.

But as I arrive at the airport hung over, unshaven, and bleary eyed, I can only offer a lame, "OK boys, sorry for being late, let's get airborne."

Silent John looks me in the eye and says, "You look like shit."

I provide an abridged version of the Margaretville bull fight and Mariachi singalong.

Bob Dupuis deadpans, "So you *attempted* to relive our wild and crazy days at Camp Pendleton with weekend liberty to Tijuana." He laughs and adds, "A little bit old for that John?"

I smile and say, "Fuck you."

I am in a coma for the entire flight to Cleveland Burke Lakefront. Silent John nudges me awake, hands me a cup of coffee, and says, "We land in 20 minutes."

I take a deserved ration of shit from the two Bu Pilots. Civilians can *never* understand the bond that we in the military feel. The two former Marine pilots are my brothers and their flippant asides are part of the brotherhood. It's a macho way of saying, *"We love you asshole and we've got your back."* But after my skull session with Dr. Linda, evidently ISIS has an identical credo.

I tell them, "No travel planned for the next few days, so, go spend time with your families. And thanks."

My cell phone has 11 messages and five texts. Lorri wasn't one of them since I had phoned my wife and provided her this partial truth pre-Margaritaville. "I'm having a series of meetings with an HBO (High Bureau Official) and spending the night at Quantico. After 8 years in deep cover with the Mafia, my wife is not squeamish about an overnight. But, it seems that my task force missed me. My arrival is met with a nervous energy of comments, questions, and observations.

Gia informs me that Sean called and is still in limbo on his return to law enforcement. "He mentioned teaching at the high school level, or even going back to graduate school for a PHD in Sociology." Gia feels that, "It doesn't sound like he'll be back."

Tommy offers, "This ain't for everybody. You gotta be half nuts to want to do this shit. Long hours, asshole bosses, unappreciative public, and people shooting at you."

Gwen observes, "You're looking a little under the weather Booker. Been south of the border?"

"That fuckin Dupuis can't keep his mouth shut."

"Wasn't Dupuis." Agent 36 laughs and informs me that, "John Canley was in my new agent's class."

"So Silent John ain't so silent." I laugh.

"You wanna confess anything El Matador!"

"Nothing happened except some case related talk, a few adult beverages, and an audition with a Mariachi band. All innocent fun. Now what's been happening here?"

The silence and wide eyes alert me to the fact that my friends and co-workers have doubts about my answer. So, I fill the silence with, "OK, I gave her a foot massage."

After some more awkward silence, Gia says, "Well, that's innocent enough."

This naive conclusion brings howls from the more knowledgeable elders and I deflect the subject by asking, "What's been going on here?"

Jun says, "Thomas and I have been busy. While you were rubbing toes, we've had 23 individuals on the Watch List detained, deported, or quarantined." She adds. "Four were serious and immediate threats."

"That's fantastic Jun."

"And," Jun says proudly, "Gia found a missing link in our plan. Actually, a blinding flash of the obvious but one which will significantly expand our efforts in preventing terrorists from entering our borders."

"I'm all ears."

Gia clarifies, "I remembered what you said about our Watch List *not* being a Stop List. You explained that people confuse the Watch List with the *No-Fly* list, which *does* prevent someone from entering the country."

"So." Jun finishes. "Gia says, *'Why don't we just transfer people from the Watch List to the No-Fly list.'*"

It takes a few seconds for this simple ploy to sink into my still foggy brain. "Wow. That *is* sneaky good. We can double our numbers while lowering the risk of being discovered."

Agent 36 agrees. "Our phony list of contagious diseases and warrants will generate some complaints but, by padding the No-Fly list we lessen the overall glare."

"The No-Fly list belongs to the Bureau so any appeals come our way. Whoever we designate to the No-Fly list can't be second guessed *or* overridden."

It's Tommy Shoulders who sums it all up. "The federal government is so fucked up. The right hand doesn't know what the left hand is doing and even if they did it would take years to get anything changed. God Bless America."

I tell Gia, "Good pick up Gia. That's *why* I wanted you on this task force. You can think outside the box." I look at Jun and ask. "Whatta you got?"

Jun says, "Had you *answered* my three calls yesterday you might *know* that the XKeyscore is up and running *and* has already thwarted a plot."

I take the verbal reprimand in stride and learn that during my Mexican adventure Michael C. Reynolds of Reading, Pennsylvania, wanted to blow up the Transcontinental Pipeline which runs from the Gulf Coast to New Jersey. Michael seemed an ambitious jihadist and was finalizing his plan with his ISIS recruiter on the encrypted website *The Dawn of Glad Tidings* and switching to major ISIS Twitter accounts, @Minbaer and @mghlli1122.

Reynolds was one of the 17 cases that Bill Garrett handed off when they went dark. Jun began monitoring Reynolds using the XKeyscore as he progressed from ideological rhetoric to planning jihad. Gia then condensed the illegally obtained conversations onto affidavits using *confidential sources* for the probable cause. Then she coordinated everything with our Philadelphia office and FBI agents arrested Reynolds in possession of enough C-4 to accomplish the plan along with a set of maps indicating the intended targets.

He is in federal custody charged with Title 18 U.S. Code § 2332f – '*Conspiracy - Bombings of places of public use, government facilities, public transportation systems and infrastructure facilities.*' It doesn't appear that he will see the light of day anytime soon. CASE CLOSED!

It's exciting to see the results of our meetings, planning, and conniving. But, it's only a beginning and as a world class pessimist, I realize that some serious shit awaits us. There are so many fronts on this lone wolf problem but so far so good.

Agent 36 asks, "So what did you and Dr. Ruth conjure up the message which will discourage lone wolves from going jihad?"

I just realized that we *hadn't* come up with the message. I'd been so impressed with Alvarez's Marine Corps analogy that we never took it to its logical conclusion at Quantico. But I *vaguely* recollect that somewhere between the Lovers Marguerita and my rendition of *La Bamba*, we had hit upon a possibility. I tell the group, "Linda is refining the wording and will get it to us ASAP." I add the thought, '*I hope.*'

Our task force spends the remainder of the day, working our specific areas of concern. It's Friday afternoon and I'd promised Lorri a shopping trip to the West Side Market Saturday morning. My wife emphasized that, "The earlier you get there, the fresher the food," so I'm planning an early night. As I am heading out the door Agent 36 says, "There *is* one other case that has a stench."

"One of the original 17 sent by Garrettt?" I ask.

"Yes, Jun has been monitoring some guy name of Joe Razone, from New York City, on an encrypted site. She asked me to review the conversation, and even though he's not talking bullets or bombs, Joey has my attention."

I chuckle and dismiss her with, "He's Italian so he *can't* be a terrorist. Maybe a bad barber, brick layer, or trombone player, but *not* a jihadist." I pause and add, "Unless someone insults his mother."

Gwen's not laughing, which is very unusual since she usually finds me clever, witty, and irresistibly amusing.

She says, "Our little Joey is talking some jihadist trash on an ISIS website."

"We unfortunately have thousands of idiots doing the same thing," I counter. "Why should we expend any energy on Joe Razone?"

"Because," Gwen says. "Joey is chatting about contaminating our food supply."

CHAPTER 49

"Women who seek to be equal with men lack ambition."

The alarm on Lorri's side of the bed awakens me to NPR radio. My first instinct is that scholarly people had somehow infiltrated my bedroom and are whispering something about Bach's Brandenburg Concertos, Toccata in D minor. I roll over when I determine the threat level is zero, but am rudely reminded of my promise.

"Revelry, revelry, up and at 'em Marine!" Lorri imitating a drill instructor. "I can smell those tomatoes rotting."

The West Side Market in Cleveland is a fascinating place. The land dates back to 1840 and is Cleveland's oldest publicly owned market. It's a combination open air marketplace with an interior concourse. The market is home to over 100 vendors of great ethnic diversity. They remind me of Italian carnival hucksters who entice you to their produce or fish with promises of, *'Yo, lady com'ere I got the best Baccalla.'* You can find not only fine meats and vegetables, but also fresh seafood, baked goods, dairy, cheese products, and even fresh flowers.

Lorri strolls amongst different produce booths feeling up vegetables and negotiating with guys named Vito. I trail behind like a baby duck following mommy. A few husbands give me an understanding nod as we shuffle along like patients at a state institution on meds.

We pack our goodies into a cooler and head to lunch. It's important for married couples to sit and talk minus distractions. Careers, egos, libidos, and an occasional FBI psychologist will sometimes pollute this ritual but not today. Lorri orders white wine and informs me that Nikki and Pedro are still a couple and her latest boy wonder boss has been terminated for sexual harassment. I counter with coffee and ask, "Did he put the moves on you?"

Lorri chuckles, "I'm *almost* old enough to be his mother."

"Maybe, but you're still the prettiest girl I know."

"You are so full of it, John Booker. But I do love you."

OK, I have a pang of guilt from my south of the border adventure with Dr. Linda, even though *nothing happened!*

We spend the remainder of the day bonding which is marriage speak for *doing those things recommended by your spouse.* In my case, it includes three checks off my honey-do list, a dinner at Lazzaras, and a movie featuring a bunch of thirty-something actors whose names I can neither recognized nor pronounce. All in all, a pretty good day in the Booker marriage.

I awake to a rare sunny Sunday November morning, grab a cup of coffee and the morning paper. My usual default section is Sports but something catches my eye. It's a two-inch headline on the front page of the *Cleveland Plain Dealer*.

BOSTON MARATHON BOMBING COULD HAVE BEEN PREVENTED.

The story accuses the current administration of political correctness, which resulted in a mosque policy that caused the death of innocent Americans. The reporter, Florence Kuhns, accompanies the article with photos of the bombing chaos and the brothers, Dzhokhar and Tamerlan Tsarnaev. Evidently, The Boston Marathon bombing could've been prevented had the FBI been allowed to surveil mosques. Who'd *thunk* that?

CHAPTER 50

"The tongue like a sharp knife... Kills without drawing blood."
— Buddha

Columbus Ohio – The Present

The pleasant boy who came to America as a skinny 13-year-old is now a 22-year-old angry man. Abu sports a full beard since the Prophet Muhammad declared that believers of Islam should be different from the Jews, Christians, and Pagans. He no longer wears western clothes such as jeans but adheres to the strict Muslim dress code of Kufiyaa, a rectangular checkered head scarf along with a black rope band, and a white Thobe, which is an ankle-length long robe.

Jabar has overheard his son on the cell phone speaking of assault rifles and suspects that Abu is in possession of *some* type of weapon. Atwa, his friend from middle school, is a constant presence in his life. It was Atwa who began Abu's indoctrination concerning infidels and the nonbelievers. During one such lecture in Jabar's home, Atwa boldly challenged him.

"You have become one with the unbelievers!"

"I have many Christian and even Jewish friends who do God's will and treat us with respect and kindness," Jabar patiently explains. "The sad truth is that Islam is a religion of peace, which has been distorted by blind apostates who misinterpret the Koran for evil purposes."

Jabars mention of Jews and Christians enrage Atwa who spits, "God's curse be upon the infidels! Evil is that for which they have bartered away their souls. And you Jabar, have incurred God's most inexorable wrath. An ignominious punishment awaits you."

Jabar counters with, "Muslims are not bloodthirsty people. Islam is a religion of peace that forbids the killing of the innocent. Islam also accepts the Prophets, whether those prophets are Mohammed, God's peace and blessing be upon Him, or Moses or the other prophets of the Books."

Abu points his finger at his father and hisses, "Father, the prophet Muhammed has said, *'I shall cast terror into the hearts of the infidels. Strike off their heads, strike off the very tips of their fingers.'*"

Atwa and Abu storm from the house, Abu says, "Let us seek the counsel of Benoit at the mosque. We have been made impure by your father's words."

CHAPTER 51

"Think ya used enough dynamite there, Butch?"
Butch Cassidy and The Sundance Kid

"Well at least you waited until Monday morning."

"You have severely pissed me off, John, and betrayed our trust."

"Calm down roomie, and think about this."

My cell phone rings on a dreary Monday morning as I'm headed to my favorite Starbucks to see Donnie Osmond and get my fix of caramel macchiato. Tony Daniels has been pissed off at me on *many* occasions. There was the time at New Agent training when I scored the White-Collar crime exam from some upper classmen. The FBI Academy has an honor system similar to West Point and Annapolis but neither Tony nor I can add or subtract, let alone explain a net worth investigation on the exam. "This is gonna get us booted out." He whispered in our dorm room.

"Naw, this is gonna get us through the white collar exam."

My logic, though ethically flawed, was going to save us plenty of heartburn. Any two exam grades below 85 during New Agent training means your seat is empty Monday morning. Sayonara, gone, adios, arrivederci, unemployed, *and* time for a career change. So, my rationalization for cheating on a FBI exam is self-preservation and the probability that neither of us would *ever* work white collar crimes. We had no problem with the other training blocks, but Title 18 of the US Code dealing with insider Trading and Bank Fraud was like studying Czechslovakian.

My roomie had been ambushed an hour ago at the Puzzle Palace by Director McKissock who innocently inquired, "Tony, do you know anything about the Sunday *Cleveland Plain Dealer* story on the FBI dropping the ball on the Boston Marathon bombing?"

I'm chuckling and say, "And that's why I *didn't* tell you. So you could truthfully say, '*I know nothing.*' "

Tony counters with, "Cut the Sgt. Schultz imitation. The Director's not an idiot and knows your little task force operates in Cleveland. He *also* knows that we were roommates, and that I was one of the ten people who knew about the Marathon screw up."

"But it was *not* an FBI fuck up. It was our Muslim-loving jihad ally in the White House at the time who decided that mosques were off limit."

A few seconds of silence before Tony says, "OK, but from now on, I want in the loop. I want to know *everything* you're doing so I won't be caught holding my putz and looking like an idiot."

"You remember the last time you made that demand."

Tony says, "No." But he's fibbing because he clearly remembers the time he demanded that I keep him updated on the Cairo mission. When I told him that our task force was considering torturing and possibly whacking a few terrorists, Tony laughed nervously and terminated the conversation.

"OK roomie, I'll keep you in the loop."

"Good." Tony, now calmer, says "So, is there *anything* else I need to be aware of? Any ticking time bombs, booby traps, or trip wires that are out there?"

"There is." I say somberly. "I have forged several official government reports involving source information on terrorist activity at mosques."

The silence continues for at least 30 seconds before Tony terminates our conversation. I'm guessing that the Deputy Director has other pressing business.

The weekend at home revitalized me. It had been a very long time since my Bu phone had not chirped during a weekend. I enter the task force area and find Jun, Gwen, Gia, and Tommy Shoulders staring at computer screens. I notice remnants of pizza lying on greasy cardboard boxes, personal hygiene items like toothbrushes, some female spray things, and a half-naked Tommy Shoulders. Tommy is shoeless and down to his skivvies. "Should I ask any questions, or just keep my trap shut?"

He looks at me and says, "Spilled some chili all over me."

Gwen laughs and says, "Booker, you're a trained investigator. Can you spell *ménage à trois*?"

I correct Gwen. "There are *four* of you." Then I comment, "I can't wait to hear this one."

"Been working our asses off." Tommy says seriously.

Jun explains. "Friday night, I intercepted an ISIS communication bragging about their finances. They actually displayed images of currency in the form of small gold coins and American cash. I simply used a GPS program I developed to determine the longitude and latitude of their stash, then parlayed Google Earth to confirm the location."

Gia adds, "ISIS has been known to operate many businesses to ensure its cash reserves remain healthy. After taking Mosul, ISIS looted nearly half a billion dollars from banks in Mosul and the other northern cities of Tikrit and Baiji."

"So did we communicate this actionable Intel into the right hands, which is the military?" I wonder.

It's Gwen who replies. "Not directly. That would lead *right* back to our illegal operation."

"I'm sure that the Pentagon is not going to act on anonymous tips."

"Duh, we figured that one out for ourselves." Gwen chuckles. "I called Stanley from State. He's their cyber security chief so anyone would assume that Stanley made the find."

I comment that, "Stanley's a tight ass and he'd be suspicious why we'd *share* something this big."

"He was at first but I convinced him that we had a hip pocket asset who couldn't be burnt. So, I sent him our incontrovertible evidence, stressed that we had to act quick, and promised a romantic dinner."

"He bought it?" I wonder.

"Made him a hero at State. He forwarded our stuff to the Pentagon and they seemed to have most of the Intel anyway except for the location of the money. Stanley may get a promotion for this."

Tommy explains, "The military airstrikes yesterday destroyed the huge bank and all their gold coins. Even the timing to bomb the bank was carefully chosen. The airstrike was conducted at dawn on Sunday when ISIS operatives were working overnight but at a time which would limit civilian casualties."

Gia adds, "They haven't announced the bombing mission to the public until they get some SIGMINT (Signal Intelligence) confirmation, but they're 95% sure ISIS's credit rating just tanked."

"And why didn't anyone call me?" I ask, pissed that I had not been informed of such a critical piece of our mission.

It's Gwen, my closest confidant who explains, "Look John, nobody works harder than you. You're the only one of us with a family and Lorri's been putting up with you being *gone* for years. Seven years undercover and then 2 years on the Cairo case. When you left early Friday, we decided to work a few more hours. We hit upon this ISIS bank late Friday my first instinct was to call you, but I knew that we could handle it and that Lorri deserved the time with her hubby."

Although I appreciate the sentiment, I am a certified thrill junkie and just missed some *thrilling* shit. "Job well done." I say stiffly then pause and realize that I'm being a selfish dick so I add, "That really is *fucking* great and I couldn't have picked a better team."

The group takes turns filling in the missing pieces of what will become known as *The Two Ton Bank Bombing*. Gwen tells me that, "Stanley kept whining that he'd get in trouble if we were wrong."

"How'd you convince him?"

"Combination hard data and 'hard on,' " Agent 36 explains. "He's a cyber geek so he was able to check and recheck our data. And whenever he'd begin to waver, I'd tell him what I was wearing."

"And people think I'm a deviant."

Tommy says, "U.S. forces dropped two 2,000-pound bombs on the bank and a Defense Department video shows what appears to be thousands of pieces of paper and coin currency literally going up in smoke as the pair of bombs hit."

Gia adds, "A U.S. Defense official believes that millions of dollars in currency was being stored in the facility, which now lies in ruin. This loss will significantly hinder ISIS's ability to recruit lone wolves."

"I am duly impressed, but next time give me a call."

Jun shakes her head and warns, "This is good but they still have plenty of dough left. I've been working on two additional financial fronts."

"Which are?"

"The BITCOINS riddle and transferring money out of the accounts of ISIS sympathizers who fund their evil." She asks me, "Do you have the routing and account numbers where you want the money transferred?"

"You ready to go on that?"

"I'm close."

I go to my desk, grab a scrap of paper with a series of handwritten numbers, and hand it to Jun.

"Should I ask *where* the money's going?"

I shake my head. "Not now, but I'll tell you where it's *not* going. It *won't* go to any government, *including* our own. They'll only waste it on entitlements to illegal aliens or studies on migrant raccoons. If we get some of that blood money, it'll go to benefit people in need."

CHAPTER 52

"He has all the virtues I dislike and none of the vices I admire."
                                                    Winston Churchill

Several weeks later two events occur almost simultaneously. Based on the *Plain Dealer*'s exposé, Congress convenes a committee to investigate the administrations cover up of a politically correct mosque policy, which contributed to the Boston Marathon bombing. Conservative legislators on the hill milk this SNAFU for every moment of camera time on C-SPAN and nonstop righteous indignation on FOX News.

The committee parades victims of the Marathon bombing before the cameras who retell the events of that tragic day and how their injuries and loss of loved ones have affected their lives. The legislators grill Chicken Shit Walt and other administration officials from their lofty perches and demand that the President modify his policy.

Congressman Taylor Griffin asks Walt, "According to your *own* agency, the government's sweeping surveillance of our most private communications, as exposed by Edwin Snowden, do not include Mosques and Muslim affiliated facilities. Supposedly this is done to protect the sensibilities of innocent Muslims who worship in Mosques. My question to you, Mr. Deputy Director, is *why?*"

Tony later confided that Chicken Shit Walt almost fainted when Congressman Griffin proclaimed that *someone* would be held accountable. In today's government, no one is *ever* held accountable.

A week after the Congressional hearing ends, Director Gary McKissock visits the former Vice President. Joe Rider is a consummate politician who covets the Presidency. He has already mentioned a run at the White House in the near future. The Director and Rider have played several rounds of golf followed by a few cocktails at the Army-Navy clubhouse. They have a good old boy rapport both having served as U.S. Attorneys.

McKissock begins the meeting with, "Mr. Vice President, this mosque policy has tied the hands of law enforcement." The Director mentions the *Cleveland Plain Dealer* exposé and the negative implications that the *previous* administration *could* have prevented the massacre at the Boston Marathon. He adds that, "Some recent polls indicate that 77% of America *support* lifting this unwise ban on mosques."

The former VP smiles and says, "Off the record Gary, I'm with you on this mosque thing. But, the guy who just left the Oval Office leaned a little toward *them.*"

"*If them* are radical Muslims then *we* have a problem. It's my job to stop *them* before they blow up more of *us.* These 77% are the same people who'll be voting in the next few elections. The lone wolf brothers who detonated those bombs at the Marathon have a zero sympathy factor. So, anyone running for office should distance themselves from this mosque policy."

'So whatta you want from me? I have no official standing."

McKissock counters with, "No but the Democrats consider you their leader and Republicans need some cover from the Dems in Congress. But they're terrified about offending groups like CAIR and the ACLU."

The former VP gets the unspoken message and is mum. The Director uses the silence and continues with, "Since October 2011, mosques have been off-limits to the FBI. Surveillance or undercover sting operations are not allowed without high-level approval from a special oversight body at the Justice Department dubbed the Sensitive Operations Review Committee (SORC)." McKissock pauses and asks, "Can I ask you question?"

"Of course Gary, we go back a long way."

"Why is it Joe, that not a soul, not even me, is aware who makes up this body, or what criteria they use to review our requests. The names of the chairman, members, and staff are kept secret." McKissock pauses and asks, "Why is it necessary to *hide* the people who decide whether or not to protect the rest of the country from radical Muslims?"

The former Vice President explains that, "*You* know why the committee was formed Gary. Pressure from Islamist groups who complained about government stings at mosques. Allegations are that the FBI routinely violates the civil rights of Muslims."

"That's absurd Joe," McKissock interrupts. "Obama caved to some Muslim fringe group screaming racism when we conducted a *legitimate* undercover sting on a California mosque. We had information from reliable sources that jihad was routinely discussed by several members. We were later proved right but it cost lives. Excuse me for saying this, but the President's decision had *nothing* to do with civil rights. It's just *another* concession to a group of extremists who want to set their own rules in America."

The VP concedes, "I'm in a tough situation. As a former federal prosecutor, I never looked at ones' skin color, religion, or race. I prosecuted the *crime* but politics is a different animal with different agendas. I actually have less decision-making ability as the former Vice President of the United States than I did as the U.S. Attorney for New Jersey."

McKissock nods sympathetically. "I understand Joe but sooner or later you have to grow your balls back because before mosques were excluded from investigations, the FBI launched dozens of successful sting operations against homegrown radicals inside mosques, and disrupted dozens of plots against innocent American citizens across the United States. If only we were allowed to continue, perhaps the many victims of the Boston Marathon bombings would not have lost their lives and limbs. We weren't even permitted to canvass Boston mosques until four days *after* the April 15 attacks, and Justice forbade us to check out the radical Boston mosque where the Muslim bombers worshiped."

The unspoken political implications hang in the air. McKissock hands the former VP a thick manila folder and says, "Joe, I need your help."

Rider understands the subtle shift of power with the use of his given name. McKissock continues. "These are 27 reports from 27 *different* FBI field divisions where reliable informants report current terrorist activities at mosques. The most radical is in Columbus Ohio. Use it as the additional ammunition when meeting with your fellow Democrats. I'm a team player but I will no longer stand by while politicians tie my hands. I'm considering resigning if the mosque policy stands." McKissock pauses and adds, "And, I won't remain quiet."

The VP nods solemnly and offers, "I'll talk to some of the Congressional leaders this week, but it *won't* happen immediately. They based their campaigns on the premise that Muslims are peace-loving folks. The problem is," "The VP pauses and concludes with, "they *actually* believe it."

McKissock is no longer in the mood to continue the verbal jousting. He rises and says, "I understand sir, but as Henry VIII said, 'Defer no time, delays have dangerous ends.' " The Director smiles and ends the meeting on a pleasant note. "Great seeing you Mr. Vice President, give my best to Debbie and let's play some golf."

Seven weeks later the Democratic Chairwoman of Policies and Procedures subcommittee announced that her committee will *revisit* his mosque policy. When asked by a reporter to shed some light on the secret Special Operations Committee, the Chairwoman deflects with, "This committee has, and will *continue* to perform, a needed oversight function. Law enforcement occasionally strays outside the boundaries of common sense and even our constitution. We all require some oversight. But, releasing the committee member names will only make them targets of those individuals who believe that all Muslims are terrorists."

I'm happy that our efforts have begun the ball rolling but it's not a done deal. Muslim groups will scream *"racism, bigotry, intolerance'* and CAIR, along with the ACLU, will file Fourth Amendment legal motions to squelch any mosques intrusion.

The morning sky is filled with dark cumulus clouds. I drive north on I-71 toward downtown Cleveland passing the Wal-Mart where Captain Kopka was almost impaled by an arrow. Seems funny now and it actually *was* funny when it happened. Cop humor.

I'm not a big fan of meetings since nothing rarely gets accomplished. But my purpose of this *particular* meeting is to tell my group of misfits that I love them and appreciate their hard work.

The group assembles in our sequestered space and I begin, "So far so good. You guys have kicked some terrorist ass. We saved lives in Minneapolis, input 2747 STOP and DETAIN entries into our port of entry computers, and to date, 1777 individuals with terrorist ties have been *denied* entry." I pause and notice I have their full attention.

"No telling how many of those terrorists would have done harm to our loved ones if not for you, in this room. The mosque policy is under review and we made a deep cut into the ISIS treasury by the bank bombing. Gwen scored the XKeyscore which allows us to follow encrypted messaging and thus prevent *more* jihad Johns from killing. I just wanted to take a few minutes and thank you."

Agent 36 interrupts with, "You done with the pep rally? All we need is a campfire, guitar, and the words to 'Kumbaya.' "

Everyone laughs and I understand that this particular group of nonconformists doesn't require backslapping or 'Attaboys.' They'd rather have free food and trips to Cairo.

Jun fills in the awkward silence with, "John, thank you for your kind words, but we are *very* busy so although Confucius never said this, he *should* have." A pause then, *'Half the time, men think they are talking business, but, they are actually **wasting time**.'* "

We all laugh and I agree with, "Touché my Chinese friend. What's up with the BITCOINS and terrorist funders?"

"An interesting phenomena. A few years ago, a hospital paid a $50,000 ransom in BITCOINS to hackers who infiltrated and disabled its computer network. The hospital was rendered unsafe since it was totally dependent on the net."

"I remember that," Gia adds. "It was the Hollywood Presbyterian Medical Center. I was in the private financial sector at the time so I'm somewhat familiar with BITCOINS. Basically, it's an online currency that's hard to trace. It's become the preferred way for ISIS to collect ransoms."

Jun picks up the narrative. "Almost *impossible* to trace but there is a tool called *Block Chain*, which can track any transactions."

"You lost me Jun," I say. "I had to steal the white-collar exam at New Agent Training."

Jun explains, "I simply add the bit coin address to the search field at *blockchain.info* and use a program developed in my native China and we'll be able to track any incoming transactions to that address."

"What's a block chain?"

"A block chain is a transaction database shared by all nodes participating in a system based on the BITCOINS protocol. A full copy of a currency's block chain contains every transaction *ever* executed in the currency. With this information, I can discover how much value belonged to each address at any point in history."

Gia has an MBA from a John Carroll University and seems fascinated by Jun's convoluted explanation of nodes and chains. She asks, "How can you do that?"

Jun says, "Because every block contains a hash of the previous block. This has the effect of creating a chain of blocks from the genesis block to the current block. Each block is guaranteed to come *after* the *previous* block chronologically because the previous block's hash would otherwise not be known. Each block is also computationally impractical to modify once it has been in the chain. For any block on the chain, there is only *one* path to the genesis block."

"You lost me at chains and whips." Tommy Shoulders chuckles.

I look at my cyber expert and ask. "Bottom line here Jun. Can you take ISIS's BITCOINS?"

"Yes."

"My final question. Can you wipe out the accounts of those individuals and corporations who fund ISIS?"

June locks eyes with me. "I may not be able to zero balance all those identified accounts, but I can put a severe hurt on ISIS bottom line."

By my beer math we originally had seven major goals which are now reduced to *four*. While I'm patting myself on the back Joe Razone is dispensing two naturally occurring toxins, nicotine and solanine, into the U.S. food supply.

CHAPTER 53

"We have top men working on it right now."
Raiders of the Lost Ark (1981)

Agent 36 is focused on Mr. Joseph Razone. There's something about him that creeps her out so she's made Joey her pet project. Currently, Gwen and Gia are staring at computer screens following postings of Garrett's encrypted group of 17. Jun programmed *all* 17 subject's transmissions on split screens which alternate every 60 seconds thus allowing task force members the ability to monitor conversational *snapshots*. If a particular asshole is talking jihad shit they're able to hit a computer key and focus on them. In addition, Jun has programmed certain *tripwire* words and phrases that automatically sound an alert.

Gwen tells Gia, "Razone's ranting about the meaning of jihad. According to Joey, the Koran describes Jihad as a system of checks and balances, that Allah set up to *'check one people by means of another.'* When one person or group transgresses their limits, and violates the rights of others, Muslims have the right and the *duty* to *'check'* them and bring them back into line."

"Code for beheadings and bombs," Gia offers.

"Joey's been chatting all day with several bin Laden wannabees, which is *not* a crime and not that unusual. It's also *not* a crime *nor* unusual to research toxins that could poison food supply." Gwen concludes, "This Guido is either a chemistry major at NYU or up to no good."

Gwen grabs one of Garrettt's 17 files who graduated from social media to encryption. She opens Razone's folder and reads aloud, "Joseph Anthony Razone is a 32-year-old white male, born in Brooklyn, NY. Went to Catholic school but it seems he had a falling out when the local priest refused to give last rites to his father because he wasn't a member of the parish."

"That's rude."

"Joey thought so and went to the rectory and beat up the priest. No charges were pressed but Joe switched teams and began his radicalization by turning to the prophet Mohammed. Six months later Joe began signing off every e-mail with the tagline, *'Jesus is not God but the slave of God.'* "

Gia comments, "Nothing too radical so far. Thousands of us get a case of disbelief with our religion and search for the perfect church. I know plenty of ex-Catholics who became unhappy with all the guilt and strict doctrine. They find some boutique church which practices everything from the occult to snake worship."

"I have a few of those friends," Gwen agrees. "But none of them recently went to Syria on a pilgrimage."

"Still nothing illegal," Gia observes, "But, there is *plenty* of circumstantial evidence. Is Joe mentioning any specific type of toxins?"

Gwen peers at the screen and says, "Yea but it don't make sense."

"Why?"

"I know that smoking is bad for your health but...." Gwen pauses and asks Gia to, "Google *nicotine* as a potential mass toxin."

Gia pecks away at her iPhone. She raises her eyebrows and hands the phone to Agent 36.

"Holy shit girl, I gotta find Booker." She pauses and adds solemnly that, "This asshole is getting ready to poison our food supply."

I am currently meeting with Bruce Gombar discussing what is known in government as *Administrative Matters*. They generally include time consuming trivial topics. In this case Bruce is complaining about my use of Peggy for task force matters. Bruce explains that, "Peggy is assigned to the JTTF and although I don't mind her typing an occasional report for *your group*, it seems that *your group* has been monopolizing her time."

The emphasis on "*your group*" is not lost on me. Bruce had a mini seizure when I initially stole Gwen, Tommy, Gia, and Sean on a case he knew nothing about. I decide on the honey instead of the bee and say, "You know Bruce, there's no reason I can't give you a brief on our case. I know it'll stay just between me and you."

Bruce leans in and says, "As the FBI supervisory agent of the Joint Terrorism Task Force, I *do* have a need to know." He pauses and leans in some more. "So what's this case?"

"Before I give you the brief, I want to resolve this entire Peggy thing."

"OK."

"Peggy's the best," I say. "And for this case, we *need* the best. So, give me Peggy full time and I'll get the Deputy Director to assign any other secretary in the entire Division."

Bruce gives my offer some serious consideration and mumbles, "*Any* secretary, *and* a case brief?"

"I promise."

"Well, that squad nine gal, I *think* her name is Wiseman, is a hard worker and well-organized."

I chuckle and say, "You mean *Marty the Chest* who recently went from a C cup to double Ds?"

Bruce laughs and admits, "I'd say that I hadn't noticed but that'd be a lie. Even Harvard men appreciate a good rack. Now what case are you working on?"

I lower my voice and ask, "Remember Area 51 in New Mexico?"

Bruce nods and says, "Roswell, New Mexico. Supposedly a space ship crashed and we have aliens stashed in government bunkers there.

But….," Bruce pauses as he connects the dots in his Ivy League brain. "That's *supposedly* all conjecture and urban myth."

I stand, lean over and whisper, "Well, it's not."

Bruce gives me a solemn nod and I exit stage left. Agent 36 grabs me and says, "I may have a lone wolf ready to go jihad."

"Talk to me, Gwendolyn."

Agent 36 gives the abbreviated version. I look at her and say, "We need to speak with Mo."

We head back to our office area and dial up Mo's extension at the Puzzle Palace. I stole SAC Williams' tarantula conference gadget when he was at lunch. I rationalized that I needed it more than him.

FBI Unit Chief Agent Mohammed Askari is in charge of the ISIS Unit at Headquarters. *Mo,* as he is known to our little group, had his finger severed by terrorists in Cairo rather than admit he was an undercover agent. That, my friend, took *major* gonads, and because of that valor we were able to eliminate a sleeper cell of terrorist who were destroying our nation. Fred and Ray Kopka rushed him to a Cairo hospital where he met trauma care nurse Anpu. They married a short time later, and moved to Virginia. Mo received the FBI's award for Valor, and was promoted to the puzzle palace.

I personally believe that a promotion to Headquarters is generally *not* a good thing because, unlike the military or police departments, once you reach the initial rung on the FBI supervisory ladder, you *never* work the field again. As in, NEVER.

Most people join the FBI to lay hands on bad guys, or for high speed pursuits, undercover work and busting down doors with your buds. No one joins the FBI for the repetitive thrill of initialing reports and attending meetings. But Mo, like Tony Dennis s, is one of those rare bosses who can make a difference sitting behind a desk. Mo embraced his role and became the acknowledged expert on ISIS within the intelligence world. Not bad for a nine-fingered guy born in Luxor Egypt.

"Hey Mo. It's Booker and Gwen."

"John and Gwen. How is my best man and Anpu's maid of honor?

Mo and Anpu were married in Parma, Ohio, at Chuck Peters' bar and grille. I had the honor to serve as the best man and Agent 36, as maid of honor. The sad part of the story is that Chuck, a former Marine chopper pilot, died of a brain aneurism 4 months ago. He medevac'd me in the initial Gulf War by landing in a hot Iraqi LZ, saving me from becoming camel fertilizer. It seems that all of the good guys have been dying lately.

"How's the hero of Cairo doing?" Gwen asks.

"Busy, Gwen, *very* busy. This ISIS unit is nonstop chaos. The problem is that nobody took ISIS serious *until* it was too late. The JV team my Egyptian butt!"

"Our previous President seemed to care more about global warming than global peace."

"Our priorities are backward," Mo agrees. "The Bureau *should* be nonpolitical but all our meetings end with someone asking, '*Now, can anyone see a political down side to our decision?*' "

"I know that Bill Garrettt's been keeping you updated on our case but we need to pick your brain on some *related* ISIS stuff."

"At your service John. I owe you my life *and* wife, *but*, you owe *me* a finger."

We laugh and Agent 36 asks, "One of our encrypted cases is researching poisoning our food supply. Any *specific* ISIS talk from their leaders on that topic?"

Mo pauses and finally says, "Don't tell me that they're *actually* planning it."

"Planning what?"

Mo explains. "During some special ops raids in Syria our military recovered terrorist manuals and documents. They found hundreds of pages of U.S. agricultural documents that had been translated into Arabic. A significant part of these training manuals is devoted to agricultural terrorism—specifically the destruction of crops, livestock, and food-processing operations. Many had explicit references and plans on the use of natural toxins as poisons. ISIS actually referred to the U.S. supermarket employee who deliberately contaminated ground beef with an insecticide containing nicotine."

Gwen says, "This is not good. Our guy specifically mentioned nicotine."

Mo continues with more bad news. "Lone wolf ISIS sympathizers intent on poisoning America's food supply are difficult to detect. The FDA feels that the public health impact of just *unintentionally* contaminated food cause 76 million illnesses, 325,000 hospitalizations, and 5,000 deaths from foodborne illness *annually* in the U.S."

I interrupt Mo and ask, "But our food distribution process is so spread out. Maybe they can hit an area or region but could they *significantly* reduce our food supply nationwide?"

"The short answer is, yes." Mo explains, "ISIS would have no problem obtaining toxins to launch an attack. The CDC's infectious disease experts have concluded that sabotage of food and water is the *easiest* means of biological or chemical attack. In addition, the CDC experts explain, the centralization of food production in the U.S. and the global distribution of food products give food a *unique susceptibility*. America has many points of vulnerability to sabotage in the food production and food distribution processes. We're talking well over 100 million Americans being affected."

"So." I conclude. "Unless we stop Mr. Razone, we're looking at a catastrophic event."

CHAPTER 54

"You cannot strengthen the weak by weakening the strong."
L.K. Samuels

I immediately call our New York office and speak with the Assistant Director, James Clastrom. Though we'd never *officially* met, AD Clastrom had me transferred from the Manhattan Detention Center to the federal Metropolitan Correctional Center. It was a foggy New York midnight when I stopped for a red light at 143rd and Lexington. I should add that at the time, I was deep under with the remnants of the Gambino's and heading back to my UC apartment. I had consumed one of those 13 course bent nose dinners in the back room of Carmines and my stomach was rumbling. Anyone living or visiting New York City is painfully aware that there's often no convenient place to piss or crap.

Some urban commando on controlled substance decided to carjack me. I had indigestion and since discussion didn't seem to be an option, I shot him twice in the knee. The NYPD arrested me and discovered I was a mob associate. It was a ticklish situation since the NYPD felt my claim of self-defense was a cover-up for a mob hit.

Clastrom knew I was operating in NYC and secured a court order transferring me to federal custody. Then nature took its course and I called my mob boss, who bailed me out. Just for the record, the Mafia consider black guys subhuman. Though I don't share that opinion, shooting some low life thug was considered a public service and greatly enhanced my *rep* with the Guidos.

"Mr. Clastrom, it's John Booker."

"You been arrested again?"

I *think* he is being facetious and say, "No sir. But I *do* need another favor."

I explain my food poisoning concern and request that Mr. Razone be placed under 24-hour surveillance. Clastrom listens patiently until I finish and asks, "Do you have an arrest or search warrant?"

"Not yet, but we're working on it."

"I suggest you do so quickly. We have 19 million people in this region and from what you're telling me, this homegrown terrorist can significantly reduce that number."

"Can you locate Razone in the meantime and keep an eye him?"

I provide some specifics to the AD and 95 minutes later Special Operations Group (SOG) is on site at Razone's apartment building in Brooklyn. *But* Joey is not at home.

I call Dr. John Goodrich at the FDA, which is the abbreviation for the Food and Drug Administration. We make some small talk and I say. "I'm looking into the lone wolf problem, specifically the feasibility of terrorist poisoning our food sources with toxins."

Goodrich's silence is my first clue that this may not be a surprise topic. He says, "That's possible." Another pause. "Do you have anything specific?"

This guy's either nervous or kin to Silent John. Since I'm on the clock I get to the point, "Dr. Goodrich, I need you to give me some straight talk. Can nicotine cause mass casualties if introduced at some point in the food chain?"

Goodrich suddenly becomes downright gabby. He explains that nicotine can be released into the air as fine powder or liquid aerosol spray. The spray allows the perpetrator to be in close proximity minus risk. Small quantities can contaminate an assortment of agricultural products and cause mass casualties."

"What products?"

"Fertilizer, the crops themselves, chicken feed, fisheries, food processing plants, and even cargo ships and containers. Anything from the dirt where crops are planted to the supermarkets that sell the finished product."

"If you were going to poison our food supply, where would *you* strike?"

Goodrich hesitates in thought and finally asks, "Somewhere with easy access, little security, but could do the most harm to the most people. Does your suspect have a scientific background?"

"I didn't say we had a suspect."

"An FBI agent wouldn't contact me for a scientific lecture on bioterrorism, perhaps a college student assigned a research paper."

"Well, hypothetically speaking, our suspect has no scientific expertise, but he is adept at computer research."

"Then I'd concentrate on food processing or manufacturing plants."

"Why food processing?"

"The food processing and manufacturing world have tremendous employee turnover. Working conditions are poor so owners hire transient workers and do not conduct background checks." Goodrich pauses and adds, "And, there are hundreds of large food processing plants in New York State."

"What exactly is a food processing plant?"

"Food processing is the transformation of raw ingredients into food. You take raw food ingredients to produce marketable food products that can be easily prepared and served by the consumer. The processing involves activities such as mincing and macerating, liquefaction, emulsification, and cooking. Then options such as boiling, broiling, frying, or grilling. So." Goodrich concludes. "It would be *extremely* easy to introduce a chemical agent into the process."

"How would we *hypothetically* know that someone's been nicotine poisoned?"

"At one time, nicotine was used in the United States as an insecticide and fumigant; however, it is no longer produced or used in this country for this purpose. Nicotine affects the nervous system and the heart. Exposure to relatively small amounts can rapidly be fatal."

"Thanks Doctor. Anything else I should know?"

"Yes. We always knew that this day would come."

"It hasn't come *yet*."

Besides being blessed with wonderful mammary glands, Agent 36 also finished first in her law class at Yale. I ask, "Do we have enough for a search warrant on Razone's home?"

"We do, but *only* if we include our illegal encrypted intercepts. Our *legal* PC is limited to Razone's ramblings on social media, his conversion to Islam, and trip to Syria. That's very thin unless we can tie it into the nicotine thing."

"But he didn't start researching and discussing nicotine until he went encrypted."

"So." Agent 36 concludes. "We can either commit perjury on an affidavit stating Razone discussed nicotine on open social media or do it the hard way."

"You'll look good in prison orange."

"Not my best color, but I can make it work."

"We run a real risk if we claim the nicotine intercept on public sites. Because if Razone goes to trial we'll have to produce those exerts. Plus, his attorney can verify that his client did *not* mention nicotine on the public sites by simply doing a past check. Then *all* of our evidence is tainted."

My cell phone chirps and caller ID indicates my Mexican squeeze. We hadn't spoken since her big toe was in my mouth. She says, "Well how's my Mariachi Man?"

"Was I bad?"

"You were great, John. Inhibitions are overrated."

We laugh and she says, "Although this is an *official* call, I do want to thank you for a memorable evening. We'll have to do it again."

"I agree. Perhaps an Italian theme. I do a mean Sinatra."

"Been giving this ISIS recruiting message some thought. The logical thing would be to covey the hardships that one would face from going lone wolf, but that actually has the *opposite* effect. I was stumped until I went to the Mall on Sunday."

"Where you passed the ISIS recruitment kiosk running a special on *message*."

"I was actually at *Macy's* and noticed some 14-year-olds acting out. They were being rude and some adults attempted to control them, but that only heightened their behavior. Then a few older kids came by and embarrassed the troublemakers, calling them *immature* and *uncool*. This worked like a charm so I suddenly realized that, it's *not* the message but the *messenger*."

"A blinding flash of the obvious," I observe. "Anything else?"

"Yes, individuals attracted to ISIS need an *alternative*. Getting back to our Marine Corps analogy, ask yourself the question, *if you couldn't join the Marines, what would have been your second choice to fulfill that need of adventure and belonging?*"

"That's great stuff Linda." I say. "Let me run something else by you. We're tracking a lone wolf who seems intent on poisoning our food supply. In your professional opinion, do all lone wolves have similar behavior traits?"

"Be more specific John."

"When I was under with the Italians, they had no problem whacking somebody, *but*, they had no desire to die while doing it. There were *no* guinea suicide bombers. But these truly radicalized lone wolves seem intent on going down with the ship. Explain to me that mind set."

"That could take a while."

"So just answer this *one* question. How could suicide be justified under the supposedly peaceful religion of Islam?"

"It *can't* be justified John, but your question is flawed."

"It's a very simple question." I counter.

"Suicide *is* against Islam, but martyrdom is *not*."

It takes a good 5 seconds to grasp her meaning. And then it suddenly makes sense.

"Thanks Linda. You've been a tremendous help in this case. I owe you big time and I plan to repay my debt." A *slight* sexual innuendo but I omit the more explicit mention of anything to do with *sucking toes* or *massage*.

She tells me that, "I'll hold you to it, John."

It's difficult to mentally switch gears, but I have Joe Razone on my mind and *he's* contemplating mass murder. I return to our Mush Room and gather the troops.

"OK," I begin, "Gwen, brief the group on Joseph Razone."

Agent 36 provides the case details including the Syria visit and the nicotine chats on encrypted sites. She plays the role of a prosecuting attorney making opening arguments. The consensus of the group is that we do *something*.

"The New York office has Razone's apartment under 24-hour surveillance but he's not home."

Gwen explains, "Razone makes his living as a day trader so he can work from anyplace as long as he has access to the internet. We'd discussed writing an affidavit for a search warrant to access his apartment *and* computer, but we'd have to include the nicotine stuff which we illegally obtained."

"We'd also have to appear before a New York magistrate or judge and that's one of the more liberal federal districts in America. We'd be tipping our hand to our New York agents and place them in a legal jackpot."

A frustrated Tommy Shoulders declares, "We need to get out of this fucking office and head to New York. I'm sprouting hives from claustrophobia."

"I agree," I say. "We leave tomorrow morning but timing is critical. If we approach Razone too *soon*, we'd be rolling the dice that he's in possession of evidence. But our one advantage is that he thinks he's electronically invisible." I pause and gather my thoughts. "Gia, I need you to find out who Razone's been gabbing with on the phone. Call Wayne Morris at New York Telecom."

"Who's Wayne Morris, and won't he ask me for a subpoena?"

"We don't have time for the snail pace of courts. Just tell Wayne that Booker says it's important." I add, "He's a retired cop but if he gives you any crap just remind him that I still have the photos of him with Porsche."

"The car?" Gia wonders.

"No, *the* stripper at the Crazy Horse." I sum up with, "Tommy, Gwen, and I will head to New York in the morning, Jun and Gia remain here and monitor Razone electronically. Gia, call me as soon as you get a copy of Razone's cell bill. Questions or comments?"

Tommy says, "Yea, a question. How do you get a jihadist woman pregnant?"

Gwen and Gia repeat, "Don't know, how *do* you get a jihadist woman pregnant?"

"Dress her up as a goat."

Jun chuckles and says, "Thomas, my dear friend, you are such a child."

I contact the FBI pilot and say. "Gas it up Bob."

"Where to this time. Uzbekistan or maybe Tibet?"

"The Big Apple."

"That's so beneath you Booker, first Minnesota and now New York, very uninspired locations."

"You need to work on your banter Dupuis. See you in the AM at Burke Lakefront."

I spend the remainder of the day attending to details. The framers of our Constitution were pretty adamant about *due process*. This means that the government can't just snatch you up or search your home minus probable cause. Sometimes even those guys got it wrong.

It's about 6 PM when Jun says, "John, come look at this."

Jun seems excited which is not her usual placid demeanor. She says, "May have found a way to further defund ISIS."

I laugh and say, "*Defund* is a nice word for *stealing, pilfering, embezzlement,* and *larceny.*"

Jun counters with, "Stolen oranges *also* have Vitamin C."

"Very Zen, Jun."

Jun points to her computer screen and explains that, "The Arab world is playing a dirty double game. Nations like Saudi Arabia, Qatar, Dubai, Egypt, and especially Kuwait claim to oppose ISIS, but turn their head when rich patrons provide money to fund terrorist activities."

"Double dealing rug heads."

"America cannot understand this dichotomy in the Muslim mind."

"So are you saying that *all* of America's allies in the Mideast are actually our enemies?"

Jun clarifies with, "Israel is our *only* true friend. The remainder of the Arab world view America as a necessary evil, a dense rich giant who can be manipulated. They actually desire our annihilation."

"So how can we cut off ISIS from their money?"

"ISIS is rapidly expanding, but that's a double-edged sword because they have increased costs. This makes them vulnerable because if we can cut ISIS off from their financiers, it is similar to cutting off the blood supply to the brain." Jun pauses. "I've identified three key terrorist financiers, including 'Abd al-Rahman, Khalaf 'Ubayd, and Juday' al-'Anizi."

Jun sips from her hot tea and continues. "Rahaman is the individual who helped ISIS transfer funds from Kuwait to Syria and has helped pay for foreign fighters traveling from Syria to Iraq. Significantly undermining ISIS's financial base would require rolling back the group's access to local Syrian and Iraqi income sources. Israel has attempted to interrupt the flow of funds from reaching ISIS, but have had little success. To ensure that their contributions actually reach Syria, Saudi donors are encouraged to send their money to Kuwait, long considered one of the most permissive terrorism financing environments in the Persian Gulf."

"Bottom line here, Jun. What can you do?"

"I'd been looking at this problem backward by attempting to identify the various electronic transfers going *into* ISIS. That was proving difficult so it struck me that ISIS has three main sources of money. They steal it from banks when they capture cities, they accept it from sympathetic financiers, or they collect it in BITCOINS in extortion or kidnapping payoffs."

"Well we blew up their bank, you figured out the BITCOINS puzzle and that leaves the large donations from sympathizers."

"I believe that I solved this third puzzle on dealing with these financiers. When tracing the funds at their origin proved difficult, I realized that it is far easier to start with the electronic monies *already* transferred into their account. I simply identify the routing and account numbers *after* they are deposited into ISIS accounts and work back."

"Let me see if I got this straight. Bad guys transfer money into several or many accounts used by ISIS. You already identified these ISIS accounts. But even if you zero out the *ISIS* accounts it's only temporary because the sympathizers will just keep sending more money."

"Correct. It's similar to putting air into a tire with a slow leak. I can remove the air from the tire but if someone is continually pumping new air, then the car continues to travel."

"I get it. So whatta we do?"

"For starters, I've identified 43 foreign bank accounts of individuals *and* corporations identified as funding ISIS activities."

"Are these corporations *total* ISIS fronts or do they serve any legitimate purpose?"

"All are *for profit* lawful enterprises engaged in products or service like electronics, petroleum, or import/export, and *all* have a deep-seated hatred of the United States. The irony is that most of these business owners conduct commerce with America."

"How much of a financial hurt can you put on these ISIS financiers?"

"Any international corporation maintains several accounts or subcorporations. So, although I can't *completely* bankrupt them, I *can* put their financial survival in question."

"What's the blowback? ISIS will naturally suspect the U.S. and they'll be a price to pay in official government inquiries and even counter cyber-attacks on American companies and individuals."

Jun Chuckles and informs me that, "Have you ever observed the shell game?"

"A sleight of hand with three inverted cups. I've lost a few bucks in New York trying to find the pea."

"Well, think of the three cups as the U.S., Russia, and China and the pea as ISIS money."

"I got the visual."

"These three nations *alone* possess the expertise to launch a complex cyber-attack and all three would be *immediate* suspect if millions of ISIS dollars go missing."

"But wouldn't that cause some heartburn for our government?"

"Russia and China are our adversaries and they, as well as the U.S., will deny any involvement. These denials will be met with suspicion by the *other* two nations, and all *three* countries will be pointing fingers at each other. But *I* can point an electronic finger of guilt by inserting a trace portal leading back to my native China. This portal will indicate that they are the guilty party."

"Why China?"

"It is my retribution for their falsely accusing my parents of treason, seizing our property, and killing my mother and father."

Her words move me, so my emotional response is raw, "Go for it Jun..... *fuck* them Chinks." I understand that this is not the most sensitive comeback given Jun's Chinese ethnicity.

But Jun actually smiles and tells me, "You have been spending too much time with Thomas."

CHAPTER 55

"Oooh! Somebody stop me!"
The Mask (1994)

As we board the Bu plane at Burke Lakefront airport, Joe Razone is parking at the Amalgamated Food Processing plant in upstate Albany, New York. He has been dumping toxic amounts of nicotine into tons of food for the past 4 days.

An hour or so later, Silent John Canley touches down at Kennedy where we are met by the NY JTTF supervisor. Special Agent Joe Pistoli is a former HRT (Hostage Rescue Team) guy. The FBI's HRT is our super SWAT team comprised of our best jocks. They can run, shoot, rappel, and Bruce Lee karate your ass if need be.

"Welcome *back* to New York," Pistoli says. A reference to my undercover days in NY.

"Well at least I don't have to say *fugettabouttit* after each sentence."

Joe laughs and says, "I heard that Chicken Shit Walt did you in."

"You heard right. Walt lacks both a sense of humor *and* a pair of balls."

"I also heard that Chicken Shit got those balls handed to him at some Congressional hearing."

"Poetic justice, Joe."

"We're still looking for Mr. Razone. Hasn't been home or at his usual haunts."

"Did you get that list of possible targets?"

"You asked for agro-terrorist targets in the New York area involving the *entire* food chain. That includes facilities of bulk storage of raw food materials, warehouses storing related items like condiments, lard, butter, preservatives, salt, pepper, etc., and food product facilities where *secondary* ingredients are kept for later use. There are also dairy plants where lots of milk are stored in vats and industrial scale bakery warehouses where ingredients like flour, yeast, etc. are stored. Then a few miles north of the city we have crops, livestock, fertilizer, and dirt." Williams pauses and concludes with, "So, the *short* answer is, that New York is a target rich environment for food-related terrorism."

I smile and say, "Good job Joe, but it appears we're not able to concentrate on any *one* site."

"I have SOG doing a 24 at Razone's apartment and we've done some ruse interaction with his neighbors posing as salesmen or old acquaintances. Appears that Joe is a pleasant guy who keeps to himself. One female did say that he was a flirt."

"*All* Italians are flirts," I say. "Did anyone talk about Razone spouting radical Muslim shit?"

"Nothing."

"Let's head to Razone's apartment."

Joseph Razone resides in a fifteen-story apartment building in Bedford-Stuyvesant. It used to be a seedy area but is in the process of gentrification. As we approach the neighborhood, Pistoli cues his mic and announces, "JT 1 inbound, any changes?"

The radio crackles with a female voice, "Same, same JT1."

Gwen and Tommy sit in the back seat of the Bu car and have been relatively quiet. I tell Pistoli that, "Gwen and I will take a look see at Razone's apartment. Maybe bump into someone who can shed some light. Tommy, I want you to standby on your cell in case I need you."

Pistoli makes a mild protest. "Do you really want to heat up Razone's floor?"

Of course, Pistoli is right because many a case has been blown by being too aggressive on surveillances. If you 'hinky' up the target, they often disappear. But I say, "Gwen is an expert at extracting information from males. I get to play her dimwitted boyfriend."

It sounded like bullshit because it *was*. We exit the car 2 blocks from the apartment building. Gwen grabs my arm and says, "I've been playing your girlfriend for a few years now. We're wearing this thin because people are *never* going to believe that someone as classy and gorgeous as moue' would date some Neanderthal like you."

"Normally, you'd be right, but one look at you and they'll just assume you're some low-price hooker with a silicone chest, and I'm a rich successful philanderer."

Her punch in my ribs is *not* very playful. Just as we're about to enter the building, I remind Gwen that, "*Last* time we entered an apartment building arm in arm, we shot a terrorist who was on his way *out*."

Gwen sighs and says, "Ah, the fond memories of past dates. You are *sooo* romantic Booker."

Razone's lair is on the 7th floor and as we stand at the elevator Gwen says, "I got a feeling that we're not searching for unsuspecting folks to play *where's Joey?*"

"Of course not. We're going to bag his apartment."

Dirty little FBI secret. Gwen and I would *not* be the first two FBI agents to illegally search a domicile. This *frowned upon* investigative technique is normally used to gather intelligence, since it can't be used to gather evidence. I tell Agent 36 that, "You and I will make sure the apartment is empty, then I'll MacGyver our way inside."

A year or two after I joined the Bureau, I attended the '*pick and lock*' in-service at the FBI Academy. I finished first in my class having apprenticed in South Philly as a teenager. The elevator in the old building is both slow and jerky, which is *never* a good combination. The car lacks an inspection sticker validating the safety of this metal coffin. We exit the elevator, having to step *up* a good 6 inches, into a musty, empty hallway. There is a pungent smell of ethnic cooking emanating from a nearby apartment. I motion Gwen to rap on Razone's door. We wait a good minute and I rap a little louder. Still nothing so I extract my little burglary kit and tell Gwen. "Give me a heads up if we get some hallway visitors."

Razone's door has a pin tumbler lock consisting of a cylinder called a plug inside a housing called a shell. I recall this particular lock from my FBI training because it's one of the easier locks to pick. To defeat this lock, I'll have to employ a basic single pin-picking technique or SPP. I insert my pick and finagle for a few minutes before I hear a click. "We're in."

Agent 36 comments, "You *never* cease to amaze me Booker, next you'll be telling me that you play the violin."

"Actually a harmonica, but not very well, *and* only when drunk."

The apartment is surprisingly neat and well decorated in early Italian motif, which includes lots of wrought iron, large gaudy chandeliers, and even a pissing statue. It's a one bedroom place consisting of a combined kitchen, living area and breakfast nook in addition to the bedroom and full bath. "You bag the bedroom," I tell Gwen.

"My favorite room."

Searching is a science. Usually when someone loses their keys inside their home, they conduct a *scattered* search. They'll flitter from room to room often returning to an already searched room. Most of the time, they'll search only part of a room. It's best to separate the space into grids and search each inch of each grid. I begin in the living area, searching chairs, cushions, underneath any object like tables, floor lamps, and testing objects for hidden compartments. Moving on to the breakfast nook and then to a hallway closet, I check the waste baskets, underneath the sink, draperies, and windows. I'm also looking for any related clues such as reading material, notes, computers, and flash drives. Twenty minutes have elapsed since we entered and I can hear the clock ticking in my mind. Gwen reappears and says, "Nothing except some porn stashed underneath his bed."

"I keep saying, he's *Italian*. But if he's a day trader then he needs a computer and why the hell is he out of pocket."

Gwen says, "Maybe he's just on a trip, holiday, or visiting family. That'd explain why there's no computer at the apartment. He can work anywhere."

I nod at her logic and say, "Help me search the kitchen."

Gwen pilfers the cabinets removing dishes, bowls, and coffee cups and proceeds to the silverware drawer. I open the refrigerator and notice some Tiramisu covered by a clear plastic dome. The Italian pastry is a personal weakness so I'm seriously tempted to help myself. Then I notice that next to the Tiramisu is a can of PAM, which is a spray used to prevent food from sticking to pots and pans. Lorri uses PAM at home, but never refrigerates the can so I scan the ingredients which include: Canola, palm and coconut oils, wheat, flour, silicon dioxide, artificial flavor, soy wheat and a propellant. It seems to contain enough food products to justify refrigeration so I place the PAM back and check the freezer, and behind and under the refrigerator. Gwen finishes about the same time and she says, "Nada."

I'm both disappointed and pissed. "Let's get out of here." I say.

We stand in front of the refrigerator and Gwen asks, "Does Joey have anything good to eat?

"A good assortment of Salami, Cappicola, and Prosciutto and some Tiramisu sitting next to a can of PAM." I pause and ask Gwen. "Do you refrigerate your PAM?"

"I actually do. Read somewhere where refrigeration prolongs the life of the ingredients."

"Joey must've read the same article."

As we start for the door, Agent 36 adds, "The cold is also supposed to help direct the aerosol spray."

I take three steps and say, "Can you repeat that?"

"The article said that refrigerating the PAM aids in controlling the aerosol spray to provide an even coating."

It hits me like a ton of bricks on the forehead. Just yesterday, Dr. Goodrich from the FDA explained how nicotine can be dispersed to poison the food supply. He said that, *'Nicotine can be released into the air as fine powder or liquid aerosol spray. Even small quantities can contaminate an assortment of agricultural products and cause mass casualties.'*

I grab the can of PAM and am tempted to spray some in the toilet. My convoluted logic is that if it *is* Nicotine the water will somehow negate the effects. Gwen reads my mind and says, "Don't even think about it."

Common sense prevails and I place the PAM in a large plastic zip lock bag. As we are about to leave I feel some hunger pangs and pilfer Joey's fridge of the Salami *and* the remains of the Tiramisu. It's probably going to be awhile before we can eat.

CHAPTER 56

"He slimed me."

Ghostbusters (1984)

Agent 36 and I muster back with Pistoli and Tommy. Gwen has the PAM hidden inside her bag, which in addition to the usual female fare also contains two guns, bullets, a handi-talkie, and possibly a rocket propelled grenade. I really don't want to know.

We provide a sanitized version of our visit. "Spoke with three people," I lie. "Two didn't know Joey and the third one hadn't seen him recently."

Pistoli raises his eyebrows and says, "Didn't know you'd be gone that long. Was getting worried about you guys."

I recognize a facetious remark when I hear one but don't currently have a believable comeback so I say, "Thanks for your concern." I'd muted my cell phone and realize that it's now vibrating non-stop in my pocket. Caller ID indicates that Dr. Goodrich desires a conversation. Since I was going to contact Goodrich anyway this seems like a good time to chat.

"Agent Booker, are you busy?"

"Just doing some food shopping. What's up?"

"We've been tracking symptoms which are very disturbing given our recent conversation."

"Nicotine poisoning?"

"Yes. Seems like we've had a rash of unexplained heart and nervous system disorders like MS, CVA, epilepsy, and aphasia."

"I got the MS, epilepsy, and heart problems but what's CVS and aphasia?"

"It's *CVA*," Goodrich corrects. "But the short answer is CVA is similar to a stroke, and aphasia, a loss of speech."

"Why is this unusual?"

"The CDC monitors statistical data comparing norms for every identifiable disease or malady. When a certain disorder or disease spikes, then they look for reasons. There have been many examples of this such as the recent case of water contamination in Flint Michigan, but one of the more publicized cases involved the activist Erin Brockovich."

"I saw the movie."

"Yes, it occurred in Le Roy, New York, when a toxic spill caused water and ground contamination. This triggered symptoms of facial tics and verbal outbursts among teenagers. Doctors could not determine the cause of the mysterious illness which effected the nervous system until Brockovich sued the chemical plant and produced hard data."

"So what are your saying, Doctor Goodrich?"

"We tested some of the affected patients and there were trace amounts of nicotine in their system."

"Is there a region or specific area in the country in which these cases are isolated?"

"Yes and that's the strange thing. It's within a two-hundred-mile radius of LeRoy New York."

"I'm not familiar with LeRoy, where is it located?"

"Just outside Albany."

"How many people have been affected and are there any deaths?"

"Our best numbers indicate 247 affected with strokes, heart attacks, and the beginning symptoms of speech loss. So far eight, mostly elderly people, have passed with heart-related issues, all of whom tested positive for nicotine poisoning."

"Have you identified patterns of the patients, such as attending an event, common water source, eating at a chain restaurant like that Chipotle E. coli outbreak?"

"No but the CDC is checking food, water, or other ingested commodities now."

"I may have something for them to check," I say and choose my words carefully. "Look at food products originating in food processing or manufacturing plants."

"Will do. Anything else?"

"I'm sending a sample of possible nicotine contaminant to our FBI lab. I'll get back to you."

"If this is the beginning of an agro-terrorist act involving nicotine, then the death toll can reach epic numbers. But if you can discover the distribution source we may be able to minimize the casualties."

"How much time before we reach epic?" I wonder.

"Not much."

We say our goodbyes and promise to keep in touch.

I need some time to digest the latest developments and make a plan. I inform Williams, "Let's head to your office."

Gwen and I pile into the back seat of the Bucar. I report on my conversation with Goodrich and this triggers a lively conversation, which becomes white noise as my brain attempts to determine our knowns, unknowns and next move. We'll get the PAM tested for nicotine. A positive doesn't really change the game plan, since we can't use the evidence in a trial. But it'd be nice to confirm Razone's our man.

As far as any proactive plan, it consists of hoping that Razone shows at his apartment. But having him in pocket is only the beginning. According to Jun, Razone has gone quiet for the past few days. Nothing encrypted *or* non-encrypted.

Gia reported that Razone has one cell phone listed in his name, and has not *made* or received a call for the past 13 days. Gia and Jun are currently determining the subscriber data for every incoming or outgoing call over the past 12 months. Once they identify the callers, they'll run the names through every single data base in our law enforcement arsenal looking for callers with criminal records, terrorist ties, or any connection with chemicals. This may take the better part of the day. I sadly conclude that we don't have a *next move*. We are in a holding pattern *awaiting* Razone's *next* move.

But while we are awaiting Razone's next move, he is *not* waiting. Because twenty minutes ago Razone contaminated a shipment of packaged cookies, sugary breakfast cereals, and processed meats including *Salami*. The *only* good news in that scenario is that Razone *probably* wouldn't poison his own Salami, which is next to the Tiramisu.

We reach the New York office, which is located next to Little Italy and Chinatown. I had spent many a day eating pasta smothered in gravy, cheese, and accompanied with brazzoli, sausage, and meatballs. But that was during my undercover days and *before* Fat Tony was decomposing on a Staten Island land fill. I'll admit that I had a heads up on the hit but Tony was a piece of shit who deserved death. Chicken Shit Walt didn't agree and feigned righteous indignation that the FBI could have prevented a murder. Walt was further incensed when he heard my explanation of, *Yea, I knew he was gonna get whacked, but some people need to die.* Two weeks later Chicken Shit whacked *me* and I was banished to the Cleveland FBI office.

But Karma is a powerful equalizer and the gossip mill is betting that Walt will retire after his embarrassing testimony on the hill. Only a shallow person could bask in the revenge afterglow at the expense of a fellow agent, but I can't help myself. Walt's both a coward *and* a poor leader.

I decide to toss the Salami in the trash after my conversation with Dr. Goodrich. No chance tempting fate and besides, Joe Pistoli made a detour to Angelina's Deli. Angie is an elderly Sicilian lady who makes the best heros in New York City. Crusty bread, fresh meats and cheeses, and a combo of olive oil, mayonnaise, and mustard. We sit in the JTTF area with Nana's victuals spread around a table and discuss the case.

Gwen places the PAM canister inside an evidence envelope and then that packet within a larger manila envelope. She scrawls *'Special Agent Bob Dupuis'* in red ink on the outer envelope. One of the JTTF agents is dispatched to Kennedy with instructions to, "Give this *only* to Special Agent Bob Dupuis, do *not* make any stops, and do *not* open the envelope." I call Bob on his cell phone and alert him to expect a visitor. I conclude with, "Get the package to the FBI lab and make sure they know that its contents contain, *'Possible bio-terrorism contents – handle with care.'* "

"Then what?"

"Then get back to Kennedy and stand by. This case has a lot of moving parts."

As I am finishing up Angie's Salami Hero Gia calls. She says, "Wanted to give you an update. Razone was basically a loner but some of his more interesting outgoing calls involved two Muslim males listed in our Intel files as militant."

I interrupt Gia and wonder, "What's militant mean, any other specifics?"

I hear paper shuffling and she says, "Not much, the only notation is from an informant of *unknown* reliability who stated, that Mustaf and Ashid spout violence against infidels at the mosque. It's the same mosque that Joey attends. But there are two other calls that caught our attention. One call to a gun store in the Bronx and....I'm saving the best for last.....Two months ago there were two phone calls to the Amalgamated Food Processing plant in Albany, New York."

"Gia that's some outstanding work." I pause and ask, "Length of calls?"

"What?"

"How long did Razone stay on the phone each time?"

Gia checks her notes and says, "The first call lasted 11 minutes and three weeks later, 77 minutes. Why?"

"That last call was probably a telephone job interview. I want you to call Amalgamated, demand to speak with the plant manager. No one else and find out if Razone is an employee."

"Wow, that's a great pick up. I'll get on it and call you right back."

I brief the group on the gun and Amalgamated Food Plant in Albany. "My money is that Joey Razone's first call to Amalgamated was a request for a job application, he filled it out, send it back, and the second call was his phone interview. According to Dr. Goodrich of the FDA, these food processing facilities will hire anyone."

Agent 36 points a finger at me and says, "Didn't you *also* say that Dr. Goodrich told you that the nicotine cases were isolated in and around the Albany area?"

I look at Joe Pistoli and ask, "How long will it take to get to Albany with lights and sirens?"

CHAPTER 57

"Leave the PAM and take the cannoli."
John Booker

The answer is 225 miles but in New York one measures travel not in distance but in time. Emergency lights and sirens have little effect on New Yorkers so it takes an hour just to clear the congestion. Joe calls ahead and has New York state troopers clearing the road ahead. Normally the trip would take 3 ½ hours but we actually make it in 3. I'm tempted to contact the local police and have them charge into Amalgamated and snatch Razone but there's too many land mines in that scenario. So, I have Tony Daniels contact the owner of Amalgamated with a request to stop *all* shipments. I stress that the owner not alert anyone at the plant *why* shipping is suspended, but it is imperative that it immediately ceases.

We are leading a four-car caravan of agents and put on notice officials from the EPA, Homeland Security, FDA, and EMT. Pistoli, Shoulders, Gwen, and I are in the lead car and Tommy asks, "What's the plan?"

'Good question' I think and since we're in mixed company I give the party line, "Grab the plant manager, have him point us to Razone and give him a chance to surrender."

Tommy sarcastically offers, "So we can't just shoot him?"

"We can," Gwen says seriously. "According to the Geneva Convention, residents from Brooklyn are considered foreign nationals and can be shot on sight."

Pistoli laughs and says, "OK, I know when I'm being screwed with."

"This is not as complicated as the Mall of America," I reason. "Razone has already poisoned his last victim. The only wildcard I see is if he's armed and wants to take one for Allah."

Tommy adds, "I can only hope he does."

My caller ID indicates Gia so I interrupt our take down discussion. She confirms what my gut has been screaming and says, "Joseph Razone has been an Amalgamated employee for 2 months."

I thank Gia and she signs off with, "Good Hunting."

"Gia confirms Razone is an employee and wishes us *good hunting,*" I brief the group.

Gwen chuckles. "I do believe that our little Gia has come over to the dark side."

"So we grab the plant manager, and have him identify Razone, then bum rush him," Tommy confirms.

Pistoli offers, "How about if we have the manager call him to the office, then we'd have him in a contained area."

Tommy disagrees, "May make him suspicious and he might go postal *before* he gets there."

"We have to assume *two* things," I begin. "One, that he is armed with a traditional weapon, and two, that he is armed with a bio-terror weapon. Our goal is to isolate him and prevent him from using either one."

Gwen says, "I think it's safe to assume that the management is not aware that Razone is contaminating their food. So, we confide in the plant manager to gather Intel on the plant, Razone's work area, proximity to other employees, will strangers strolling the area cause suspicion, and so on."

"And it's also possible Razone may have some ISIS sympathizers on the floor with him, so we confide in management *only*. When we get ten minutes from the target, we cut off the lights, sirens, and have the agents behind us peel off. Have them stage at a nearby location and wait." I ask, "Agreed?"

Pistoli nods and says, "Agreed. We don't want to give Razone any advanced warning."

"Ok," I continue. "The four of us enter the plant and proceed to the office. No visible badges, guns, or raid jackets. We ID ourselves only to the manager and inform him that we have an arrest warrant for Joseph Razone. We stress that we don't wish to interrupt the plant's operation. Joe, you remain in the office, which will double as our command post. We'll communicate with you via cell phone and you can coordinate any action with the troops."

Pistoli doesn't seem happy to be excluded from the party but my strategy is three-fold. First off, any criminal with a guilty mind would become suspicious if approached by three white males with cop eyes at his workplace. Second, our small group has been operational in many tactical situations and we are simpatico. Third, we may do things that are not Bureau kosher. I continue with, "We'll ask that the manager take us on a *pretend* tour of the plant, which wouldn't seem that unusual. When we get to Razone's location on the floor, we ID ourselves and hope Razone surrenders."

I ask, "Anything else we need to consider?"

Gwen says, "I've been tracking this guy's conversation on the net, and he's the real deal."

"What's that mean, Gwen?"

"It means that Razone is *totally* radicalized. He not only studies the Quran; he *believes* every violent word. Brenda in Cleveland was a jihad hobbyist and Gus in Minnesota was an idiot loser. "But," Gwen pauses and turns toward me, "Joseph Razone will become a martyr for Allah in a New York second."

The onsite plant manager is Jake Beck. He's a beefy, red-faced guy who may be sampling the processed food. I show him my creds and explain our presence. I ask to see the personal file of Joseph Razone. There's a photo of Joey attached to his folder and I compare it with his New York State driving license photo. I've occasionally arrested the wrong person so I'm happy to see that the two Joeys match.

"Mr. Beck, we need your cooperation. It's strictly voluntary but I'd like you take us on a tour of the plant. Alert us when we're getting close to Razone's work station."

Beck says, "No problem. My cousin's a cop and I support law enforcement. I don't know what this Razone did, but I want him *out* of my plant."

Any take down is fraught with danger and unknowns. People are unpredictable and psychotic extremists are *extremely* unpredictable. They do not respect life whether it be yours *or* theirs.

I ask Mr. Beck, "You good with this?"

He nods and as we enter the industrial area of the facility Beck seems stiff. He walks robotically with his eyes locked forward. I say, "Be casual. It's a tour so just smile and point. Stop and speak with the employees and don't be in a hurry."

This seems to relax Beck a bit and I add, "When we get close to Razone's work station, say the words, *'This is one of our more critical areas.'* "

Beck repeats the words and we continue to meet and greet some employees along the way. Evidently, the plant is sizable because we're fifteen minutes into the sham tour before Beck points and utters, "Up ahead is one of our more critical areas of the facility."

The space is the size and shape of a football end zone. It has four large metal cylinders, approximately 10 feet high and 8 feet wide, all connected by some assembly type belt. It unfortunately provides excellent cover and concealment.

I notice Joey Razone immediately. He has the typical Italian physical traits of large nose and black curly hair, overflowing from his hard hat. He stands a solid 5'11" and must be into some serious weightlifting. His back is turned toward us and he seems busy with some task involving a large metal vat. A female worker stands next to him and they are engaged in conversation. Beck's eyes get that look of a deer just before the semi-truck strikes and I say, "You're doing great. Nod if Razone is the guy next to that female worker forty yards to our left."

Beck nods and I say, "Just keep talking and head in that direction."

We're about twenty yards from Razone when the female worker notices us and turns her head. Razone follows her eyes and turns in our direction. I notice that the female is smiling but Razone is *deciding*. I've seen that look a few times from fugitives who are deciding whether to run or shoot. Presently, Joey is determining the threat level: friend or foe, fight or flight, butter or margarine.

Mr. Beck's body language is not good and Joey can smell his fear. It is time to *shit or get off the pot*, as my cop father would counsel me. I reach for my 9MM, but Joey is one step ahead and grabs the female worker by her neck. I later learn that the hostage is Lois Dutchman from nearby Poughkeepsie. I observe two actions that occur almost simultaneously. Jake Beck retreats backward in the direction of his office and Joseph Razone has a 9MM pistol aimed at Ms. Dutchman's head.

Shoulders, Gwen, and I have our weapons drawn and using our command voices say, "Drop the gun Razone!" or in Tommy's case, "Drop the *fucking* gun you *fucking* cocksucker!" It's a cop thing.

I can read Shoulders's mind. He wants a clear head shot and is shuffling his feet in order to minimize hitting the hostage, who Razone uses as a shield. Joey notices Tommy's dance and rams the muzzle of his pistol into Lois's temple. She shrieks and I turn to Tommy. "Don't," I say.

The Cleveland cop gives me a nasty look but stops his ChaCha. It's not that I have an alternative plan but I'm *hoping* one will eventually present itself pronto. My gut says that Joey *won't* commit suicide by cop so I'm feeling a surrender.

"Mr. Razone," I say in a civil tone. "We're with the Federal Bureau of Investigation and all we want to do is *talk*. Don't do something you can't undo."

Just for the record we law enforcement officers lie all the time. Razone has *already* murdered eight elderly people with his nicotine poison, which he can *never* undo. A civil conversation at this moment seems *farfetched*. Perhaps *after* Joey's in handcuffs.

Razone's comeback to my *'just talk'* bull is straight from the Quran (8:12), *"I will cast terror into the hearts of those who disbelieve. Strike off their heads and strike off every fingertip of them."*

Gwen whispers, "Doesn't seem he's about to surrender, Booker. And, I just had my nails done."

Razone quoting the Quran seems strange coming from the lips of some Brooklyn Guido. I'm still leaning toward him surrendering, but the hostage has become a wild card in what would have been a fairly simple shootout. My brain ticks off options. Joey's finished poisoning people, so our immediate concern is saving the life of Lois Dutchman. Realizing that this Mexican standoff cannot last indefinitely, I make a decision. I whip out my University of Google degree in Psychology and channel Dr. Phil.

"Mr. Razone, we're going to leave now. We understand that you have strong religious beliefs and we at the FBI recognize and support *all* faiths. We wish you *As-salamu alaykum*. Peace be upon you. We'll let you get back to your job."

My retreat approach seems to temporarily confuse Joey because he's worked himself up into a confrontational frenzy. But I've been to this rodeo before and seen a hundred Joeys acting tough on the street. I'm betting that he's just some wannabee punk from Brooklyn who views ISIS as the latest social fad no different than Occupy Wall Street or Hari Krishna. When push comes to shove, Joey won't die for some foreign ideal anymore than he'd die for his Flatbush softball team. I also doubt he'd kill Lois Dutchman from Poughkeepsie. It's one thing to be three steps removed from your faceless victims by poisoning them, but quite another to look that person in the eye. My strategy is to deny Razone an audience in this ISIS Shakespearean saga. I realize that I'm betting with someone else's money, but at this moment in time, it seems like our best bet.

I turn to leave but both Gwen and Tommy remain rigid in their shooting stance. "Let's go," I say in a conversational tone.

Agent 36 hisses, "Not funny Booker!"

Razone screams another exert from the Quran (2:207), "*And there is the type of man who gives his life to earn the pleasure of Allah...*" He pauses, locks eyes with me, and says in a conversational tone. "And, I am *that* man."

The tone of his voice send chills down my spine. I think, '*This guy ain't fucking around,*' and I suddenly remember two recent conversations with Gwen and Dr. Linda.

Agent 36 cautioned me before entering the plant that, '*Joseph Razone will become a martyr for Allah in a New York second.*'

And just an hour before, Dr. Linda warned, '*Suicide is against Islam. But martyrdom is not.*'

This subtle difference in distinguishing between suicide and martyrdom forces me to reassess my tactical position. Joey is prepared to die at this very moment. Jihad is not just some passing fancy to be outgrown and as Gwen said, "Razone's the *real* deal."

Lois Dutchman's body is rigid with terror, so I'm not expecting her to join the party as an active participant. Our options have *narrowed*. I acquire site alignment on Joey's head with my 9MM Glock but Joey's no dope. He shuffles his feet which in turn makes Lois much more of a target than Razone.

While I'm contemplating options Razone forces the action. He demands, "You will drop your weapons now."

"Not an option Joey," I reply.

Razone calmly points his 45 caliber at Lois Dutchhamn's foot and pulls the trigger. My first reaction is that the powerful weapon is loud followed by the thought, *"I really didn't think he'd do that."*

Lois screams and slumps but Razone maintains his human shield in a powerful chokehold using his massive arms. He smacks her head with the side of his pistol and says, "Shut up or I'll blow your brains out."

Dutchman simmers down to some intermittent sobs and Joey repeats, "You will drop your weapons *now.*"

It's decision time and our options have narrowed. We can drop our weapons, continue the Mexican standoff, or start shooting. Option one will probably result in our *own* deaths, option two accomplishes little, and option 3 guarantees Dutchman's death. I decide on the head shot, concluding it's become our best and last option. I tell Joey, "OK, we'll drop our weapons, but I'd like your word as a devout Muslim that you won't kill anyone."

Since many Muslims are degenerate liars I'm not shocked when Razone says, "You have my word."

I turn toward Gwen and Tommy, "OK, he's given us his word and *I* believe him."

Tommy and Gwen know me well enough to know that I don't believe *anyone* let alone some Italian jihadist from Brooklyn. This is their signal that what I say next will be some type of message. I say, "We're going to drop our weapons and I'll go first. Then Tommy, and finally Gwen. I don't want *any* tricks or *head* games. I look at Gwen and emphasize, "Especially from you Gwen, No *head* games."

Agent 36 give me a smile that alerts me that she's on board. It's the same impish smile she beamed in Cairo just before strangling the 300-pound imam to death. She says, "OK, no *head* games."

I slowly place my weapon on the concrete floor and look at Tommy, "Now you, Tommy."

My overall strategy is threefold. Muslim men consider women inferior and a step above camel shit. Therefore, Gwen presents the *least* threat to Razone. Second, by dropping our guns one at a time, Joey's attention will be on the person in the act of placing their weapon on the floor, and third, Agent 36 is our best marksman. She routinely qualifies as expert with every weapon in our arsenal.

Although Tommy understands the plan he hesitates and seems unable to move. I realize that Cleveland Detective Tommy Shoulders surrendering his weapon to this punk goes against every molecule in his body. So, I add, "Do it, Tommy!"

Tommy makes an exaggerated movement by raising his gun hand into the air. He bends at the waist and slowly, ever so slowly, places his weapon on the floor. Tommy loudly curses at Razone to further deflect his attention from Gwen. And as Tommy's 38 Smith and Wesson touches the concrete a loud retort startles everyone. I grab my pistol and glance at Razone. He is slumped over but still standing and *still* grasping his weapon. Lois has fallen to the ground and begins sobbing.

I run toward Razone and notice blood pouring from the right side of his head. We make eye contact and he is once again in a decision mode. Since I now understand the ROEs (Rules of Engagement) and know Joey will take one for Allah, I shoot him in his gun hand. I step next to him, kick him in the mouth, and take his gun. He spits out several teeth and glares my way. I say, "Sorry, I got carried away. My bad."

Gwen grabs Lois and places pressure on her wound. Tommy joins me and points his revolver at Razone's temple. It's fortunate for Razone that I'm present since Shoulders placed 38 slugs into the temple of three Cairo terrorists. I pat Shoulders back and say, 'Not now, Tommy."

I contact Pistoli and say, "Get the EMTs to the office ASAP, we have some wounded. We also need to evacuate this entire building and seal it off. Interview every employee to make sure they're not a Razone sympathizer. Then we'll need some chemist from Homeland Security to deal with the nicotine. Amalgamated needs to conduct a nationwide alert and recall all their products. Get them off the supermarket shelves, vending machines, and any other place they distribute."

"Got it."

I make a half-hearted attempt to stop Razone's bleeding and ask Tommy to search the immediate area for any more weapons or evidence. Joey's awake and lucid. The head wound is deep but a graze. I find some greasy rags from a nearby counter and tie them tightly around the two wounds to stem the blood.

"You doing OK?" I ask with little sincerity.

Joey actually spits at me as I'm tying the knot on the bandage. "That wasn't nice," I say and then break his nose with my fist. "Oops, sorry Joe. My bad, again."

Tommy returns and in his hand is a can of PAM. "You're shitting me."

I take the can of PAM and kneel next to Razone. "We need you to cooperate Joey. Names of any accomplices, information on how many shipments you contaminated, where you secured your gun and chemicals, stuff like that. Do you understand me?"

Razone nods and I'm thinking he just *may* cooperate.

"So how 'bout you doing the right thing and be a good Catholic boy. I'll hear your confession and grant you absolution," I tease.

Razone spits blood at me again and says, "Fuck you."

I actually chuckle and tell Razone, "Now that's more like the tough Brooklyn wop I expected. You had me confused spouting all that rug head shit. OK Joey, you just made a choice."

I turn to Shoulders and say, "Tommy, this place is about to get crowded. Help Gwen in getting Lois some medical attention. On your way out, block off the entrance to this area. It's a crime scene and I'll be the only one to clear it."

"Got it," Tommy says, and begins to leave.

"Tommy!" I say.

He turns back and I say, "Leave the PAM, take the cannoli."

CHAPTER 58

"Don't be silly... you're taking the fall."
The Maltese Falcon (1941)

Gwen and I accompany Razone inside the ambulance to the hospital with Tommy following in Pistoli's Bucar. Joe will stay behind and supervise the crime scene, which will keep him busy for days. There's 201 employees to interview, quarantine, the CDC, ERT (Evidence Response Team), FDA, and several other alphabet agencies. A few hundred agents from the New York Division are currently in route to Amalgamated to get the job done.

We sit on the ambulance jump seat a mere two feet from a prone Razone as EMT techs work to stop the bleeding and check his vitals. I ask, "How's he doing?"

Rhonda the EMT says, "Head wounds bleed a lot but the round didn't enter the cranium, so he's looking at some minor surgery. The hand is actually more serious since the bullet lacerated a tendon. The good news is that the EM doctor will clean and close the laceration, then recommend tendon repair to a specialist at a later date."

"Thanks," I say but think, *'What a waste of time. Razone's hand will be the least of his worries.'* I can save them the effort, because Razone and I spent some quality alone time.

The justice system is *not* just. Razone is a U.S. citizen who will lawyer up and *never* cooperate. The only option on the table will be the death penalty or life in prison without parole. Joey's a lone wolf, and has no information worth trading, so the taxpayers will be liable for several million dollars in trials, appeals, and housing. Razone will become a symbol of the oppressed and gain minor celebrity status. Women will write him on death row and offer to marry him, and he'll probably get a book deal. Nobody gets a book deal these days.

So, I made an executive decision. As Razone lay bleeding and semi-conscious on that concrete factory floor, I opened his mouth and sprayed pure nicotine from his PAM canister. If Rhonda the EMT is correct, Joe will survive the two gunshot wounds, the kick in the mouth, and punch on the nose, but he'll die a slow and painful death as the poison attacks his nervous system. Fuck him and anyone who would accuse me of denying him due process, or the oft used *innocent until proven guilty.* He deserves some excruciating last moments on this earth and I'm happy to assist Karma. I can understand the actions of some Mohammed born in Syria and brainwashed as an infant. But Razone is a special kind of scum because he betrayed his own country.

My cell phone has been chirping nonstop. I ask that Tommy call Jun and Gia to brief them while I make a call. I notice five *missed* calls from my roomie. "Tony, we just finished up on this nicotine case in New York."

"That's an understatement. It's all over the national news. *FBI in shootout with terrorists planning bio terrorism.* The Director wants to know why he has to learn about his agents through CNN."

"First of all, it wasn't *terrorists.* It was only *one* misguided Italian from Brooklyn."

"John, this ain't the time for your bullshit. Director McKissock wants you at the Seat of Power tomorrow. Be ready to explain this little clandestine operation you got going. One rumor has you hiring a Chinese national and providing her access to SAP (Special Access Programs)."

"Not true!" I say and alibi with, "She isn't on the government payroll."

This is *technically* accurate since I am paying Jun with monies she skims off the ISIS financiers and BITCOINS.

Tony terminates the conversation which has been a trend lately. I may be able to put off a meeting with Tony citing an upset stomach or a bad hair day, but not Director McKissock. I call Bob Dupuis and ask, "Did you get that PAM can to the FBI lab?"

"Done. It was only a 40-minute flight and they had an agent waiting at Dulles."

"So you're back in New York?"

"Awaiting your majesty and his court."

"Cut the sarcasm Bobby, been a rough day."

"I've heard. You seem to have a knack for the front page."

"It just happened a few hours ago. How'd it get in print?"

"Front page on Google, AOL, Bing, and all the other search engines. You really *need* to join us in this century."

"And you and Silent John *need* to get a room in Cleveland tonight. I need a hop to DC in the morning."

"You know something Booker."

"What Dupuis?"

"I'm living vicariously through you."

I laugh and say, "Get a life."

I notice 3 missed calls from Jun during our PAM escapade. I ask Tommy if he'd briefed Jun and Gia.

"Gave them the skinny. Why?"

"Jun's been reaching out for me."

"Forgot to tell you. She needed your ear on something."

We arrive at LaGuardia and after we get to cruising altitude I call Jun, "What's up?"

"Nothing urgent. It can wait till tomorrow."

"Have to go the Puzzle Palace tomorrow, but I have some time now."

"Well, I've been transferring funds from *them,* and just wanted to give you a balance update."

"I hadn't even thought about that part of the operation. Whatta we looking at?"

"Twenty-seven."

"I thought it be more than 27 grand."

I chalk up the silence to dropping the call while scooting past cell phone repeaters at 327 knots. I say, "Hello, you there?"

"Yes John, but it's not 27 thousand, it's 27 *million.*"

CHAPTER 59

"Well, here's another nice mess you've gotten me into!"
Stan to Ollie.....
Sons of the Desert (1933)

I'm feeling like a third grader summoned to the principal's office. I sometimes forget that the Federal Bureau of Investigation is a paramilitary organization with a defined chain of command. In equivalent military terminology, I am some infantry 1st Lt. in a distant outpost while McKissock is the Chairman of the Joint Chiefs. He can courtmartial my insubordinate ass, then order a firing squad. With my federal pension in jeopardy, I decide to act contrite and apologize liberally. My explanation will include, half-truths, exaggerations, and some boldface lies. Hey, I'm in survival mode and another dirty little FBI secret is that field agents are more stressed out meeting HBOs (High Bureau Officials) at the Puzzle Palace than a terrorist in a warehouse.

Tony confirms, "McKissock is pissed. *Extremely* pissed. He received two calls yesterday. The Attorney General wondered why FBI agents were executing an arrest warrant minus the *warrant*. His U.S. Attorney in New York complained, quite vehemently, that he had no *heads up* on a major bio-terrorist case in his district. He was *particularly* troubled that every news outlet in the world stuck microphones in his face and demanded details, of which he had *none*."

"I stepped in it good, huh?"

Tony actually sighs. "The FBI is rapidly changing. *You* have *not* changed. Twenty years ago, our mission was simple; we put bad guys in jail. We were a band of hard-charging brothers who drank together, caroused together, stood as the best man or godfather for a brother agent. We loved each other and couldn't wait to get to work in the morning. If you did your job the bosses had your back. Those days are gone. In today's FBI, everybody goes their own way at 5PM. We don't know the name of another agent's wife or kid, and we spend our days attending seminars on diversity, affirmative action, and GLTB recruitment." Tony pauses and finishes with, "Just do me a favor and try to play nice. No more vigilante actions and keep me in the loop so I can cover your butt. We good?"

I was 100% simpatico with my roomie until he got to the *vigilante* stuff. He's correct that the Bureau *has* changed. The FBI's *forgotten* our basic mission, it's become political, and too dependent on the Justice Department to conduct our investigations and we've forgotten how to develop human assets. Our rules of engagement (ROEs) are too restrictive, precedent court cases have tied our hands, and we no longer fight to win. ISIS believes we are soft and continually poke sticks in our eyes and we respond with rhetoric and hesitancy. They challenge us to engage them but we don't, and *that* is the reason why we require some freelancing.

But what I say is, "I'm good."

"The Director is waiting, John," Tony reminds me and adds, "he's not in any mood for your bullshit."

Tony walks me to the Director's office and turns to leave. "You're not coming in?" I ask.

"You're on your own roomie."

"Any words of advice?"

Tony tells me that, "The Director doesn't mind your cowboy *fuck the system* antics. He read between the lines on your Cairo rodeo and ignored little indiscretions like waterboarding, operating illegally on foreign soil and the bullshit report you submitted. McKissock understands that field agents sometimes operate off the books but he's hearing that you went *way* off the reservation."

"Like what?" I ask, but can already guess that a PAM can *and* Razone's mouth are part of the equation.

Tony says, "The Director wants the truth." My roomie pauses and reconsiders, "In your case maybe a *version* of the truth. McKissock just wants to rein you in for your own good and the *good* of any case that may go to court. He doesn't want the headlines to read *'FBI rogue agent sentenced to life in prison.'* " Tony pauses and pleas, "Just humor him, OK?"

I tell Tony, "I know that you've had my back roomie, and I *know* I make it difficult."

Due to my many previous verbal scoldings, I can recognize a *genuine* ass chewing when I see one coming. Many are halfhearted and lack passion and sincerity. McKissock has his game face on but begins with the carrot, "You and your team did an outstanding job in New York." He pauses, leans forward, and points his finger at me. "*But* you also put many people at risk with your total disregard of our arrest procedures. You didn't utilize SWAT as required in high risk arrests, you informed the plant manager that you had an arrest warrant, but didn't, and obviously had *no* intention of, securing a warrant, *since* you failed to notify the U.S. Attorney's office in that jurisdiction."

McKissock pauses and asks, "Any answers, John?"

"No sir, *except* there were some exigent circumstances."

"That was a comment John, but *not* an answer. You had several hours to do it the right way. Deputy Director Daniels, at *your* request, contacted the owner of Amalgamated and ceased all shipments. Therefore Mr. Razone presented no *immediate* threat. But *you* felt the need to confront Razone and your actions caused a Ms. Lois Dutchman from Poughkeepsie, New York, to sustain a serious gunshot wound."

"*But* we probably saved her life." I realize that my initial plan was to just sit here and absorb the lecture but my pie hole isn't on board yet.

McKissock reminds me that, "This is *not* a discussion Agent Booker. The Attorney General contacted me and reminded me that she's *my* boss. She then demanded that I conduct an OPR investigation into this entire nicotine case. Specifically, what was our probable cause, where was our arrest warrant, and did an FBI agent, namely *you*, attempt to murder an unarmed and helpless subject."

"What murder?" I ask, suddenly *very* concerned.

"Razone claims you held him down and squirted concentrated nicotine into his mouth. The Doctors confirm that Razone is likely to die within the next 30 days from nicotine poisoning."

My brain is scrambling to come up with something plausible. Our probable cause *was* illegally obtained by Jun, *so* if I can resolve that *one* issue, then the other two disappear. I can claim that once we found the PAM inside Razone's kitchen we had the PC follow the bread crumbs to Amalgamated. Once there, eyewitness accounts will corroborate that Razone pulled a weapon and shot his own hostage. As far as the attempted murder beef, the *only* two people in that room were Razone and myself. And, Razone will be dead long before any investigation concludes.

The Director interrupts my mental scheming by asking, "Well, *do* you have any answers, John?"

"Razone's full of shit. I actually made every attempt to *save* his life by *stopping* the bleeding." I pause at this point since I can't answer the Director's other questions and attempt to redirect the conversation with, "Mr. Director, I'll have an FD 302 on your desk by close of business tomorrow which will contain verifiable facts that refute *all* those accusations."

After the Cairo case I *know* that McKissock is a pragmatist. He accepts my MO of massaging a policy but he'd *never* add *murder* to that list. Killing Razone was a public service. Squirting nicotine into that assholes mouth was the ultimate irony. I'm reminded of that biblical saying, '*Those who live by the sword, will die by the sword.*' I suppose I should feel *some* remorse in ridding this world of Joey from Brooklyn, but I don't.

The Director nods his head and says, "OK John, by close of business tomorrow. Now let's talk about lone wolves."

I breathe a sigh of relief until the Director asks, "Something odd is going on with our lone wolf problem."

Since I'm not sure, what the Director knows, it seems prudent to say, "Yes sir." Then wait.

McKissock has a smirk on his mug. I've seen that identical expression on my wife's face and it's usually followed by some trap. "In addition to your excellent work on the Minnesota and New York case, ISIS seems to be having a run of random bad luck."

There's definitely a land mine somewhere near. I offer, "I've read some of the Intel bulletins but am not up on the details." Then I add, "I've been pretty busy."

"Well, allow me to update *you.*"

I nod and the FBI Director informs me about the two-ton bank bomb that destroyed millions of ISIS dollars. "The State Department did a fantastic job identifying the bank's location and coordinated with Defense."

"Occasionally, the State Department will surprise you."

McKissock frowns and follows with, "*And,* there's also been an *inexplicable* increase in the number of individuals denied access into our ports of entry during the past six months. Custom officials report that some 13,000 individuals have been detained, deported, or denied entry just in the past six months."

"That's great," I mutter.

"Yes, it is John, and get this." Pregnant pause. "Most of those individuals are primarily of Mideast origins." He waits again but I'm not biting, so he asks. "Isn't that peculiar?"

"It is," I say but McKissock's silence prompts me to add, "isn't it?"

The Director locks eyes with me and it's reminiscent me of a *who-blinks-first* contest. He wins and continues, "Then we've picked up chatter that some major financiers of ISIS had their bank accounts cyber hacked for millions of dollars." More silence and a stare. "It *seems* that China is the culprit. What do *you* think John?"

I give the FBI Director the same innocent gaze I offered Father Cilliberti in 10th grade at Bishop Neumann High, when caught peeking at Nicky Stamato's trig exam. "Good stuff, Mr. McKissock."

"It is and there's some *more* good news." A pause, a stare, and, "*Someone*." Emphasis on the *someone*. "Leaked a story to the press that the President's mosque policy impacted the Boston Marathon bombing."

I offer, "And isn't the President about to rescind that reckless policy *because* of that leak?"

McKissock nods. "It did take *that* newspaper story to force the President's hand."

"Well then, the leak was a public service, because *before* that mosque ban the FBI prevented 57 potential attacks originating at mosques. We demonstrated that mosques were used to shield the work of terrorists from law enforcement scrutiny, and then, the President initiated that idiotic ban."

The Director adds that, "Radical Muslims *were* falsely hiding behind the First Amendment and taking advantage of Special Operations Committee."

"That committee is just a Muslim front operated by our own government."

"Unfortunately, I agree but that stays between us. The Vice President assures me that the President assured *him* the mosque policy will be reversed."

"When?"

"Soon." The Director frowns and adds, "But *soon* to politicians could be an eternity. Our *new* marching orders concerning mosques should allow agents to monitor religious or political speech whenever the *facts or circumstances reasonably indicate* violent crime or terrorism. And, the decision will be *ours* to make and not some committee."

"So we'll be able to use informants or plant intercept devices at mosques if we have reliable information."

The Director nods and says, "As a former U.S. Attorney I argued that mosques and other Muslim organizations involved two or more people, and that constitutes a conspiracy if there is *any* discussion advocating violence."

I observe with some pride that, "We seem to be getting a handle on this lone wolf problem."

McKissock pauses and sets the bear trap. "As I said before, it *seems* that ISIS is having an *unexplained* run of bad luck which is effecting their recruitment of lone wolves. Do you know anything about *all this bad luck, John?*"

I shrug and say, "No sir." But I do believe that the Director knows that I *know* he's tacitly approving my clandestine operation as long as I don't murder anyone else. At least, that's *my* read.

McKissock continues. "Then, we come to the 33 sanctuary cities in the U.S. We know that local law enforcement *won't* deport illegals for crimes, but they *will* expel individuals with contagious diseases." He pauses, picks up a notepad, and begins reading, "Diseases like HIV, African sleeping sickness, bubonic plague, chicken pox, cholera, dengue fever, hepatitis A through G, leprosy, meningitis, rabies, smallpox, and, my personal favorite, bacterial vaginosis." He replaces the pad on his desk and stares at me.

"Wow."

"Wow?" McKissock repeats. "And get this John. It seems that *only* Muslims have contracted these terrible diseases. Mexicans,

Guatemalans, Hondurans, and even Canadians seem extremely healthy while living illegally in our great nation."

"Wow."

"Wow?" McKissock repeats again. A"nd I've been told that a civilian, actually a Chinese national, is working alongside your task force with unrestricted access to our FBI files."

I nod and admit, "Yes sir, that's *mostly* true but we needed a cyber security expert and Jun's the best. We did a background on her and she's clean."

"Two things, John. The FBI has the best cyber security experts in the world, and, second, this *Jun* must pass an extensive background investigation just to receive a secret clearance." McKissock pauses once again and warns, "Of course Hillary Clinton escaped indictment on cyber security access issues. Perhaps you can also use the *incompetent* defense."

"We'll take care of Jun's clearance and I'll visit Hillary's attorneys for some advice."

McKissock warns, "Just be careful, John. I need you to take care of this lone wolf thing, just do it right." The Director smiles and adds, "Well, in your case, *almost* right."

"Am I free to go?" I say, only half in jest.

"You are, but expect a call from a deputy assistant director on this OPR investigation. The result will be forwarded to me and I'll adjudicate the matter."

My immediate reaction is that McKissock is giving me both a warning and a lifeline. He's basically saying, *'Do what you have to do to mitigate this lone wolf thing, but don't go too far, and this OPR thing will disappear.'*

I'm feeling much better until I ask, "Who's overseeing the OPR investigation?"

"DAD Walt Maulbit."

"Chicken Shit Walt," involuntarily escapes my lips.

CHAPTER 60

"Inconceivable."
The Princess Bride (1987)

I'm back inside the safety of our task force office the next day and dial my roommate. "You disappeared yesterday."

"I had a meeting over in Langley."

"Well I got my ass handed to me."

"Look, John," said Tony seriously, "I told you the Director was pissed. Attempted murder is way past his comfort zone."

"Razone is a terrorist who given the opportunity would kill your wife and three children."

"I don't know what happened in that factory, and I don't wanna know. If I was there I probably would've held Razone's mouth open, but most FBI agents are wired differently. They view that type of law enforcement as *way* over the line."

"Then they're hypocrites because that line moves all the time."

"That's how *you* see the world John, but it's that *line* which separates us from the barbarians at our gate. If everybody threw away the rule book it'd be anarchy."

"Our world has changed and those rules are outdated. Now terrorists dictate the rules."

"You may be correct but the Bureau is a massive bureaucratic institution with rules. Most agents break some rule every day and never get caught but *you* are on *everyone's* radar." Tony pauses and throws me a lifeline. "Just get your shit together on that attempted murder beef and the rest will disappear."

"I doubt that, Tony. The Director assigned Chicken Shit Walt for my OPR and that man may spray PAM down *my* throat."

"I *assigned* Walt to your case and there's a reason for that."

"Can't wait to hear this."

"Deputy Assistant Director Maulbit dislikes you." He pauses and adds, "Immensely so, and he wanted you fired over that undercover mess. Walt actually went to McKissock and accused *me* of assigning one of my lunch cronies to whitewash the matter and you *did* skate."

"Nobody felt bad about some dead mob guy, and besides, I had nothing *directly* to do with his death."

"You *really* don't get it. For Walt and *most* FBI agents you *were* complicit because you could've stopped it by alerting your contact agent. We had a responsibility to prevent that murder, no matter his status as a member of organized crime. You *should've* been fired so Walt is intent on nailing your ass this time."

"So you assign my sworn enemy to investigate me so he can get even?"

"My logic is that Walt would probably go directly to Justice if I assigned *any* other DAD. Then we'd lose control. But if he personally conducts the invest and can't prove the attempted murder we slap your wrist for the minor constitutional violations which seem to be your specialty. This wouldn't be your first or *last* suspension, but it'll satisfy Walt."

I think about it for a few seconds, "Got it. Machiavellian with a little Tony Soprano thrown in."

"I hope you didn't spray poison into a helpless subject's mouth. But if you *did*, then get very creative *very* quickly."

I alert Tony that the Director will be e-mailed my post op report on the Razone matter by close of business (COB) today. His final words are, "Make it good."

There are several pressing matters that will consume my next ten hours. There's the consequences of Razone's poisoning processed foods *already* on supermarket shelves, vending machines, and homes of unsuspecting citizens. The FDA has used every mass media technique in their toolbox warning the public to check lot numbers and dates printed on specific processed foods. The good news is that even those citizens who've consumed the tainted food can be aggressively treated since physicians are aware they're dealing with nicotine poisoning.

Then there's my promised report to the Director due by close of business today. That's going to be a work of art since it'll include some fancy word smithing. I'd painted myself into a Fourth Amendment corner by entering Razone's apartment minus a search warrant. If I had some PC (Probable Cause) then I can claim exigent circumstances. Finally, I am expecting a call from Chicken Shit Walt who *never* liked me and now has the opportunity for the kill shot.

I require a few creative minds with a devious bent and on cue, Agent 36 and Tommy Shoulders enter the office. Gwen says, "We stopped for coffee at your Starbucks and Donnie Osmond said he misses you."

"Been getting my caffeine fix at airports and Circle K gas stations lately."

Tommy says, "Wanted us to give you a message."

"I can't wait."

Tommy's already chuckling, "Donnie said that he tried the unicorn and it hurt his behind."

My voice mimics a hissy fit and I say, "That bitch! Here I confide a dark secret to my soulmate and he blabs it to the world."

"Not your best gay impression, Booker." Gwen offers, "How'd the meeting go with McKissock?"

"I need some advice."

There's just the three original amigos in the office. We've flown halfway around the world, endured several shootouts with terrorists, and attended the funeral of a member of our team. So my two compatriots can recognize the serious tone in my voice. I won't confess to killing Razone, but that's not necessary. They *already* know and would have done the same thing. Hell, they already *have* done the same thing in Cairo. I begin with, "McKissock suspects that we didn't have any PC to bag Razone's apartment, and without that, the remainder of the evidence is tainted."

The group spends fifteen minutes discussing options but none will pass an OPR smell test. We seem stuck at the illegal encryption interception on Razone's computer.

Jun enters the room and announces, "I found a deli that has homemade Jalebi."

"What's that?" Tommy wonders.

"A delicacy in India. It's made by deep-frying batter in pretzel shapes, then soaking them in syrup. You top it off with a crystallized sugary exterior coating." Jun takes a bite and places a bag on the table, "Try one." She offers.

Tommy dips a Jalebi into his Starbucks, takes a bite, and pronounces it, "Good shit."

Gwen informs Tommy, "I thought you were on a diet?"

"I am. My goal was to lose just 10 pounds. Only 15 more to go."

Although I enjoy *anything* with a crystallized sugary exterior, I left my appetite at the Seat of Power. I hadn't intended on including Jun *or* Gia in this particular conversation. Gia is a new agent and although she's been privy to some questionable FBI practices, nothing yet of a firing offense. And, Jun is a civilian and could be pressured to testify against yours truly. Just as I'm about to ask Jun to excuse us it occurs to me that our sticking point involves computers and encryption. So, I decide to make some subtle inquiries. I ask Jun, "Is it possible for an encrypted conversation to revert back to non-encrypted?"

"Give me an example John, I'm not following you."

"OK. Say we're monitoring some lone wolf on open social media like Facebook, then they go encrypted. Computers are always doing strange things that we can't control, so, is it possible for that encrypted conversation to just revert back to open source?"

"That was at the core of the San Bernardino case where the FBI demanded that Apple provide them the key to defeat the encryption on the terrorist's cell phone."

Tommy argues, "What bullshit! Apple argued that if they provided us the back-door key, we'd use it to illegally listen to conversations without a legitimate warrant."

Agent 36 and I look at each other and laugh. She says, "Tommy, that's *exactly* what we're doing here."

"But we're *only* doing that with *guilty* assholes."

Jun runs interference for her friend, "Thomas is *actually* correct. The Chinese have a saying, 'The superior man understands what is right; the inferior man understands what will sell.' "

Gwen laughs and asks, "You *sure* that was Chinese?"

"Well, back to your question on encryption," Jun says. "There is Phonotactic Reconstruction (PR). It's in the research stage and I've been working with my colleagues to bring it online. PR is used to *predict* clear text words from encrypted sequences. It segments sequences of the VoIP packets into sub-sequences mapped into candidate words, then, based on rules of grammar, hypothesizes these sub-sequences into whole sentences."

"English," I plead.

"Sorry." Jun smiles and says, "Basically, we're able to reconstruct the conversation by guessing and predicting the original sounds used within the original transmission."

"Does all that mean that encryption can unexplainably go unencrypted?"

"Yes. We've had sporadic success so it is *theoretically* possible to *unencrypt*."

"Can you write up how that happens in technical language?"

"I can, but due to the proprietary nature of the research, it will lack some of the specifics."

"Just include plenty of technical mumbo jumbo," I say and add, "Can you get me that report sometime before 4:30?"

The chubby former stripper/cyber security expert nods and heads toward the Mush Room.

Gwen surmises that, "So your OPR defense is that FBI HQ was *legally* monitoring Razone on social media. When he went dark, his case was referred to our task force as per our standing procedure. *Our* SOP is to continue monitoring Razone social media accounts in case he returns to open sources."

I pick up the narrative and say, "And *'who'd a thunk'* that Razone suddenly materializes on *open* media threatening nicotine terrorism. This provides us the exigent circumstances to bag his apartment, and everything else becomes legally kosher."

"Very conniving," Gwen observes.

I turn to Gwen and Tommy, "Jun may be the premier cyber guru on the planet, but Chicken Shit Walt is a career bureaucrat and the first thing he'll do is take Jun's report and have FBI cyber people poke holes in it."

Agent 36 smiles and offers, "Well, we do have a cyber mole in the Puzzle Palace."

"Who's that?"

"A member of your own fraternity."

"I wasn't in a college fraternity."

"Not a *college* brother." Agent 36 chuckles. "A Marine brother."

"Bill Garrett," I say. "He *is* the FBI's Cyber Security Unit Chief, so any confirmation review will go through Garrett."

My clock is ticking. I have till Close of Business (COB) today to transmit a report to the FBI Director which rationally justifies our ignoring the Fourth Amendment of the Constitution. I punch in Garrett's personal cell phone number. "Billy, how's it going?"

I ease into the point of my call with some small talk. I purposely mention our shared Marine Corps experiences before I say, "Bill, we both know that I don't know shit about computers, but I'm a little jammed up with the B."

I explain my OPR predicament but stick to the approved script, "And, all of a sudden, Razone appears on the open net and is planning a bio-terrorist attack on our food supply. So, *we did what FBI agents do and rushed to his apartment, where we found the evidence which save thousands of lives.*"

Garrett knows I'm full of shit, but he patiently waits for the *hook.* "I'm submitting a report to the Director that explains how this encryption thing may accidentally reverse itself. It'll have sound scientific justification. You'll probably be the one to evaluate it and determine if it's bullshit or not."

The silence indicates that Garrett is attempting to process both the obvious and hidden implications. Bill is a cyber stud and knows my report will be mostly fiction, but he's also aware that our nation is in peril and political correctness is tying the hands of law enforcement.

"Who's the DAD on the OPR?

"Walt Maulbit."

"Chicken Shit Walt," Garrett says. "He's a total asshole, but the good news is that he's a *dumb* total asshole. Send me the report and I'll do what I can but," he warns, "make it good with plenty of cyber jargon."

"That's definitely *not* an issue. Thanks, Bill and Semper Fi."

I purposely added the *Semper Fi* as some type of subliminal loyalty reminder.

Gia strolls in and her formerly jet black silky Asian hair is a now swirls of red, purple, and blue. Tommy wonders, "What the hell happened to you? Looks like you were attacked by some angry interior decorators."

"So you like it," Gia says puffing up her red bangs with an index finger. "Gwen took me to her beauty salon in Parma."

Agent 36 adds, "Benny the Beautician is a 300-pound genius of the asymmetrical blunt cut with apricot color. He's also had five 300-games at the Parma Bowling Alley."

"A true renaissance man," I note. "I personally like the *do* but the SAC is gonna order you to lose the rainbow. Just tell them I assigned you some undercover stuff."

"I think she looks great," Agent 36 opines.

"Let's get inside our cone of silence room and I'll brief you on my meeting with the Director."

As we enter the Mush Room, Jun looks at Gia and says, "The hairdo is *not* very Feng Shui."

Tommy comments, "Don't know what that means but it don't sound like a good thing."

I begin with, "I have some good news. We seem to be having a profound effect on ISIS lone wolf recruitment efforts." I run it all down. The bank bombing, pilfering the financier accounts, the STOPs at our ports of entries, the sanctuary cities deportations, the thirteen thwarted mass casualty plots, which include Gus and Razone, the move to rescind the mosque policy, and the suspension of the Special Committee.

Tommy says, "I didn't realize we were doing *that* good."

"We are, and it's all because of you guys. Goes to show what a mobile, agile, and hostile band of brothers can accomplish when not constrained by bullshit policies made by agenda driven politicians."

"So, what's next?" Gia wonders.

There is a loud and consistent rap on the door. This is somewhat unusual since we are technically not part of the Cleveland Division. Our task force is TDY to HQ, this room is off limits, and all of us can be reached via cell phone.

I open the door and it's Peggy. She appears somewhat harried and says, "Sorry to bother you John Booker but I told him you couldn't be interrupted. But he told me, *I'm ordering you to get Agent Booker to the phone now!'* "

I smile and say, "It's OK Peggy, you're not in any trouble. Who's ordering you around?"

"Says he's Deputy Assistant Director Walter Maulbit."

CHAPTER 61

"You can rule by fear or you can rule by love. Fear works better."

Al Capone

Columbus Ohio

Abu rents an apartment close to the Omari Mosad mosque located near downtown Columbus. He's broken all ties with his former life, which include his parents and younger sister Faisa. This mosque is frequented by U.S. citizens with radical sympathies, many of whom depart the Ohio mosque and engage in lone wolf terrorist activities. The city of Columbus, Ohio, may be considered a quaint Midwest city but it's a magnet for some word-class jihadists. Four individuals who previously attended the Omari Mosad mosque have been involved in major terrorist attacks on U.S. soil. All of them informed authorities that they acted *alone* in the name of Allah.

Abu shares the apartment with his friend Atwa but the two young men spend their days at the mosque being *educated* by Benoit Nurab. He is a 42-year-old visiting imam from Libya and knowledgeable in Islamic hukum. Benoit is a large man with a perpetual glare who enjoys the prestige given only to those who speak with Allah. He leads discussion groups in a small room off the main prayer area and his prized students are Abu and Atwa. All but one of the regular attendees fervently embrace Benoits's inflammatory speech.

Faisal Habib is a devout Muslim *but* believes that Islam is a *not* a religion that condones the slaughter of innocent women and children. Habib debates this issue with Benoit by quoting the Quran, "*O Prophet! strive hard against the unbelievers and the hypocrites and be unyielding to them; but be not a butcher of babies.*"

The imam is a scholar of Mohammed's teachings and refutes Habib with quotes from the prophet, "*And be not weak hearted in pursuit of the enemy; It is not for a Prophet that he should have prisoners of war until he slaughters all of the unbelievers.*"

Habib reluctantly nods to the powerful imam rather than openly oppose him. Abu is the most fanatical member of the group and Benoit fuels his rage with generalizations. "America loves the Jews and will kill our brothers to protect Zionism."

"But the Jews are in Israel. Why is it America's fight?" Abu asks.

"When the Jews stole our land and renamed it Israel, thousands of American Jews left the United States and resettled in Jew-land. Every time an Israeli rocket kills our brothers, America also has blood on their hands. The Jews displaced Palestinians from their homeland leaving them robbed of life, property and dignity. The Americans protected the pigs with their military."

Abu wonders, "Why did they steal our land?"

"Because it was *always* their goal to conquer the entire world," Benoit clarifies. "The latest western military efforts are consistent with the aggression of the past religious crusades fought between Catholic and Muslim forces over the *Holy Land*."

"So this aggression toward the true believers is not new."

"The imperialistic United States divided the Middle East after World Wars I and II. Then they invaded Iraq on the false premise of weapons of mass destruction. They desecrated our sacred cities of Mecca and Medina in Saudi Arabia with their military bases. These infidels remain on our holy ground to this day."

Habib counters with, "But Allah received retribution when our martyrs destroyed their New York skyscrapers and Pentagon."

Benoit's voice rises with anger, "And this led to *more* Muslim blood." He calms himself and continues. "*Before* America invaded Iraq in 2001 many Muslims still viewed the U.S. in a positive light, but *after* the slaughter of our babies in Iraq, Syria, and Afghanistan, Muslims worldwide now regard American as Satan."

"And they *continue* to kill our family with their bombs," Abu adds.

"America uses the term *National Security* to justify their slaughter of Muslims, but their wars are fought on *our* soil. This is why we must wage jihad on *their* land. They tell the world that their motive is not imperialistic but they readily trade our blood for oil."

Both Abu and Atwa are silent. Benoit's epistle has replaced their curiosity with hatred and their fear with courage. Benoit smiles knowing he has done his job. He says, "*The Quran, 3:169, declares that those warriors slain in Allah's way are not dead, but alive.*"

Atwa agrees, "We must *punish* the Americans for their sins against the prophet."

Benoit asks, "Do you wish to be Allah's warrior?

Abu nods and says, "We are true believers and wish only to serve our Master."

"True believers forsake their lives for principles of faith and religious deeds. They wage jihad and fight with zeal in Allah's way, thus attaining martyrdom."

CHAPTER 62

"You seem to be the best possible proof that evolution has stalled."

Chicken Shit is a tall, slender geeky guy who wears colorful suspenders and matching bow ties. This combination *doesn't* work for him. Our last conversation occurred after I failed to notify the B that some wise guy was about to sleep with the fishes. Walt was the Deputy in charge of covert ops *but not* a fan of undercover cases. He's stated on more than one occasion that UC agents are hot dogs trying to escape the office. Perhaps, but undercovers work 15-hour days, deal with psychopaths, minus their badge and gun, and put very bad people in jail. With that said, the FBI office can be just as dangerous. An OPR investigation concluded that although I exhibited bad judgement, *"Agent Booker"* was not *directly* complicit in the murder.

After a 30-day suspension Walt ordered me to report to FBI HQ, with suit and tie, where he unceremoniously and emphatically informed me, *"You dodged a pink slip this time but agents like you will fuck up again, and I'll be there to stick it up your ass."*

My response of, *"You're not my type"* may have been clever at the time, but unwise. This will be our first *chat* since that day.

I pick up the outer office phone and punch line one. "John Booker," I say.

Deputy Director Walt Maulbit conjures up his most officious voice and says, "You stepped on your dick *again* Booker, but this time not even Tony Daniels can save you."

"Who is this?" I ask, knowing that Chicken Shit Walt has already red-lined his anger gauge.

"I'll tell you who this is, Special Agent *Booker*. It's the guy who's going to put the cuffs on you for attempted murder."

"Oh," I say as if recognizing the voice. "I thought you were *still* testifying before that Congressional committee. Heard it wasn't going too well."

"I know it was you who leaked that story, Booker, and I intend to place you under oath and ask *that* specific question."

"Is that in *addition* to my attempted murder beef?"

"It'll bring me immense satisfaction forcing you to admit that you leaked my name to the press. And I'm seriously considering subpoenaing your reporter girlfriend."

Two thoughts immediately come to mind. First off, since I'm facing an attempted murder charge I'll perjure myself in a New York nanosecond concerning some bullshit leak. Besides, the story I leaked was true. I verbalize my second thought to Walt, "You can't force a member of the media to testify. Eric Holder went after James Rosen and he ate a whole lot of humble pie."

The silence is a result of Chicken Shit Walt processing my spot-on rebuttal. He finally says, "I am personally conducting this OPR investigation so get all your bullshit out now, because when we meet, you won't be so contemptuous."

"I can save you a lot of time, travel, and aggravation. I never leaked that story, and I didn't attempt to murder that asshole terrorist who, by the way, killed innocent Americans." I realize that statement included two big whoppers but who's counting.

Walt isn't listening to reason anyway. He says, "You are a rogue agent Booker, I know it and you know it. You can't do anything the right way, the FBI way, the *legal way*. I'm going to enjoy relieving you of your credentials."

I'm tired of this banter since its only purpose is to harass me. "I'm pretty busy now Walt, can I help you with something?"

"You'll be getting an official notification of the OPR investigation through your SAC. Once you're officially notified, I'll be seeing you."

"You know where to find me." I say and terminate the conversation.

I sit at the desk and take stock of my tenuous situation. The attempted murder charge is the most serious matter *but* it is also the weakest. It's my word against Razone's and he will *not* be a sympathetic witness. It's also a good bet that Joey boy will be dead long before the justice system can schedule a trial. The leaking of information is also a dead end since I plan to lie under oath, and Florence Kuhns can't be forced to divulge a source. In the few cases where prosecutors threatened media members with contempt of court, it always backfired and caused lawsuits and bad press. So, my most vulnerable issue is the warrantless search which *could* get my ass canned. But if Jun can produce a plausible explanation on how Razone's encrypted messages could inexplicably morph public, it's game, set and match. I get to continue my game of WAR with Chicken Shit Walt until one of us surrenders. It won't be me.

But first things first and that includes my written report to the Director. I decide on feeding the monster a healthy dose of bullshit. Government bureaucrats adore reports. I imagine some of them using official files as porn while masturbating and screaming, *'Oh God, what a perfect FD 302, and...with an attachment.'*

The more words, charts, and graphs equal a quality document. I hit the *'memo'* icon on my Bu laptop and begin my yarn.

To: Gary T. McKissock, Director, Federal Bureau of Investigation
From: John Booker, Special Agent, Cleveland Division
Subject: Razone; et al: file number 35- 6247
Pursuant to our conversation on 3 March, the following is a case summary concerning the arrest of Joseph P. Razone, in Albany New York.

Background: Joseph Razone of NYC, came to the attention of the Special Terrorism Task Force, (STTF) following a referral from FBI Headquarters Unit Chief, Bill Garrett. Following investigative procedures Garrett had been tracking Razone on open social media. Razone frequently discussed jihad and espoused radical Muslim tenants of killing the infidels. When Razone's communication on known terrorist websites ceased, Garrett referred the case. As per SOP, the STTF placed Razone's public internet account under electronic surveillance (ELSUR) and on 15 March, Razone reappeared on a website which was encrypted. This involuntary exchange from encrypted to non-encrypted conversations, though rare, is feasible and is explained in Attachment One.

The remainder of my fairytale includes how we followed the crumbs from the apartment to the food processing plant. It explains why an exigent search of Razone's apartment was necessary and concludes with Razone's claim that I sprayed pure nicotine down his throat with a PAM can. This particular piece of the report requires the most succinct explanation of, '*Mr. Razone's claim of malicious spraying poisonous nicotine directly into his mouth never occurred. I can only assume that his frequent transmitting of the poison into PAM canisters caused him an unintentional but deadly exposure.* Translation, "He's full of shit!"

I attach Jun's convoluted seven-page attachment of technical IT words and hit *SEND*. My hope is that Bill Garrett remembers the Marine Corps motto, *Semper Fidelis*. (Always faithful).

The Bureaucracy can sap your energy. It's a subtle but continuous drip, drip of bullshit, which adds up. *Much* of your day is expended on stuff which has nothing to do with your job. My conversation with Chicken Shit Walt exhausted me but there's one more item on my list today. Jun's been withdrawing millions from ISIS financiers. The money is sitting in an offshore account in Antilles. I considered Dubai, Panama, and Singapore but the Antilles have high levels of bank secrecy and a solid economy. Unlike the United States, the Antilles allow you to set up accounts that hide the names of the real owners, using trustees as go-betweens. My first choice was Gwen to act as my go-between but I'd be exposing her to serious jail time. So, I dusted off my undercover identities and became both owner and trustee.

It took me about a week to design a process that would convey the terrorist money into informant hands, who would then be ratting out the *terrorists*. The irony is a beautiful thing since terrorists are now funding terrorists to snitch on them.

I transferred ten million dollars from my offshore account into a separate Antilles fund. Jun set up a website titled *Jihad Joe*, which promised millions of dollars to anyone who provides information on terrorist-related activities. The information is limited to terrorism and information must result in a solid lead. You get more dough if arrests are made, no questions asked.

We copied the Crime Stoppers model, which offers money to citizens who provide information for *any* criminal activity. They are assigned a personalized number instead of divulging their name and, if the tip proves accurate, they collect their dough. The main difference between Crime Stoppers and Jihad Joe, (I thought it a clever but nonoffensive name) is that Joe will pay ten times the amount for verifiable information. It's actually a skewed variation of a Ponzi scheme whereby we steal money from the terrorists and use it to catch them.

Americans believe that the majority of Muslims strictly adhere to the doctrines in the Quran and Sharia law. Although that may be true, there's a significant number of them who will sell their soul for money. They are as depraved as Italians when sex and money are involved.

To assure that no roads lead back to our little group, Jun takes the tips and forwards them to the FBI ISIS tip line. This toll-free number was created specifically to track Americans who may have joined or are planning to join ISIS, and accepts anonymous tips. And the FBI supervisor in charge of that operation is our good buddy Mo Askari.

The President still hasn't rescinded his mosque surveillance policy and the clock is ticking until *more* innocent civilians die. Hopefully our Jihad Joe program can fill the void in keeping an eye on mosques. I've been at the Jihad Joe website for about three hours when my cell phone vibrates an incoming text. It's SAC Mike Williams and the message is, *'Need to see you ASAP.'*

SAC Williams is sitting behind his massive desk with a smirk on his handsome face. Williams could be the poster child of the FBI with brown hair, steely eyes, and chiselled chin. He points to a chair and says, "This seems to be a pattern with you John."

I smile and say. "This doesn't look like we'll be discussing the Indians chance to make the playoffs."

Williams smiles back and says, "No, but that doesn't seem likely." He pauses and picks up a document. "You have a particular talent for pissing off HBOs (High Bureau Official). Recently, it was Unit Chief Lewis when you suggested she could benefit from sex *and* a seaweed diet."

"I can guess who I pissed off this time. Chicken Shit Walt."

Williams stifles a chuckle and says, "Good guess and I'm required to read aloud the charges and have you sign your understanding of the OPR process. Although in your case you probably have this form memorized. And, since it includes a criminal charge, I must advise you of your right to remain silent."

The SAC does his due diligence and hands me documents which I sign and initial in several places. He asks if I have any questions.

"I do. OPRs are *administrative* matters. Normally, an agent *must* cooperate or be fired for insubordination. The attempted murder is a *felony* so why doesn't the Albany PD have jurisdiction?"

"Because," Williams explains, "DAD Maulbit understands the system. He knows you can take the Fifth on any question involving spraying nicotine into Razone's throat, but, he *can* place Gwen and Shoulders under oath and force them to provide information on the nicotine thing. Basically, he's using the OPR to gather evidence which he'll turn over to the Albany prosecutors. And," Williams concludes, "he *may* ask you questions about what happened leading up to your initial contact with Razone since that's part of the administrative inquiry."

I gaze at the official papers and notice that my sworn statement will take place on April 21. I've got six days to work my magic.

Williams says, "We've already had this conversation, John. As I told you before, you *really* need to retire if you beat this latest jam."

"This attempted murder charge is bullshit. Didn't happen and can't be proved."

"Well, I guess you haven't heard the latest."

"Nope, been busy in the Mush Room. What's up?"

"An hour ago, Joseph Razone died."

"I don't wanna sound insensitive, but that's good news on two fronts. First off, Razone murdered several elderly people and second, his death puts a dent into Walt's murder investigation."

"That would be true if the Amalgamated Food processing plant didn't have cameras."

CHAPTER 63

"We find the defendant incredibly guilty."
The Producers (1967)

"Cameras," I repeat.

Williams nods and says, "This is between you and me, but DAD Maulbit called me an hour ago and gave me the heads up that he was sending this OPR notice. We got to talking about your case. Told me that you were a disgrace to the FBI and that he *finally* had the goods on you. Said he personally reviewed *all* the interviews on the Razone case and noticed that the manager casually mentioned the cameras. He sent two agents to Albany with a subpoena."

My stomach just did a back flip. I say, "That's not a problem." But I think, *'Holy fuck, that's a big problem. I'm going to jail.'*

Williams and I shoot the shit for a few more minutes but I don't recall one word. My brain keeps flashing, *'You forget to check for cameras. What a fucking rookie mistake.'*

I return to our area and slump in my chair. "What was that about?" Agent 36 asks.

"Williams' official notification of my OPR."

"You knew it was coming, so why the sour puss?"

"Been at it for nine straight hours. I'm going home and recharge my batteries."

Gwen has always claimed to be my female clone. When we first started working together I'd tell her an occasional fib for her own good. She'd raise her finger and say, *Bullshit!* She somehow knew *every time* I lied. So I decide to say little more and leave. I reaffirm, "I'm fine Gwen," and head for the door. I'm almost outside the room when I hear, "Bullshit!"

On my way home I decide to stop at the Arrow Café for a sit down with Ray Kopka. When the terrorists planted 5 Kilos of coke in my car it was Ray who made the drugs disappear from the evidence locker. The retired Cleveland police captain was our father figure in Cairo who kept us from attempting several ill-advised strategies. If I could totally confide in anyone it'd be Ray Kopka. It's dark by the time I park my Bucar on St. Clair Avenue and enter the Arrow Café. Kopka has added a few inches to his middle since his retirement, which is a residual effect of owning a Croatian restaurant.

"Well if it isn't John Booker in my humble eatery? Pigs *do* fly."

"The B is picking on me again."

There's a few customers pecking away at their food. I notice a stout lady exiting the kitchen balancing a tray. It takes a few seconds to recognize Bunny, a waitress from Fryman's Deli. She winks at me while dropping some plates off at a nearby table. I rise and Bunny gives me a hug, "Well if it isn't Johnny Booker. Long time, no see."

"Been a little busy. Whatta you doing working here?"

Bunny jerks her thumb at Kopka and says, "The boss man and I are doing the hoochie coochie."

Ray smiles and says, "Bunny's the best waitress in Cleveland, so when I opened this joint I stole her from Fryman's." He adds, "They're still pissed."

"Then one night," Bunny continues, "we were here all alone and Ray bent me over the kitchen counter."

Kopka gives me a shit eating grin and says, "That's about it." He tells Bunny, "Booker and I have to reminisce here, get two glasses and the Maraska Kruskovac."

I vaguely recall my last time at the Arrow. It was the night the team scored a trifecta and shot Brenda, Bruno, and Vito. We stopped to see Ray and he got us hammered with some Croatian rotgut. The liquor's name had a lot of vowels and consonants. My hangover was reminiscent of a morning following liberty in Olongapo, Philippines. Bunny returns with the booze, pours us a glass, and heads back to the kitchen.

"So what'd you do this time?" Kopka asks. "Insult another boss, a late report, or maybe something really serious like telling some female G-man she had nice hooters."

"None of those. I'm actually accused of murder."

Kopka says, "Was it a righteous shoot?"

"Didn't involve a gun."

"Run someone over with your car?"

"Nope. Poisoned some terrorist."

"They use to give medals for that. The feds are getting *way* too sensitive."

I provide Kopka the details beginning with our clandestine cyber operation and finishing with Razone at the Amalgamated Food Processing Plant. He nods and says, "Bastard had it coming. You sure they filmed the final act?"

"No, but they must have *some* film. The plant manager gave a statement to our NY agents stating they had cameras covering Razone's work station. OPR is heading to Albany as we speak to get the film."

Kopka rationalizes that, "You and I both know that all surveillance systems have glitches. The cameras malfunction, aimed at the ceiling, dirty lens, out of focus, the tape runs out, and a bunch of systems film over the old stuff. You've got a lot of outs here."

"You're right but it'll just be my luck that this *one* time, it all worked perfectly."

Kopka always makes me feel better. He has an ability to make the most hopeless situation seem ordinary. I limit myself two Maraska

Kruskovac's and head home. Ray makes me promise to keep him posted and if things *don't* work out, "I'll bring you good Croatian food every Sunday in the grey bar hotel."

The jail reference is gallows cop humor but it *never* fails to cheer me up.

I head home and find Lorri immersed in her stained glass hobby soldering some wild flower design. My wife is a very talented artist who is gifted in several disciplines such as oil paintings, pottery, calligraphy, flower arranging, woodcarving, and even glass blowing. She asks me how my day went. I lie and say, "Good."

Most marriage experts advise to share your troubles with a spouse. I believe that is a recipe for disaster. Nothing's accomplished by alarming your best friend that their life may be seriously transformed? Sharing my problem wouldn't change a thing and would only serve to be a dark cloud in our relationship. Besides, it's even money I can outwit Chicken Shit Walt but the cameras are the wild card. Lorri and I sit at the kitchen counter and feast on some reheated lasagna.

Our marriage has never been better. My undercover days in New York put our union under some severe strain. I was being an asshole and placed the case before my wife and daughter. Then there was my drug arrest followed by Cairo which brought us to the brink of divorce. But the marital ship turned around and Lorri commemorated that renewal with a framed calligraphy parchment which reads, "*The definition of a good marriage is falling in love with your mate again and again.*"

I have that framed inscription hanging in my office. It's one of my most prized possessions.

Lorri sips a white wine and tells me, "Nikki called and invited us to some spring football game. Just to let you know, Pedro is part of the equation."

Although *not* an Ohio native I have followed Ohio State for over a decade. The Buckeyes have won 8 national championships, 37 conference championships, 35 Big Ten titles, 4 division championships,

10 undefeated seasons, and 6 perfect seasons. In other words, they are considered a religion in the Buckeye state.

The football game sounds good, but the Pedro thing is beginning to piss me off. My little girl is too young to get serious with *any* guy let alone some *beaner*. I *do* realize that Pedro is *not* the issue but rather that my Nikki is becoming a lady who is about to replace her dad with another guy. Irrational, I realize, but most fathers will admit to some similar feeling.

"When's the game?"

"April 21."

This date has been seared into my brain matter. It is the day of my OPR interview and though I am certifiably incorrigible, even I won't chance, *"Can't make it Walt, going to a football game."*

I *also* can't tell my bride, *Can't make the football game, I'm a murder suspect,* so I say, "Oh darn, I'm scheduled to testify in court on a case I worked a year ago."

Lorri gives me the *look.* It's a combination of raising the eyebrows accompanied by a frown. The *look* is specific to job-related issues. She says, "Well, I'll be the one who represents the parental unit. Nikki will be disappointed but it won't be the first, *or,* last time." Her words peg my guilt meter as intended.

I say, "Ohio State is a pleasant 2-hour drive. I'm sure you can handle it."

My wife attempts to hide a smile, so I walk behind her and kiss her neck. I trace my finger down her spine and around to her side. Then I begin tickling her which is a family no-no since my wife is particularly ticklish. Lorri grabs my hands and turns around. She kisses me and says, "I understand John, but I miss being with you." She pauses and adds, "I'm sure Pedro will miss you too."

"That kid had *better* graduate medical school and not the typical wetback who ends up on a roofing crew."

Lorri laughs and says, "I better get a hotel reservation tomorrow."

"Why the rush?" I ask. "The spring football game is basically a glorified practice."

"That's what I thought but Nikki said they'll be over 100,000 people."

CHAPTER 64

"I was going to the worst place in the world, and I didn't even know it yet."
Apocalypse Now (1979)

Four days before the OPR.

Rose Egan was a rookie agent *prior* the attack on 9/11. She savors those pre-terrorist days when criminal activities in America *didn't* involve beheadings, WMDs, and suicide bombers. FBI agents who entered on duty *after* that horrific day view these crimes as their *new normal*. The SAC of the Cincinnati Division is reviewing the JTTF (Joint Terrorism Task Force) status report.

Egan studies the document and pens comments on several cases. One case involves a Palestinian exchange student at Xavier University with ties to Hamas. She assigns an accounting agent to another case involving three local businesses sending money to foundations that front for terrorist groups.

And last, but not least, she reviews five ongoing cases which she unofficially refers to as her Facebook Fun Five. The Bureau has established protocol on certain words or phrases that are considered *tripwire*. A computer program will recognize these words on open media sources and *red flag* the individual IPS account for additional monitoring. Then the FBI CART team will focus on these conversations and should a subject go encrypted, they refer the case to Bill Garrett.

The SAC determines that nothing in the report rises to the level of actionable Intel. The Facebook Five persist in their usual anti-government rhetoric praising Allah and while viewing ISIS propaganda videos. They seem to approach the legal line of violating the law but stops short. Her instructions are to, 'Continue Monitoring.' This latest generation of 20-somethings seem a particularly unstable and immature group of malcontents.

Rose scans the last section of the report titled Source Intelligence and the final entry grabs her attention. It concerns the President's mosque policy and her recent conversation with Cleveland SAC Williams and agent John Booker. Although she agreed with Booker that the mosque restriction is horseshit, Egan didn't appreciate his lecture on her responsibility as a SAC.

She rereads her agent's FD 302, "Faison Habib, a source of unknown reliability, advises that Nurab Benoit is leading discussion among several members of the Omari Mosad mosque concerning harming infidels. Habib did not have specific information on targets, timeframes, or methodology. It is recommended that Habib be opened and assigned as cooperating source. Introduction of an undercover agent is not feasible because the discussion group is limited to long time members of the mosque. Habib has stated a willingness to provide information on this group to the FBI."

The Cincinnati SAC would normally approve the request to open Habib as an FBI informant. He would rate top echelon status in the war on terrorism having access to a mosque which is considered a hot bed of jihad activity. But Egan's dilemma is that any FBI strategy would require Habib to attend the mosque, which is not permitted. Because, once Habib becomes an official FBI informant, he is prohibited from visiting the mosque for purposes of gathering evidence. It's the classic Catch 22 and Egan is pissed at our commander-in-chief. She picks up the phone and dials the Cleveland FBI office. SAC Williams was a mentor to Egan and if *he* trusts agent John Booker, then she would too.

At this very moment Nurab Benoit is packing five vests each with 38 pounds of explosives. They'll be worn under the outer clothing with the pockets loaded with ball bearings and screws, though everything from the bomber's wristwatch to his bones essentially becomes shrapnel with this tactic. The explosives connect to a detonator, which in turn electronically connects to a cell phone. Abu, Atwa and four other soldiers watch intently and seem fascinated with the process.

"You have been chosen to be soldiers in Allah's army," Nurab informs the group. "If you can kill a disbeliever, especially the spiteful and filthy Americans, then rely upon Allah, and kill him in any manner or way however it may be, their blood and wealth is legal for you to destroy."

"It is our destiny," Abu says.

"We will soon be with Allah," Atwa agrees. "Our life is his."

Abu adds, "And our death is also his."

Benoit points a finger at Abu and corrects him, "You will *not* die Abu. You *were* dead and He gave you life. Then He will give you death, then again will bring you to life on the Day of Resurrection and then unto Him you will return."

"We are martyrs Abu," Atwa says. "Martyrs are guaranteed the highest rank in Paradise. We will be brothers forever."

Benoit explains that, "Suicide is a sin of weakness in Allah's eyes *but* martyrdom is an act of deep piety. We are willing to sacrifice 100 martyrs of Allah to bring about the death of single American."

"If we had more soldiers," Atwa says, "then we can kill *more* infidels."

"Muslims who do *not* join the fight are 'hypocrites' and warned that Allah will send them to Hell if they do not join the slaughter." Nurab pauses and quotes the Quran. *"Let those fight in the way of Allah who sell the life of this world for the other. Who so fighteth in the way of Allah, be he slain or be he victorious, on him, We shall bestow a vast reward."*

Abu asks, "Will these vests kill many infidels?"

Benoit smiles and informs his charges, "It will level buildings and kill many, many, of the Near Enemy."

Abu smiles and tells the group. "This is good and I am honored to be an instrument of Allah."

"I will be with you my brothers. To guide and encourage you on your journey."

Benoit *didn't* clarify that a handler or *guide* often accompanies a suicide bomber to the proposed scene of an attack. In addition to guiding and encouraging the attacker, the handler sometimes triggers the explosion remotely by use of a cell phone or other wireless device. Benoit has decided that he will ignite an explosion that will be ten times more powerful than the ISIS suicide vests that rocked the Belgium airport. Witnesses described *that* scene as apocalyptic with blood and *'dismembered bodies everywhere'* after just *two* blasts destroyed that terminal on March 22, 2016.

Peggy texts me on my Bu cell phone. "SAC Williams wants you to call him."

My immediate default is something concerning my OPR but the SAC informs me that, "Rose Egan wants you to call her."

"Why?" I ask, since SACs rarely break the chain of command.

"She said, it was nothing urgent, but wanted to pass on some local Intel on lone wolves."

I dial the Cincinnati FBI switchboard and say, "SAC Egan."

After passing muster with two more keepers of the gate, Egan says, "Thanks for the quick call back, John."

An SAC referring to a brick agent by their first name isn't an invitation to reciprocate. The standard reply when conversing with a *male* SAC is "Boss," but somehow *Boss* sticks in my throat with a female so I opt for, "No problem ma'am." Yes, I am a sexist pig, but I *do* surround myself with strong women.

"First off," Egan says, "I didn't realize that you were the *Cairo* John Booker last month. Congratulations on a job well done."

"You're welcome but I had a lot of help."

"You recall our conversation on some vague terrorist activity at a Columbus mosque?"

"I do."

"Well, it's become a bit more specific."

"That's usually a good thing," I say. "But you sound like it isn't."

"Excuse my English but I'm the daughter of an Army Drill Sergeant, and this mosque policy is a cluster fuck."

I laugh and say, "We speak the same language. I was a jarhead."

"I wondered why you were so *in my face* when we last spoke."

"The Bureau shrink diagnosed me with STFU disorder."

"That's a new one on me."

"It's a condition where one just can't Shut The Fuck Up."

Egan laughs and then gets serious. "We have a mosque in Columbus that seems to be on every bucket list of jihad wannabbes. Several of the major U.S. terrorist attacks involved someone who filtered through the Omari Mosad mosque."

"So I take it that something's going on there and our mosque policy prevents you from doing your job."

"We have a source who's been part of some discussion group on the brink of going jihad."

"Where and when?"

"That's the problem. If we open him as a source and send him into the mosque, we violate the President's policy. But if I do *nothing*, I violate my oath to protect and defend this nation."

I'm not about to suggest some abuse of a presidential policy to a boss, so I remain mum.

"Your SAC advised me that you head up some special task force on lone wolfs. This seems to be right up your alley, and besides, even though Columbus is part of the Cincinnati Division, it's closer to Cleveland."

"You mentioned Cairo. Then you must know that a hip pocket source made that case."

I should mention that a hip pocket source is an individual who provides information but refuses to testify or be identified on paper. As far as the FBI is concerned they are ghosts and exist in the *hip pocket* of the agent. They used to be standard fare but a few strayed *far* off the reservation and made the practice a liability nightmare. Dr. Suehad Faison, a gorgeous Egyptian college professor, was murdered by a sleeper terrorist cell in cahoots with the North Korean government. She was my hip pocket source in the Cairo case, but that's a long and *very* complicated story.

Egan doesn't mince her words. "Of course I knew. Every SAC was briefed by the Director due to the national security implications." She pauses and her voice becomes playful. "And, if you're interested, I operated a few hip pocket sources in my day."

I do believe that SAC Egan and SA John Booker have just reached an unspoken agreement. We are on the same rogue page, but one that doesn't exist in the FBI Manual of Investigative Operational Guidelines (MIOG). I say, "This mosque case seems to fall within the parameters of our task force."

Rose provides me the name and contact number of Faison Habib. We tacitly understand that Habib will become my hip pocket source with no paper trail leading back to Ohio. And according to Saint J. Edgar Hoover, *'If it isn't on paper, it doesn't exist.'* So, in my Clintonian brain, we are *technically* not in violation of the President's directive on mosque surveillance. This may constitute fucked up logic but when one works for the government it seems totally reasonable.

I smile and rationalize that if I *am* caught, the B can just add this latest infraction to my existing felony tab.

CHAPTER 65

*"Only those who will risk going too far, can possibly find out
how far they can go."*

T.S. Eliot

Three days before the OPR

"Tommy Shoulders and I make the two-hour drive from Cleveland to Columbus. Detective Sergeant Thomas Patrick Shoulders of the Cleveland Police Department is an interesting guy. Plainspoken, profane, and a hard charger who is smart and understands what makes bad guys tick. He was Ray Kopka's partner during the great East Coast blackout and became a member of the task force by default. It was my good fortune since Tommy became a central figure of the Cairo case and dispatched three of the five terrorists. He's probably not clinically sane but he *is* extremely loyal.

"So here's the scoop."

I begin with Habib and explain the nuances of a hip pocket source versus an approved FBI source, Tommy's eyes glaze over and he stops me with, "A snitch is a snitch is a snitch. You feds can somehow fuck up a one car funeral."

He's right since most local police departments don't have the funds to pay informants so basically *all* their sources are of the hip pocket variety. End of discussion on that narrow legal distinction. I move onto the OPR matter, which is much more significant to my well-being *and* freedom.

I tell Tommy that, "You're going to be interviewed, under *oath*," I emphasize, "and asked questions about what happened in that food processing plant."

"No problem. Just tell me what you want me to say."

I smile and thank my friend for his unconditional loyalty but warn him that perjury on a murder charge can put him in jail for five years."

"It's our word against Razone's," Tommy says. "And he's in nicotine heaven so he *can't* say words."

"No but they have his signed sworn statement *prior* to dying that I sprayed pure nicotine down his gullet. And he *may* have mentioned that you handed me the can of PAM."

'So we just both deny it. It's some greasy Italian terrorist's word against two upstanding civil servants."

I'm trying to bring up the camera issue. It's a delicate legal matter that's considered prima facie evidence of a cold-blooded murder. A jury may not *like* Razone but they like cop vigilantism a lot less these days.

I decide that Tommy Shoulders *can* handle the truth and am just about to mention that we were caught on film when Tommy says, "And since I erased the tape we don't got squat to worry about."

"What did you just say?"

"Thought I told you but I guess we were busy that day."

Tommy explains that after he handed me the can of PAM, he went to the office and noticed a recording system off in a side room. "I just rewound the tape to the point where we came into Razone's work area and erased everything after that."

"Have I told you lately that I love you?"

"You may have fucked a unicorn but I personally don't roll that way."

We spend the next five minutes giggling and trying to talk but can't get two words out before laughing and punching each other's arm. Perhaps Dr. Linda is correct in her diagnosis that law enforcement officers are a group of seriously disturbed individuals.

We find Habib at a McDonalds near the German village section of Columbus. It's an upscale area and on the opposite side of town from the mosque. He's a tall lean guy in his late 30s dressed in a black Thobe Kaftan and sandals. I ask if he'd rather go somewhere else or talk in the car, but he tells us that he's comfortable right here. We make some small talk and I try to get a read on his motivation to betray his countrymen. Habib seems like a nice guy but I've been fooled by a few seemingly cordial guys who will insert an ice pick into your eyeball if you stare at them too long. He tells us that he's originally from Lebanon but picked the wrong team when Qaddafi was overthrown, so he exited stage left to America. His time in America has softened his hard-core beliefs that Jews and Americans are Satan, though Habib maintains his faith in Sharia law. Before we get to the specific details I always ask a simple question to every snitch, "So, why are you cooperating?"

Habib does not hesitate and says, "I do not believe that Allah intended for innocent babies and children to die in his name. Benoit uses the Quran to justify any *act* of violence."

We ask Habib why he believes that Benoit will act on his militant rhetoric.

"Benoit has been moving a small group of disciples in that direction for some time. There are six men who worship Benoit and trust his every word. I attend his sermons because he is considered a scholar in the Quran but he uses this holy document for his own agenda."

"You haven't answered the question."

"I would occasionally question Benoit's call for jihad and he has since banned me from his small group of disciples."

"That still don't add up to some imminent attack."

"No but Abu is a member of his group and he spoke with me a few days ago. It was this conversation which made me contact the FBI."

Habib pauses and says, "Abu said, '*I cannot die Habib.*' I asked what he meant and Abu replied. '*Martyrs for Allah will bring you to life on the Day of Resurrection and then unto Him you will return.*' "

That little aside definitely answers my question and sends a chill down my spine. This Abu fellow seems ready to die. We spend another thirty minutes discussing strategy Habib can use to elicit information from Abu. I'm especially interested in target, time, and method. "Can you go to Benoit and get back in his good graces?"

"He would be suspicious and it may force him to act prematurely. I *can* speak with Abu and discuss Allah's plan for his disciples. This may provide some indication of their plan."

"You're placing yourself in some serious jeopardy. What happens if anyone finds out you're cooperating with the FBI?"

"I believe you know the answer."

"Yes and the FBI is prepared to provide enough money for you to start a new life someplace far from here."

"That is very generous," Habib says. "But that place does not exist."

My intent is to provide Habib a shitload of ISIS snitch money if he can stop an attack. But all roads will lead back to him so he's probably correct in his assessment that with 1.6 billion Muslims in the world, Habib can run, but not hide.

We request that Habib frequent the mosque and engage Benoit's disciples in the rhetoric of jihad hoping that one may spill the beans. I hand him ten thousand dollars in an envelope and say, "Take it. Use it to loosen some tongues."

Habib reluctantly takes the envelope and promises to call me daily with an update. He leaves and I still don't have a take on what just happened. My gut is screaming that Habib *believes* something bad is going down, but, many promising leads end up in the investigative shredder.

We return to our office space around 3PM and find Jun, Gwen, and Gia at work. Jun's tapping keys on her computer, Gwen's on the phone, and Gia is writing something on a legal pad. They stop and Agent 36 asks, "Anything worthwhile?"

"The guy *seemed* legit." I begin. "And if he is, there's some bad shit coming our way. Some *really* bad shit."

Gwen says, "Talk to us."

Tommy and I take turns relating our conversation with Habib. They ask a few questions but the most important ones can't be answered. Although we have the *who,* we're missing the *where, what,* and *when.*

"Suggestions?" I ask the group.

"Twenty-four-hour surveillance," Gwen offers. "If not at the mosque, then at their homes."

"Thought about that. But could we lose our advantage of *having* a snitch."

My phone alerts me to the fact that Bill Garrett desires my ear. "Excuse me." I tell the group.

Since my continued employment with the FBI depends on the FBI cyber unit chief, I am a tad bit apprehensive. "What's up Bill?" I say going with a casual undertone.

Garrett plays along and says, "Not much. Just thought I'd call and say hi." He pauses and says, "Hi."

"Quit fuckin' with me Billy."

"OK. I've got some good news and some bad news. Whatta you want first?"

"The bad. I'd like to end this conversation on a positive note."

"We'll don't get your hopes up. Chicken Shit Walt forwarded me your justification on how an encrypted communication can mysteriously appear on the open net."

"And." I prompt.

"Sorry to say John, but it was a load of technical bullshit. Lots of untested hypothesis and faulty cyber theories. But to the unknowing eye, it was *quite* impressive."

"We still on the bad?" I ask.

"We are. And the Deputy Assistant Director attached a personal note. It seems that he's already decided that your explanation is bogus."

"That's *definitely* not the good."

"Not it isn't. Walt felt that he has enough web expertise from his many scathing e-mails to make this technical decision."

"Then why'd he send you the report?"

"Because he understands if you appeal any disciplinary action, he'll need me to sign off." Bill pauses and adds. "Walt also made a veiled threat to make sure I agreed with him."

"What was the threat?"

"Sign off on my assessment or I'll make your life miserable."

"That isn't so veiled."

Garrett actually chuckles and says, "Pretty direct but it also pissed me off. I don't handle threats well and I've got my 25 years so Chicken Shit Walt fucked up on two counts. First off, I hate bullies and secondly, I *really* hate bullies."

"When are we gonna get to the good?"

"Now." Garrett chuckles. "I just hit *send* on my reply to our Deputy Assistant Director. It basically says that your explanation is based on sound cyber principals and then I thanked him for his personal note."

"Is your ass hanging out because of me?"

"Nope. My thank you included the following. '*I appreciate your concern for my career advancement and will treasure your words of encouragement for all time.*"

"That's fucking brilliant Billy. You got him by the balls. Walt's arrogance is also his weakness because if a copy of that e-mail threat is leaked, Walt'll be forced to retire."

Garrett is silent for a second and finally says, "Just thought you'd want to know. Semper Fi."

CHAPTER 66

"Run, Forrest, run. Run, Forrest!"
Tom Hanks Forrest Gump (1994)

Two days before the OPR

I'm feeling good as a new day begins. Tommy took care of the photographic evidence on the murder beef and Bill Garrett rendered our search of Razone's apartment kosher. I'm actually looking forward to my grilling by Walt. Chicken Shit won't divulge that the Amalgamated cameras crapped the bed or that his cyber expert validated my encryption defense. The asshole will remain in character as an arrogant bully but minus any evidence, his *only* move is to threaten and intimidate a confession out of me. Maybe I'll act terrified and beg for mercy or perhaps do my Robert De Niro impression, *'You talkin' to me?'*

I briefly celebrated my unofficial acquittal last night with the gang at The Arrow Café. I'm beginning to acquire a taste for Kopka's Croatian drain cleaner. But I made it home in plenty of time for a nightcap with Lorri. She knew something was up when I walked in the door and announced, "I'm home Lucy, where's *little* Rickie?" I often quote lines from I Love Lucy when in a frisky mood. Don't know how it started but it's my usual default mode when drinking or horny, *or* both. Lorri reluctantly plays along until I begin imitating Fred Mertz.

I share the good news that her hubby has, *once* again, escaped the occupational Grim Reaper. Lorri mentions that, "This is becoming a recurring theme with you. Last year it was insubordination, assault, and drug charges. Now it's murder and unlawful searches. What's next John, pestilence and plague?"

My response of, "Lucy, I got some 'splainin' to do!" is met by a Swedish glare, so I revert to a humble John Booker. "It's a long story, hon. Let's talk."

We spend the next two hours minus cell phones or television. It's like our old days in college when our bookshelf consisted of six cinder blocks and three planks of wood and our one phone had a cord. My bride has the right to be angry, frustrated, *and* fed up. She signed up for the undercover absences but not the irresponsible behavior of a certified thrill junkie. It'd be different if my high-wire act wouldn't affect my wife and daughter, but they'd suffer greatly if I fall.

Lori asks, "Have you thought about retiring one of these days?"

I nod and lie. "Think about it a lot."

Lorri chuckles and says, "You are such a bullshitter, John."

"That obvious?"

"Only because I know you so well. Being a FBI agent is *not* what you do, it's who you *are*."

"But the FBI is changing and so are my days of running and gunning. Guys like me will soon be placed inside a glass case with a sign, *'Break only in case of national disaster.'* "

My bride chuckles and agrees, "The Bureau *does* seem to be more of a hindrance these days."

"Maybe Chicken Shit Walt is right and I *am* some rogue cowboy who can't do it the right way?"

Lorri reaches across the counter and places her hand on mine. She looks me in the eye and tells me that, "Perhaps, but you're *my* cowboy and people are alive today because you care, *and*, all the Chicken Shit Walts in the world don't."

I squeeze her hand and say, "I love you." I stand and lead my bride into our bedroom. Our lovemaking seems different this time. It's been awhile since we let go and simply enjoyed the experience. *Old married sex* is filled with the distractions of everyday life. Your mind strays and at some point, the goal becomes reaching the finish line, but Lorri and I seem engaged, mentally, physically, and spiritually. It's also been some time since we had *sweaty* sex, which has always been my personal standard for quality. We lay still for a while both reluctant to return to the real world. Lori leans toward me and says, "I feel closer to you at this moment than I have in a long time, John."

I nod and say, "Ditto." Not my best comeback under the circumstances.

Lorri and I kiss goodnight, which ends the official portion of our altered state moment. Before my wife twists into her pre-sleep position, she says, "I can't wait to see Nikki in two days."

Her mention of the Ohio State spring football game is a reminder that my OPR is the day after tomorrow. In some ways, I'm looking forward to my game of thrones with Chicken Shit, since I'm holding four aces and can see Walt's hand of seven high slop.

* * *

One day before OPR

I rise the next day at 0527 full of vim and vigor. I have no idea what *vim* is but that's how I feel. Lorri was asleep when I left and I *may* have detected a smile on her face. The Starbucks is located right off the I-71 exit at Middleburgh Heights. Donnie Osmond is his usual manic self, holding court with the early AM regulars. Donnie has *outed* me as a FBI agent so I endure some unique questions, comments, and asides. Question: "*Did Hoover really wear a dress and makeup?*" Standard answer: "Only for formal occasions." Question: How did the FBI let Hillary off the hook?" Answer: "We really fucked that one up. Question: "*Have you ever shot anyone?*" Answer: "It's been a couple of weeks."

Donnie seems especially happy to see me since he comps my caramel macchiato and says, "I have a new boyfriend John. He reminds so much of you."

I ignore the softball pitch hanging there and opt for, "Congratulations Donnie, you look happy."

Donnie beams and raises his hand to his face. "Does it show? O' *my* God!"

"I can't stay and shoot the shit Donnie. Got a busy day."

"And I was gonna tell you all about Guy."

"Guy's his *real* name?"

"Do you think gay people have aliases. What are we John, fugitives?"

"Probably, since most people into arts, entertainment, decorating, and wieners use different names."

"You are such a homophobe Johnny," Donnie says, "but I still love you." He pauses and adds, "Have a nice day." I think his middle finger was part of the sendoff.

I arrive at the office at 0612 and greet the night duty agent, Joanne Overall, with, "When do you get off third shift?"

Joanne is a fantastic agent who pissed off her supervisor for telling the truth. She's an investigative superstar leading the Division in arrests and convictions. During a biannual inspection, the inspector wondered why she transferred a fugitive case *after* she discovered the killer's location but *before* she made the arrest.

"I didn't transfer that case. Why would I do that after working my ass off for 8 months?"

"So who did?"

"My supervisor."

"Why'd he do that?"

Joanne hesitates not wanting to get on the wrong side of her boss. "I'd rather not say."

The inspector assures her that, "Don't worry, this conversation is confidential."

She decided to trust the earnest inspector and reveals, "My supervisor transferred it to his asshole drinking buddy who had *no* stats. He was worried that his lazy incompetent friend would get dinged on inspection without some arrests or convictions to show."

The inspector commiserated with Joanne declaring, "That's unethical and I'll get to the bottom of it!" He *immediately* confronts Joanne's supervisor who drops the *incompetent* dime on her. *'Agent Overall has attitude issues and her work performance is lacking.'* The bottom line being that Joanne is rewarded for her honesty with the 30-day graveyard shift. Lesson learned: *never* trust members of the Boy Wonder fraternity. They can be coldblooded and heartless creatures.

I enter our office space and put on a pot of coffee. Tommy is a creature of habit and should be walking through that door within the next 20 minutes. This Columbus mosque case is not officially opened since we can't paper a file with source information of an unopened source. Hip pocket sources are frowned upon by the management.

Habib has been contacting one of us three or four times a day. He's making some progress on getting Abu to drip and drab some details about the pending jihad. After evening prayers at the mosque last evening Abu seemed excited and began quoting several passages from the Quran concerning jihad and martyrdom. According to Habib, Abu ended his rant with, *'Paradise is near.'* This is not a good development and I need some creative thinking. None of the principals involved in the alleged plot are on social media, whether unencrypted or encrypted. We could do always do a full court press with either surveillance or snatching them up and some hostile interrogation.

Our waterboarding of Jabar in Cairo produced the names of the four terrorists about to purchase a nuclear suitcase bomb. The asshole liberals who swear that *enhanced interrogation* is useless should spend 10 minutes with my task force. The sad part is that the politician's rationale prohibiting waterboarding is flawed. It's uncomfortable enough to make you cooperate but has no lingering effects like a *beheading*.

I decide to check the FBI Intel bulletins to determine if any sabers are rattling elsewhere.

Tommy arrives 4 minutes late and he says, "Fuckin' elevator." He looks at me and asks, "Whatta you reading?"

"FBI Intel bulletins and recent statistics."

Tommy chuckles and says, "You feds generate way too much paper. Allow me to share the locals' version of statistics. *'Cleveland PD statistics indicate that terrorists commit no jihad after they've been shot.'* "

I laugh at tell him, "We got some decisions to make."

"Why now?"

"Something bad is happening. My belly is screaming to shit or get off the pot."

"Could be indigestion," is Tommy's reply but he's also an adrenalin junkie and sitting around an office results in hyperactivity.

"We'll have a powwow with the rest of the group and decide on a course of action."

Tommy tells me, "I'm going into the Mush Room and input some STOPS at our ports of entry."

"How's that going?"

"We're up to thirty-three thousand Abba Dabba Dos who won't be driving taxis or working the night shift at a 7-11."

"Well put. But haven't you run out of excuses?"

Tommy shakes his head and explains that, "It's fucking endless. Been going down our category list and this week's category is infectious diseases. I'm about to inflict some bin Ladens with small pox, hepatitis, malaria, Ebola, yellow fever, meningitis, and the ever-popular Zika virus. Next will be mental illness week and I'm thinking about inventing some new ones like *Asshole Syndrome*."

"I'll call you when the girls arrive."

My roommate, the Deputy Director, is also an early riser. We were always the first two in our classroom at New Agent training. Tony answers the phone with, "If you're calling me to beg that I get you off the OPR hook, have some dignity."

"I left my dignity in a beer bottle in Tijuana 20 years ago."

"You rehearsing your lies or will the truth set you free."

"Actually, I'm not sweating Chicken Shit Walt's inquisition. I'm calling to pick your brain."

"You sound pretty confident roomie. *Too* confident."

"Walt's out of his league on this one. His OPR gun is loaded with blanks."

"Wanna share something?"

"Not about that but I do need an adult opinion on a case." I brief Tony on *most* of the Abu development leaving out our blatant disregard of the mosque policy. I chalk up our Intel to a confidential source and ask, "What's your tubby gut telling you?"

"I'm on that seaweed diet you recommended but it sounds like you may want to surveil that location, that is," Tony pauses and offers his disclaimer, "as long as it's not a mosque, which we're prohibited from doing."

"You are starting to sound like everyone else at that Puzzle Palace."

Tony ignores my shot and says, "I was going to call you this morning anyway. I met with the Director yesterday. He had the current numbers on the lone wolf problem. It seems that just a few months ago, we had active cases in all 50 states. But, since you've formed your task force this lone wolf riddle has been significantly mitigated."

"We'd do a lot better if those assholes on Pennsylvania Avenue allowed us to do our job."

"They're never gonna do that, but listen to these numbers. ISIS recruitment is down 62%, partly because their message became significantly less inspiring, but more so because their transmissions seemed to have hit some weird electronic wall. Know anything about that?"

"Nope."

Then, there's the matter of ISIS funding down 77% which has seriously disrupted their entire operation. Can't pay their soldiers, buy bullets for their weapons, or parts for their transportation."

"'Bout time these assholes had a run of bad luck."

Tony chuckles, "Now we come to the matter of STOPs at our ports of entry. They're up some 72% and get this, 98% of those barred from entering the U.S. are Muslims who were on the WATCH LIST, *or* listed in Intel files as having terrorist affiliations. Know anything about *that*?"

"Nope, but it sounds *highly* unusual," I comment.

"How about *another* curious happening. All 33 sanctuary cities have seen an unexplained number of illegals arrested on outstanding warrants like murder, pedophilia, and sex trafficking. In other words, crimes that *even* liberals have a tough time overlooking."

"*Finally* there's some justice!" I say with a phony gospel fervor.

"It seems that *only* those of the Muslim persuasion have these sudden outstanding warrants. Who'd thought?"

"You sound like you're accusing me of *something*, but I don't know what."

"Anyway, Director McKissock wanted me to tell you that *whatever* it is that you're *not* doing, just keep it up."

"I'm pissed at McKissock. If he thinks I'm doing such a great job, why did he OPR my ass for violating the bullshit regs that's reducing the number of lone wolves?"

"Like I told you before, McKissock can forgive a lot but not cold-blooded murder. If DAD Maulbit can't prove that *one* charge, the Director will dismiss the others."

"You wanna talk about cold-blooded murder. Let's talk about the Americans ISIS beheaded on camera, or the Turkish pilot they doused with gasoline and lit up, or how about all those Christians they slaughtered, and who can forget the kids they threw off mountains?"

"But don't you understand that we aren't like them. If they reduce us to their level of savagery, then they win."

"In case you've haven't noticed, they *are* winning," I counter. "And that's the problem. Bureaucrats spout the same bullshit about rules of engagement. Terrorists are savages and have no rules. Our military deployed in Iraq and Afghanistan can't chamber rounds, or engage the enemy *until* they are fired upon first. We're not allowed to surveil a mosque because we'll hurt some rug head's religious sensitivities. Well fuck them and fuck McKissock."

Tony says, "You don't mean that John."

"The fuck I don't and if you wanna know the truth, I sprayed poison down Razone's mouth because he deserved to die and I no longer trusted our justice system to do the right thing because, the only people getting convicted these days are the good guys."

There's an awkward silence and I'm suddenly aware that I placed my best friend in an ethical trick bag. It was unintentional due to my inability to *shut the fuck up*. So, I fill in the quiet with, "Look, I didn't kill that asshole even though I should've. I'm just breaking your balls because I found out that Chicken Shit Walt has video of what happened between me and Razone. That's why I'm not worried, so don't *you* worry. It *never* happened and the proof of my innocence is currently in the hands of my worst enemy, who'll *have* to clear me. Now that's some poetic justice, my friend."

Tony seems to buy my bullshit since it makes sense. He says, "Good luck. Call me after the OPR interview."

"Luck is for rabbits, but I'll call you anyway."

I grab my second cup of coffee for the day and in walks Jun and Gia. "Good morning ladies. We're going to have a sit down as soon as Gwen arrives."

Gia wonders, "Something going on?"

"Could be Gia. Our mosque is on the front burner. We may be saddling up sometime today."

"Don't you have an OPR tomorrow?"

"Crap. You know I actually forgot about that," I fib.

"Is that because you routinely get OPR'ed?"

"Hadn't thought about it that way, but Chicken Shit Walt is seriously lacking in evidence."

"How's that?"

"His entire case boils down to *two* issues. Proof that I poisoned Razone but Joey is currently indisposed and having maggots eating out his eyeballs. And secondly, *can* conversation switch from encrypted to open source. Walt's own cyber expert says it's possible."

Agent 36 strolls into the squad area and comments, "Anything's possible, Booker, but in your case, there's usually some scam involved."

"Let's go into the Mush Room for some secret squirrel conversation."

I gather the troops and begin. "Tomorrow is my OPR conducted by Chicken Shit Walt. Some of you may be interviewed. None of you were in that room when I arrested Razone, so just tell the truth." I give Tommy a nod and continue. "The other issue could be sticky. You'll probably be asked if you have knowledge of this task force monitoring encrypted communication minus a warrant."

Gia interrupts with, "Can we refuse to cooperate?"

Agent 36 replies, "No. You can only invoke your Fifth Amendment right in a criminal case. Since none of us are the target of the OPR, it's considered an administrative matter and we either talk or get fired for insubordination."

I continue. "I'm not going to ask anyone here to perjure themselves. They probably won't fire me for the encrypted beef so do what you gotta do. I won't be mad."

I know that Tommy Shoulders and Agent 36 will fib on my behalf. They routinely lie whether under oath or under water. Since Jun doesn't officially exist, it all boils down to Gia Olson, the Italian/Swedish/Korean who shot Brenda in the back. I stare at the rookie agent and she shrugs her shoulders and says, "What's encryption?"

Everyone takes a second to grasp the implication and we all laugh. Special Agent Gia is a keeper. "We'll let's move on to a much more pressing issue; the mosque group in Columbus. Our hip pocket believes something's happening soon, and I agree." I summarize Habib's recent conversation with Abu and ask. "Options, comments, suggestions?"

"Surveil the group?" Gia offers.

"A possibility, but we already have eyes with Habib, and according to him all the conspiring takes place at the mosque. If we heat up the area, Habib's the likely suspect and they'll either kill him or freeze him out completely."

Gwen observes, *"If* Habib is our eyes he needs to see something ASAP."

"I agree. We'll go proactive with him, so the question is how?"

Tommy asks, "Have Habib supply them with weapons or money?"

Gwen agrees that, "That's an idea. Make Habib useful to them and they'll confide in him."

"But." I remind them. "He's not privy to the jihad discussion. Remember, they froze him out when he argued with the leader, Benoit."

"He's still part of the mosque and Abu seems to trust him."

"It seems we need a face to face with Habib." I turn to Tommy and say, "Get him on the phone. We'll meet Habib in three hours at our usual place."

Shoulders hits Habib on speed dial and says, "Went to voice mail."

"He may be at the mosque." I pause and give it some thought. "Let's load up in three cars. Tommy and I, with Gwen and Gia going solo. We'll stage at the Bob Evans right off exit 147. Make sure you have your diddy bag and a change of underwear. Questions?"

"What about your OPR?" Gwen asks.

"If there's nothing urgent in Columbus, I'll come back and deal with that."

It's 11:53 AM when we arrive at the Bob Evans parking lot. Tommy attempted five more calls to Habib, all going to voicemail. We have an unofficial folder with information on the mosque group including basic pedigree information of DOB, POB, Country of Origin, Current

Address, SSN, and height and weight. We're still optimistic since it's not that unusual for an informant to go missing for a few hours or even a few weeks. It happens all the time, but, my gut tells me that Habib is not your typical source. He impressed me as genuine in his concern about random genocide.

Since we're all Type As sitting around a Bob Evans is not easy. Our brains are wired for action and our imaginations will always conjure up the worst possible scenario. I resist the urge to storm the mosque. An hour passes and before I send Agent 36 and Tommy to do a drive-by the mosque and Habib's apartment looking for his blue Toyota Celica. No joy on the car. Two hours later we loosely bracket the mosque area laying back one block in a three-car triangle. We sit through evening prayers and into early evening. People in the neighborhood have been eyeballing us and a black and white patrol unit pulls behind our car.

An officer approaches from the rear and motions for me to lower my window. Officer Hyler smiles and asks, "Car break down?"

"FBI," I say holding up my tin. "Working a fugitive case."

"Maybe I can help," Hyler offers. "I know most everyone in this area."

"That'd be great," I lie. "Name of Patrick Fitzsimmons. Suppose to have a girlfriend in this area. We have several units looking for his car, a 2009 Ford Escape, Idaho *partial* license plate of DH56."

"I'll keep an eye out for the car. You have a business card with a cell number?"

"No card on me, just call our Cincinnati office."

The patrol car leaves and I decide that we've burned ourselves for tonight. I cue the mic and say, "Rogue Gallery one to RG units. We're breaking off. Meet at the staging area."

Back at the Bob Evans parking lot I check my watch. It's 10:10 PM and I am the target of a criminal inquiry some nine hours from now in Cleveland, Ohio. I tell Gwen, "Check local hospitals and jails tonight. If no luck there, then find a hotel and get a good night's sleep. We'll find Habib in the morning. I'll be back as soon as I can."

My drive back to Cleveland is quiet and I use the time to think. Habib wouldn't go out of pocket without letting us know. Something happened and my gut says that Habib has disappeared. The only question remaining is if he's dead or alive.

CHAPTER 67

*"You have no respect for authority, you are belligerent, insubordinate,
and should be taken out and shot."*

Catch-22

Cleveland – OPR Day

I arrive at the Booker heavily mortgaged split level in Strongsville,
Ohio, at 1 AM. Lorri is awake and reading a book in bed. It's one of
those historical fictional accounts involving guys with Fabio hairdos
on the cover. My wife is a veteran law enforcement spouse who *acts*
nonchalant but anxiety is always close to the surface.

"Everything OK?"

"The usual drama involving snitches."

"I know you John, and I get a feeling that it's not the *usual* drama."

"You're a very perceptive woman," I say and head for the
bathroom. "I just got some heartburn, where's the Pepto-Bismol?"

Lorri is still reading after my quick shower and as I climb in bed
she says, "Quit the Booker bull, John, and talk to me."

"I have a bad feeling that a group of radical Muslims are going to
kill people." I pause and add, "Soon."

"Do you wanna talk about it?"

"I've already discussed it to death."

Lorri chuckles and says, "Bad choice of words." She turns back to her book and says, "You'll stop them, John."

I give my wife a kiss and say, "I'm up early so I'll try not to wake you."

"I'll give Nikki your love."

"Almost forgot, you're going to the spring football game. Tell Nikki I bet 300 bucks on the home team and inform Pedro that if he ever makes my daughter cry, I'll castrate him."

Lorri chuckles and tells me that, "You *already* informed him of that."

I *didn't* forget that my wife is heading to Columbus, Ohio, home of Ohio State *and* the radical mosque. But, we have no credible information of a pending attack, let alone a, *who, what, where, when,* and *how.* I considered contacting SAC Egan but her options are limited. Gwen Googled, *Springtime Events in Columbus, Ohio,* and 27 major activities are scheduled. There's the Azalea Festival, Wounded Warrior Marathon, the Ohio State spring football game, and several art festivals. It would be irresponsible to close down an entire city with no credible threat. I even considered issuing some type of general warning but those cautionary catchphrases of, *'If you see something, say something,'* are meaningless. Most people just scratch their head and wonder, *'what the hell am I looking for?'*

* * *

Friday - 0537 - Cleveland

I awake fifty minutes before the alarm clock so I kill some time at the kitchen counter jotting down OPR notes. No matter how many scenarios I turn over in my brain, the OPR is a waste of time. Razone is dead and there's no evidence I killed him, and Garrett validated our cyber fairytale. Another consideration is Chicken Shit Walt's approach knowing he has no evidence. If it were me, I'd cancel the interview and say, *'My bad, we got nothing.'* But Walt is an arrogant asshole who feels that I already beat several Bu raps so I'm due some justice.

I arrive at Starbucks and Donnie Osmond is slinging some special involving the coming of spring. He says, "It's a tulip macchiato John, delicious."

I grab my tulip flavored coffee and linger at the counter to bullshit with my favorite barista. "How's Mr. Right?"

"Who?"

"The guy that reminds you of me?"

"Guy stole my heart *and* my credit card. The bastard."

I say, "Too bad I'm straight."

Donnie smiles and says, "Well, so is spaghetti until it gets hot and wet."

I laugh and tell him that, "You are one fucked up person."

"You know John, when I first found out you were FBI, it took me by surprise."

"Why's that?"

"I always thought those guys lacked a sense of humor."

"A communist, socialist, and a liberal enter a bar." I wait until Donnie asks, "Yea?"

"Who pays for the drinks?"

It takes a second before Donnie smiles and confirms that, "Well, at least you're not a gay basher."

"I gotta run before we start discussing Broadway musicals."

Joanne Overall is completing her final midnight punishment shift. She greets me with, "I heard that you are enduring yet *another* OPR. Have you broken the Bu record yet?"

"Working on it, but there's some agent in Vegas who just robbed a casino."

"Have you ever thought about going straight?"

"I just had that conversation with a gay guy."

Joanne shakes her head and offers, "Good luck."

Why does everyone wish *'good luck'* on OPRs? Luck has nothing to do with guilt or innocence. It seems more a matter of tactical lies and manipulation.

My OPR interview is scheduled for 9 AM so I have time to either deal with Habib or worry about my OPR. Since I always enjoyed working without a net when bantering with imbeciles like Chicken Shit Walt, I choose terrorism and call Gwen.

"Any luck with hospitals or jails?"

"None. He never made it home, and his car's not at the mosque. Habib has simply gone missing."

"I should rap this thing up in a few hours and be in Columbus by three at the latest."

Agent 36 cautions, "Don't get cute with Chicken Shit Walt. You already know he can't lay a glove on you so be respectful and lie when appropriate. He's a poisonous snake and if you get too complacent, he'll bite you in the ass."

"That's good advice Gwen. But if this mosque thing wasn't on the front burner I'd go caustic on that pompous asshole."

"We'll be waiting for you."

I spend the next hour reviewing Intel bulletins, looking for specific or generic information on terrorist activities. These bulletins contain everything from reliable source information to unsubstantiated rumors. Every JTTF pools information and analysts attempt to connect the dots. They use computer analysis and incorporate intercepted chatter, social media, and deductive reasoning. Nothing seems to jump out so I visit Bruce Gombar.

"How's it hanging?"

Bruce looks up from the pile of files strewn on his desk and says, "Buried in paper. I thought Congress passed some document reduction act."

"You asked for this shit."

I should explain that unlike police departments and the military, the first line of supervision in the FBI chains you to a desk for the remainder of your career. There are meetings, file reviews, more meetings, signing a bunch of shit and more meetings. All of which occur sitting on your ass.

Bruce looks at me and asks, "Wanna talk about your OPR?"

I shake my head, "Naw, got that covered. It's a case."

Bruce perks up since I rarely confer case strategy issues. "Whatta you got?"

"May have some terrorists about to go jihad."

My brief includes the main points but omits any *off the books* activities. Bruce has an analytical mind though no ability to think outside the box. My brain resides *outside* the box so I may require the linear intellect of a Harvard law grad. He asks some questions and I provide some answers. Bruce finally concludes, "Abu seems your weak link. Have you thought about confronting him with an old fashioned hard ass interrogation?"

Although Tommy may have suggested this as an opening move, we may have reached that point. Peggy appears in the doorway and says, "Sorry to interrupt but Deputy Assistant Director Maulbit is ready for you John."

CHAPTER 68

"What an excellent day for an exorcism."
The Exorcist (1973)

Friday - 0846 - Cleveland FBI office

Bruce says, "Good luck." I just shrug my shoulders and am beginning to wonder if I require *luck*.

Peggy gives me a hug and says, "I've been praying for you."

I embrace this wonderful and spiritual person. "Thanks Peggy, I can use all the prayers you got." I add, "But *not* on this OPR thing."

The SAC conference room is appropriately appointed with rich textured wood, *real* flowers in crystal vases, and a stainless-steel espresso machine. An unsuspecting individual may be lulled into a false sense of tranquility and assume that predators would be *persona non grata*. But that impression could prove deadly. My firm belief is that the world is filled with assholes who attempt to hide that condition from the rest of society. The group sitting before me is evidence.

Chicken Shit Walt greets me formally and introduces me to two OPR goons. Jerry Spencer resembles Truman Capote and Tamara Thompson is a dead ringer for Rosie O'Donnell. Walt selected a grotesque bow tie and orange horned rimmed glass frames for the inquisition. Limp, insincere, handshakes all around and Walt goes directly for the jugular.

"No need for small talk John. You know why you're here. If you lie, that will constitute a lack of candor and you'll be terminated. You have no constitutional right against self-incrimination since this is an administrative matter." He pauses and finishes with, "Any questions before I swear you in?"

Truman and Rosie are scribbling furiously into notebooks. Rosie occasionally meets my eyes and when she does, I smile and she immediately drops her gaze. I'm sitting on one side of the conference table with Walt positioned at the head and the two junior headhunters across from me.

I say, "Yes, *if* this is merely an administrative matter, then you really *can't* ask questions about murder?"

Chicken Shit is prepared. "Mr. Razone, *before* his untimely death, accused you of *intentionally* poisoning him. This action, *if true*, ultimately caused his death. Since Mr. Razone was in federal custody at the time, we can question you about the circumstances. Today is a fact-finding matter on that one issue as well as an administrative investigation into charges of unauthorized access, unauthorized intercepts of private conversations, falsifying official documents, lying to FBI officials, unauthorized search and seizure, and a few other miscellaneous allegations."

"I understand that I'm required to truthfully answer questions on administrative matters *but* my right to counsel is constitutionally guaranteed on criminal matters. And murder is criminal."

Walt's red face turns crimson and he seethes, "You are going to lecture *me* about constitutional rights Agent Booker. That is a joke in light of your blatant disregard of *anything* statutory."

I'm about to answer when Rosie O'Donnell interjects, "At this point, there *is* no active investigation of murder. The local New York coroner ruled Razone's death *incidental* self-poisoning. He attributed death to his ongoing exposure to nicotine. Razone made his accusation to FBI agents while in *our* custody, so we are required to investigate. *If* evidence corroborates Razone's accusation, we'll refer the case to the Albany PD. This preliminary process doesn't rise to the level of invoking your Fifth Amendment right of self-incrimination."

Walt explains that, "Agent Tamara Thompson is the Legal Division Unit Chief and has researched this specific matter."

"That sounds all officious and I'm sure you're an excellent attorney Rosie." *That* was an unintentional slip of the tongue. I say, "Excuse me, *Tamara*, but isn't a victim's dying declarations admissible in a *criminal* case?"

The silence in the room confirms that I hit a legal nerve.

Rosie's answer is more legal double speak. "I'm sure you conducted many proffers, John. Well think of this as a proffer. You get to discuss Mr. Razone's allegation and nothing can be used against you in a legal proceeding. *But* we get to decide if you're being truthful. If we determine that you're not, we *cannot* use your statements to prove our case. We must obtain independent corroboration."

Chicken Shit Walt has heard enough. He warns me. "Here are your options *Mister* Booker."

His emphasis on the *Mister* instead of *Agent* is a cautionary warning that I can transit to civilian status in no time. Walt continues, "You can either lawyer up at which time we'll conclude this OPR inquiry and you'll be fired for insubordination, or you can answer our questions truthfully."

Since I'm already aware that the evidentiary deck is stacked in my favor I'd rather not get a pink slip. I'd ultimately win the case but *after* two years of serving lattes with Donnie Osmond to pay the mortgage. I lower my head and concede, "OK, you win. I'll cooperate." As I raise my eyes Rosie is staring at me so I wink at her. She begins to reflexively smile but bites her lower lip to stop.

Walt nods at Truman who grabs his legal pad and reads a canned legal disclaimer citing what can happen as a result of an OPR investigation and concludes with, "...*and if found guilty, you can be terminated from the rolls of the FBI. Do you understand your rights and agree to provide statement?"*

"I do." And resist the temptation of adding, *'I now pronounce us man and man.'*

Chicken Shit smirks and begins the inquisition. He phrases his questions as statements of fact. This interrogation technique was last used by Attila the Hun.

"You illegally hired a Chinese cyber security expert and provided her access to top-secret government information minus a security background check."

"We conducted a top-secret background investigation *prior* to her access."

Walt actually smiles and says, "We checked the FBI files and there *is* no such top-secret background investigation."

"Check again," I challenge.

When Walt *does* check the electronic files, he'll find a complete and satisfactory top-secret clearance investigation on Jun. Several days ago, Jun actually cleared *herself*. She answered the hundreds of questions on the application and created a sixty-four-page fabricated report. The investigation includes employment and personal references as well as her college transcripts, interviews with co-workers, and the required history starting with her birth in China to her present status as the CEO of her own cyber security firm. Gwen signed off as the interviewing agent then Jun back dated the document using her computer magic. The completed packet was inserted sequentially into the appropriate electronic file. End of that problem. Next!

Walt hisses, "We *will* check that matter and since you stated for the record that your Chinese friend has a top-secret clearance, you just lied. Lack of candor is grounds for dismissal."

He's waiting for my response and I almost blurt out, *'Nanna Nanna, Boo, Boo,'* but I say, "My candor is not lacking *Mister* Maulbit." Two can play at this *Mister* game.

He glares at me and continues to the next charge. "You had no probable cause to search Mr. Razone's domicile, and therefore conducted an illegal search. This series of mishaps resulted in Mr. Razone's execution."

I'm tempted to say, *'I'll take constitutional violations for two hundred, Alex.'* But *actually* I say, "I forwarded you the explanation. We were monitoring Razone on open media based on a referral from Headquarters. He electronically disappeared for a few weeks so we assumed he went encrypted. During a routine scan, *on open media*, Razone popped up."

"What you are spouting is scientifically impossible." Walt points a bony finger at me. "I'll give you ten seconds to change your mind and tell the truth."

Since I know that Walt is bluffing I shrug my shoulders and say, "It happened." His own cyber expert determined that it *is* possible but I can't front Bill Garrett.

"So is that your official reply!" Walt screams.

"Yep."

Walt turns to Truman Capote and warns, "Make sure you clearly note Mr. Booker's response."

"Yes sir."

"Now on to a more serious issue." Walt pauses for effect and says, "I want to make sure, for the *record*, that we are about to probe into allegations that you caused the death of Joseph Razone by forcing him to ingest a liquid spray which you *knew* to be poison are voluntary."

"I fully understand *Walt*." I hadn't intended to say *'Walt'* but you can't un-ring that bell.

Just as I'm about to apologize the emotional dam burst and Chicken Shit explodes, "You are a poor excuse for a federal agent. A foul-mouthed hot dog who went undercover to escape the duties of *real* FBI agents. You have no respect for authority, the chain of command, or our policies and procedures. You assaulted your last supervisor and should've been fired had your rabbi, the Deputy Director, *not* intervened on your behalf."

"Was that a question or a comment?" I ask innocently. Rosie O'Donnell actually smiles.

Walt isn't through playing *Jeopardy* and says, "You maliciously sprayed poisonous nicotine into Mr. Razone's mouth?"

"No."

"No what?"

"No, I did *not* spray poison into that terrorist asshole's mouth, but, I'm not too bothered by his agonizing death."

Walt smugly asks, "You *sure* that's your answer?"

"I am."

"What would you say if I told you that the Amalgamated Food Processing Plant had cameras covering every inch of that plant?"

"Then I'd be *extremely* worried if I *did* whack Razone." I pause and continue with, "*But* I didn't. Next question."

Truman Capote opens his briefcase and extracts a white envelope containing a DVD disk. He slides the envelope toward me so I can read, '*Copy, Razone/Booker Amalgamated Food P.P.*'

Walt tells Truman, "Play the tape."

The OPR agent dutifully inserts the DVD disk into his laptop computer, hits play and turns the screen in my direction. Truman cues the video to start at the moment Gwen, Tommy, and I enter the Amalgamated office. Absent sound the images reveal our conversation with Jake Beck the plant superintendent. After a period of time, we begin our sham tour in route to Razone's work station. Our images electronically pass between multiple cameras as we progress between work stations. We eventually enter Razone's work area and Truman hits *Pause*. Evidently, Walt rehearsed this little Greek tragedy for maximum tension. It would have been a fantastic bluff had Tommy Shoulders not erased the remainder of the video.

All eyes are on me with the expectation that I'll fold like a wet Bangkok suitcase. I say, "Well, this *is* certainly an unexpected surprise.

Cameras. I'm shocked!" I realize that my performance is a bit over the top, so I somberly add. "Cameras, really?"

Walt is beaming like a Cheshire cat who caught the rat. "So, you *admit* that you poisoned Razone."

"Maybe, but first, I'd *really* like to see the end of that video."

"You really *don't* want that image imprinted on your brain for all time, John." Chicken Shit is suddenly my wise and sympathetic elder concerned for my mental well-being. He leans toward me and suggests, "Just say it, John, and you'll feel so much better. I'll go to bat for you and recommend some federal country club prison. We'll get the Bureau psychologist to testify that you've been under tremendous strain, your combat record as a Marine, three years undercover with the mob and working nonstop on that Cairo case. You have many mitigating circumstances."

There is a bizarre irony to Walt offering the Bureau psychologist on my behalf. I can imagine Dr. Alvarez testifying on my behalf, *'Agent Booker was under immense stress so I stuck my big toe in his mouth.'*

I have reached my limit for this bullshit and say, "OK, I *do* want to give a statement."

The three OPR goons poise pens over paper in anticipation of my murder confession. I scan the faces starting with Walt, then Truman and finally Rosie O'Donnell. I wink at her and ask, "Ready?"

They nod in unison and I say, "Jerry, you look like a more effeminate version of Truman Capote, *if* that's possible. Tamara, you bear a striking resemblance to Rosie O'Donnell although if I wasn't married and we were sharing a bottle of tequila, I'd jump your bones. Deputy Director Maulbit, you probably know that your nickname is *Chicken Shit Walt* because you are a bully, coward, and major league asshole." I rise and ask, "Did you guys get everything or would you like me to repeat my official statement?"

As I'm heading for my car in the subbasement, I think, *'I really need to self-censor myself."*

CHAPTER 69

"Doesn't expecting the unexpected mean that the unexpected is actually expected?"

Friday – 10:15 AM – Interstate 71

My two-hour ride on I-71 south is a blur of jumbled thoughts. I'd intended to play a passive role in the inquisition but my hissy fit and theatrical exit junked that plan. Even though I'll beat the OPR rap, my heart is racing. Had I *finally* gone too far with my foolish need to incessantly poke the authority bear in the eye? It's barely 10:15 AM and my premature provides extra time to locate Habib. If there *is* anything to this jihad thing, he's the key.

I call Gwen and say, "On my way."

"That's strange," Agent 36 says. "OPRs usually last half a day."

"Well, Chicken Shit Walt ran out of bullets."

"I highly doubt that."

I ignore her and switch subjects, "Any changes?"

"None. We've been making the rounds of the mosque, Habib's apartment, Abu and Atwa's place, and re-contacting hospitals and police stations."

"Shit!"

"What's wrong?"

"Have you checked the morgues?"

"Relax Booker. We're not rookies. No Habib, dead *or* alive."

A thought crosses my mind and I wonder aloud, "Any John Does sitting on slabs?"

The silence is my answer and Gwen says, "I'll get on it."

"Call me back. I should be there in about an hour."

My next call is to my wife who just happens to be on the same interstate, some fifty miles ahead. "How's it going?"

Lorri's voice is playful and upbeat. It's the voice of a mother about to see a child no longer in the nest. "Almost there. The game's not till 3, so Nikki and I are going shopping and have lunch first. My wife chuckles and adds, "I'll probably have to endure *more* GOOEY cheese with Nikki and Pedro. How's your day going?"

"Going great," I lie. She has no idea that I just testified under oath as a murder suspect while struggling to find terrorists intent on jihad. I very much wish that my wife and daughter avoid crowds today so I suggest. "You guys *actually* going to the football game. It's going to be crazy with thousands of drunks shoving and pushing."

"I hear you John, but Nikki has her heart set on it. The spring football game is a religious experience at Ohio State."

"Call me *after* the game hon. Love you."

"And I *really* love you, John."

"*Really*? What a nice adjective."

"Well sometimes we just use, *I love you*, as a tag line to end a conversation. But I want you to know how special you are John Booker, and that I'm a lucky gal."

"We both know that I'm the lucky one." I pause and tell my wife, "I'll see you tonight Lorri."

Lorri says, "It's a date."

As I'm passing the Worthington exit my phone chirps. Gwen says, "Habib is toes up at the Fairfield County morgue."

"I'm sure he didn't slip on a banana peel and hit his head."

"Close." Agent 36 says, "Habib is actually *minus* his head."

"Any details?"

"Not much. It's a rural county next to Columbus and yesterday some fishermen found a headless body. The Coroner sent finger prints through the system and there was a hit on Habib's immigration paperwork."

"No other details or crime scene evidence?"

"None, but Tommy and Gia are heading that way as we speak."

"Get them back," I say. "There's nothing useful at the morgue. Where are you?"

"Half of block from the mosque. Got tired of sitting around."

"You *do* know that you're in violation of an executive order signed by our former President."

"He may have been *your* President but Vladimir Putin has bigger balls and I was always attracted to a guy who'll wrestle a bear shirtless."

"Don't get burnt."

"I'm a female with big tits sitting alone in my car doing Sudoku puzzles. Shouldn't arouse any suspicion."

"Poor choice of words."

"It's a talent. What's the plan?"

"Wish I knew, but, it definitely won't include sitting on our asses anymore."

* * *

Friday – 11:07 AM –Columbus Ohio Mosque

Benoit lays out the six suicide vests on the floor inside his small prayer room. The imam is mindful that law enforcement is prohibited from searching the mosque. Islam is slowly creeping into the DNA of America. The Koran has become part of the curriculum taught in hundreds of schools and Sharia is the law in several U.S. cities. There are cabinet and subcabinet level Muslims serving in agencies such as Homeland Security, CIA, NSA, *and* the FBI. Muslim judges sit on federal and appellate courts and there are 19 Muslim members of Congress. Muslims have penetrated all three branches of U.S. government and one outcome is that mosques are now off limits to law enforcement. Benoit smiles when he reflects that American hypocrisy and political correctness permit surveillance at churches, synagogues, and temples, but *not* at the locations of their sworn enemy.

Several days ago, Abu approached Benoit and mentioned, *"Habib has been making inquiries about our activities."*

Benoit expelled Habib from his prayer group due to his frequent challenges of Allah's teachings. His attempt to penetrate the privacy of his prayer group using Abu is bothersome. Habib was aware that Abu is unstable due to his mental illness. The imam encourages Abu to take the pills to stabilize his behavior, but he complains that they make him drowsy. Habib had become a liability so Benoit ordered Allah's soldiers to confront the unbeliever with the sword.

Benoit has been planning today's jihad for over a year and would not risk a last-minute set back. The date was chosen to coincide with an event that would insure maximum death and destruction. Men, women, children, *and* an American institution all in one location. It will be discussed in hushed tones by the faithful for centuries. That is the reason soldiers of Allah took their first step to Paradise by beheading Habib.

The imam gazes at his charges who are prepared to become martyrs and says, "The prophet Muhammed has decreed that his word be spread through jihad. He divided it into *dar al-Islam* (abode of Islam) and *dar al-harb* (abode of war). The aim of jihad is clear: to establish God's rule on earth by compelling non-Muslims to embrace Islam, or to force them to accept second class status if not *eradicate* them altogether."

The six men ranging in age from 19 to 27 nod. Benoit lowers his voice and says, "Think not of those who are slain in Allah's way as dead. Nay, they live, finding their sustenance in the presence of their Lord and rejoice in the bounty provided by Allah." He pauses and almost whispers, "Some of you have family who are devout disciples of Allah, and will be those left behind. Visit your loved ones and though you may not discuss your fate, you should soothe any past transgressions which may block your journey. Be back at the mosque no later than 2:30."

Abu and Atwa stand on the sidewalk outside the mosque. Atwa says, "I will visit my mother and her mother. They are all that is left of my family. And who will you choose Abu?"

Abu thinks for a moment. "My parents have embraced American values. They have Jew friends and can no longer be disciples of Allah. They will not make the journey to Paradise, but my sister Faison is pure and performs the good deeds of *da'wa* (missionary activity). She reads the Quran and says her daily prayers. I will visit my sister."

Atwa hugs his fellow soldier in Allah's army and says, "We will soon be in Paradise, entitled to special status for this is our Judgment Day."

Gwen perks up when two young men exit the mosque and stand conversing on the sidewalk. She grabs her binoculars, focuses on the twosome, and recognizes Abu from photographs supplied by Habib. The other guy resembles Atwa, but Gwen can't be sure and mumbles that, '*these Muslim guys all look alike.*' Abu hops on a moped and Agent 36 starts her engine. '*A bird in hand,*' and all that stuff she thinks.

* * *

Friday –11:08 AM– Ohio State campus

Ohio Stadium is the fourth largest on-campus facility in the nation with seating capacity of 104,944. Nestled on the banks of the Olentangy River, Ohio Stadium is one of the most recognizable landmarks in all of college athletics. Built in 1922 at a cost of $1.3 million the horseshoe-shaped stadium is a monument to college football. The Ohio State football program has always had a special fan base, but on this spring day, Buckeye Nation is expecting more than 100,000 fans. This constitutes an attendance record which is unusual since the spring football game is *practice*. The Ohio State offense plays the *Ohio State* defense.

Lorri, Nikki, and Pedro are back at the GOOEYZ Grilled Cheese Restaurant at the South Gateway Campus Alley. There's a 25-minute wait and a server explains that a customer sued the restaurant claiming their gooey cheese caused his bypass heart surgery. Ever since the legal action went public, the restaurant has been packed. It's a very confusing world these days.

Nikki says, "Too bad Dad couldn't make it."

"You know your dad. He's working one of his big cases, but he sends his love and says he bet $300 on Ohio State."

Pedro wonders, "Doesn't he know that Ohio State is playing *Ohio State*?"

Lorri smiles and explains, "Nikki's father has a somewhat offbeat sense of humor."

Nikki suggests, "Don't ever let him know he got to you. If dad senses any weakness, he's relentless."

"Your father's very nice, but, I choose my words carefully around him."

Lorri says, "You're dating his daughter and no man will *ever* be good enough. John will push and push. He's probing for any weakness, so my advice is to be yourself and speak your mind."

Nikki adds, "But not *too* far. He shot one of my boyfriends because the guy had an earring."

Pedro laughs and says, "I *think* you're kidding *but* knowing your dad, I'm not sure."

"What time do we have to get to the stadium?"

"Game starts at 3, so we better get there by 2:30?"

Lorri checks her watch and says, "It's 12:41, we have an hour or so to do some shopping."

* * *

Friday – 12:42 PM

Agent 36 calls me and says, "Subject moving eastbound on High Street."

"I'm not familiar with Columbus. Give me a cross street."

A brief silence the Gwen tells me, "High and Whitehall."

"10-4" I say and load the information into my GPS. Gwen is 23 minutes from my location. I follow the robotic British voice of Sarah to *"turn right in 200 feet."*

As I turn right on Hamlet and left on Front Streets Gwen updates me. Ten minutes later she transmits, "Subject stopped at a residence. Entering a home located at 23171 Albert Avenue"

I load the address into my Garmin and Sarah provides my ETA at 18 minutes.

Five minutes later Agent 36 tells me that, "I just checked this address. It's Abu's parents' home."

"Be there in about 10. Call Tommy and Gia and give them your twenty."

"On it."

I'm caught up in the excitement of the chase, but, have no idea what we'll do once I get there. My training agent, Mat Raymond, was a former logistician in the Army. He continually reminded me that in law enforcement operations you *must* plan for *every* conceivable possibility. "But," he warned, "Every once in a while, you just gotta say fuck it!" This seems to be that occasion. I mentally run down our PC and it includes plenty of circumstantial combined with illegally obtained evidence. The Omari mosque, Benoit, Habib, and Abu's recent talk of jihad. I can't include Habib, who is a verboten unofficial hip pocket source and I'd have to admit violating the President's mosque policy to attribute Habib's info. *But,* since my rogue snitch is dead, I may be able to construct a string of official sounding bullshit. This brain exercise could go on forever so I go to Mat Raymond's plan B, *"Fuck it!"*

Our Bu radios are on a scrambled frequency. I cue my mic and announce, "Hello sports fans, Gwen has the eye but we'll need a little get together and talk this thing through. Tommy, my twenty is the BP gas station three blocks west of target location, corner of Albert and Washington."

"10-4."

Tommy Shoulders and Gia pull beside my car. He rolls down his window and says, "What's 8 feet long and wrapped around a lump of shit?"

Gwen repeats, "Don't know, what *is* 8 feet long and wrapped around a lump of shit?"

Tommy waits a beat and says, "A turban."

"Not one of your better ones." I comment but notice Gia laughing. Maybe Bruce Gombar is *right*, and Gia requires a more traditional Bureau experience. To date, she shot a teenager in the back and now finds Tommy Shoulders amusing. I shake my head and brief them on how we arrived at this place. I finish and ask, "Ideas?"

Tommy being both direct and astute asks a few questions. "Do we think Abu and his group is about to go jihad?"

We have a brief discussion and the consensus is '*Yes.*'

"Can we get a warrant for the mosque, his house or anywhere else in Columbus?"

A big fat '*No!*'

"Who can we lay our hands on who *may* have knowledge of this jihad?"

That'd be, '*Abu.*'

"So." Shoulders sums up our options, "We can continue this circle jerk or snatch that camel jockey and find out what's up."

I check my watch and it is now 1:27 on a sunny Friday day in April. We decide to snatch Abu using a traffic stop pretext. If given the opportunity, we'll pick a crowded commercial area away from Abu's present location. Tommy and I will do the ruse stop with lights and siren. Gia and Gwen will be close by if things go to shit. Their exclusion by gender is calculated since Muslim men do not respect women and we don't need Agent 36 smacking Abu upside his head.

In the meantime, I position Gia a block from the target location essentially bracketing the area. Everyone's on board with the plan. Tommy jumps into my car and I ask, "Do you have your Taser?"

* * *

Friday - 2:03 PM- The Horseshoe

Lorri can't believe the mass of humanity as she enters the Horseshoe. She's seen crowds this size on television but never could imagine the effect on her senses. The stadium actually vibrates and the pandemonium of color, smells and sounds border on chaos. She closely follows Nikki as Pedro leads them in single file toward their seats. Young fans hoop, holler and the Ohio State band horn and drum section add to the fever pitch. The aisles are nearly blocked with students excitedly exchanging high fives, munching on nachos and gulping beer. It seems that spring fever combined with Ohio State football has created a holiday mood.

"This is unreal." Lori comments

Nikki says, "You should come to a regular season game."

"No thanks honey, don't think my heart could take it."

"You can't play the age card mom. Most of my friends meeting you for the first time think you're my sister." Nikki pauses and adds, "My *older* sister."

They find their aisle and crawl over some students who have scarlet and grey painted faces. Pedro points to three seats near the twenty-yard line about twenty rows from the field. Lorri finally relaxes and says, "Good thing your father isn't here. He'd be complaining about how these kids should get a job and quit acting like idiots."

"Was dad a party animal in college?"

"He had his moments. I'll leave it at that." Lorri points to the mass of humanity and comments, "I'd hate to have to evacuate this place. It'd be impossible to move."

* * *

Friday – 2:04 PM – Abu's house

"We got movement."

"10-4 Gwen."

"Subject westbound on Albert. Coming at you Gia."

A few seconds later Gia broadcasts, "Got him."

Gwen confirms, "You got the eye."

Surveillance is basically an art form. Someone must *always* be responsible for having an *'eye'* on the target less you hear that sickening statement of, "*I thought you had the eye.*"

Gia calls out, "Subject on a red and white moped doing the speed limit. No helmet and wearing a white jacket. Approaching Washington Street. Coming your way John. Seems about to turn northbound on Washington."

Abu actually passes the BP gas station where Tommy and I sit. I tell Gia, "We'll fall in behind you. Keep the eye until we get away from this area."

"10-4."

I pull behind Gia's task force car, which is a nondescript Chevy Impala. The Korean/Italian/Swedish FBI agent seems intent on not losing Abu. The moped turns onto Washington Street, which is a series of stores, restaurants, and vacant buildings.

"He's heading back toward the mosque," Gwen advises.

"How far is the mosque?"

"Another 3 or 4 miles."

I look at Tommy and he nods. I cue my mic and say, "We'll take the eye, Gia."

Gia slows and allows me to pass. Abu is about 50 yards ahead with four cars between us. I ask Tommy, "Ready?"

"Born that way."

Detective Shoulders places our emergency blue light on the dashboard and I close the gap. We swerve into the middle turn lane pass the remaining cars then pull directly behind the moped. Abu doesn't seem to be aware of our presence. Our car is only some ten yards behind when I flip the toggle switch for the siren. At first Abu ignores the obvious blare which allows Gwen the opportunity to pass Abu. This places our target in the same position as the vanilla cream inside an Oreo cookie. I close the distance to about five feet and Tommy hits the loudspeaker, "FBI, pull over, now!"

Abu tilts his head backward and we make eye contact. It's not the look of cooperation. I transmit, "Be aware, subject may run."

Gwen and Gia both acknowledge with a "10-4."

Abu lowers his upper torso which serves to reduce the wind resistance and usually precedes a significant increase in speed. The sound of 125 CC engine at maximum thrust is high pitched. I know that Abu can't outrun us but if he reaches the mosque our plan has '*shit the bed*.' Abu's *getaway* strategy involves using his smaller vehicle's maneuverability which is a decent plan. The moped is only capable of reaching a maximum speed of 28 mph, which doesn't sound that fast but within the confines of an urban area, it's sufficient to disappear. Gwen is probably our most aggressive team member and when Abu attempts to swerve ahead, she mimics his movement. This turns into some weird synchronized motorized dance as they swerve back and forth, only inches apart. Gwen realizes that this dance can't continue for long so she hits the brakes. Abu's moped hits Gwen's back bumper and he literally goes airborn. He actually lands on the front hood of the Bu car and lays there motionless. Gwen is out of her car and Tommy and I are sprinting toward the scene. Just as the three of us are about to approach the living hood ornament, Abu sits upright and slides off the car onto his feet. He's reaching inside his tunic and we react by unholstering our weapons, screaming, "Hands, Hands up!"

Abu has his own pistol which I recognize as a 45 caliber. He has the weapon at his side and pointed at the ground. Abu stares at three pistols aimed at his center mass and seems frozen as we continue to demand that he drop the weapon. He smiles and raises both hands into the air, surrender mode. I take a deep breath thinking the worst is over and take a step toward Abu. He slowly rotates his weapon toward his right temple. I scream, "No!"

Abu pulls the trigger and the powerful bullet enters and exits his skull along with brain matter.

Tommy turns to me and nonchalantly observes, "Well, we *may* have miscalculated that boy's commitment to Allah."

* * *

Friday – 2:35 – The mosque

Benoit realizes that something is wrong. His most fervent disciple is late. Abu is the one believer most eager to enter Paradise on this glorious day. He often utters the refrain, *"O Allah, that there is nothing more beloved to me than to fight in your cause and join you."*

Benoit forbade his soldiers the use of cell phones and personal computers for the past two months reminding them that, "The FBI has many agents who inspect the internet and airwaves for the servants of Allah."

So even though he cannot contact Abu, the Fatwah is not in jeopardy. Benoit did not share any details of today's jihad with his soldiers. And, since law enforcement is forbidden from hiding microphones or placing informants inside mosques, they cannot stop destiny. The target and time are known to *only* Benoit, but when he reflects on the likelihoods of Abu's absence, none can be good.

Atwa and his five remaining soldiers sit before him with piercing eyes. He tells the group, "Muhammad said: 'I have been ordered to fight against *all* the people until they testify that there is no god but Allah and that Muhammad is Allah's messenger.' "

Benoit understands his mentor role because even Allah's most devoted disciples may suffer doubts about the hereafter. No matter how enthused a martyr seems, it's just *not* natural to blow up your own body. So, on this glorious day Benoit must motivate and engage their minds *until* he can detonate their vests. The imam will ignite them simultaneously by transmitting a signal on his cell phone. That's because they're so easy to construct and deploy." Bombers use the cell phone as a typical remote control: to send a signal via radio airwaves. The signal energizes a relay connected to a blasting cap, which in turn detonates explosive material.

Although remote controlled toys and keyless entry devices set off bombs too, cell phones remain the most popular. That's because they're convenient in a variety of ways:

Using 1200mA x 3.7-12 volts, they have just the right power.

They have time synchronization capabilities.

They have an extremely accurate alarm clock function.

They include a vibration circuit that can be addressed by phone number or function.

They allow for worldwide usage.

It's impossible to track where they come from and where they go — especially if they're disposable.

It's easy to get inside their circuitry.

They're easy to conceal.

Their highly unstable batteries are easily ignited.

This remote-control signals radio airwaves and energizes a relay connected to a blasting cap which detonates the explosive material. Cell phones have an extremely accurate clock function synchronization capabilities and allow for distance and even worldwide usage.

It is Atwa who asks, "Where is Abu?"

"Abu will meet us."

Benoit lifts a vest from the table and holds it before the group. "This weighs 19 kilograms or 38 pounds. None of you will have difficulty with its weight. Do *not* carry anything in your hands since coolers, seat cushions, or bags are often searched by security. The temperature outside is 62 degrees so most people in the crowd will be wearing light coats or windbreakers." Benoit pauses and points to a scarlet and grey windbreaker on the table. He continues, "This will cover the vest and not arouse suspicion. You will enter Gate 22 and walk slowly to your assigned section and seat which is on your ticket."

Benoit points at Atwa and tells him, "You have a special assignment, Atwa. Once the infidels hear the sounds of Allah's wrath, they will squeal like pigs and flee toward the exits. There will be pandemonium and they will be forced into a massive cluster with nowhere to go. You will place yourself in the middle of this group and meet Allah."

The imam *doesn't* share information of the residual carnage on the suicide martyr. Once the vest is detonated, the explosion resembles an omni-directional shotgun blast. Much of the energy wave rolls upward, ripping the bomber's body apart at its weakest point, between the neck bones and lower jaw. It accounts for the curious phenomenon in which suicide bombers' heads are severed clean at the moment of detonation and are later found in a state of perfect preservation several yards away from the torso's shredded remains.

The steel balls, which measure 3 to 7 millimeters in diameter, constitute the most lethal shrapnel and is responsible for about 90% of all casualties caused by this kind of device. The vest's tight constraints and the positioning of the explosive pouches, channel the energy of the blast outward. Human beings within 100 yards will be decimated.

Benoit directs the four men to prayer rugs facing east. They kneel and lay their heads forward in prayer. The imam says, "Allah has made this promise to you in the Quran, CHAPTER 22-Al-Hajj, verse 58: Those who leave their homes in the cause of Allah, and are then slain or die - on them will Allah bestow verily the goodly provision of Paradise."

* * *

Friday – 2:45 PM – Washington St. Columbus

The car chase and subsequent bullet in the brain thing has triggered some mild interest in the immediate area. Crowds are forming and police sirens wail off in the distance. But our clock is ticking and we can't afford to spend hours at the crime scene debriefing the locals. I'll need Tommy and Gwen's experience for this pesky terrorist thing, so I sacrifice Gia. "We need to get going." I tell her. "You *need* to stay here and explain this mess."

Gia is smiling and wonders, "What would *that* explanation be?"

"Good question. The truth, *but* if that fails just keep repeating the FBI refrain of, *'national security, no comment.'* Just tell them we're working a terrorism-related matter, and Abu was a subject in that investigation. While attempting to interview him, he ran, and rather than chat with the FBI, he blew his brains out."

Agent 36 adds, "The cops will probably make some wisecrack that putting one in your brain is *usually* preferable to *chatting* with the FBI."

Gia laughs and says, "I got it here. You guys go and have some fun."

I turn to Gwen and say, "You've totally ruined this impressionable young agent. Now, she'll have to go back to the academy for some reprogramming." I turn back to Gia and say, "Any problems, just call SAC Rose Egan, and tell her John Booker needs some cover with the locals."

As we are jogging to our cars Gia's slight voice can be heard saying, "Good Hunting."

Agent 36 is following close behind in her Bucar and I que my mic and tell Gwen, "Take the lead. You have our location in your GPS."

"The mosque," She concludes. "We back to stealth *or* we going rogue?"

"I'm tired of being good. Let's go Cairo on their ass."

* * *

Friday – 2:59 PM- The Mosque

We pull up in front of a large tower called a minaret. It's used to issue the call to prayer five times each day and on this Friday afternoon the tower is making noises. The three of us stand near the entrance and Gwen asks, "How we playing this?"

"Habib described some private prayer room that Benoit used for his group."

Tommy finishes my thought with, "We'll ask for a look see."

I push open tall ornate doors and notice a large wash basin used for ritual washing before prayer. I later learn it's a called a wudu, used to wash hands, faces, and feet for purification. Since we're not here for hygiene we walk past the bird bath and enter a gigantic hall. The bare room is devoid of pictures, furniture, and statues, which Muslims believe to be blasphemous. A niche in one of the walls, called a mihrab, shows the direction that the worshippers should face toward Mecca.

Though its main function is a place of prayer, mosques offers a variety of services such as Sunday schools, Arabic classes, Quranic instruction, youth activities, marriages, funerals, and potluck dinners. This *particular* mosque has a reputation for community activism with several smaller rooms set aside for that purpose. It is inside one of these rooms that Benoit planned his jihad.

A few men stare at us. It's obvious that we don't belong since Agent 36 is minus the mandatory head scarf and Shoulders resembles some demented derelict. His wardrobe and facial expression rarely fluctuates. Blue jeans, pull over shirt or hoodie dependent on the outside temperature and a perpetual scowl. A man garbed in Bisht cloak approaches us with an air of authority. "Can I help you?" he says, with the tenor of a man who has *no* intention of helping.

I quickly flash my Creds and say, "Special Agent Walt Maulbit, FBI." My identity theft won't pass any serious inquiry, but it'll certainly cause Chicken Shit some heartburn later.

The man stares at me with disdain and asks, "And what makes you so *special* Mr. Maulbit?"

This isn't going well so I default to caustic, "Well sir, my Italian mother, God bless her soul, always thought I was pretty special, because I could fart *God Bless America*. Wanna hear it?"

Kalif glares at me and demands that I repeat *and* spell my name. This little spelling bee maneuver is designed to intimidate me so I feign a look of insecurity and slowly spell, "M-A-U-L-B-I-T."

It turns out this arrogant asshole is the imam of record for this radical shithole. Benoit holds the power but Kalif is the face, and, an ugly one at that. His face resembles a country road under construction with ruts, a large bulbous nose, beady eyes, and warts.

"You must be aware that the FBI is not permitted to enter this house of worship."

Agent 36 attempts to diffuse the situation with her charm, "We understand sir, but have a pressing matter and need your help."

Kalif replies with, "We do not recognize your authority and you will please cover your head as you insult the prophet Muhammed and our faith."

This is the first time in modern history that Agent 36's tits have failed to neutralize a man. Gwen stares at the imam and tells him that, "This is Ohio, Bubba, and that subservient shit don't cut it here."

Kalif is about to respond when Shoulders tells Kalif to, "Shut the fuck up before I arrest your smelly goat ass for mopery."

Tommy seems to score one for the good guys since Kalif's not accustomed to having his authority challenged within these four walls. He is temporarily speechless as he gauges this scruffy guy who now seems to resemble an angry, mangy Rottweiler. He concludes that I'm the only sane one in this insubordinate group and tells me, "I will allow you one minute to leave, at which time I'll call your office, and you will lose your job and pension."

It's decision time and I'm no longer in the mood for verbal gymnastics. "Can we speak with you for one minute, sir, in a more private place and we'll be gone."

Kalif is deciding whether to go verbally jihad on my ass but is wary that Tommy will go postal on *his* ass. He angrily agrees and says, "One minute, follow me."

We follow Kalif to an office. It seems the conventional workplace with a large desk, scattered papers, two filing cabinets, and stuff on the walls. Kalif remains standing and looks at his watch, "One minute." He warns.

I give Tommy a nod and say, "It concerns an individual by the name of Mr. Taser."

Kalif immediately responds with, "I do not know this person."

Tommy seems preoccupied and evidently missed my cue so I say, "Tommy, isn't that the guy?" He looks at me and I repeat more slowly and louder, "Don't we need to find Mr. *Taser* right now?"

Shoulders nods and says, "Let me check my notes, we could be in the wrong place."

He fumbles inside his pocket while closing the gap between himself and Kalif. I attempt a distraction by pointing to some painting on the wall and ask, "Is that some desolate place in sand land?"

As Kalif is forming a reply, Shoulders takes two quick steps and Tasers Kalif in his neck. The imam shudders as the electrical impulse interrupts the regularly scheduled programming to his brain and his muscles scream, *'What the fuck just happened!'*

We lock the door and cuff the imam who has fallen to the floor. Shoulders used Mr. Taser in Cairo on another imam with similar results, so we know the drill. Kalif's brain will regroup in 2 to 5 minutes so we can't risk leaving him alone.

I tell Gwen, "You stay with this asshole while Tommy and I bag this building."

Agent 36 smiles and takes the Taser from Tommy who says, "It's OK if you kill this guy just like the other jamuck in Cairo."

I add, "That'd be two imams in *two* years. You'll be considered a specialist in whacking Muslim clerics and can teach the course at Quantico."

We exit the office and find several other doors in this area of the mosque. Some have designated signs like *Day Care* or *Classroom,* but many are unmarked. We take turns opening the doors and most are empty. The Day Care has kids running around and an elderly lady looks our way. I bow and say, "Building inspectors, wrong room."

The next door is secured with the most rudimentary tumbler cylinder lock. I insert my pick and push the pair of pins upward and out of the cylinder. We enter and notice an empty room configured like a classroom with several chairs facing a desk. Tommy searches the desk and I open a closet door. It's dark but I notice several hanging jackets one of which is bright and catches my attention. I pull it off the hanger and hold it up in the light of the room. "Look at this." I tell Tommy.

He pauses and turns toward me. It takes several seconds before Shoulders says, "Holy fuck!"

I am holding a brand-new Ohio State scarlet and grey windbreaker. I ask, "You thinking, what I'm thinking?"

"Let's get going."

CHAPTER 70

"Have fun storming the castle."
Billy Crystal – The Princess Bride

Friday – 3:42 PM – Ohio State Stadium

We grab Gwen and pile into one car. My brain is running down options but it becomes all jumbled. My wife and daughter are somewhere in that stadium along with suicide bombers. I check my watch and it's now 3:42. The game was scheduled to start at 3 so I tell Gwen, "Call someone at the stadium and order an evacuation."

Gwen thinks about this for about 5 seconds and says, "Three things; one, *who* do I call, two, *will* they believe that I'm an FBI agent, and three, will they *risk* a mass evacuation for an unknown caller?" She pauses and adds, "I don't think so."

I make three attempts to contact Lori and Nikki on their cell phones but neither answers. Lorri's phone is usually in her bag and the crowd noise would make it impossible to hear the muffled chime. I call SAC Rose Egan's personal cell number, "John, this is unexpected, is everything OK?"

"No and I don't have time to explain, but you've *got* to contact someone at Ohio State and have them immediately evacuate their football stadium."

"What is going on?"

"There are suicide bombers at that game. I don't know how many, where, or what they look like, other than they'll be wearing Ohio State windbreakers."

Egan correctly observes, "Most people in that stadium will be sporting scarlet and grey colors. Let's talk about this."

"We don't have time to talk. It's time to act."

Egan tells me that, "I'll contact the chief of police at Ohio State. They have their own police force with arrest powers. I'll also contact the Ohio State police and send 100 FBI agents there ASAP. But *if* we attempt to declare a mass evacuation, this will cause panic and many injuries when 100,000 people stampede toward the exits."

"My wife and daughter are at that game."

"I'm so sorry John, but maybe your info is wrong, maybe it's not today or the stadium. Let's play it safe for now. Trust me."

"I *don't* trust you. Because you and the rest of the bureaucrats can't make a decision," I shout. "My family is at that game!.....fuck you, I'll handle it..."

As I'm terminating the call I hear Egan say, "Don't go doing something you'll....."

* * *

Friday- 3:44 PM- Ohio State University -The Horseshoe

Benoit tells the five men that he envies them since they will soon be in Paradise. "But Allah has resolved that I remain and serve him in this hell called earth. *You* are his chosen ones on this glorious day."

He stops the van in the 5-minute loading/unloading zone near Gate 22 and says, "Slay the idolaters whenever you find them and let them find ruthlessness in you."

The men exit the van in their Ohio State windbreakers looking like a bunch of college students late for the game. Atwa is the last to leave tells Benoit, "I can feel that Abu is dead. You said that he will join us, but, it is *us* who will join him."

Benoit nods and drives off toward the parking lot. He positions the van a safe distance from the blast and flying shrapnel. Two cell phones lay on the dashboard. One will detonate the vests of the four soldiers and the other will ignite Atwa's special surprise. Four vests contain 38 pounds of plastic explosives enhanced by ball bearings and nails, but Atwa is sporting the mother lode of all suicide vests. Forty-seven pounds of Octanitrocubane, which is the most powerful non-nuclear explosive known to man. A few ounces can destroy an airplane and 47 pounds is capable of causing structural damage to people, dormitories, and classrooms one mile away.

The Ohio State offense has scored 14 points on the Ohio State defense when Benoit ignites four of the five suicide vests. These soldier martyrs are seated in sections 16B, 24A, 17A, and 21D. Benoit chose these precise seats after researching the virtual interactive seating chart on the web.

Their strategic positions afford maximum casualties given the burst radius, incline of stadium style seating, and the sheer mass of human beings packed within the blast area.

The four simultaneous explosions instantly kill 1369 men, women, and children including a third of the Ohio State marching band. Another 447 will die within the next year, with 1008 wounded, many with severed limbs. The mortality rate in the semi-enclosed stadium area is 57% of victims within 200 feet. The remaining 43% will survive the blast but sustain traumatic amputations, burns, lacerations, rupture and middle ear damage, abdominal hemorrhage and perforation, globe (eye) rupture, concussion, Traumatic Brain Injury (TBI) without physical signs of head injury, and the severing of major arteries, all resulting from flying debris and bomb fragments.

It is the deadliest attack on American soil since 9/11.

Lorri is immediately aware that the explosions are not part of the festivities. Realization comes to the rest of the masses in stages. Thirty seconds after the initial blasts reality is confirmed by the screams of the wounded. The confusion and devastation is so massive that those still ambulatory run blindly in all directions.

She tells Nikki and Pedro to "Stay put."

* * *

Friday-4:07 PM- The Horseshoe

We're about a mile from the stadium when the earth rocks. A chip of concrete hits the roof of the car and we all flinch. Our emergency lights and sirens are having little effect as people scramble away from the blast area. Cars are now careening toward us as people are in survival escape mode. Our car comes to an impenetrable barricade of cars, people, debris and bodies about 200 yards from the stadium. As I'm bailing out of the car, I tell Tommy and Gwen, "I'm going to find my family, you can do what you want."

My brain is no longer in law enforcement mode. I can care less about a crime scene, aiding the wounded, or assisting in the evacuation. My wife and daughter's well-being is all that matters. I have no idea of where I'm going or what I'll do when I get there. The first gate I approach is blocked by bodies who have been trampled upon and form a human barricade. As they attempt to gain their feet another barrage of people come crashing upon them trying to escape the carnage behind them. The fear blindly propelling them is the possibility of another blast.

I notice a 20-foot cyclone fence, which forms the first line of separation between the gate area and stadium proper. My adrenalin allows me to leap a third of the way up as I snag the metal with my fingers and stabilize myself with my feet. Another burst of energy and I'm over the top, taking two rappelling steps downward before dropping the last 8 feet. I notice that Gate 22 to my right is still a human cluster fuck of bodies so I head left.

* * *

Lorri is searching for an exit. She concludes that since the bombs were detonated simultaneously the stadium now provides some degree of safety for Nikki. She feels better that Pedro is protecting her little baby girl and her goal is to get the three of them to safety. People are running in every direction, many screaming, some limping, and some with gaping face and head wounds. She stops and attempts to gather herself and think logically. She looks at blue directional charts on the concrete walls and notices that Gate 22 is a handicap entrance. They are usually wider and more accessible so there should be a better opportunity to exit. Lorri follows the arrow and begins a circular route in search of a way out of this hell.

I'm in full gallop and about to enter the field area when I hear an enormous explosion in the distance. Three seconds later I am flying through the air and then darkness.

* * *

Three days later I regain consciousness in the ICU of the Cleveland Clinic. A nurse notices my open eyes and asks, "How you feeling?"

I'm having difficulty hearing her and my attempt to ask, '*How's my wife and daughter?*' comes out as gibberish. She calls the doctor who appears and offers, "I'll speak into your good ear." Dr. Mann bends over the bed rail and tells me that, "It was touch and go, but, you seem to be one tough guy. You had blast lung injury which is usually fatal, but that was actually the *least* serious problem. There were third degree burns, a burst ear drum, ripped soft tissue and rapid blood loss. We even had to remove five ball bearings from your stomach and lung."

I try again and mouth, *'How is my wife and daughter?'*

Dr. Horace Mann quickly says, "Your daughter is fine. You need your rest." He turns a small lever on my IV which releases some knock out juice and I'm heading back to dream land. Just as I am dozing off I realize that my wife is dead.

EPILOGUE

Seven months later – The Booker Home

The good news is that my Lorri died instantly. Atwa's powerful explosion killed an additional 854 people, and wounded 1875 more. Nikki survived without a scratch and I thank God that he spared my little girl. Consistent with Lorri's wishes, she was cremated and her ashes spread into the ocean off the coast of North Carolina. We'd spent many summers at Emerald Isle and it was her favorite place on earth.

Benoit escaped and the rumor has him back in Libya. Nikki has been by my side for the past six months. I'm now ambulatory but not all that motivated to move. I insisted that my daughter get on with her life and that includes finishing her degree. Pedro also sat out the semester and became the man of the house. This unfortunately included sitting my ass on the toilet and helping me bath and shave. I've grown to like and admire the kid since he's kind and good to my Nikki. I haven't called him a *beaner* or *wetback* once. Tommy, Gwen, and Gia come by a few times a week but my heart isn't in the game. Our banter lacks energy and the pep talks seem repetitive.

Our little task force practically eliminated lone wolfs in America, so mission accomplished, but I can't get too excited. Jun put a severe crimp on ISIS recruiting by blocking and substituting their message on the net. She neutered sanctuary cities rendering them a bad place to be for Muslims.

At our Ports of Entry, thousands of Muslims on the watch list are in jail, deported, or were denied entrance into the U.S. Millions of dollars destined for ISIS is being cyber pilfered into our accounts. It's being used to buy information from greedy snitches who may quote Allah but purchase lap dances from girls named Mercedes. The task force along with the FBI 57 field offices has used our information gleaned from encrypted messaging to thwart hundreds of jihads, but not the one that mattered most.

We have a new President of the United States who changed the policy on surveilling mosques. But my wife was the casualty of political correctness and a past President who traded the lives of decent Americans to placate an ethnic group who disdains everything we stand for; who despises our values, constitution, economic system, and laws. They come to America to change those very beliefs and values that make our country great. They come to segregate themselves but take taxpayers money and then criticize those who provide them food, shelter, education, and opportunity.

Had we been able to utilize informants, surveillance, or wiretaps, we would've been able to stop Benoit long before he committed mass murder. The remaining Ohio State windbreaker we found was Abu's, but it took us too long to find that missing piece of the puzzle.

It's a gloomy Friday afternoon as I sit half watching some game show. Bruce Gombar raps on the door and we sit in the kitchen over coffee. After some small talk and gossip he says, "When do the doctors feel you can get back to work?"

"Three weeks ago."

Bruce looks confused and says, "That's great news. Everyone misses you."

"But I'm not coming back to work."

"Whatta you mean John?"

"I mean that they won?"

"Who won?"

"Them."

"Who's *them?*"

"The terrorist, the politicians, the bureaucrats. They're all the same."

THE END

ABOUT THE AUTHOR

John Ligato is a South Philly native who found himself with the lead contingent of Marines into Hue' City during the 1968 TET offensive in Vietnam. He captured the 6th NVA flag at the St. Joan of Arc school, which was displayed in the Marine Corps Museum. John was awarded three Purple Hearts for his service in Vietnam in addition to other valor awards. The American Hero channel recently featured John in a documentary titled, *Against the Odds*. For 10 years, John worked with developmentally disabled children before joining the Federal Bureau of Investigation, where he infiltrated the Italian Mafia and spent 8 years in deep cover. The 2006 movie *10th and Wolf* is a loosely based bio of his life. In 1999 John received the Attorney General's and Director's award for investigative excellence.